THE MULESKINNER

Phillip Craig

CONTENTS

PART ONE: HIS CRUCIFIXION

One

The whip hit Michael across his open eyes. Sheet lightning sprayed through his skull, knocking him back into the water. When the shimmers faded, he was in a black and white world, sitting in soft luminescent ripples in the gently flowing creek.

Michael would remember nothing of writhing, of weeping and sobbing. He rolled further into the creek, away from the lash and, as abruptly as it had begun, it ended. The Comanche dropped the whip and rejoined the other four.

Michael sat in the water, sweating, bleeding some, his world dismantling and then reconstructing along lines that were hidden in the back of his head. Each stripe delivered had exposed a layer behind the fragile unwieldy shell that he had so painstakingly assembled, leaving him naked and raw, bedazzled by all the light that was suddenly, gloriously, streaming in.

He sat in the gentle cool water breathing deeply, staring colorblind at the chaos. For the first time in his life, unafraid.

Two

He had awoken at dawn, a red smear of clouds low in the east. He crawled from underneath the wagon into the orange light. The sodden air pushed back as he passed through it. Wiping his face with a calloused hand, he trudged down a scree covered incline to where the shallow creek ran.

One of the six mules, the nasty white one, pawed the ground and snorted angrily, wanting free of the hobble and picket to drink as well. Michael gestured weakly back and knelt stiffly down, his knees in the water, the fabric of his trousers darkening. He cupped both hands and splashed the cool clear water over his face and neck, into his mouth and eyes. Droplets collected on his sparsely fuzzed chin. He sat back, letting the warm air rest in his chest like smoke.

The low crimson light reflected off the rippling surface of the creek in gold shimmers that sparkled and held his gaze, snagging and unraveling his foggy mind like a loose thread caught on a rusty nail. Silent, inside and out, Michael's brain indulged itself and hour-like moments passed in quiet harmony, his mouth slack. The spell broke when the cross white mule snorted and stamped more fervently.

Michael's being reluctantly stumbled back. He lifted his eyes. He stared uncomprehendingly at the rippled reflection in the creek of five silent terrible Comanche sitting ponies painted for war.

Three

Comanche is anUte word that means people who want

to fight all the time. This band had been pushing hard for three weeks and had struck a dozen times at what was opportune and vulnerable and then had evaporated onto the plain. Their rampage had left a dozen bodies spread lifeless on the dirt, women raped, and men mutilated, livestock slaughtered, crops trampled and set to flame, homes only smoldering cinders. Oblivion in their wake and terror before them, they were tired to exhaustion. Now, they were on the run.

Near them, and against them, rode Rangers. A troop had been tirelessly pursuing the raiders within several days of the first killings. As severe and inexorable as the Comanche, as ruthless and vicious, they paved the Anglo inroads. Only direct and relentless force would serve and they prosecuted their duty with unrepentant rage. Peace was not an option; only ever a ruse. Understanding would never come nor the desire to be understood. They saw no common ground and the common ground was all that both sides wanted.

The Comanche had doubled back the day before but a lucky Ranger, seeking far for game, had come across sign fresher than what they had been following . It had saved the troop a half day's useless circling. It was enough. The moon shone full and low and they had been able to follow the tracks most of the night and were now, after two weeks of coming up short, all but on top of their prey.

Four

The feeling that they did not have much time to waste gnawed at them but they had needed badly to eat. They could feel the pressure of being hunted. They had felt it in some degree from birth, but they also thought that they had gained a breathing space and that this was worth the pause.

The white man's wagon was loaded with plank lumber,

kegs of nails, and carpentry tools, with which the endless tide of settlers eroded their division. They were out to kill white people, one of whom was staring dumbfounded at them as their ponies splashed across the creek.

Two of the men relaxed their mounts mid-stream, their blowing ponies dipped their foamed muzzles to drink, while the other three circled past Michael, portentously surrounding him. All of it happening with casual grace.

Michael wet his pants, the stain spreading across his front; his body from the waist down seemed to empty of life. His knees went numb and his thighs were painfully tired. He knew he could not stand, much less run.

The rising sun blazed directly into his eyes and he wished he had put on his hat. Involuntarily his right hand twitched up to shade the blinding glare. And that is when it went from the bad to the inevitable.

The provoked Comanche attacked as a group. From behind, one lashed out with the butt of his lance to the middle of Michael's back while. From the front, another galvanized his pony from nuzzling the cool water to springing right through Michael, striking him hard in the chest. Struck twice from two directions, he sprawled breathless to his back.

The unshod hooves of the ponies stamped nervously by his head and he cowered curled up half in the creek, half out. Two of the warriors trotted away from him, splitting off into separate directions to scout.

The warrior atop the pony that had struck him down, continued leisurely on and loped to the wagon. He rode around it. The wagon was long with high sides, supported by four tall spoked wheels. He stopped adjacent to the bench at the front and leaned agilely, far off his barebacked seat, to better see something that had caught his attention. He scooped it from where it lay coiled and loose on the floorboards.

Five

The father a jackass, and the mother a nag, the progeny inevitably favor a certain disposition. Mules are renowned for stubbornness; but stubbornness can only be achieved when first there is a great strength, a powerful will, and little intelligence.

Mule-skinning was not the act of removing the hide from the obstinate hybrid but the occupation of those few whose like-mindedness made them ideal for driving and managing mule teams. The fact that the job did not actually call for decortication, did not stop those select few from trying to do it a little at a time while the animal was still drawing breath. The accepted method of making a mule do what a mule did not want to do was never to offer the carrot but to liberally apply the stick. A stick would do but the tool of the trade was what was misnomered a bullwhip.

Named perhaps for the material from which it was constructed rather than the circumstances of its use, fifteen feet of softened leather was woven onto a foot-and-a-half of stout wood. The softness, the suppleness, the flexibility, was precisely what allowed it to overcome the stiffness and rigidity of the mule's nature. Application took both talent and training. Improperly applied it had an unforgiving habit of redressing its user's inadequacies with proverbial backlash. The height of finesse was to send a de-amplifying ripple along its length; the ripple increasing in speed as it approached the end which could then snap with enough velocity to surpass the speed of sound. The volume and suddenness of the subsequent boom near the animal's head was usually enough to motivate most mules to a change of behavior. Failing that, they would simply get a beating.

Six

Michael sat quietly. His body trembled but his mind held firm. Welts and lacerations covered his torso and limbs. His eyes were watering so badly he seemed to be weeping. He could only discern vague shapes without color.

But, however colorless and indistinct, the world was now stable and organized and intelligent, its many facets laid out before him like the pieces of a grand puzzle. And the final telling piece, the one that brought the image to life, had fallen into place, landing home with the thunderous sound of the whip-crack.

Whatever was to become of him, now held no terror. His fate was no longer of his own choosing, nor was it in the hands of any man. He was merely a piece of that puzzle, his place preordained. His course was settled and it would be futile and unholy to try to deviate from this new black and white path. He waited with infinite patience for the next thing to unfold.

The Comanches had found food. The five men had dismounted and were busy with separate tasks. Two cut out one of the brown mules and led it around the wagon out of view of the other animals. They wrenched the mule's head and brought it to the ground, cleverly tying off its legs and pressing it flat. One man straddled its neck and twisted its head upward, while the other deftly and deeply cut its throat. The blood came in dark gouts and was soaked up instantly by the bone-dry sand. Magically, dozens of flies appeared and hummed noisily to breakfast around the growing stain and in the open wound.

Another brave stood atop the wagon's load of lumber and hurled kegs of nails, with good aim, at sharp rocks, where they burst like bombs to his great satisfaction, scattering the long square nails. A fourth gathered dry mesquite and broken kegs and built a fire to roast freshly butchered mule meat.

The fifth was their leader. The one so handy with the whip. He was lean and graceful and possessed of a marvelous economy of movement. The whip was still in hand as he admired its construction and utility. He had been familiar with riding crops and horse whips and recognized immediately its purpose. His natural abilities with tools and weapons brought him the respect and admiration of his fellows as he turned those talents to mayhem and violence. He searched unhurriedly through a wooden crate of carpentry tools stowed forward under the wagon driver's bench.

Michael seemed to be forgotten but he was aware that every one of the Indians was tuned to him peripherally. Four were squatting or standing near the little fire either holding skewered meat over flames or eating. As one the braves and Michael turned toward their leader. He stood erect on the wagon's bench, one foot braced on the side rail. He was tall for a Comanche, almost five and a half feet, and his pose and stillness lent him a regal bearing. In his left hand was the neatly coiled whip, his right held a new tool. His eyes narrowed and darted from the nails to the white man and he was certain he knew how to make use of the long-handled iron-headed hammer he hefted.

Seven

Downstream, thirteen Rangers paused without dismounting and let their horses drink. A gangly, but large, beardless youth dressed drably in black shifted impatiently, his right foot twitching in the stirrup.

Ranger Peter was named for Jesus's right-hand man. His parents had been long on religion and short on literacy. They were intolerant in the extreme of anything or anyone that smelled of the seven deadly sins. Being firstborn of eleven he had received the fullest impact of their devotion. To circumvent gluttony, they starved. To refrain from pride, they wore unostentatious black and rarely spoke. To shun greed, they remained dirt poor. They sidestepped envy by a strong sense of their superiority. However, their zealousness could not go the distance and sloth, lust, and wrath were transmuted into virtues.

Peter had enlisted with the Rangers, reasoning correctly that barely surviving on an underworked and overpopulated farm was the greater of two evils. It also had the added allure of allowing him the opportunity to vent some of his own wrath. After the upbringing he had had, Peter felt strongly that he really needed to kill someone.

Peter, who had coveted his neighbor's horse, borrowed both the animal and his daddy's double-barreled fowling piece and applied to the Rangers. He was tall, armed, well mounted, murderous, self-righteous, and did not speak even when spoken to, easily checking off the list of requirements for the ideal Ranger. That had been over two months prior and, much to his frustration, he had yet to fire his weapon in anger.

But now his excitement was brimming; filled he was with anticipation and energy, even after a grueling day's and night's ride. The sun had risen. God was with them. And the subhuman savages were close to hand.

Known to his fellows, and to his face, as Puritan Pete he had, in that short amount of time, managed to carve out a place in the unit as the unlikeable friendless loner. But this very morning he felt he would be the one to lead these men. That it was his time to come to the fore and show himself to be the hero, the brave example, to the men who had chosen to largely ignore or dismiss him.

Not wanting to miss his moment, Peter stayed close to the right of the Ranger captain, a seasoned veteran sure to recognize his audacity and courage.

Captain John 'Red' Martin had had a good Irish Catholic

upbringing which was more Irish than Catholic - more bending of the elbow than the knee. His locks and whiskers and the bright hue of his nose gave him the handle that nearly everyone used to the exclusion of his Christian name. His violent temper and the unpleasant drunken rages, that his great size and strength made truly frightful, also added to the nickname's validity.

His men loved him like they loved their own drunken violent fathers and would do anything brave or foolhardy to keep his favor. And Red delighted in their devotion. When reasonably sober he was not a violent or petty man and was conscientiously concerned with the welfare of his troop; both as an entity and as individuals.

As Red's big roan gelding cooled, he studied the panorama that stretched away upstream. He decided it was time and called softly to his men to check and ready their weapons.

He turned and, though mildly surprised to see the Puritan there, he grinned and said, "Puritan Pete, me boy, where there's smoke there is fire." Then in his strong melodious voice, that carried so well in the warm wet air, "Now is the time, lads, make me proud and please don't get none of yourselves killed!"

With a, "Yah," he spurred his horse forward, towards a thin column of white smoke less than a mile distant.

Eight

They dragged Michael, who was neither kicking nor screaming, by his bruised and bleeding arms and propped him up against the high side of the wagon. Three held him there while one gathered a half dozen of the three-inch long square-headed nails from where they lay littering the plain.

Michael could still not see well enough to understand

what was transpiring and only a part of him knew he had been moved and had been placed with his back to the wagon, his arms outstretched as if trying to touch the big wheels to either side. He was trying to comply, to help those that were helping him to stand but there was little energy in his legs and it was only by leaning hard on the wagon, that he managed to support his weight.

He had withdrawn himself away from the pain of the beating and the horror of the circumstance and his eyes blearily settled trancelike on the horizon. He heard the hammering rather than felt the new addition to his torments.

In a way, it was rude of Michael to be late to his own crucifixion and the handy brave wielding the hammer was beginning to feel like an unappreciated host. Michael stared through him and showed no signs of discomfort. The brave needed some reaction from Michael. He was tired to exhaustion and in no mood to be thwarted. His raid had been bloody but not profitable. He had no captives or horses to show and retribution had been swift and persistent in its pursuit. The bullwhip lying coiled around his neck, like a tame serpent was the only meager and tangible trophy he had acquired. Michael's unresponsiveness was disconcerting and unsatisfying. He did not like what he did not comprehend.

He impulsively struck Michael a short sharp blow with the hammer to the forehead. The blow opened a cut between Michael's eyes and there was immediate heavy bleeding. It covered his eyes like a curtain dropping.

The strike jarred Michael into the present. He knew exactly where he was and what was occurring. The two worlds, one material one ethereal, he had been occupying since the whip had struck his eyes, merged. The schism he had straddled, dissolved, and the pain and profundity he had been experiencing as separate realities came together, magnifying both actualities tenfold.

The blow had opened his skull and enlarged his mind. In a bright flash of insight, he understood the larger picture and the meaning grafted onto it. The three concentric spheres of Heaven, earth, and Hell were laid open. He could understand their order and structure and was keenly aware of the weft and warp of their intertwinings. The fabric of sacred and secular were overlapping at their boundaries where angels and demons wandered, doing their sacred and profane works in the same spaces and time. And the locus of this overlap was the turbid sphere wherein mankind dwelt. He saw people occupying territory in all three realms: their feet rooted in Hell, their spirits aspiring to Heaven, and their actions filling the middle ground, determining the final direction of their destination.

Michael realized he had been shirking his duties, fleeing from his destiny, and that he would pay dearly for it. Michael knew now who he was, on which side he was allied, and who his adversary was.

The warrior held Michael's head up by his hair and the white man looked right into him, through the mess of blood, sweat, and tears that marked his spiritual deflowering. Drooling, quivering, his pupils pinprick small, Michael's clear voice spoke the name of his tormenter.

The brave spoke only a little English but he had a knack for language, as he did all tools, and there was no mistaking Michael's intent or the syllables of the name he gave him.

"Satan."

Nine

The Rangers had covered the mile between themselves and the site of Michael's degradation and liberation, in less than five minutes. They had had to do little more than follow the creek, for though the water did not flow in a straight line to Michael's camp, the distance had been small enough for Red to surmise that whoever was responsible for the rising white smoke was encamped near the creek's bed. It would have been faster to travel the shorter direct way across the flat expanse, but the winding path of the water in the small ravine it had cut, afforded his men some protecting cover with which to conceal their approach.

Surprise and caution, careful planning and daring, were the paradoxical bread-and-butter of the guerrillas' strategy. Life on the frontier was far too short without adding unnecessary risks. With a gesture of his arm, Red signaled to his men to stop. All of his troop knew to keep one eye on their leader in such situations and all of them were aware of what Red meant when he lifted his left hand and waved it backward. But not all of them responded in the usual well-rehearsed manner. All but one of the Rangers brought their mounts to a quick and quiet halt.

The exception of good military discipline was the over-excited and under-observant person of Puritan Pete. He flew past his fellows as if they were standing still, which they very nearly were.

Red had intended to divide his force and come at the as yet unknown party from two non-opposing directions. To keep his men out of the lines of their own fire he would send them in, one from the creek side, and the other, with himself in the lead, bisecting the first line of attack at a right angle; catching whatever awaited them in a potential crossfire. He also had intended to warn his gallant and trigger-happy boys to assess the situation before opening fire. One never knew what to expect in the field, as evidenced by Pete's disregard for rehearsed and understood gestures. Although he was fairly certain he had caught up to the war band, he did not want to be responsible for the massacre of a party of innocent emigrants.

Red watched open-mouthed as Puritan Pete raced by him. Then his mouth filled with curses. He yelled and gestured to approximately half his men to continue their course along the creek and for the rest to follow him up the slight incline and ride directly toward the column of smoke. His cursing changed its object from the Puritan to less specifically directed profanities as he noticed the sudden swelling of the thin column to billowing clouds of dense black smoke.

Ten

They took brands from their cookfire and started the wagon ablaze. It burned reluctantly at first, black smoke hiding the timid orange flames, but steadily the flames grew, struggling to breathe in the densely stacked lumber.

Michael believed that Hell could not wait for him but was coming to claim his wayward soul. Satan and his archdemons had crucified him in a gross parody of the Christ's heroic sacrifice. The heat from the fire and the smell of smoke merged his last moments on earth with his future nether worldly abode.

Understanding God's plan had come too late to save him. He had made his choices early in life and his death was coming on before he would have a chance to redeem himself. There would be no second chance. The debt had to be paid.

His life passed in review. He saw that he had started out with a much better chance at salvation than one should reasonably expect. He had had the benefit of Christian instruction. Born to the wife of a Methodist minister in the lowlands of Scotland, the tradition of the family was to give the first-born male the auspicious name of an archangel to encourage piety and commitment. It was a little un-protestant to be named for an angel - the belief in such creatures seemed to border on Catholicism - but the Burns' family had an innate stubbornness that transcended faith and they continued with the practice.

Michael's father had been named for God's herald, the

trumpeter Gabriel, and had followed his father into the ministry. Like his namesake, he knew his purpose was to announce the presence of God to all. To the greater fulfillment of this ideal, he felt himself, his wife, and his only son, called to take ship to America, then overland to the very edges of civilization.

Michael's mother was from less hardy stock. The close, cold, and unhygienic circumstances of shipboard life had brought on a disease of the bowels. It quickly worsened with each passing mile during the exhaustingly hard travel west in the bone-jarring back of a wagon. They buried her shortly after crossing the Mississippi.

Michael knew the loneliest day of his life when his father, himself, and a meager few fellows placed his mother in the damp earth of a harsh land that was not her home. Michael had carried her feet.

His father preached over the casketless corpse in its muddy hole. He spoke eloquently about the beauty and joy that belonged to those that went repentant and contrite. But Michael knew that his mother had died in darkness, in delirious agony, writhing in her own bloody shit, in the stinking bed of a rickety wagon. Any humility she had departed with, came only from pain and regret.

Michael had few memories of his mother's affections and the only touch his father shared was through the intermediary of his belt or a switch. Michael clearly remembered the brutal awareness of the futility of reaching out by word, look, or touch, to his father for comfort or connection in the very hour of her death. The loss they should have shared, pushed them apart. Michael felt himself an orphan. He buried his faith with her. Her death and his father's indifference proved what he had previously suspected: that the world was without purpose or meaning. There could be no God in desolation. As the dirt was shoveled over the thinly shrouded corpse, he envied and hated her.

His father's eyes only flickered past him, the same as

for everyone else in the group standing meekly graveside. Michael was obviously no more a relation to him than to any one else on that wide prairie. And Michael felt no more tied to his father than to the rotting emaciated woman in the pit. And he drew some comfort from that freedom.

When he walked away, three years later at the age of fourteen, it was not as a runaway; his father would have had to wanted him to stay for him to be called that,. On the frontier ,fourteen was old enough to be on his own. He walked away with a sense of relief, being finally alone in body as well.

Michael learned that walking away solved most problems, and, on the frontier, there was always a vast emptiness to walk into. His loneliness was his comfort. In the next ten years he made no friends and no attachments. He drifted without purpose, speaking only when necessary.

Nailed to the side of a wago, Michael was sorry he had walked away and so far. He had been a coward. He heard, above the crackle of fire, two heralding barks of thunder, the trumpeting of his destiny. As death drew him down, Michael, with all his soul, yearned for salvation, yearned for God.

"Father," he whispered. "Hast thou forsaken me?"

Eleven

Pete's shotgun carried two long tapering octagonal barrels, designed for the hunting of ducks, geese, doves, and quail. Firing it from horseback, at a gallop, at furiously moving targets, Peter was fortunate not to have shot himself or his horse. He charged across the creek, screaming. More than forty yards from the Indians, he discharged first one barrel, then the next in rapid succession.

The warriors were more startled than fearful, and more

from Pete's screaming than from his marksmanship. They vaulted onto their ponies and took up reins and weapons, looking in all directions for more enemies.

Peter, his hat brim blown back against his crown, his body hunched forward, had assumed his fellow Rangers had followed his lead and were right behind him. Unaware of his solitude, he continued his charge straight at the now armed and mounted Comanche.

One of the warriors, bow in hand, nocked an arrow and loosed it at the Texan. The shaft carried great force at close range, burying itself feathers deep in the chest of Pete's horse. The gelding took several more lunging strides before its legs gave out all at once and it pitched forward onto its head. Its weight and momentum plowed a deep furrow in the loose sandy ground.

Pete let go of his gun, which went floating slowly away from him. His feet lifted free of the stirrups, and his buttocks levitated up from the saddle His hat separated from his head. Weightless he hovered above his dying horse. His feet touched ground in front of the sprawling animal as if he had been playing leapfrog with it. His momentum pitched him forward, his knees buckled and his torso bent at the waist. He rolled like an acrobat and, as much to his astonishment as those who observed, he came once again to his feet, stumbling and flailing his arms, framed by a cloud of dust.

As he staggered past, the warrior instinctively leaned sideways off his pony and, with a tremendous forehand blow, struck Pete with the hammer on the side of his head. Pete's head shattered and collapsed. His body spun and slammed down in a grotesque parody of his horse's death.

His hat floated gently down, puffing up a tiny dust cloud, landing a foot further on from Peter's head.

Twelve

Red, in the fore of his half of the troop, crested the rise and came into view of those at the wagon. The other half were behind a bend in the creek and still out of sight of the Comanche. To the warriors, it seemed they were being attacked from only one direction, but that onslaught was enough to make them flee. The sight of a half-dozen bearded whooping Texans charging them, pistols blazing orange fire and gray smoke, horses kicking up clouds of dust, did not terrify them: the Rangers were too few in number. However, the Comanche way of battle required room to maneuver their agile ponies to advantage. They hoped to engage the Rangers in a prolonged chase, where their lighter swifter mounts could literally ride circles around the slower Texans. Although the white man's guns gave them greater firepower, they were clumsy and slow to reload. Once emptied, they left the bearers vulnerable to swift attack. Given enough time and space, they would gradually wear their heavier pursuers down and pick them off one by one.

All the Comanche but one wheeled and dashed at a tangent to the Ranger's charge. Their way in one direction was blocked by the large wagon and the panicking mule team. Not wanting to ride in a direct line away from the Rangers guns, they turned toward the creek bed.

Their leader was unable to follow them as his immediate path was blocked by the body of Puritan Pete and his dead horse. His only option was to ride directly away from the Rangers. His vulnerability inspired him to a display of courage and defiance. He would lead the Rangers away and his war band would take them in the rear.

He kicked his pony and leaned his body far over so that his pony's flanks shielded him. He scooped up Peter's hat and, righting himself as he rode away, waved the trophy of his kill tauntingly, whooping in a high pitch. The moment was shaded though, for in leaning down for the hat, he lost the precious whip, its coils slipped from his neck and traded places with Peter's worn headgear.

Thirteen

Red had heard the twin blasts from Pete's piece over the pounding of horses' hooves but had arrived too late to witness the incredible demise of the Puritan. A large revolver in each hand, he led his men over the rise and onto the flat plain. Through the thick black cloud rolling from the wagon, he could see five mounted warriors and one dead Ranger.

The Indians took one quick look at Red and his men and bolted. One painted brave ran straight away from them waving something over his head and yipping his high-pitched cry. Red would have liked to have given chase to the haughty warrior but could not risk his men following him, rather than staying with the plan. And the plan was working: four Comanche were riding right into the other half of his troop.

Red and his men pulled their horses to a halt between the wagon and the creek at the top of the slope. The sudden arrival of the other group of Rangers, cut off the warrior's flight in midstream.

There was a moment of inactivity as the Rangers lined up their mounts, shoulder to shoulder, on both sides of the trap, and as the Indians realized their situation. Caught between the rock and the hard place, with nowhere to go but down, they raised their bows and lances and shrieked flamboyantly their fearlessness.

The Texans, excited, scared, pleased with themselves, vengeful, wasted no time. Most carried a revolver, some, like

Red, more than one. Some held single shot rifles as well as a revolver in reserve. The twelve men fired aimed shots until their guns emptied at the four milling trapped Comanche and their ponies. Red's Rangers were good shots, each having a lifetime of practice as well as practical experience of shooting while under duress. Four, bunched, only slowly moving targets, in a crossfire, were no challenge to their marksmanship. They thumbed back the hammers, sighted quickly and carefully, and pulled the triggers with efficiency, ruthlessness, and glee.

The warriors never returned fire. Their lances and shields dropped from their hands to sink or float away. Their bows remained undrawn as they weathered the hail storm of round lead balls. Their white teeth and white rolling eyes flashed against their black face paint, as projectiles smacked meatily into their muscles, bones, and organs.

At the first shot, one warrior pitched off his mount and lay face down in the creek with his legs tangled as balls puckered and splashed the water around him.

Another pony reared up when a ball struck its flank. Its rider flipped backward, slipped from his seat. His shoulders and the back of his head bounced off another frantic, wounded, bounding, pony before he landed on his side with a flopping splash. His rearing horse was then shot squarely in the heart. Its hind legs buckled and it fell slowly back and to its side, covering its owner's head and chest and pinning him beneath the shallow water. His legs kicked and jerked as he drowned, untouched by lead.

A third must have been an obvious target, for shots whacked persistently into him from both sides. He slipped off his circling pony and landing in the water in a sitting position, where his head was blown open from behind. He slumped forward, his shoulders resting between his bent knees as his injured mount ran blindly in the water downstream. After only a few long desperate strides, it broke a foreleg and stumbled, landing on its side, half immersed and screaming relentlessly.

When the shooting stopped, only one brave remained

mounted. His body was draped over his wild-eyed stamping pony, one arm and one leg to each side, his head turned to one side, his face resting tenderly on the crest of his pony's neck, his back pocked with four holes and one leg splintered at the knee.

Red's men only stopped firing when their guns were empty. Some immediately began the laborious process of reloading. Others, their ears ringing, surveyed the scene through the haze of gunpowder and wood smoke. One Ranger, stood in his saddle. He gestured and shouted frantically for Red to look behind him.

Red's first thought was that the taunting hat-waving brave had returned to take them from behind as they reloaded. Each of his pistols had one unfired chamber, as he had carefully counted his shots. With the hair rising on the back of his scalp, he turned in the saddle and raised a gun. But saw no screaming savage. Just a crucified white boy calmly looking him in the eye as he was about to be burned alive.

Fourteen

His pony flew. He leaned forward against the neck until his eye was almost level with his mount. Their heads rolling in time to the gallop, as if they were one beast. His right hand gripped the hammer and was also tightly woven in the pony's long main. His left held the hat and he used it to quirt the animal's flank.

This was life: galloping a fleet pony, escaping and outwitting his enemies, riding free and fast. It was the best of moments. He was young, clever, and bold - a Comanche. He would live to fight on. He would father sons. Without courage, strength, determination, and independence a man was at the mercy of fate; he would be like dust blown whichever way the wind gusted. Riding a galloping pony across the wide expanse changed that. He was now the bird of prey liberated on those very same winds. Armed, audacious, dangerous, predatory, he could soar on circumstance; go where he wished, take what he wanted and leave those pathetic earthbound creatures that tried to restrain him, far below.

He glanced backward to check the closeness of his pursuers and saw, with both disappointment and relief, that there was none. Wary of a ruse, he only let his pony slow slightly. He veered to his right as he struggled to see, from several hundred yards, what had happened to the Texans and his companions.

Through the haze of smoke, he could make out nothing more than the burning wagon and the outline of the mounted Rangers along the top of the rise overlooking the creek. He could not see the other Comanche. Nor was there anywhere to be seen, even a dust trail leading away from the wagon in any direction other than his own. He brought his pony up and turned it.

It was his ears that finally told him the whereabouts and fates of his fellows and friends. The muted pops of gunfire drifted to him like a chilling wind.

Fifteen

Michael had a perfect view of the massacre in the creek. Even though he could only make out indistinct colorless shapes, he had seen how the wily Satan had escaped by ruthlessly sacrificing his archdemons.

The fire had been started at the rear of the wagon and was now burning nearly its entire length. The plank lumber that was Michael's freight, was dry, seasoned wood, but being stacked tightly, it could not draft well enough to burn all at once and only the top planks were afire. The wagon itself was only smoldering and, although Michael was uncomfortably hot, he was not being burned. He could feel the flames and smell the smoke but did not know from where the fire originated. It seemed more that it was he who was moving into a fiery place, not that a fire was moving to overwhelm him. He was surprised when the avenging horsemen rapidly dismounted and approached him.

Michael smiled at them but, having little practice, he could manage only a lopsided grimace. God's grace had not come to him in this world and, in these, his last moments, he had seen ordinary men, good men, annihilate the demons; something he had failed to do in his short life. In a whisper, and without envy, he wished them all the blessing that should come to brave men in the final reckoning.

Mixed with the crackling and popping of the burning wood and the shouting of the Rangers, Michael thought he could faintly hear a lone voice that was at once close and far away. It sounded remarkably like his own. It seemed to ring inside his own bruised brain. The voice was hoarsely screaming one word over and over.

"Help,' it said. "Help!"

Sixteen

Red leapt from the saddle and holstered his revolvers. He dashed to where Michael was nailed to the wagon. The boy was wide-eyed, bloody and bruised, and was screaming to be helped. Red wanted to help but, when he comprehended the circumstances, he was at a loss as to how to free him.

Red was joined by most of the men who all shouted suggestions as to how best to affect a rescue. Some felt it wise under the dire conditions to just rip his pierced hands away, others, that they should search out the proper tools. One, who was taking the fire very seriously, thought it would be fastest to chop Michael's hands off at the wrist and went so far as to draw his knife.

When Red saw the flash of the knife, he knew he had better begin making decisions before his men, in their panicked efforts to save the unfortunate boy, killed him. He told his men to step back, shoving them clear with bearlike swings of his arms. He faced Michael and crossing his arms in front of himself drew both pistols which were holstered butt forward on a single belt. First with his right, then quickly with the left, he fired his two remaining rounds into the plank Michael was nailed to, shattering and splintering the wood only inches out from Michael's pointing fingers. The two shots were insufficient to burst the heavy boards but his men had the idea and, without being ordered, those that had reloaded, used their pistols to good effect.

Through the powder smoke, Red could see that the board was smashed through and he bellowed to cease fire. He holstered his guns and moved in, taking Michael around the body to carry him away. But the boy and the cross plank were still secured to the wagon by an upright post just to the left of Michael's spine. Michael stopped screaming when the gunfire began and the moment Red held him his legs gave out. Red struggled with the limp body trying to hold it up and free it from the wagon without yanking against the still secured hands. He could tell the board was not free and understood why. He cursed himself for not seeing the upright and for the desperate idea of trying to shoot him free.

The others saw the difficulty. One jumped forward and, grabbing one end of the shattered board, began heaving and jerking to free it from the wagon. The board bent but did not loosen. Yet the bending encouraged the others to add their strength and soon, on both sides of Michael, many pairs of arms strained and heaved at the stubborn wood.

There was a sudden sharp crack as the board split where it had been nailed to the upright and Michael's arms came together to limply embrace Red, several feet of wood hanging from each hand.

Coughing and eyes streaming, the Rangers staggered quickly away from the hotly burning wagon, and Red carried the sagging body to safety.

Seventeen

Michael had been surprised when they attempted to rescue him. He had considered his fate sealed and did not know what it might mean when they suddenly stepped back and commenced firing toward him. He reasoned that his rescue was beyond them, but being good men, they were simply doing the kindest act in their power and we're going to put his body out of its misery; as they would shoot an injured horse on an old dog.

Michael tilted his head back and closed his eyes, letting his breath stream slowly out between his lips. His attention narrowed, concentrated on the sensation of the spent warm air brushing softly through his mouth. He relaxed completely, relinquishing all efforts to hold himself firm. Energy and breath and thought fell away from him like dreams escaping an awakening mind.

Without reflection or comment, he let himself drift silently from the torture of the flesh. He floated unencumbered and passive down a stygian corridor of quiet, without emotion or thought, in a state of total receptivity. His consciousness was wide open and clear, like a crystal pool of still water. He wafted through time and space toward an unlocatable place that was anchored only in a moment of eternity. He was in a limbo of anticipation, the calm before the storm, a final unmoment of essential being.

His soul gently quivered in expectation, and that mild

action jarred loose a bubble of self-awareness that floated slowly up from the mud of his flesh, through fathoms of detachment, toward the surface of experience.

He heard a voice with a Gaelic accent, similar to, but more melodious than his father's. He opened his eyes to see a beard and mustache framed mouth. Partly lip-reading, he struggled to make out the content of what was being spoken to him.

Red was saying, “I'd wager you believed yourself to be a goner.”

Eighteen

Red shouted instructions to his men as he knelt straddling Michael. He and Michael had locked eyes. Michael's face was relaxed, Red’s was cheerful, flushed and excited. Neither one attempted to look away from the other. Red gave his orders without breaking eye contact and assumed correctly that they would be carried out satisfactorily and without supervision.

Some of the men remounted and rode off to scout the area, but most of the Rangers remained and picketed their horses and moved Michael's mules down closer to the creek. Smoke from the wagon fire was hanging heavily in the still humid air, making the immediate area of the camp uninhabitable. No one attempted to save the wagon from burning, for the fire had spread to all its parts and the heat from the flames was too intense to allow approach.

Red had the bulk of his men seeing to the clearing up of the battle site. They waded out with Bowie knives drawn to dispatch the wounded. Although the Comanches were all quite dead, two ponies needed their throats cut before the scene was finally quiet and free from the sounds of pain and struggle. The creek was burbling soothingly. The wagon fire crackled and burned almost cheerfully, if hugely. The horses all stood with their heads down still working to catch their breath. The Rangers spoke to one another softly and only when necessary. After the mayhem of only a few minutes before, it was as if the earth were trying to enforce a calm by the steady working of the fundamental processes. The Rangers, coming back from a place of violence and instinct, attuned themselves to nature's mandates, and we're gently drawn into normalcy; moving away from the thin line that separates life from death.

Red was handed a wooden canteen of water. He uncorked it, and gently lifting Michael's head, put the spout to his lips and slowly dribbled in a small amount at a time, patiently waiting for Michael to clumsily swallow. He crooned and encouraged him, complimenting him for each successful gulp as if Michael were an infant. Red had a powerful paternal instinct, and Michael's open face and otherworldly, though bloodshot eyes, reminded him of his children when they were newborns.

Michael, for his part, felt like a newborn, or perhaps a reborn. The shapes and textures that soaked into his eyes had become sharp, clear, though quite colorless. He could distinctly see every whisker in Reds beard as separate and singular, different in all respects from every other whisker, and worthy of notice and study. He felt his mouth and throat evolve from parched to moist, from brittle to supple, from hot to cool. He felt his stomach expand and loosen as the water painted its lining a piece at a time. All sensation was so complete that it was both pleasant and painful, an assault and a caress. This dichotomy suspended Michael in the middle, neither retreating nor embracing. Without responding either emotionally or physically, he simply accepted, with no need to act or react. Where he was right then was as good, or as bad, as anywhere else he might be.

Red smiled at him and lowered his head to the earth.

He stoppered the canteen and set it next to Michael's head. A Ranger named Luke had arrived with a set of pliers they used to extract horseshoe nails and Red looked grimly away from Michaels' eyes to Michael's hands.

Luke was a short, bandy-legged man, with a wispy yellow beard, and thinning hair under a wide-brimmed farmer's hat. He was no doctor, not even a horse doctor, but he handled all the on-the-spot doctoring. It was not that he was especially skilled or experienced, but he possessed a steadiness of nerve, and an unflinching disregard for the sufferings of his comrades that allowed him to start, and finish, any grizzly procedure - no matter how painful to the patient.

He put one foot on the plank beyond Michael's fingertips and planted the other firmly on Michael's wrist. The nails had been driven cruelly deep into the hand and the palm had bled and swollen and risen like bread dough to engulf the nail head. Luke had to press the pliers down hard and fish about, before finding a grip on the spike, causing blood to well up and pool in the slightly cupped palm. Red looked away, but Michael watched unblinkingly, his gaze never faltering and his expression never altering, as Luke straightened up, using his back and legs to pull on the nail, which he had to wiggle and work back and forth to free.

Luke opened the pliers and removed the bloody nail from the jaws where it had stuck. He casually tossed it aside and for the first time looked at Michael's lacerated and cracked face. He was curious as to whether his patient had remained conscious, most men thrashed and moaned when he did his doctoring and needed to be held down, unless they had had the good fortune to pass out. He was startled to see that not only was Michael wide awake, but calm and attentive.

His brow furrowed and he asked, "Don't that hurt, boy?"

"Yes sir, it does," Michael replied in a monotone, his face deadpan.

Nineteen

A pair of Rangers had headed out in pursuit of the one Indian that escaped the massacre and easily found his trail, if not the sight of him. The trail ran straight for a couple of miles, then gradually circled back, but soon it verged into a third direction, leading away from their camp.

Their horses were tired. They had ridden hard all the previous night, and sprinting about in the sweltering heat was fast eating up the last of their resources. This was not the kind of country one wanted to be afoot in and, rather than risk their mounts on what would most probably prove to be a fruitless chase, they reluctantly decided to turn back.

They did not like to quit. It was not in their natures, and it ate at them for the entire slow walk back toward the smoking wagon. But, giving up on this trail was not the same as giving up on this man. He had attacked the people it was their job to protect and killed one of their own company. They would follow up on this until their sense of vengeance was satisfied. No matter how long it took, or how far the trail led, they would extract eyes for an eye and teeth for a tooth. Persistence and perseverance were the watchwords of rangering and these two men spent the next quarter hour swearing to each other that, though they had lost a battle, they would win the war.

The one they had been pursuing knew he was being chased, and, although his pony was only scarcely better rested than the bigger horses of his pursuers, it was of a heartier breed and more used to hardship. His pony's small size made it more efficient, his own small stature and lightweight equipment meant that the animal carried less of a burden. When push came to shove he was willing to ride his mount into the ground. He had no doubt about his ability to elude the dogs on his trail, but evading them was only the beginning. He would remain in the area waiting for a chance to revenge himself.

He had lost horses and men to the whites, and though he had killed and destroyed, the invaders were gaining ground. It was not just his life, but the very survival of his people that depended on his success and the success of warriors like him. European diseases had decimated his tribe; sick forty-niners passing through on their way to the promise of the California goldfields had brought a devastation many times greater than the Comanches had ever suffered in open war with the settlers. With their numbers depleted, it was more difficult than ever to deter the endless flow of trespassers.

It was not a game to him, not a silly point of pride. His tenacity was born of dire necessity. A coyote chasing a rabbit was not just running for his supper but for his very life.

Twenty

The returning scouts lent themselves to the task of clearing the creek of corpses. They looped braided leather lariats around the necks of ponies and Comanches and, wrapped the other end around the horns of their saddles. They then spurred their horses out of the creek and well into the brush, dragging the bodies a hundred yards or so from the creek bed. They had no intention of burying anything, they only wished not to be troubled by the soon-to-come stench or the workings of scavengers. Although life was cheap, meat was at a premium in this environment, and by the next morning, there would be little left but the bones.

They placed the four dead braves shoulder-to-shoulder in a neat row, but they left the ponies in a casual heap several yards away. Half a dozen Rangers milled about the Indians, curious about their enemies. In life, there was nothing more terrifying than a Comanche warrior in his black warpaint and regalia, armed to the teeth, as beautiful and dangerous as a cougar. In death, they were small and pitiful.

They were nearly naked and what they were wearing was worn and dirty. Their weapons seemed primitive and makeshift next to the mass-produced and machine-like firearms of American factories. Their jewelry and ornaments were made from bits of bone and seashell and cheap trade goods or the occasional small tidbit of looted precious metal. They were short, barrel-chested, and bandy-legged. Their faces were prematurely wrinkled and dried out, and they all showed signs of past diseases or poorly healed injuries; crooked limbs from broken bones that had not been set straight, ugly scars from cuts that had suffered infection, smallpox scars, and cloudy eyes. These young men were old before their time. Barely in their twenties, their lives were well past the average halfway point for their people. The story their bodies told was of a hard savage life of meager sustenance and little hope.

The Rangers went through the Comanche's few belongings looking for souvenirs and trophies but found little worth keeping. The sight of death, even of dead Comanches, was not novel. Their own lives were scarcely longer or easier. But that scarce amount was noticeable and quantifiable.

Little of the Rangers belongings or clothes were of their own production, but had been made elsewhere and then purchased. This implied a network of support spanning thousands of miles and involving millions of people. They were merely the vanguard of the huge ever-expanding empire of industrial civilization. The Comanches, with their stone age appearance, seemed already an anachronism. It was only by remembering the deeds and capabilities of braves like these that the Rangers kept from feelings of pity and remorse.

They walked or rode back to the camp feeling an insecure satisfaction over their morning's work. They had to remind themselves that they had met the enemy and carried the day, they had done their jobs, earned their pay, and furthered their cause. And with every step away from the corpses of their enemies, their backs became straighter, their chins lifted higher, their resolve became tighter, and their pride shifted to find its own stability.

Twenty-One

Michael was freed from his bondage and was sitting up. Luke removed the tattered remnants of Michael's shirt and, with the canteen of water Michael had sipped from, irrigated the lacerations on his chest, back, and face. The skin had mostly held and Michael had more welts than wounds. When enough blood had been washed away to distinguish between the two, Luke produced a clear bottle of diluted grain spirit and dribbled it sparingly, though thoroughly, into the torn parts.

Luke knew this disinfecting was excruciating and usually offered a draught of the mixture to the patient as a painkiller, but the boy remained as unperturbed as when he had removed the nails from his hands. Luke knew that people who had been hurt often went into a state of shock, but this boy seemed alert and normal in every respect other than an indifference to pain. It was strange but Luke really did not have any personal interest in Michael and soon accepted, then stopped noticing all together, Michael's queer lack of reactions.

Michael had been whipped top and bottom as well as front and back. The urine staining his trousers had never dried in the humid air and was giving off a rancid odor that was palpable over even the strong smells of smoke, sweat, and gunpowder. Excrement and open wounds were a bad mix, and Luke, with Red's help, removed Michael's brogans and then began to take off his trousers in order to be able to examine and clean his legs. At this, Michael began to display agitation and then began to thrash his legs and tried weekly but frantically to squirm away.

Terror broke Michael's calm like a rock thrown through a glass window. His fear was partly the shame of exposure but there was a deeper remembrance of pain and humiliatio, if not a specific incident. Lying buried in Michael's memory was a raw scar that he had not the resources to confront or acknowledge. Michael felt guilt and horror and helplessness over some original sin he could not, would not, put a name to. His reactions, internally and externally, where childlike in their simplicity. He was drawing away from pain, the knowledge of pain, the knowledge of good and evil.

Luke persisted, unsuccessfully, in trying to strip Michael, but Red broke off his efforts.

"Here now, son, settle down," he spoke soothingly. "Let Luke here have a look at those wounds of yours."

At the word son, Michael began to thrash even more wildly, so that Luke too had to desist. Red and Luke then stood up and stepped back, giving Michael room. Once they did this, Michael curled up and quieted down. His eyes were clamped shut and he was shivering, but he was no longer fighting or trying to move away.

Red glanced sideways at Luke and Luke answered Red's look with a shrug of his eyebrows. Red then cautiously approached Michael, as if he were a skittish colt, careful not to alarm or startle him.

"I mean you no harm, man." When Michael did not respond Red tried a different tact. "Hey, tell us your name. What's your name, now?"

Michael's eyes popped open at the question, startling Red. "Burns." He said once and then again louder and more clearly, "Burns."

Red looked over his shoulder at Luke, and, with the relief of understanding in his voice, said, "He says he's burned, his legs must be burnt."

Turning back to Michael, confusion replaced understanding in his face for Michael was gently shaking with laughter. Then Michael slowly uncurled, lay back in the dust. Consciousness left him.

Twenty-Two

Red stood over the body of Puritan Pete, which lay as it had fallen. The bulk of the Texans had been busy doing everything else that they possibly could to avoid the task of dealing directly with the death of their newest member. Red, busy and fascinated by Michael, had simply forgotten about the dead boy and had not asked anyone to look after him. Luke had checked for signs of life in the Puritan as soon as he had dismounted but, finding none, had left him to see to Michael.

After Michael passed out, Red and Luke finished stripping him and cleaned his legs. Finding no burns but many welts and a few lacerations, they had thrown his ruined clothes aside except for the shoes which they refitted to Michaels bare feet. They covered the shoed but otherwise naked Michael with a thin blanket - not to keep him warm, but to prevent the sun from finishing what the Indians had started. Michael's face was freckled and fair and the rest of his body looked as though it had never seen daylight. He was pale as a corpse where he was not bright red with welts.

The other rangers returned from their various tasks and joined Red in a ragged silent circle around Pete. Kneeling, Red rolled the body over and methodically went through the pockets but found nothing at all. He stood up and told his men to start digging a grave.

"Get his clothes off before he soils them," he said quietly. "Our friend over there can make use of them."

Red turned away and begin filling a clay pipe with tobacco from a small tin kept in his shirt pocket. He stooped and broke off a dry twig of mesquite and lit one end of it from the back of the wagon which was still burning, but only in places and with much less fury. He lit his pipe and smoked as he watched his men work and the wagon burn. The sides had burned away and some lumber had spilled out but the wagon still stood upright on its wheels. His men scratched and hacked a shallow narrow trench only a few feet from the corpse and just barely large enough to fit it. They were tired and Pete had never been worth much effort.

Red tapped his pipe empty on the large flat palm of his hand and stowed it in his pocket. He gestured for the naked body of Puritan Pete to be placed in its grave, which two Rangers did, folding his arms across his chest.

The ragged circle reformed with hats off and heads bowed. They shifted from one foot to the other, looking mostly at their toes but occasionally glancing at Pete's smashed head.

"Naked he came into this world and naked he will be leaving it." Red stood behind Pete's head, speaking softly. "He had courage though, courage but no sense. This boy is dead today because he forgot discipline and did not remember he was part of a troop." Red looked up and around at the faces of the men. "You bastards are expected to think on your feet but you are also expected to do as you are told and not act like this turnip and get the lot of us scalped." There was a low murmur of agreement from around the circle and Red looked down again. "But he was a Ranger, and he was just a boy, and I won't say another bad word against him. Let's hope this Puritan was pure enough to get himself into heaven. Jesus have mercy on us all. Give him an earth bath."

The Texans chorused an amen - mistaking Red's musings for a eulogy - and either moved away or began pushing dirt over the remains with the edges of their boots.

Twenty-Three

The Comanche rode away from the Texans for half the day and then, swinging wide, rode back towards the Texans for the rest of the day and into the night. He hobbled his exhausted pony several miles from the Ranger's camp, on the far side of the creek. He carefully, slowly, made his way closer.

The sounds of scavengers brought him to his companions. Two coyotes, snarling and competing with each other, quickly relinquished the field to the newcomer without argument, sneaking off to watch bright-eyed and anxious, prancing with quick dancing steps, for some opportunity to reclaim their meal.

The dead ponies had occupied most of the coyotes' attention but the braves have been violated greatly during the day and evening by birds and flies. Their corpses were stinking, bloated and maggot-filled, and mice and rats, bolder than the coyotes, were hard at their work, gnawing the flesh from the bone.

The survivor squatted low and motionless for more than an hour, exasperating the impatient nimble coyotes with his still presence. He had come to see, and for the seeing to strengthen his resolve, to feed his wrath. Instead, it opened his mind to accept the futility of war with the white man, this war his people could not win.

He was transformed in that hour, hiding in the brush in silent vigil. He was no longer a warrior fighting for his people; he had lost that honor when he had lost his comrades. He was now the anger, the vengeance, of a destroyed culture. He would exist only to punish the white man, to extract in blood and suffering some small payment for what had been taken. He hated, and his whole being fused around that hate.

Twenty-Four

Michael awoke naked, except for shoes, but hot and sweating, under a thin scratchy blanket. Judging by the dim iridescence of the sky and the stirrings of the many Rangers lying around him, he knew it was just before the dawn. He knew where he was and remembered everything that had happened, except for how he came to be naked.

Upon remembering, he experienced a brief moment of panic, for it was at about this time of morning, one day before, that his life had begun a transformation. The terror lasted only the briefest of moments and faded quickly into the background. He had metamorphosed into someone who had no stable ground for a seed of fear to sprout and grow. His forgotten hysterical reaction of the day before, was more turning away from something ugly, than a flight from something he feared. He had seen hell and survived a kind of purgatory; what then was left to be the unknown? His world was ordered and predictable, and his place and meaning in it were well-defined. He knew he moved about simultaneously on different planes and only one of these planes held an illusion of mortality. He knew that everything, including the immediacy of emotion, was transient and therefore mostly false.

He was relaxed and rested. The day before he had woken up weary, today he was aware of no stresses. He had no dread of living, nothing to make him want to retreat back into the cocoon of sleep, and nothing to make his sleep uneasy.

He was aware of the many lines and points of pain that criss-crossed his body, but unless he concentrated on them, they did nothing to disturb him. His sight was clear though colorless but, as there were only stars to look at, he felt no need to focus. He lay quiet and still, his mind relaxed an open. He did nothing but breathe in and out. Without thinking about it, he was aware of all the Rangers and whether they were asleep or awake. He was aware of the two Rangers on guard duty, and of the horses and mules. He was also aware of someone else out on the periphery of the camp, someone who did not belong, who was leaving with the fading darkness.

Michael knew his task on this earth. A struggle was taking place and he had been redeemed to play a part in it. The stakes in this battle were the souls of all humanity. God and the Devil, vied each and every moment of every day and night for even the most insignificant of territory. Every loss was a great loss, and every victory a terrible victory. As the archangel Michael, had fought and defeated Satan in the primal cosmic war, casting Satan out of heaven, Michael Burns was now prepared to assume the mantle of his namesake and be the earthly avatar of that archangel; sent to cast Satan, in his many guises, from yet another plane. Michael had been chosen by God to be his right hand on this battlefield. He would be God's avenger: the archangel himself incorporated into flesh.

Michael rolled from under the blanket and fought his way to his feet. He stood swaying in the gathering light, unconcerned by his nakedness. He gazed out in the direction of the evil presence but he felt it slipping away, already too far gone to be addressed.

He knew who had been out there and who's form he had been wearing. He was unperturbed that Satan was escaping, for he knew the battle was only beginning, and that there would be many meetings. Michael was facing the creek, just like he had the day before, but this time Satan was leaving, rather than arriving. That, in itself, was a small victory.

Michael walked swiftly down to the creek and waded into it several steps Cool water soaked into his brogans and gave his whole body relief from the heat. The sweat dried on his back. He shivered slightly when a faint breeze caressed him, gooseflesh appearing on his arms and head. A mule whickered softly.

The sun was rising in the distance but its brightness

was muted by the revealed presence of storm clouds on the horizon - black, billowing, ominous, but far away. The wind picked up and was blowing toward him, he could feel it on his face and chest - the cautious herald of the thunderstorm.

The storm's coming was an inevitability As Michael's bloodshot battered eyes watched its advance, he saw illuminated, in a dazzling burst of a spider's web of lightning, poised on the top of a small rise, silhouetted against the clouds, in the middle of the rain and fury, perhaps its catalyst, most assuredly at his ease, a lone rider. The figure's malevolence was palpable and his hatred was aimed unerringly towards Michael, carried to him on the storm's winds.

In that flash, Michael and his enemy recognized and acknowledged and mirrored each other, and came to an agreement.

Not today, they understood, but soon.

PART TWO: HIS RESURRECTION.

One

The white mule stood as much apart from the other mules and horses as possible. Even though it was hobbled and tied to the other animals, she would slide away or snort and stamp threateningly if approached too closely.

All the other beasts were various shades and mixes of darker hues, and although not a snowy white, the mule had no spot of color or shadow upon her other than black hooves, pupils, and muzzle. As if aware of her distinctive appearance the mule acted with a kind of vanity, and sulked or became violent if not treated with a certain deference. If not hitched in the front of the team she would drag her feet and bite the mule in front of her, if not fed and watered first, she would bray and kick in the mule equivalent of a temper tantrum. She would remember every slight and injustice and would extract some measure of retribution, even had she to wait days for the opportunity.

Because of its haughty demeanor, teamsters had named the creature Her Highness and usually referred to her as, “her royal fucking majesty.”

Highness was none too happy at the moment. Not only was she placed in close proximity to lesser animals, she had been roughly handled and then neglected by men who did not belong to her court. The shooting, the fire, and the killing of a mule, horses, and men, had grated on her nerves and created a cold anger that turned Her Highness into a hunter. Patiently she awaited a moment of opportunity, her long ears flattened back.

She had dozed fitfully through the night and, come morning, had been aware of Michael being up and about. Highness was especially attuned to the Muleskinner's presence. Not that she liked Michael overly much, she simply regarded Michael as a valued and polite servant. she would do Michael the favor of pulling his wagon because Michael treated Highness with preference and patience. This relationship was the standard by which Highness demonstrated her place in the hierarchy.

When Michael failed to respond to a gentle wicker, Highness's mood became even darker.

Red awoke at dawn and, propping himself on one elbow, surveyed the camp. He saw Michael standing naked but for shoes in the creek, and beyond him on the horizon, he saw the beginnings of a storm. He thought it remarkable that the boy was on his feet, and strange that he should be standing around without clothes. He didn't remember that they had discarded Michael's ruined clothes and, although they had set aside Pete's clothes for the boy, they had not placed them where Michael would easily find them.

Red had drunk heavily the previous night. He had awakened with a mild headache and a very dry mouth. He moved his sticky tongue around and smacked his parched lips then decided to rise and walk to the creek ,to both drink and inform the boy where he could find clothing.

Instead of proceeding in a straight line, he headed off on a tangent to find a place to relieve his bladder. He shuffled slowly, his eyes blurry and his mind clumsy, to a place just behind the hobbled animals.

The urinating figure directly behind her was standing still and only a few feet away. Her Highness turned her head and looked at Red to confirm what her ears had told her. Her eyes narrowed, and her ears twitched in the mule equivalent of a smile.

Two

The Pruitt brothers liked to steal horses,. They would steal anything that was not nailed down, and if it was nailed down, they were inclined set it on fire. They never met a man that they would hesitate to murder and they had never seen a woman or girl that they did not want to rape.

They were well mounted on stolen horses and well-armed with stolen guns. In addition, the four of them rode with six pistoleers, half-breed Indians, and Mexicans, who, even The Pruitts considered subhuman. Very few considered trying to enforce the law when the lawbreakers were the Pruitts and their companions.

The gang had been doing a brisk trade for several years. They would steal, rape, and murder along the Texas border and across the river into Mexico. Then exchange who and what they had taken for Comanche horses and loot. The horses they could always find a buyer for and give complete assurances that the ponies had not been stolen - at least by them. In this way, the Comanche were happy, for the Pruitts would often trade them three stolen horses for two more marketable ponies. The horse traders were happy, for they would receive a steady supply of horseflesh without having to traffic openly in stolen goods. The Pruitt gang was very happy that they could make an easy living at the expense of others.

The state and people of Texas were less than pleased, however, and had placed a sizable reward on the head of each brother; a bounty no one had ever even attempted to collect. Since the gang was more than comfortable hiding out in Mexico or the Comancheria, they had eluded capture and hanging by the Rangers.

And it looked as though their luck was going to continue

to hold. They had been pursued for two days by one of the relentless Ranger companies in the field. Their Captain was hard as nails and mean as a badger, though only five-foot-two inches tall.

Captain Black had been born with the name Johan Schwartzenschimit. When he was fifteen, his family emigrated to Texas from Germany and had Americanized his first name to John; they kept the family name of Schwartzenschimit. John became hard and mean from the many fights that had developed over his surname's syllabic resemblance to the words 'short-shit'. John's first autonomous act, outside his family influence, was to sign his name on the Ranger's enlistment roster as John Blacksmith. But after several misunderstandings about his occupation, he shortened it to John Black. Later in life, he would regret not having changed it to the more common John Smith, when no one seemed to be able to resist rhyming him into Jack Black, and then Black Jack. Problems over his name, coupled with an innate lack of humor, kept Captain Jack continually irritated. This along with his German ancestry made him a commander who would tolerate no excuses for a job poorly done. And as a result, his men were as angry and on edge as he was.

Although it was very bad luck to have Captain Jack on your trail, it was very fortunate to have a thunderstorm coming up that would obliterate your tracks.

The gang was oblivious to the fact of their pursuit and was more concerned about the weather than the hand of retribution. The nine of them paused and gathered while mounted around Joseph Pruitt, the youngest and smallest of the four brothers. Joseph was the temporary boss of the gang, left in charge by the eldest brother, Beasley.

Beasley had split off from the gang three days earlier, in a black mood set off by his brother's constant bickering and fueled by his own constant drinking. It was either leave or start shooting his kin. With only a few terse words, he had gone off on his own to wallow in self-pity over being cursed with a childhood and family that was not perfect.

Joseph was flanked on his left by his brother O.C., a cheerful faced man, and on his right by his brother Price, who wore a constantly dour expression. all of the Pruitts were dark-haired, slender, and of average height, with meager coarse beards. The six other mongrel outlaws remained just far enough behind to be excluded, but close enough to overhear.

"Storm's coming'," Ocie observed loudly.

"No foolin'?" Joseph felt that he was quite clever and that his three elder brothers were less than brilliant. Joseph liked to demonstrate his superiority through sarcasm, which he considered the highest form of wit. He could take Ocie and Price down a peg with a barb but Beasley would beat him bloody if he even suspected that Joseph was taunting him.

"Yeah, just look over that way, you'll see for...," Ocie's voice trailed off when he caught Joseph's condescending look. Joseph's mouth was set in a nearly permanent sneer.

"What do you suppose we ought to do?" Price asked.

"I suppose we ought to find someplace we can stay dry." Even when Joseph was serious it tended to come out sarcastically, making his brothers feel more put out for not being able to discern the difference.

"Um, where?" Price asked cautiously.

Joseph looked at his brother with a weary face, as if years of putting up with so much stupidity were taking their toll and then, shaking his head as if with disbelief, he turned his horse sharply to the left, jostling Ocie roughly aside.

Over his shoulder, as if he did not care if he were heard or not, Joseph said, "There's that ranch the Comanches raided last spring about four miles south of here. I think there's still an adobe standing, if I'm not mistaken."

Ocie and Price fell in behind their little brother but let him ride further ahead.

"I hate it when Beasley leaves that little shit in charge," Price growled in a low voice.

"We're better off. When Beasley gets ornery, he can be

worse than Pa." Ocie had several jagged scars and a crooked nose from his father.

"Someday that little shit is going to need my help and he's going to wish he was kinder to me. And you. Right now I wouldn't piss on him if his hair were on fire, I tell you what."

"Well, he's right about that Adobe, if it still has a roof, even if it is out of our way," Ocie said, it hard for him to hold a grudge.

"Yeah well, he'll get his one day I'm certain, and I'll be there to laugh, I tell you what. If Beasley were here he'd whoop his little ass black and blue and you know it."

"If Beasley we're here now he'd whip all our asses and you know that's a fact."

Three

"God Damn it!" Red shouted so loudly that his voice cracked and became a hoarse shriek.

He was lying on his belly, his head lifted like a turtle's, his eyes watering and his face crimson.

"That fucking mule kicked me." His tone disbelieving.

He squeezed handfuls of sand and his legs squirmed ineffectually. The Rangers, only half awake, ran to Red's side and milled around him not knowing what to do. Luke, ever unflappable, pushed through the confused mob and squatted down in front of Red's face.

"She break your back?" he asked calmly, and with no more gravity, as if he were asking if Red had had his breakfast yet.

"You heartless son of a bitch!" Red came to his hands and knees and made a grab for Luke, but pain cut his rage short, he curled in on himself, his mouth open in a gasp of agony.

"I believe your back ain't broke if you're able to get up like that. Want me to shoot that mule for you?" This was Luke's way of demonstrating some emotional involvement.

"No. Don't shoot it." The voice was urgent and not Red's. Luke turned slightly without rising and saw Michael, naked but for shoes, looming over him. "Don't shoot my mule."

"All right, I won't." Luke was a little unsettled by Michael strangeness. His request, his nudity, and his general oddness conjoined to make Luke want to placate the boy.

"Maybe you want to get some clothes on, fella." He suggested it not out of prudishness but in hopes of removing the disturbing presence.

Red was bellowing to be helped up and so Luke turned away from Michael and he and several others lifted Red, carefully setting him on his feet. They watched silently as Red staggered a few steps at a time, hunched over, holding his back with both hands, his elbows sticking out to his sides as if in some grotesque comical bird imitation.

His aimless reeling march brought him right up to Michael, who reflexively reached out and took Red by the shoulders, steadying him. Red stood swaying, his eyes closed, held firm in Michael's grip. He was cursing inarticulately, but fluently, with every outgoing breath in English, Spanish, and Irish.

Michael understood pain. He knew it altered and isolated a person. He was not feeling any pity for Red but he recognized a fellow traveler, and he bridged his own alienation to accompany Red for a portion of his journey.

Red opened his eyes after a while and the two men looked at each other for several moments. Michael's patience and acceptance calmed him. Although the pain was still as intense, he was able to master himself, and began to choose his actions rather than to just react.

He left Michael's hands and walked with a degree of control over to where he had made his bed. Slowly, gasping at the effort, he sank to his knees and lay down on his side with his legs drawn up slightly.

"Luke, you bastard you, come here and see if all me bones are in one place. And one of you slack-jawed little girls fetch me bottle. The rest of you stop gaping at me and find something to do or I'll have your arses for me breakfast." He closed his eyes again.

Luke knelt down behind Red and began poking and probing, none too gently, on Red's spine and ribs. One of the Rangers searched through Red's belongings and brought him a glass corked bottle half full of clear whiskey. He uncorked it, and leaned down and tapped Red on the shoulder with it. Red opened his eyes and accepted the bottle, making pained faces all the while.

"Bless you, my son, you're one of the good ones. Give that naked boy dead-Pete's clothes," he told the bottle bringer. "He'll fry in no time walking about in his birthday suit."

"You should look to yourself captain. Your horse is out of the barn there, you know."

Red mumbled an expletive and set the bottle down in the dirt, screwing its base to plant it firmly. Using both hands, he tucked his manhood away and buttoned up.

"Pissed meself too," he said and reached for the bottle again. Never one to guzzle his liquor, he took several small sips that added up to a guzzle.

"Can't find nothing broke, but your back is all twisted up bad." Luke had stopped his prodding. "That kick made you a hunchback, Red."

"Then I'll be needing more whiskey," he said. "Tell the boys to settle in, we're going to rest here for a couple of days."

Luke and the other Ranger walked away, leaving Red to his drinking. They had expected to remain here for a time anyway; the men and animals had been driven hard for the past few days and needed to catch their breath. Now that they had put a stop to the Comanches, there was no place they needed to be with any urgency.

Red's drinking did not bother the troop, many men they

knew drank too much. The sight of Red nursing at his bottle was a familiar sight that eased the Rangers' worries about their captain.

Luke walked up to Michael and, speaking clearly, he pointed to a pile of clothes. “You can have the dead fella’s clothes there. I think whatever you might have had with you got burnt up.”

Michael nodded and went to the pile and begin dressing, pulling the dark pants on over his shoes. Luke stood nearby, studying him. “Them savages must have given you a good wallop on the head judging by that lump on your brow.”

Michael nodded again.

“It’s strange to me seeing you dressed in the Puritan’s clothes like this.”

“Why’s that?” Michael asked, buttoning up the gray shirt that was a little tight around his shoulders.

“Pete was kilt by being struck on the head just like you was, except a little more on the side. You got kind of the same build as the Puritan. Seeing you dressed in his clothes, with that big knot on your face, it's like he rose from the dead or something. Guess you got a harder head than Pete did. His caved in like an egg.”

Michael touched the lump above his eye. The flesh was swollen and tender, with a knot on the bone underneath, but he could feel that the skull was solid and whole.

“I believe the only reason you’re alive and he's dead is that little bit of difference where you was hit. A man's life can be measured in fractions of an inch, it seems.” Luke was interested in anatomy.

Michael noticed the bullwhip lying where it had been dropped the morning before. He picked it up, coiling it carefully.

“That’s one thing of yours that ain't been burnt up, but I can't imagine you would be too happy to see it. It's what they beat you with wasn’t it?”

“No,” Michael said. “I want this.”

"Suit yourself. You can come with us till we come to a town, I suppose. We're going to stay here a day or two, though, and rest up."

Puritan Pete's shotgun had been leaned, barrel up, against his saddle. Whip in one hand, Michael picked it up by the leather sling attached to its forearm and trigger guard. "Can I have this?" he asked, holding it up.

Before Luke could respond, a big drop of rain splattered on his face and was quickly followed by a rapidly growing shower. The storm had arrived. Without answering Michael, Luke moved rapidly off to find his hat and some shelter. All the Rangers, Red included, moved away from the creek to higher ground.

Vested in his new somber black clothes, Michael lifted his bruised and battered face towards the dark thundering heavens. He raised his arms, shotgun in one hand, whip in the other. "Thy rod and thy staff," he said. "They comfort me."

Four

Beasley Pruitt rode through the violent summer storm like it was a perfect spring day. The tempestuous weather fitted his inner climate like a hand in a glove. For the brief hour that it lasted, his horse trudged doggedly on, his head lowered.

The rain had not reduced the temperature, only raised the humidity, and when the sun broke out and the dark clouds dwindled to a dull haze, the only real difference was his clothing was heavy with water and steaming.

He rode for an hour more, neither looking to the left or to the right, not concerned with anything other than putting miles between himself and his brothers.

He didn't love his brothers, he did not like his brothers,

but he seemed unable to be rid of his brothers. Wherever he went, whatever he did, they were invariably there, near him, doing what he was doing, making him murderously angry.

He didn't need them, they needed him. He made the decisions, came up with the plans, and saw them followed through. Without him, they would wander aimlessly, pissing people off until someone had the good sense to hang them. He was living his life and they were his persistent ubiquitous shadows. His most frequent command was that they should shut the hell up. Sometimes that was all he said to them for days.

Although he was riding away from family, he was also vaguely riding toward other family. Both parents were long dead but he had a sister who resided in a shithole of a town less than six miles further on. Mary, though younger, had been part mother and part friend to him in an unwholesome and disjointed way since before their Ma had died. He rarely quarreled with her, and would often do as she asked, even though he considered himself an order giver, not a taker.

His brothers he had sent to meet and trade with a band of Comanche that they had done well with before and should be able to do well with again even without him. His brothers were innately violent and he had no doubt that they would acquire horses or be killed trying. Either outcome would suit him just fine. He'd also told them to scout a certain ranch for livestock that might be worth stealing, then meet him back at their sister's. His last order before he turned his horse was to tell them all to go straight to hell.

His mood improved as the day wore on and the distance between himself and his brothers increased. Just as he was considering stopping and making a midday meal, he sighted a man camped with two browsing horses a mile ahead. A lone traveler and good horses were a welcome opportunity for a horse thief. He loosened his revolver in its holster and angled his horse in the direction of the man's camp.

At a leisurely walking pace, it took his horse half an hour

to arrive within speaking distance. The man stood waiting for him with one foot back and a large bore rifle cradled in his arms. His eyes were narrowed and squinting, even though his face was shaded by a slouched-brimmed black hat with a rattlesnake-skin hatband. The rifle's muzzle was casually, but unmistakably, pointed at Beasley. Beasley could see from where he was that the hammer was pulled back to half cock, with the man's thumb resting firmly on the cock and his finger squarely on the trigger.

"Good day, Sir," Beasley greeted him. "You might be mindful where you point that rifle, Sir, tends to make a body nervous."

"Ye don't look like the scary sort to me." The man had a gravely solem and deep voice that cut through the air.

"Well, it would be a sad story to be shot by accident." Beasley smiled, his teeth were crooked but big and shiny white.

"Would not be an accident if you were to be shot today. Ye can be shore of that." He sounded very sure.

"My name is Beasley Pruitt." Beasley waited to see if his name would be recognized.

"How are ye, Mister Pruitt?" he asked, his manner changing abruptly. "I'm Sam Johnstone. Rattler is what they call me. Ye going to dismount or stay perched up there where I have to squint at ye?"

"I would be pleased to join you for a while. Not too many travelers out here and a person finds himself tiresome company after a time." Beasley was dismounting as he spoke and even turned his back on the man and his rifle.

"Happy for the company, and if ye have any coffee to share ye will have made yourself a friend." He shifted the rifle to point at the ground.

Beasley produced a burlap sack from his belongings, which were draped across the rump of his horse. He shook it, and the beans rattled. "Well then, friend. I'll make us a fire."

As Beasley gathered sticks and brush, he studied the man

and his camp. He had obviously been caught without shelter in the storm as well, and had spread his clothes out over bushes to dry. Most of the garments were of buckskin and there was a heavy coat made from a blue and red trade blanket. Sam himself was naked from the waist up except the much-worn hat. His torso and arms were dark brown and muscular. He covered himself below the waist with a soft skin loincloth and artfully fringed deer-hide leggings and high moccasins. Though his body was supple and straight, Beasley guessed that the man would be firmly into his fifties for his face was lined and worn, and his beard and long hair had considerable gray. In addition to the caplock rifle, he had a long knife in a beaded sheath, and a tomahawk suspended from a belt decorated with bear's teeth. Around his neck on a thin leather strand was a four-inch-long rattlesnake rattle flanked by two delicate fangs. Sam was taller than Beasley by many inches and walked in and odd careful manner.

Though far from the Rockies, Sam was obviously a mountain man. Beasley, like most children, had been raised on the colorful tales of Kit Carson, Jed Smith, and Bigfoot Wallace. Like Daniel Boone before them, the mountain men were considered the quintessential frontiersmen and were elevated to mythic stature. Beasley tried to summon some disdain for the older man but found himself unable to push back the awe and respect.

Though the beaver trade was played out by the mid-thirties, and those famous few had moved on to other adventures, there were still those who trapped and lived hard and solitary lives in the cold high country. Sam seemed old enough to have been a contemporary of the originals, both genuine and fabulous.

Killing an authentic mountain man would be sacrilegious and boast-worthy. Beasley sat across the little fire and simmering pot from Sam and sorted through his feelings, and calculated his odds. The old man's quiet, and his sharp-eyed watchfulness, was unsettling his normal overconfidence and made him feel childish and fidgety. Most folks were easy to shoot, as they were either unsuspecting or afraid.

"Where are ye headed to in this wide world?" Sam asked suddenly.

"Home, I suppose."

"Are ye unsure if it is home ye are bound for or if where ye are bound for is not home?"

Beasley had to decipher and then ponder for his answer. "Both."

Sam absorbed that without comment.

"Looks as though you are far from where you started from," Beasley stated.

"Yaw," Sam replied with a slow nod.

"Where are you going to? If you don't mind my asking." Beasley felt like a boy fishing for a bedtime story.

"Unsure as well." Sam brightened. "I am in search of warmer climes after what occurred in the mountains."

"What do you mean?" Beasley bit the bait and all his murderous thoughts faded away.

"Blackfeet, son. Blackfeet is what happened to me. Waugh, there was never a less sociable or hospitable creature created than a Blackfoot, I'm here to tell ye."

"You've never made acquaintance with a Comanche then." Beasley sneered.

"Met them I have, and was duly impressed. However, they haven't the wiles and demon like cunning of the Blackfeet. This vast flatness requires boldness and does not stimulate a devious nature, is my thoughts on it. The Comanche seem like they just want to kill ye in all haste. The Blackfeet want to play with ye for a while before easing ye out of this life." Sam finished his coffee and hung his chipped ceramic mug upside down from a bush's branch.

He seemed lost in his own recollections but, with a sharp turn of his face to Beasley, he continued. "I had set my traps in a high marsh that was rich with beaver and was working profitably through the winter when I found sign that my camp had been scouted. I picked up fast and headed down but the savages were waiting for me. I had been herded and corralled. I was relieved of all my possessions and the fruits of my winter's labor. They even took the clothes from my back and the horse from beneath me.

"They kept me tied and afoot, and goaded me along with pricks from their lances. They informed me they were taking me to their village to let the squaws and children commit all manner of deviltry to entertain the tribe with my sufferings. They promised to take my eyes and tongue last. To keep me helpless and mutilated, for their ridicule. And when they tired of me, they would cut off and roast bits of me to feed their curs."

"What did you do?" Beasley was all in.

"I bided." He breathed in and out noisily. "I bided but no opportunity for escape presented itself. They were ever vigilant. I weakened from their abuses and grew desperate. When they paused to rest their mounts, one brave turned his back to me and commenced to relieve himself. In impetuous anger, and not reasoned judgment, I kicked that savage a hard blow to his spine. I heard it snap, and, as he had been facing the edge of a chasm, he fell far. Some of the band went for me, the others rushed to retrieve their confederate.

"I wasted no time and ran up the side of the mountain. I chose no trail and went where their horses could not follow. They chased me on foot. Though my hands were tied my fear of torture and dismemberment was greater than their wrath for I eluded them for the day and blundered higher through the night. Each time I fell, I rose and moved again. My body was torn and bleeding from the hard edges of the earth and trees. My nakedness kept me active though, for, sweating as I was, the cold would find me the moment I relented.

"I did not stop until there was no higher to go. From my peak I could see, far below and far away, the band moving again toward their village, one brave draped across his horse.

"But my trials were only just begun. They had abandoned

pursuit but left me to freeze and starve. From my vantage, I could see much of the world, and I cursed its hostile indifference. There is no colder winter than the Rocky mountain winter. When ye piss ye must keep your pecker swinging lest the stream freeze and tie you in place 'till the spring thaw. The dry wind is like sharp knives and the sun never finds the valley floor. I suffered every moment torture more hellish than anything them noble savages could have devised.

"There is little fuel for fire that high up and I had no means to create a spark. I knew if I slept, I would not arise. I tumbled and fell back the way I had come. I staggered back onto the trail they had taken me. My mind was gibbering. I dreamed as I walked of hairy upright monkeys half my height again, whose oversize footprints I followed. Those fantastic beasts led me unerring to the camp of six trappers where I appeared a spectral and frightening apparition under the glare of a full moon. I know not how many days and nights later.

"They coaxed me into a shelter. Ladled rich beavertail broth into me and laid me under buffalo and bearskins five deep between two roaring fires. And, though I baked for a night and a day and regained the full faculty of my reason, I lost most of my toes and both my ears.

"I recuperated with those blessed men for the rest of the winter without shedding any further extremities, and come the spring, I went with them to rendezvous and got myself outfitted again on loan. I spent the next winter trapping to pay back my debt and acquire a small stake, but I'm here to tell ye that the cold was so hard on my flesh, so deep in my bones that I cursed my life and the world unceasingly. My trial had deprived me of any ability to stand up to the unforgiving winters.

"So, I left the mountains when the thaw come and headed down and south. I spent a year in New Mexico with the senoritas but, even there, the winter was more than I could bear. I continued southerly until the land flattened and the sun was always on me. Though I fear I may have overdone it, as this side of the earth is warm enough to melt the very rocks." He flicked a drop of sweat from his nose, it sizzled in the ashes of the fire.

Beasley shook his head slightly as if coming out of a dream. He finished the bitter dregs of his tepid coffee.

"That is good yarn, mister, any of it true?" He wanted Sam to know he was nobody's fool.

Sam looked at him unflinchingly, "Well, if'n it ain't," he said. "It ought to be."

Beasley considered that and tried to see if Sam had ears but the thick hair and slouched hat made it impossible to discern. Right then Beasley decided to kill him. And if the old man had ears he would cut them off and feed them to a dog.

Feigning interest he leaned forward examining Sam's rifle. "Is that a Saint Louis Hawken?" he asked.

"Yaw."

"May I have a closer look?"

"Yaw." Sam removed the percussion cap, lowered the hammer and handed Beasley the rifle.

Beasley went through the motions of examining the heavy piece that he had hoped to shoot its owner with. He stood and held it to his shoulder, sighting at nothing. He thought he would draw his pistol and shoot Sam in the face but when he looked down Sam was drawing circles in the dirt with the tip of his long knife and watching Beasley's hands.

Beasley handed the rifle back. Sam stuck the knife in the ground and recapped the piece, putting it at half cock and back into the cradle of his arm.

"That firearm of yours is of interest to me. I have been considering acquiring one for some time now. May I?" he held out a hand.

Beasley hesitated but complied. He wished to appear trusting and therefore trustworthy.

Sam leaned his rifle against his shoulder. He held the pistol with both hands. He looked at it from all possible angles even down the barrel. He worked the hammer and the trigger carefully, grunting at how the cylinder turned with the action. He held it up to the sun and grinned as its blued barrel glinted. He sighted it at arm's length, squinting one eye shut. He turned away from the sun and shaded the pistol with his body.

"Samuel Colt, New York City" he read out loud, pronouncing every letter slowly as if sounding it out.

He abruptly turned back and handed the pistol back to Beasley butt first saying, "It seems all the finest people are named Samuel."

Beasley took the gun and stepped back a pace. The old man had left the rifle leaning against his shoulder. Sam was just sitting in his still way, smiling slightly at him.

"Now," Beasley said. He raised the revolver, cocking it as he did so. The moment it was settled on the old man's chest he pulled the trigger.

There was a metallic clap but the pistol did not fire. Beasley froze for a moment, caught in the act of attempting murder. Sam rose, fluidly and powerfully. He raised his rifle to his shoulder bringing the hammer to full cock. The dark hole of the muzzle seemed enormous to Beasley at such close proximity. Beasley frantically recocked his gun and squeezed again but with the same unsatisfactory result.

"Cock it again and I will kill you," Sam told him, his voice soft and pleasant. "I have never killed a white man but I will take your scalp if further provoked. Set that piece down now, I am through playing with ye."

Furious Beasley did as he was told.

"I see that I have finally acquired a revolver. I will take it, and powder and ball and other paraphernalia ye may have as well. In fact, you had best leave all your worldly goods here with me."

"You're robbing me?" His astonishment was genuine.

"Yaw. As I see it, I am taking a chisel away from a baby." He gestured with the rifle. "Now go, before I take a switch to ye. Ye may keep your horse."

"I will kill you for this." Beasley promised.

"Then I had best just shoot you now." Sam sighted down the barrel.

"No!" Beasley held his hands up to ward off the impending round. "Wait, I'll go. I won't hold no grudge, I swear."

"Then go. Unhitch your belongings and don't forget to leave the holster. And refrain from saying anything more that might aggravate me."

With shaking hands, Beasley untied the pack and let it fall. He was saddled before it hit the ground and turning his horse when the old man spoke.

"Boy," he said. "It was all true." He retired the gun to its crook and removed his hat, hanging it on the muzzle. With his free hand he pulled away the hair on the side of his head and, where an ear should be, there was only scarred flesh.

Beasley raced away at full gallop.

Sam lowered the rifle when Beasley was out of range. He picked up the revolver, blew dust from it, and replaced the three caps.

Five

Just before sundown, Captain Black rode into Red's camp at the head of his troop. Red had been hard at his bottle, which stood mostly defeated, as an analgesic to the considerable discomfort brought on by the mule's unprovoked kick. It had not truly alleviated the pain but had mitigated the suffering. Red's mood was merry and nasty.

He watched Michael with a peculiar fascination. He found himself happy to follow the young man's doings as if watching a play. Michael at present, squatted at the edge of the swollen and fast flowing creek, scraping off his meager beard with a borrowed razor. Red smiled as he watched.

The long thin low clouds left over from the storm, gathered crimsons and golds and oranges gradually over hours, tinting the harsh barren landscape a feminine pink. The prolonged setting of the sun cast a serene quiet over the troop. Everyone slowed, becoming idle, and they smiled at each other companionably.

Red was dozing he realized, as the crunching of boot soles on gravel roused him.

"People coming, Capt'n," Luke said. "More Rangers it seems. Want me to help you up?

"Hell no." The pink had faded and grays were prominent. In the last of the light Red squinted through his inebriation to try and focus on the approaching band.

"That's Black Jack, that is. The little cunt thinks he's Santa Ana. Makes his men ride tight like that."

Black led a column of twos, seven layers deep, with the pair in the rear leading pack mules and spare mounts. Flanking the column were four Lipan Apache scouts carrying long lances and riding decorated pintos, two to a side. Michael had to step away from the creek as they forded it at a walk.

"Well, thanks to Dad, it's the tiny German come to our rescue," Red announced to the camp. Most of his men laughed as did a few of Black's.

Black's troop spread out to either side of him as he halted his lathered horse at Red's feet. Red sipped from his bottle.

"Greetings, Admiral Rednose. Is there a purpose to your being here or is this just where you fell from your horse?"

"I've been earning me pay. Keeping Texas safe and whole, freeing us from the terror of the Comanche. We put four of the weasels in the ground and saved a drover from the fires of perdition."

"Looks like you put one of your own in the ground as well," he said, pointing at Pete's mounded grave with his chin and grinning.

"Are you going to set up there on your high horse all

night?" Red asked, his face losing all its humor.

"We have business to consider, you and I. I will see my men camped properly and then we will talk." He led his men downstream.

"Properly, me arse," Red muttered into his bottle. Red had never given his men orders as to how to camp and was not to be embarrassed that his men did not sleep in neat rows. "I suppose he instructs them as to how best to shit and piss as well, he does."

"Them Germans like things a particular way, I have noticed." Luke opined.

"As if that makes life work." Red drank deeply, draining the last.

"Want me to make you coffee, Red? Luke asked.

"Hell no."

Six

Michael sat close to one of the several small fires, oblivious to the men with whom he shared it. The night was warm and the fires were not necessary but they were cheering after the rain and helped the Rangers be companionable. He ate grits with beans and bacon that had been given to him for supper. Other than speaking his name in response to introductions, he had given only monosyllabic replies that made a conversation with him futile.

The talk around the campfire was bawdy and crude. The Rangers were bachelors mostly, young and healthy, and because they were untroubled by any immediate needs their conversation easily turned to women. As if trying to balance the preponderance of masculinity present, they felt nearly constant curiosity and preoccupation about the physiological components of the half of the human race not represented in their ranks or on their bodies.

Loneliness and isolation were so much a fact of Michael's past that he accepted it as a natural unquestioned state. His self-generated lack of inclusion created no bitterness or hostility. He could not imagine why anyone would want to talk to him or what he could possibly have to say that anyone would care to hear. He did not blame others for not reaching out to him, and he did not know to take responsibility for his own insulated condition. He knew worse than nothing about women and so felt no ability to participate conversationally. The Rangers simply assumed his quiet was the product of his brutalization and that he wished to be let alone.

His father had insisted vehemently that children should be seen and not heard and Michael had been raised not to speak until spoken to. Both rules had been enforced with the very real threat of a switching.

Michael had scars on his back and bottom that predated his injuries at the hands of the Comanches. For speaking out of turn or any other infraction of the rules, his father would give him a cold look and quietly tell him to go out and cut a switch. If Michael failed to return with due speed his punishment would last longer and have more energy.

After being handed the cut branch, his father would instruct him to remove his shirt, drop his trousers, and lean over the table upon which they ate their meals.

His father favored dividing the blows into groups of ten, occasionally even exceeding the one-hundred mark. After each ten, Gabriel would pause to rest his arm and preach to Michael for him to cast out Satan and cleanse himself of evil and blasphemous thoughts.

The beatings were persistent enough that Michael still habitually slept on his belly. As Michael grew older and more withdrawn, the whippings became less frequent but more intense. The day Michael left he had been sent out to cut a switch for failing to say grace in a loud and clear enough voice.

The double bind of being beaten for talking and not talking loudly enough, was more than Michael could stand. He stood facing his father's house, the sun setting behind him, tears of frustration trickling down his cheeks, telling himself in a quiet voice that it was not fair, that it was not right.

An hour later he was several miles closer to where the sun had set, still crying, still muttering to himself, and trailing the three-foot willow branch in the dust behind him.

The rest of that night was vague in Michaels memory. He had slept somewhere out on the prairie and, upon awakening knew, that it was impossible to go home. He left the switch where it lay and went off to make his way in the world with a mixture of dread and relief.

Michael's mother had never switched him, although he very clearly remembered her slapping his face with bone-rattling force on several occasions. Being switched or whipped with a belt or struck with a hand was not an unusual method of child-rearing in Scotland or America at the time of Michael's youth, and so he never questioned the act itself, and never questioned that he was a loathsome, worthless, stupid, lost-cause, who deserved what he had received.

He had few memories of his homeland other than a cold damp stone house, oatmeal and butter for breakfast, and bathing in a large metal tub the evening before Sabbath.

He only sketchily remembered his mother bathing him, but she continued to do so long after he was capable of washing himself. He never tried to avoid the bath the way many boys his age resisted cleanliness. It was the only time that he was touched in a non-violent way. His baths were lengthy and thorough, his mother stroking with her bare hands, cleaning every part of him slowly and without a scrub brush or cloth. She undressed and dried him and at no point during the course of the hour or more would she make eye contact. Often the washing would continue until the bathwater had lost all its heat and Michael's teeth were chattering.

The bathing ritual went on into Michael's preteen years.

They ended when one day his father entered unexpectedly and became enraged over what he saw. Michael had been standing naked, his hair tousled, his mother kneeling in front of him drying his legs with a coarse towel. As she wiped the towel slowly up and down his dry leg, she leaned heavily against Michael as if for support, her cheek pressed up against his erect penis. Gabriel had beaten both Michael and his mother that night; calling her a harlot and lascivious and him unnatural and vile. The next day Gabriel announced to a silent family that they were leaving for America, and soon after that, his mother was dead.

Michael would often wash his hands and face but almost never bathed completely. He would often look at and be aroused by a woman but this only confused him; mixed as it was with anger and shame. He remained a virgin.

Michael stared at the stigmata on his palms, the voices of the Rangers registering only as background noise. He assumed himself cleansed and purified by his ordeal, and that his fleshy self had been purged of all his earthly and base desires. To be liberated from the requirements of nature was a source of great relief to him. It freed him from having to explore or feel the pain of exclusion from an entire area of life that terrified and confounded him. It was a fear he no longer had to confront, an enigma he need not decipher.

Michael knelt and thanked his creator for all he had done for him.

Seven

Mary Pruitt knelt in the pasture behind the livery stable earning a living. The pasture was well-used, but unoccupied at present by any of the four-legged residents of the livery. It was so thoroughly speckled by road apples that Mary had to take care when she chose a spot to kneel.

Before her stood the stablehand, his pants draped over his shoes, his face turned up as if enraptured by the Milky Way, his eyes, however, screwed tightly shut.

Mary was not the only whore in the little town, but she had carved herself a sizable portion of a competitive market by possessing a physical asset that set her apart from the other women. She was missing her top two front teeth. This feature, rather than diminish her attractiveness to the opposite sex, created a niche in the oldest profession that kept her fed, clothed, housed, and drunk. Her unique dentation created a mystique that made Mary, and the service she provided, seem not only unusual but exotically tantalizing. Rather than lay her down or bend her over, men would invariably ask her to kneel, as if in prayer, before them.

Except for the skill acquired by constant practice, Mary was probably no more creative or talented at the act than any other adventuress, but evidently, the idea of a mouth with fewer sharp obstacles brought her more attention and remuneration then if her plain round face had been left unmarred. In addition, many of her married patrons came to her in the rationalization that oral sex was not cheating, and they need not then feel the requisite shame.

Although when she smiled sincerely she kept her lips pressed firmly together, Mary was actually quite content with how her uniqueness had changed her career. She did not care to have sweaty farmers and cowboys crushing her down with their weight, or humping her and grunting like goats. Specialization allowed her a degree of control that most prostitutes lost the moment the money changed hands. Sometimes a man would get rough and grab her hair and try to force in more than she was willing to accommodate, but she had learned to keep one hand wrapped around the base of the penis and the other tugging firmly on their stones. If she felt herself put-upon, rather than gag, she would squeeze hard with both hands and bite down with her remaining teeth until the fellow's passions were replaced by a more urgent need to respect Mary's boundaries. Should any man take offense at this tactic and try to repress her further, she would produce a pocket revolver and not hesitate.

She had been kneeling in front of her new best friend of the moment with her head bobbing up and down, for less than two minutes when his legs went soft and wobbly and his hands reached up and pulled his hat down hard over his ears and he said, "Oh my Lord, my Lord, that is good."

She continued to pump her hand up and down the shaft while she turned her face away and spit a large gobbet of jism onto the dirt. Sometimes she would take her face away entirely and let the man spill his seed directly onto the earth, but usually, she accepted it into her mouth, but never any farther. She liked to leave the men she referred to as 'my stupid boys' happy. It was good business and she would normally playfully jerk at their spent members for a few moments after they ejaculated, making fun of them and teasing them crudely. Often, they would blush. She wanted them to like her.

"You don't make me work hard for my money, sweetie pie, short and sweet, I tell you what." She grinned at him, showing the gap in her teeth.

"I don't care to waste my time, it seems," he said.

"That hardly took any time at all, sugar. This little feller seems happy though. Suppose you got your money's worth." She tugged on his little feller a couple more times before letting him loose.

He bent over and began pulling up his trousers. "Damn hot out tonight," he said, attempting to steer the conversation in another direction.

"Your ass got a little cooler," she laughed and slapped his cheeks.

"It did at that." He grinned at her and took several steps away. "Smoke? He asked, pulling makings and paper from a sack he had under his shirt

"Yeah, roll me one, and let's have a drink from your bottle. She helped herself to a jug perched on the top of a fence post, where they had left it two minutes earlier, and took several deep pulls.

"You got an empty leg, I never knew a woman to drink the way you do."

"It's something I learned from my Pa, only thing worth a damn thing I ever got from that bastard, I tell you what."

"Mean drunk, was he?"

"Just plain mean." She looked down and all the play went out of her face. "He was the one knocked out my teeth."

"What you do to make him do that?"

"I wouldn't stop crying while he was fucking me."

He choked on his whiskey, "Shit Mary Maggie you shouldn't say such things."

"Why not? It's the truth."

"Well, I guess no one wants to hear it like that is all."

"Bastard climbed on me when I was ten years old and didn't get off until I was seventeen when Beasley shot him in the head. The day after they buried him, I went and shit on his grave. Bastard!" Mary drank deeply from the jug and then passed it back.

"Beasley shot him? Damn, he's one tough man your brother. What'd your ma have to say about that?"

"Nothing. That bitch was long gone. Died when I was ten. I suppose that's why he.... Hell, Beasley ain't that tough. I'd a shot the bastard myself. Beasley was the first one of us to steal a gun. He didn't shoot him on my account anyhow. Had plenty enough reasons of his own, I tell you what." The last was not true. Beasley had shot his father to stop him from raping his sister and Mary would always be grateful for it. 'Don't you say nothing bad about my brother. He isn't what everybody thinks he is."

The stablehand knew that Beasley was exactly what everybody thought he was.

"Hell, I just meant he was right to shoot him. Took a lot of balls is all I meant. I ain't stupid enough to be saying nothing bad about him." He wished he had not said that last part for fear of Mary taking offense at the implication, but she was too drunk now to read between lines.

The talk of incest was arousing to him. He had a clear image of Mary, who, even now, was thin, small, and girlish as a ten-year-old, squirming underneath some big faceless drunken brute. Mary almost never consented to intercourse. She was rarely asked, and when she did, she insisted on being on top. He thought she might be drunk enough that if he worked it carefully, he could be that big drunken brute in his fantasy - although Mary was twice ten now. He handed her the jug.

"Drink up there darling, the night ain't over yet."

"I'll stick all night if you got the coin, but this whiskey is buying you nothing." She drank from the jug, spilling a trickle down her chin. She's reached out with her free hand and felt his crotch. "Well, look who woke up. That little feller need me to hum him another lullaby?"

He sidled closer to her and put his hand on her breast. "We could find us a place to lie down that would be nice."

"Pay first, or I'll be taking this jug and leaving." Her voice hard and serious.

He quickly released her breast, tossed away the last of his smoke, and dug into his pockets for cash, handing what he came up with to her without looking at it. She dropped her cigarette, which lay glowing on the dirt, pocketed the money and led him off into the pasture.

"Lay down here sugar, mama take care of the rest." He undid his trouser flap and lay on his back. She straddled his knees and bent her head down but he held her hands back.

"I was thinking we might do something more than before." He pulled her gently but against her resistance.

"Don't know that I want to fuck you." Mary did not like being held like that.

"Now Mary, you took my money, you owe me what I

want." He was grinning and trying to sound sweet even though they were now nearly wrestling.

Mary did feel some obligation since she had taken the money and it was more than he had paid before. She was tired and drunk and thought it might just be easier to comply and, knowing him, get it over with quickly.

"All right, sugar, I'll ride you." She lifted her skirts and sat down on him, using her hand to ease him inside her. Slowly at first and then with more speed and force, she lifted and fell on him, her hands on his chest.

Casually he caressed her arms, keeping his eyes closed. Then suddenly he grabbed her firmly and rolled them both over. He thrust into her and smothered kisses on her face through the tangle of her long dark hair while she struggled and twisted her mouth away, more concerned with avoiding being kissed on the lips than escaping from underneath him.

Mary felt helpless and weak; two things she'd not felt in a long time. Her head was reeling from the whiskey but even more from the feeling of being unable to draw a breath. She was hot beyond endurance, and the stifling pressure was making her begin to lose consciousness when he froze noiselessly, held still for a few seconds, and rolled himself off.

Mary gasped for air and concentrated on not vomiting. He lay quietly next to her, breathing deeply and buttoning his trouser flap.

"Girl, you sure earned your money that time. Damn it's hot."

Mary rose laboriously to her feet and smoothed down her skirts. Her thinking was slow and foggy. She was not sure what had just happened, how much she had consented to, and what she had a right to be upset about. She had taken his money and agreed to fuck, but she also knew she had been tricked and taken advantage of.

"Mary, why don't you fetch us that jug? Another drink will cool my ass off." He knew that Mary was mad and that he had pushed his luck. It was a bad idea to make a Pruitt an enemy and he hoped to get her so drunk that she would not remember enough to get him killed.

Mary was having trouble holding onto a train of thought, but a drink definitely did sound like a good thing. She walked the few yards back to the corral fence and returned with the jug. He had sat up and was smiling at her.

She stood over him, removed the cork with her teeth and spat it at him but it fell short. She lifted the jug with both hands and drank until the last was gone. The jug was heavy, hard, fired clay and was difficult to hold up. The cheap whiskey burned a slow path down her throat but it seemed to clear her head, making room for an intense anger to well up.

She lifted the jug overhead, then with all her strength, sent it flying straight at his head.

He had seen it coming but had not expected it and was not entirely able to avoid being struck. It bounced off the side of his head without breaking, knocking him onto his side and causing his hat to fall off. His head swam and sparks shot across his vision. He did not know how well he could walk but he knew he had better try.

Mary drew her small revolver from her skirt pocket, and, although she fired four times, she was not able to hit him as he fled. She was swaying badly, her arm unsteady, and he was running in a zigzagging stagger that was difficult to follow.

"Cocksucker," she yelled after him. "I'll shit on your grave you fucking bastard!"

Mary tried to aim another shot but lost her balance and stumbled to her knees, smearing her dress with horse manure. Shots and screaming did not always cause alarm in her town, but they sometimes attracted the curious and Mary looked around to see if anyone might be coming to investigate.

The horses in the corral were stamping and milling about nervously, but no one else seemed to be interested. Mary was not afraid of being in trouble over a shooting that killed nobody, she just did not want anyone to see her crying.

Eight

After dark, Black sat down cross-legged at Red's fire. He sat to Red's right but faced Red rather than the fire. He stuffed a clay pipe with tobacco and lit it with a coal from the fire. Red was sipping from a new bottle and Jack watched him with a superior expression.

"Care for a swig, Blackjack?"

"No."

"Sure, and it might loosen that marble arse of yours," he muttered loud enough for Jack to hear. "Your boys is all tucked in are they?"

"They are properly camped, yes."

"What are you doing out here, little Blackie, looking for whores?" Red was having a good time. His back was a dull cramp that felt far away and the relief had lightened his mood.

"We were in pursuit of a band of brigands but we lost their trail in the thundershower this afternoon." Jack did not like to admit a failure, especially to Red Martin, and so he hurried on. "But my scouts found something of greater interest."

Red would not let it pass so easily though. "You would have better luck catching folks if you didn't waste so much of your time with ordering your boys about, in my opinion. They're Rangers, little Blacky, not Queen Victoria's royal fucking Beefeaters. Take me boys, for example. A better gang of Comanche catchers in the state of Texas you'll not find as they proved to all concerned yesterday. They won't be needing me to tuck in their little arses in at bedtime."

"Perhaps if your men were more accustomed to following orders, you would not be a man short today." One of Jack's men, at his captain's request, had found out the story behind the unmarked grave and reported it back to him.

"It is how God culls out the foolish from his flock," Red growled. But he felt bad about the Puritan; Jack's taunt hurt him with the truth in it. He blamed himself but would not let a self-righteous little shit blame him. "It's a spiritual conundrum as to how you survived against his divine plan." He looked skyward raising his voice and pressing his palms together. "Thy will is truly dark and mysterious, oh Lord. Just give me a sign and I will be thy instrument in this matter."

"A drunkard is only amusing to himself. I doubt if the almighty finds you humorous."

"It is me belief that the almighty enjoys a good joke, as it is proved to me every day."

"I imagine that he might have slapped his thigh a little at having you crippled by a mule." He had uncovered that story too.

"Precisely me point. Here I lay in terrible agony and there you sit, smug and happy, at my expense. He's a cruel jokester to be sure."

He sipped from his bottle and Jack knocked out the ash from his pipe on the hard sole of his boot.

"Who were these desperate fellows who escaped your keen pursuit?"

"Thieves and murderers, led by four brothers named Pruitt."

"Yes, I know of them. You'll be needing our help to round them up, it seems." Red scratched hard with thick stubby fingers at the skin under his bristly ruddy beard.

"They are not so important now. Make no mistake, I will catch and hang those cunts and I will need no help from you to do it, either." Jack was waiting for Red to ask him the obvious but Red remained silent, sipping at his bottle, scratching at his beard. Jack assumed that Red was too drunk to follow and decided to simply tell him.

"After the storm, we rode on, trying to pick up the track, but we saw no sign of the Pruitts. However, we did come across sign of a sizable pony herd."

"How far ahead?" Red perked up. He'd not been too inebriated to follow the conversation, he was just argumentative and noncompliant. But this information superseded any personal feelings he had. A large pony heard only meant one thing: Comanches!

"The tracks were made after the storm. They could not be more than a day from here. One of my scouts also found your camp. For this task, I will need your help."

"How big was the heard?"

"Several dozen head, I would estimate."

"That means there could be more than a hundred in the band. Sure, and you might be needing more help than I can offer." He leaned back and sipped, thinking the matter through, calculating the odds.

"There would certainly be less than forty warriors, I would imagine. We have close to thirty men here as well as the element of surprise. However, if you are too timid?"

"I'm pissing myself for fear, as you can see. I think I'll be able to master meself come the morning. Those four bucks we killed yesterday most likely came from that band. I don't think I could keep me men from their throats even if they have to ride with you lot to do it." It made Red feel uneasy: he did not feel lucky about this. He marked his premonition down to his back pain and took another drink to ease his misgivings.

"We will leave before dawn then. I'll have my scouts go on ahead." Jack put away his pipe and studied Red. "Perhaps you should stay behind. I doubt if you'll be fit to ride by tomorrow morning."

"Don't you be worrying about me, Jack Black. On my worst day, I could still out drink and out fight you, and ten like you, you little bastard." He was not sure if Jack was referring to his back or the wound to his sobriety and, truthfully, he would have given much to lie where he was for a few more days but his duty was important to him. Almost as important as not letting Blackjack get the better of him.

Black wiped the sweat from his brow with his sleeve. The

full moon was at its zenith but it was muggy and warm enough to make campfires wholly unnecessary for anything but cooking and custom, and conversation.

"When it's hot like this I can't help but remember Mexico," Jack remarked.

"Ah, best to forget Mexico."

Both men stared blankly into the fire for several minutes until Luke strolled over from where he'd been sitting at another fire and sat down next to his captain.

"Have a sip of your whiskey, Capt'n?" Luke often joined Red for a drink just before sleep, and Red, preferring company at all times, but especially when he was drinking, never minded sharing.

Red passed Luke the bottle and Jack rose to his feet saying, "Well then, I shall set my scouts at their task and then see to my own rest."

"Want me to tuck you in do you?"

"No, that will not be necessary." He walked briskly away and pretended he could not hear Red chuckling at his own joke.

"You two mix like fire and water. I'd think you try to get along seeing as how you're both captains." Luke handed the bottle back and Red took several sips.

"Don't know why being captains should make me treat that little bastard with any kindness, Luke."

"I was just thinking it was a matter of respecting the rank. I know he's a prig, his men sure don't like him, but I can't see as to why you hate him so much. He just rub you the wrong way?" Luke removed his hat and ran his fingers through his thinning hair.

"No, I've known him from before the war. He's never done anything to make me change my opinion of him."

"He didn't soldier well during the war?" Luke had emigrated to Texas from Missouri less than three years before and had only been rangering for two years. Most of the famous old timers had quit the Rangers after the war, having seen enough death and bloodshed to last one lifetime. Many Rangers, like Luke, were relatively new at their jobs, not veterans of the Mexican war, and were always curious about the role their special force had played.

"We all soldiered well. We were too eager. We went down mean and angry and got meaner as it wore on. Jack, though..., he's no coward, I'll say that much for him, but he's a cold little bastard.

"I'll tell you a bedtime story about Black Jack." Red put the bottle down and screwed his eyes to Luke's. "We were in Monterey. The thing was nearly done but there were some still fighting and we were rooting them out. Meself and Jack and some others were walking to fetch our horses. There were some boys following us, little ones, urchins, orphaned by the fighting, I suppose, not more than seven or eight, just having a laugh. The sun was high and it was hot like it is today. Jack wiped his neck with his Ranger scarf but dropped it when he went to tuck it back. I was trailing him and pointed it out. But before he could retrieve it, one lad snatched it up and off he was with it.

"I remember he was smiling as he ran, thinking he'd counted coup on an Americano. I was laughing meself. Then Jack shot him with his pistol. Hit the boy low in his back. A couple of our boys laughed then, but even the worst of them stopped when the child started wailing.

"I saw me some cruelty and violence in that war but to shoot down that skinny brown babe over a bit of cloth, that was a sight I could've lived without. Jack walked over cool as can be and retrieved his precious scarf. The townspeople watched him, scared to move. I watched scared to move. He came back no more bothered than if he had swatted a fly. The boy cried and then stopped and then he was still.

"We called him Black Jack after that. Most behind his back. Me to his fucking face."

Red passed the bottle to Luke who took a small sip.

"He'll burn in hell for that," Luke said.

"We all will, Luke."

Nine

The Apache scouts had built a small fire of their own but had let it die after cooking their rations. They sat closely in a row passing the tobacco they had rolled in a page torn from a book. The blue smoke hung in curls around them with no breeze to scatter it.

They wore long hide loincloths and high fringed moccasins that came halfway up the calf. Their thick black hair was loose and their heads were wound round with calico cloth in loose turbans or were covered in wide-brimmed straw hats. Their muscular torsos were bare and nearly black. They wore no ornaments.

They kept their ponies nearby, separate from the pickets of the Texans. Their lances, tipped with broken ends of Mexican sabers, and their shields, painted with hummingbirds, bats, lightning, and the sun, were near to hand. Their rifles, butts on the ground, leaned against their shoulders. Each had a knife and either a hatchet or club, as well a bow and quiver.

They spoke softly.

The Apache spoke a different language from the Comanche and had come south into Texas before the Comanche or the Spanish. The Lipan had been the first to encounter the Spaniards and their impressive mounts. They could not steal enough of the wonderful beasts and were the first to ride mounted to war on the plains. When the Comanche came, they drove a wedge between the Lipan and the other Apache clans, leaving them isolated and vulnerable. The Lipans chose to side with the Texans in their wars with the Comanche and became indispensable as scouts and trackers. Apache scouts would prove to be the Americans' most effective tool in rooting out the elusive warriors of the southwest and would eventually hunt their own long-lost brothers.

When Black came and stood before them in the dark, they did not look up.

"I want you four saddled up and on the trail of those Comanches tonight. One of you come back before first light to show us the way."

The Apache who was called Quiet Frog nodded that he understood and after a moment Jack moved off. He was the one who all translations went through, though all four spoke enough English to understand and their Spanish was even better; they let the whites believe that only Frog could understand and be understood. The Texans assumed that Frog was their leader as well but they mostly listened to the one named Traveling Tortoise, and let the whites believe what they would.

Frog would not have needed to translate even if the others had not comprehended. They knew what was to be done and had been waiting for the captains to finish squabbling so that they could get on with it.

Turtle pinched off the glowing end of the shared smoke and pocketed the stub in his tobacco pouch. War was beginning. They would abstain from tobacco and salt and observe other taboos. They would speak in an indirect way, alluding to things rather than coming straight at them.

They quickly gathered their things, mounted, and rode out of camp at a walk. Most of the Rangers never noticed their leaving. They did not intend or need to follow the captain's instructions. They knew already where the Comanche had camped. They had also known where the Pruitts were, having picked up their respective trails shortly after the storm ended. They had kept that information, feeling that the Comanche were a greater priority than finding a few white horse thieves.

Ten

"You're welcome to come with us but you shouldn't," Red told Michael. It was still dark and Red was lying were he had been for the last twenty-four hours. He'd had Michael woken and brought to him. "I'd hate to have saved you from those ones only to have their kin fix you up. But if you want some revenge on their kind, you'll never have a better chance.

"I'll go." He would have followed even if not invited. He had fallen asleep the moment he lay down, and on his back for the first time in years. He had snored loudly, making some men vociferously regret having saved him. He had not dreamed and awoke, when prodded by Luke, instantly, feeling fresh and new.

"That's as is then," Red said. "Luke," He called and Luke appeared. "Stop being a useless bastard and go fetch me saddlebags." He gestured for Michael to sit with him.

"I don't want you thinking you're a Ranger now. If you live through the next couple of days and don't make a fool of yourself then we can discuss a future in law enforcement. You should have a taste of what's what before you decide."

Michael remained silent and Red took his silence for understanding and consent. But Michael was not really listening. His eyes were fixed on the dim red glow just cresting the horizon. He watched it blossom and fill the vast expanse with reds and golds as the huge bloody ball revealed itself. His dreamlike and sometimes nightmarish life had shifted course but had not come to grips more firmly with reality. His moments were hours, his years moments. The only real difference for him was he now felt safe.

"You listen and stay close to me," Red was saying. "If you don't, you'll end up like poor Pete there" Red glanced at

Michael and followed his gaze to Pete's grave.

Red gave him an affectionate pat, which made Michael flinch, then he used Michael's shoulder as a crutch.

"A glorious morning to be sure." He rose groaning loudly. "I wish I were alive to appreciate it.'

"Me too," agreed Michael because he thought he ought to.

"You'll need a horse, I'll ask Jack to lend you one."

"No, I'll ride one of my mules."

"I suppose that's fine. You can have the Puritan's saddle. You have everything else of his." And his life, he thought. "They're cursed animals but there is no denying that they are dangerous to mankind." He rubbed his back and tried carefully to stretch it. "I've been set upon by Britts, Mexicans, outlaws, and savages but it took a sexless half-brain to do me in."

Red changed his attention to the cookfire where Rangers gathered to collect biscuits and bacon and were noisily slurping too hot coffee from tin or ceramic cups.

"Hey now!" he yelled. "One of you inconsiderate cunts bring your Captain a cup'a." Turning back to Michael he said, "You should eat now."

"I'm not hungry." Michael had courteously eaten whatever had been handed to him but had not been hungry for two days. He was only really aware of the need to breathe and took great interest in that act. When he inhaled, he felt filled and empowered. When he exhaled, he felt relieved and unburdened, and in between, stable and centered. He felt as if he were able to breathe in light and sound, shadow and substance, absorbing it in some essential form and understanding it completely. Though he sweated in the mounting heat and humidity, he was not hot. Though he had slept little, he was not tired. Though he had been terrified, he felt no fear. He breathed and there was no past, no future, and no suffering.

A Ranger walked carefully over to Red, trying hard to balance a full steaming cup and not spill a drop.

"How are you feeling, Capt'n?" he asked handing the coffee to Red, truly concerned.

"Hurts to breathe. Other than that, I'm fine." He sipped the scalding brew and saw the concern in the Ranger's face. "Don't you be fretting about me." He grinned at the man. "I'll be fucking and fighting long after you're dead and buried. Have you any pretty sisters?"

The Ranger grinned back, "Naw, they all looks like me," and returned to his breakfast.

Red sipped the coffee, having faith that it would cut through his hangover. It was thick to muddiness, bitter and sour as they had no sugar. The band drank coffee by the gallon. They carried roasted and unroasted beans in ten-pound sacks, ground it as needed, and brewed it in a large kettle at the boil for fifteen or twenty minutes. The slightly rancid result was soupy and drunk without straining the grounds out. The men would often chew and swallow the grounds. They relied on the coffee to move their bowels which were frequently unresponsive on their limited diet. They flipped from constipation to diarrhea and some were thin to the point of gauntness. A full plate and not one exhibiting a variety was preferred, but a full belly was no guarantee against malnutrition. Coffee gave them a nervous energy that replaced actually energy. And it was safe to drink. Water alone and unboiled was unpredictably dangerous.

Luke returned with Red's bags.

"You going to drink this early, Red?" he asked in a cautious tone, assuming that was why Red wanted his bag and worried his commander would be useless during a fight.

"Shut your pan and see to your horse," he said without rancor and then louder to all his men, "We leave in ten minutes."

He opened one of the two bags connected by strips of saddle blanket and meant to balance on either side of a horse's ass.

"I don't use this anymore. I used to have a pair but its brother blew up in me hand and was no good after that. Didn't do me hand much good either." He held up his left hand and wiggled the stubs of what used to be whole middle and ring fingers. In his right, he held a massive revolver in a plain holster. He handed it to Michael.

"Don't you worry though, there is a fine chance you will come through this with all your digits. That holster ties to your saddle. It's too big to be dragging about on your person."

He produced a heavy leather pouch tied with a drawstring and tossed it to Michael. "There's the shot for it. I'll have Luke issue you some powder as well. You'll be needing more bark than just that bird gun of the Puritan's and that big dog is like a cannon."

"Thank you." Michael drew the pistol and examined it, liking the way it's great weight felt in his still swollen hand.

"Just remember where it comes from. I'll be wanting it back."

Captain Black strode up to Red, his irritation evident.

"Are you going to stand here all day?" My men are mounted and my scout is here to guide us. I'm waiting a half an hour and you haven't moved. We must be going."

Red yawned and slowly sipped his coffee.

Eleven

The Colt Walker Dragoon pistol weighed nearly five pounds when loaded. It had a nine-inch barrel and it's six cylinders would hold more than fifty grains of powder each behind a forty-four caliber ball. It was as good as a repeating rifle in a time when firing three aimed shots in a minute was considered fast shooting.

When the Texas Rangers were first formed to combat the Indian, all they had available were single shot percussion rifles and muskets. They would ride up to within range of the enemy, dismount and fire. Their foes would simply ride away, out of range, remain out of range for as long as they wished, or swoop back in while the company was reloading and vulnerable. Loading a muzzle-loading long-arm on horseback, even a stationary horse, was nearly impossible, and the Texans had no background in fighting with lance or bow. They were technologically more advanced and at a distinct disadvantage.

The invention of the percussion cap (a mass-produced fulminate of mercury compound inside a copper cap that would explode when struck) some decades earlier had been a significant improvement over the flintlock and it greatly reduced the frequency of misfires, but it did nothing to improve the rate of fire. Then Sam Colt had an idea, or rather put several ideas together.

Others had previously invented revolving chambers for flintlock rifles, but the result was clumsy and they never became widespread. Colt saw how the new caps would work well with the revolving cylinder and how the idea of multiple firing was more suited to a short-range weapon. Borrowing money, he took his hand-carved wooden prototype and manufactured a thousand pistols in a factory in Paterson, New Jersey.

The resulting gun was not a financial success and it nearly ruined Colt. Most of the guns, however, found acceptance and appreciation on the frontier, where there was a greater need for self-defense, and a freer, less reactionary attitude towards innovation.

The beleaguered and ineffective Texas Rangers were both excited and impressed with the new sidearm, and acquired as many as possible. Finally, they would face their foes on somewhat equal terms. While mounted and in motion, they now had, each man carrying two pistols, an astounding capacity to fire ten rounds without reloading. Their Comanche antagonists were both surprised and massacred when they first encountered the new guns, and the tide turned then and there in the war for Texas.

The Patterson, or Texas Patterson, as they became incongruously named, was not without its drawbacks: It had to be disassembled to be reloaded, the caliber was too light to have good stopping power, the handle was awkward to hold, and the trigger, which only extended when the gun was cocked, lacked a trigger guard.

A decade after the production of the first Pattersons, a Texas Ranger, Captain Samuel H. Walker, was on the east coast preparing to gather recruits for the U.S. Mounted Rifleman to fight in the upcoming war with Mexico. While there he sought out Colt and together the two Sams created a much-improved revolver with none of the problems associated with the Pattersons. Pleased with the new design and grateful for the Army contract, Colt called the new pistol The Walker Dragoon.

The improved gun was the first six-shooter, a massive single action revolver that at a hundred yards was as good as a carbine. The new model included an attached, hinged loading lever underneath the barrel that allowed quick and easy reloading from the saddle. The larger caliber, the longer barrel, and deeper cylinder, combined to make the gun the most deadly and powerful handgun yet to be invented, an honor it would hold for another century

The Walkers and the Rangers who used them became famous in the ensuing war with Mexico, and Sam Colt became a more successful arms manufacturer. Captain Walker, however, died in battle with the Mexicans, his namesake pistol in his hand.

The famous pistol did not survive the war either. Extensive use in the field had revealed several imperfections. The gun was too heavy and too powerful to be used by anyone but the biggest of men; the loading lever fulfilled its function well but was loose, and fell during firing, jamming the cylinder. The sheer size of it, although useful as a club when empty, made it awkward to carry and so was usually holstered on the saddle.

Colt corrected these faults the very next year, producing the Dragoon model, and went on to become rich selling smaller, lighter revolvers to the forty-niners, the Army, and anyone headed west.

The Walker remained a prized possession among those who owned the thousand or so that were manufactured, a symbol and a relic of a heroic time.

Red had loaned Michael his gun out of guilt, for the death of a Puritan, and in recognition of some connection he felt with Michael. Red no longer used the Walker if he could avoid it. Instead he carried a brace of matching Dragoons, but his offering of the special pistol was a sign of deep feeling and not something he had ever done before. He hoped the gun would impart some magic and luck to Michael, keeping him alive in a fight he had little ability to survive.

Twelve

On the evening of the day after he tortured a white muleskinner, and had led four of his companions to their deaths, he arrived at the camp of his people. He'd known the general area they would be occupying and he had known the direction they would be moving, but he was surprised to find them so close to where he encountered the Rangers. He felt a moment of mixed terror and relief that he had almost blundered further by the leading white men directly to his people. At least now he could deliver a warning about the nearby presence of their most dangerous enemies.

He did not enter the camp right away, for he was ashamed. If he had returned with much loot, many captives, and marvelous accomplishments to boast about, he would have charged in whooping amidst great celebration. As it was, he would slink into camp under the cover of darkness. He would not be able to hide the fact of his return, but a quiet entrance would announce his failure and prepare the tribe to accept the bad news and the blow to their collective pride.

No one would actually be too shocked. They would, of course, feel saddened at the deaths of their kin, but episodes like this were becoming more and more commonplace. Even their best and bravest we're meeting with little success and, weakened by disease and defeat, they were slipping into a fatalistic depression. Their doom was upon them and they were too tired and beaten to feel desperate or angry.

He dismounted and relieved his horse of his equipment, not speaking or making eye contact with any of the boys who watched the herd. He walked around the circle of teepees to his father's and quietly slipped inside. The sides of the teepee were rolled up to let in any breeze that might stir the hot damp air. His father, two of his aunts, and one of his toddling nephews we're sitting cross-legged eating stew from a communal pot. His mother was dead from white man's disease and so his aunts came to cook for his father.

His father's face briefly lit up at the sight of his only surviving child returning healthy then fell when he realized the implications of seeing him in this way.

“Have you all returned?” he asked without expectation and was not surprised when his son shook his head no. “Did any return with you?”

“I am the only one to come back to my people. We killed many whites but the fighting was hard all the way and we had to ride fast to stay ahead of the Rangers. Yesterday we were trapped by Rangers and only I escaped. I have lost much and gained only this iron club.” He held up the hammer on its long handle.

His father looked at the tool for a time then dropped his eyes. He would ask no more questions of his son and they would probably never speak of this again.

“It is not a good time for our people. Every day brings more sorrow. Our time is nearly done.” He wished to comfort his son with these words, to absolve him of his guilt, for he could plainly see that he was nearly broken by the experience, and had come home a changed and disturbed man. He feared for his son's spirit. His insight told him that his son was twisted and fragmented, and part of him seemed to be broken off. He would try to think of some way to help his son become whole again.

"Now you should eat, and then sleep. We will talk more in the morning." He leaned back and watched his family finish their meal and settle in for the night. One of the aunts left for her own bed, but the other and her son stayed; her husband was dead and she did not like to be alone at night. The one who left would tell of his return and, by morning, the entire camp would know what had happened. This was not trivial gossiping, everyone needed to know and would spare him the pain and embarrassment of retelling his story.

Neither his father nor he fell asleep easily that night and so slept past the dawn. They were awakened by the furious barking of the camp's dogs and they rose quickly to explore the reason.

Some white men, with some Mexicans and mixed bloods, we're riding into camp, escorted and surrounded by two dozen of their own warriors. These whites were familiar to them. They were traders they had dealt with on many occasions, who would give them very much for very little.

He followed his father to a shaded place where the trading would be done. The other warriors acknowledged his presence but ignored the truth of his return, and treated him as if he had not left.

Several men went out to the pony herd to bring in animals for trade. Nearly everyone else gathered around to watch and comment.

Joseph Pruitt led their packhorses to the bargaining place and he and his brothers unloaded and set out a dozen guns for display. A murmur of approval greeted this display, as the arms were badly needed and would be a huge benefit to the tribe. They also set out kegs of gunpowder and bars of lead for shot.

The meeting went swiftly and well, both sides pleased with the outcome. The tribe was now better armed and therefore more dangerous and secure, and the Pruitts, adding gun running to their list of crimes, had acquired twice the worth of the guns in horseflesh.

To celebrate and seal their deals there was smoking, drinking, and friendly gestures, all parties smiling broadly. His father and he had not participated in the trading. He did not wish to own a gun, but he was very interested in the white men and watched them carefully. He followed one of them when he broke a little apart from the others and, moving in front of him, attempted in his limited broken English to engage him in conversation.

Ocie had walked to his horse to get some water from his canteen when the young warrior stepped in front of him. He smiled at the Indian and tried to look friendly even though the warrior's grim face unnerved him. Trading with a Comanche, and especially being inside a Comanche camp, was a very risky proposition and Ocie had enough sense to be scared and wary.

"You got something you want to trade, do you?" he asked.

"No," he said speaking slowly and carefully. "I want you speak me something."

"Okay."

"What mean say tan?"

"Say tan, say tan?" He looked at the warrior without comprehending. His eyes seemed to bore through Ocie's head, making him sweat and smell of fear. "Oh, Satan, do you mean Satan? Uh, El Diablo, hey?" The warrior nodded and Ocie was relieved at first, thinking he was being asked a theological question by an Indian with thoughts of conversion. Something in the warrior's demeanor assured him that this was not the case and his relief was transmuted to dread.

"Satan, he's like a bad man, he wants to destroy...." Ocie knew who Satan was, he just did not know how to explain him to a heathen. "Oh, my people they are afraid of Satan, he's like a god. No, not a god exactly. He has horns." He lifted his index fingers to his head in pantomime. "And a tail, and he's red. He fights against us but he's not a man, not human I mean." Ocie shrugged with exasperation but the warrior seemed satisfied with the explanation; he understood entities that were not corporeal. He understood that Satan was a monster god who was the adversary of the Texans.

"I Satan. El Diablo." And then again, "I Satan."

"I believe you," Ocie said backing away.

Thirteen

Joseph gathered his two brothers to him with subtle nods and gestures. "Let's get the boys together. I want to get the hell out of here while we still got our hair."

"I think you're right about that. I hate to be around here when they find out how shit some of them guns are." Ocie was anxious to leave on any pretext. Having an Indian walk up to him and announce that he was the Devil was more than his limited capacity was willing to accept. His hands were shaking slightly and his knees felt weak and a tremble.

"Beasley'll be fit to be tied when he finds out you traded those old muskets. They'll be lucky not to have them blow up in their faces if they fire it all, I tell you what." Price was a little happy to have something to hold over Joseph and could not keep the smile out of his voice.

Joseph looked at his brother with contempt and said, "Well if he ever finds out I'll just have to tell him it was your idea, won't I?" Price's smiling feeling evaporated. The one truth Joseph knew was his older brother would never believe that it was Price's idea. He would know exactly where to place the blame should the occasion arise, but Price would never be willing to take the risk of telling now and risking Beasley's wrath.

Joseph shoved past his brothers and approached the Chiefs to say his goodbyes while Ocie and Price assembled the men and horses. Several of the Mexicans, ex-vaqueros, gathered the ponies into a remuda and started them out of the camp without waiting for the others.

Ocie sat his horse, searching through the gathered Comanches for the one who called himself Satan. Ocie was far from being religious, he killed without remorse and had never set foot in a church, but even if he did not know how to recognize the presence of God, he had plenty of experience with the works of the Devil. He felt he knew a demon when he saw one. He had not spoken of meeting Satan firsthand with his brothers and did not intend to. He had no intention either of reforming his ways particularly. He felt his soul to be long lost on that score. He thought only of putting some miles between himself and the prince of darkness and postponing their next meeting for as long as possible.

"Come on, come on, Joey, let's get going if we're going," he said, though only Price was close enough to hear. Joseph was exchanging back slaps and handshakes with several men, apparently saying farewell but actually receiving permission to depart. Intuitively he knew better than to simply leave. Just as men did not enter a Comanche camp without permission it might be fatal to exit without observing the proper forms.

"These Indians got you all scary, do they?" Price teased.

"Yeah, I'll tell you what, there's plenty to be scared of here." He checked the looseness of his revolver in its holster for the fifth time in two minutes. "You believe in the devil, Price?"

"I guess so, ain't thought about it much."

"You suppose we're going to hell?"

"Sooner or later, I expect." Price seemed perfectly calm with the notion.

"Don't that scare you at all?"

"Wouldn't be worse than where we've been, I tell you

what," Price replied.

Ocie realized he did not feel much differently than his brother and relaxed a little. He'd long been reconciled to an early death. Few people, on the frontier especially, expected to see an old age, and the Pruitt lifestyle did much to guarantee a youthful demise. He did not fear dying so much as retribution for the many things he had done. Price's words reminded him that his life had been hard and ugly from the beginning and his desire for some kind of revenge on an unforgiving world had belied any worries he had about divine justice.

Joseph had finished his leave-taking and was walking quickly toward his brothers who were holding his horse for him.

"Well come on you shit-brains, stop sitting here holding your cocks. We got places to be." He mounted and, without another word, pushed his mount past his siblings.

"Only problem with going to hell as I see it," Price said, "Is that little bastard is going to be there to greet us."

Fourteen

Red sat hunched on the back of his big roan gelding, eyes squinting, teeth clenched. Ripples of pain spasmed up and down his back and shoulders. It made his breathing laborious and painful. He wanted to retreat to a shady place and find solace and comfort in intoxication. But he had his boys to watch over and an attacked to plan.

It was well past midday and the two troops of Rangers had halted to rest and water their horses by another small creek, much like the one where they had camped, but narrower and faster flowing. All the men had dismounted except

Red, who felt it would be easier to try to rest where he was than to have to go through the challenge of dismounting, only to stand around for a short painful spell before climbing back into his saddle.

One of the Apache had traveled with them all the warm morning, guiding them, and another had been waiting for them at this creek. He reported that the Comanche camp was near and that it would take the Rangers the rest of that day and most of the night to get there, even though the scouts could obviously cover the ground in half that time. They had daubed themselves with white clay and we're carrying their shields and rifles.

Captain Black rode up to where Red sat his horse and handed Red a wooden canteen. Red swished some water around in his mouth and spat before drinking deeply. One of his men had filled his own canteen for him but had tied it to the back of the saddle where it was difficult for Red to reach without twisting.

"We should hold up out of sight till just before the dawn and then hit them from two directions before they wake up," he said, handing Jack back his water.

"My Apaches will want to stay outside the camp to chase down the ones that try to escape. They don't like to charge straight in."

"Smart bastards they are."

"Perhaps you want to sit out this fight? You look to be in great pain."

"Do I now? Here I thought I was making a great show of being brave," Red said, not answering Jack's question. In Mexico, Red had despised the officers who remained in the rear while their men fought and died under their orders. He could never send his men into battle while he stood by safe. He would have to give up his command first and he could not give up his command now: that would mean giving his men over to Blackjack.

"Your muleskinner? Can I loan him a horse?" He was looking at Michael, who stood holding the bridle of his white mule. The Rangers had brought all of Michael's mules with them, using them as pack animals and leaving them in Michael's charge.

"No, I offered him one for you but he said he prefers to ride that nasty beast. Someone ought to shave its tail. I hope it does better for him than it did for me." Red squirmed in the saddle, the leather creaking, vainly trying to be comfortable.

"He is a strange fellow. Maybe you should not have let him come along." Jack saw Red nodding maybe and thought to himself that it was odd for Red to agree with him so much in one day. "Did you give him that pistol?"

"Yes. At least the loan of it. The lad seems half dead already. He may need to get a little of his own back to come alive. I felt I owed him that chance."

"Why do you owe him anything?" Jack scoffed. "You saved his life."

"To be sure, I saved his arse going up in flames but we were too late to save his life. When you go through something like that, you'll not be going back and just picking up where you left off."

Jack became quiet and thoughtful. "You are right. Perhaps he will be of some help to us. He has cause to fight hard." He blew out a long sigh. "I for one am tired of fighting."

"You! I thought you loved to get bloody."

"I can never seem to win a fight. That wears on a man after twenty years." Jack turned and walked his horse away, snapping orders at his men to mount and get moving again.

"Why is it I'm the one showing the wear-and-tear then?" Red spurred his horse across the creek, his silver Mexican spurs jingling while he muttered, "That little fucker will outlive me. To be sure, it's all part of God's little joke."

Michael swung into the saddle, the big revolver holstered to the pommel, shotgun slung across his back, the whip coiled and secured to the saddle, and hurried his mule to catch up with Red. When Highness was close enough, she reached out and bit Red on the leg, just above his boot top.

Fifteen

He stood on a small rise just past the pony heard, their whickering and snorting floating over him in the still evening air. He faced the pink glow that was all that remained of the set sun. His back was to the rising moon, which had come up well before twilight and hung large and low in the east.

After the Texas traders had left, he spent the afternoon with his father, discussing his, and his tribe's, recent misfortunes. His father's views where gloomy to the extreme, foreseeing more defeats and eventual disaster for his people. He advised his son to seek wisdom from solitary reflection and prayer. His father believed that his own time was past and that his son needed counseling from the Spirits, not from an old man whose ways proved no longer effective in a world that had changed beyond his traditional understanding.

He felt his father's understanding to be still valid enough to be heeded and had given his father the hat that he had boldly snatched while fleeing from the Rangers guns as a sign of respect and gratitude for the suggestion.

The Comanche believe that if supernatural help was needed, all that one had to do was ask and then wait patiently for the answer. The Spirits, after all, were on their side and wanted to help the people. Asked with the proper respect they would be happy to respond, not needing any special sacrifices or promises. Unlike the more masochistic practices of some of the northern plains tribes, the Comanche simply found a quiet spot, away from distraction, and asked politely and persistently for guidance.

Sweating lightly from walking in the humid warmth,

wearing only a loincloth and moccasins, and carrying a blanket, his bow, and a quiver of arrows, he came to a rise and paused to urinate. His penis was scarred in several places from chancres that had plagued him for several years but had seemed to abide some time ago. He noticed some numbness in his right hip and upper leg recently and his vision, which used to be excellent, was now becoming a little blurry on the periphery and not as acute at night. What he had not noticed was a subtle degeneration in his thinking processes. What his father's and friends had ascribed to anger and depression was more the result of decreased mental capacity. He seemed not to be able to reason in anything more complex than a straight line. Extenuating factors and external influences often failed to modify his plans and responses, and sometimes he could not figure out what was best to do or even what his choices might be. This was one reason for the dismal outcome of his recent raid.

He tucked his member back into his loincloth and turned to spread his blanket. He lay back and looked up at the waning, just less than full, moon which was brightening and adding contrast to the darkening sky. Bats crossed his vision and a cricket chirped nearby. His legs and back ached from spending nearly three days and nights in the saddle; resting for a night and a day had allowed soreness to blossom where it had continually been repressed.

He wanted to understand himself, his new name, and his relationship to the white mule driver. He wanted to continue to fight for his people, to be a warrior, and to live his life on his own terms, but he did not know if that was even possible. He chanted his prayers and let his eyes rest on the moon.

His chanting made the ponies closest to him alert and active. The stallions soon became involved in a game of king of the hill; seeing which one could defend the summit of another low rise about thirty yards in front and to the left of where he lay. The moon was behind him now, high in the eastern sky, and, as it traveled out of his sight, he was still chanting, watching the ponies at their game. He'd been tired and, lying down in the warm air, he chanted himself into a dreamy trance. Losing the moon and finding the ponies had brought him to an abrupt awakening, startling him. He focused consciously on the stallions like an amnesiac wondering how he had gotten where he was. It seemed to him that his chanting had transported him away and returned him in time to witness something important.

A small but aggressive red stallion had commanded the rise and driven off all adversaries, even those larger than himself. He bit, kicked, and charged with more energy and ferocity than any other two put together, his viciousness more than making up for his lack of size. The larger males soon tired and gave up the fight, leaving the champion to gamble and prance his victory atop his mountain.

The yipping sounds of a pack of coyotes coming together and greeting each other, intruded into the pony heard, causing many of them to prick their ears and mill nervously. But the triumphant red stallion, full of himself and his strength, raised his head and whinnied back a warning. He dashed off his perch chasing a small white mare. His huge phallus emerging red and shining. He bit her withers and neck and shouldered her into submission then quickly mounted her. He heaved and squealed, thrusting himself into the pale mare, who stood with head lowered and legs braced. His act was quick and violent and over in just a few moments, the stallion then loping off and losing himself in the herd.

He knew he had received a vision from the Spirits. They had given him a sign and showed him a direction. He knew the actions of the little red stallion were meant to inspire him, to harden him, and to ordain his path.

He stood, excited and happy for the first time in years, and gathered up his bow and quiver. he had not understood everything about his vision and now must talk with his father and other wise men of the camp to help comprehend what he had witnessed. The moon was just beginning to set and it would be several hours before the sunrise. His father would still be asleep. He would go hunting before returning to his people. He felt powerful and confident and knew he would be successful in the hunt. He would ride into camp with a big deer across as horses shoulders to feast the old men whose advice he would seek.

He almost ran to look for his pony. Although he had not slept, he was not at all tired. He was relaxed and exhilarated at once. He knew his name and understood its meaning. He knew who he was and what he needed to do. His life would continue, his people would continue, even though everything else would change.

Sixteen

The Rangers quietly came to a halt just after the moon had slipped below the horizon. The Apaches, all of whom were with them now, communicated to Captain Black that the Comanche village was just a short distance away. They would rest here until a little before dawn. To attack while it was still dark would place them at a severe disadvantage. Their opponents would know their ground best and be better able to defend themselves and escape while the Rangers stumbled about, perhaps even shooting each other in the dark. Just before the sun rose, when it became light enough to see clearly, they would have both surprise and the light on their side.

Michael sat on his mule a few yards behind the main body of Rangers. After Her Highness had bitten Red's leg the captain had yelled at Michael to stay the hell away from him and so he had let himself fall a little behind the group even though he had no trouble keeping up. Mules are not as fast in a sprint but they can travel distances just as well or better than most horses can, and Her Highness did not like to follow anyone.

Some of the men dismounted and strolled around to stretch their legs. Others remained on their horses and checked their weapons or drank from canteens and munched on their rations. Captain Black stayed in his saddle and made the rounds inspecting his men's guns and gear, occasionally reprimanding but never complimenting.

Michael listened quietly to the night insects chirping and humming and the muffled sounds of the men conversing softly. His mind was devoid of thought, but he was feeling a growing sense of anticipation, not fear, but a mounting awareness that his destiny was at hand. Every breath he drew filled him to bursting with readiness and vigor. He was like a kettle left too long on a hot stove, he was all steam and released energy, boiling over and expanding against his limits.

He knew he was about to venture out to kill, but to him it was a righteous cause and although the Bible clearly said 'Thou shalt not kill', it also described in great detail many a killing directed by God's hand. To kill the wicked was a glad duty to the Israelite and therefore the good Christian would not hesitate to fight in the Lord's name, for the Lord's cause. Michael recognized God's hand in bringing his own avenging angel to this time and place and in this company. He would lead these men to glorious victory against the minions of Satan. He was sure of it, even though he had never fought in his life.

Luke walked his horse over to Michael and Michael leaned forward slightly in the saddle, his eyes shining unnaturally bright in the darkness.

"Red says you're to hobble the mules here," Luke said while carefully maintaining his distance from the dangerous white mule and eyeing the beast warily. "You want some help with them?"

Michael practically leapt down and went about his task of unloading the mules' packs and tying their legs together with strings of thick rawhide. He only shook his head at Luke's offer. A job that normally took twenty minutes Michael finished in five, without seeming to hurry.

"I see you're not feeling too poorly today," Luke observed as Michael sprang back up on Her Highness. "That beating those bucks give you seem to do you more good than harm."

Michael nodded distractedly.

"Ain't one for a lot of talking, are you?"

The light briefly went out of Michael's eyes and his face twisted as if the left side were at war with the right. Michael felt a brief sharp pain in his chest and a knot in his stomach. He reached out and laid his hand on the butt of the big revolver holstered to the pommel.

"I can talk," he said almost inaudibly and in a tone that was both questioning and pleading.

"I know you can talk, you just don't care to do it much."

"I'm sorry," he stammered. "I don't mean to be rude."

"No skin off my nose. "You tired? It's been a tiring couple of days for everybody. I know I could use a meal and a long peaceful sleep."

"No, I'm not tired." Michael's face was still straining but some of the shine was returning to his eyes. "Are we about ready to fight yet?"

"Can't wait to get out at them, can you? Yeah, we'll be in the thick of it by the first light. The waiting to fight is harder than the fighting, I find. You look all fired up though, can you shoot straight?"

Michael realized he had had no opportunity to practice. He had fired rifles and was even familiar with shotguns like the one he had inherited from Puritan Pete, but he knew pistol shooting was more difficult and had no previous experience with a handgun of any kind. Even his long arm shooting was mediocre at best.

"I don't know," he answered honestly.

"Well, just make sure you don't shoot one of your own and you'll be fine. Sometimes all that matters is how much noise you make more than what you can hit." Luke leaned forward and looked Michael straight in the eye. "You yell a lot and keep firing that big pistol of Red's and them cunts will be falling over themselves to get away from you. I have seen it happen that way before. And if anyone gets too close you give them both barrels without giving it a second thought."

"I wouldn't give it a second thought. I know what I'm here to do." Michael was looking directly back into Luke's eyes.

Luke was feeling a little uneasy again and wondered to himself why he continued to try to converse with the strange boy.

"That mule of yours, she sure has a strong dislike for the Captain," he said changing the subject and breaking eye contact.

"There's something about the Captain she doesn't like." Michael shrugged.

"Don't make any sense the way she keeps going after him."

"Mules don't generally make too much sense. I mean you can't reason with them. They don't think as a man would. Once they get an idea into their head, they don't ever let it go. You got to teach them right the first time because once they learn something you can't show them another way, no matter how much you try." This was the most Michael had spoken at any one time in a decade. It had not occurred to him that he had probably learned a lot about his trade over the years and that someone might find it interesting. He noticed he was enjoying talking to someone and realized how lonely he must have been all that time with no one to talk with.

"I think since mules can't breed they don't need to try to learn new things. They never have to get along with anything else cause they're always going to be alone no matter what. It makes them strange."

Seventeen

The Comanche camp was quiet and still. The dogs were sleeping in groups. The ponies were calm, and the boys who minded the herd were dozing peacefully. People slept warmly on top of soft furs and hides, the sides of their teepees rolled up halfway to let in any cool breezes that might wander through. Mothers cuddled next to their infants and the older children piled up next to one another, their arms and legs cozily entangled. The old men snored hard and the young men curled with their young wives like two spoons. Everyone was dreaming.

This was generally a good time of year for the tribe. Food was more plentiful and there was little work to be done. The trading had gone well and created a happy day of feasting and celebration. They had gone to sleep with full bellies and a renewed sense that they might preserve their way of life and somehow overcome all their recent hardships.

On the outskirts of the pony heard, in the dim glow of the false dawn, Quiet Frog, Turtle, and the two other painted Apache warriors crept forward, making their way through the herd without disturbing a single animal. They separated and each stalked toward a drowsy adolescent, their knives drawn.

Eighteen

The Apaches ran the herd off quickly and with as little commotion as possible, but sixty ponies bolting off all at once was still a tumultuous and noisy thing. The disturbance was a benefit to the Texans who were not planning on sneaking in and cutting the Comanches' throats while they slept. That was how Apaches might have done it, but the Rangers could never have managed the necessary stealth. They wanted the camp alive and in an uproar, charging in before the Comanches could organize a defense.

The attack would come from two directions. Red and his troop would ride in from the south while Captain Black's troop came in from the west. The Lipans stampeding the pony heard was a signal for both Jack and Red to begin the attack.

Jack ordered his men to form in a column of twos with himself at the lead. When his scouts, which he could not make out in the herd, set the ponies running away from the camp, he calmly gestured for his men to follow as he spurred his mount for the teepees.

Red's men assembled in their usual disorganized mob but still with Red taking the point. The men with Red had been fidgeting in their saddles, palms sweating against the smooth wooden grips of their revolvers. When the herd, which they could easily see in the dim light, began to run they shifted their attention to their captain. Red raised his arm with pistol in hand, stood in his stirrups, back pain momentarily forgotten, and drew in a deep gulp of air.

But before he could shout out the cry to charge, Michael shot past him, his white mule a blur of unmule like speed.

"Again?" He threw up his other hand in exasperation. "Damn it! Come on boys, don't let him get there first," he shouted, kicking his already moving roan into a dead run. The sweat ran cold down his back as he failed to gain on the streaking figure of the Muleskinner.

Nineteen

Michael violated the circle of teepees at a full gallop just as the sun erupted over the horizon. The double-barreled shotgun was in his right hand with both hammers cocked while he held the reins in his left. He was perfectly balanced standing in the stirrups and did not feel any jolting as Her Highness thundered into camp. His body felt as light and ethereal as a warm breeze. His eyes still could not discern any color but shapes and textures stood out hard and distinct in the sharp light of dawn.

There were already dozens of people outside their teepees, aroused by the stampeding of the ponies. A warrior burst out of a teepee, knife in hand and a desperate savage look on his face. Michael, passing him, extended the shotgun and lowered his arm, pulling one of the triggers without slowing his dash. The gun tipped upward with the discharge, belching flame and acrid gray smoke and Michael let his arm bend with the kick, raising the weapon until the barrels pointed straight up. The warrior, taking the whole of the blast in his chest at close range was spun and lifted, crashing down into the dust, to lie limply on his side, dying moments after hitting the ground.

Michael looked ahead and saw an older naked man running directly away from him. He switched the reins and kicked the mule with one foot, guiding the mule to the right side of the old man as he barreled down on top of him. He let the shotgun drop into the cradle of his left elbow, across the saddle and pulled the second trigger, firing point blank, blowing the old man's head apart in a spray of blood and brains and smoke, the tip of the barrel nearly touching the old man's long gray hair, setting it on fire.

Michael was still the only white man in the camp as more Comanche began to emerge and suddenly he was in the middle of a confused mob. The center of a cyclone of activity. He pulled hard on the reins and spun his mule around on its hind legs, scattering the Comanches away from him like water rippling away from a jumping fish. He tossed the empty shotgun to his left hand and drew the big Walker revolver from the saddle holster just as a young brave charged him barehanded and leaped up to pull him out of the saddle. Michael only had time to see that the boy had dark brown eyes and a large nose before he whipped the heavy iron barrels of the shotgun down and across the boy's head. The heavy double barrel cracked the boy’s skull and split the skin of his brow drenching his face in blood.

As the boy dropped dead to the ground, the mob was shattered by Red and his Rangers arriving with a hail of lead and the sharp crack a pistol fire. A moment after that, Black Jack led his column inside the teepee circle. The Comanches who had not already fled or died broke and ran, either to escape or to find cover. The Rangers split up into small groups and pursued the Indians, snapping shots at anything that moved, not having or taking a moment to discriminate between men or women, old or young.

Michael stood in the stirrups and took careful aim at a large man running across a clear space in front of him some thirty yards away. He ran in a crouch, among fleeing women and sprinting mounted Rangers. Michael led him carefully without using the pistol sights and hit him high in the chest, just under the collarbone. The man fell to his knees then to his face and tried to crawl away using only one arm to drag himself desperately onward.

Michael was the only still form. He sat his mule amidst the screaming shouting frantic swarm like a rock in the surf. The air was thick with dust and powder smoke. It hung heavily in the windless battleground, swirling only when people and riders cut through it or another pistol blast exhaled a fresh current into the mix.

Out of the smoke, a warrior appeared suddenly to Michael's left side and raised a rusty short barreled musket. He was only a few feet away and Michael could see the opening of the muzzle centered perfectly on his torso. He cocked the revolver and began to swing it around but, even as he did so, he knew he could not shoot the man before the man shot him. He clearly saw the man's finger jerk hard on the trigger and was opening his mouth to yell, when the breach of the gun exploded with most of the blast and shrapnel flying backward into the man's head. His hands mangled and his face a bloody blinded ruin, he fell backward and squirmed and writhed, the shattered musket lying in pieces around him.

Michael surmised then that he was invulnerable. He was under God's hand at that moment doing God's work. What he shot at he would kill. Those who shot at him would miss or die as this man had died. He was invincible as long as he remained true and faithful to his purpose. He'd been purified in the waters of pain and torture and risen from the death of a life deluded. He was the Archangel incarnate, the living vengeance of God. He felt light as a bird and as insubstantial as a gossamer thread. He felt radiant and magnetic.

The mortal Michael Burns was huddled, quiet and scared, deep inside him. In this moment of chaos and violence, his divine Angelic aspect was prime. He was exalted in the power, the grace, the liberation. He was relieved of morality, pity, fear, want, and judgement; there was only duty.

And there was Joy. Rapture even.

The pale mule under him, a being pure and sexless, was his wings, his flight, his mobility. They would act with one mind and together they would destroy the servants of Satan.

Michael and Highness dashed off in pursuit of a big man in headlong flight. He was ushering a woman who held a baby in one arm and the hand of a little girl in the other. The man kept looking over his shoulder and pushing his family ahead of him. The baby's arms flailed wildly from the woman's bouncing gait and the little girl, too big to be carried, was being dragged more than led.

As Michael bore down on them the man looked back again and seeing Michael nearly on top of them turned and threw up his hands, interposing himself between Michael and his family.

Michael shot him in the chest and Highness shouldered him aside like a stalk of tall grass. Michael then shot the woman in the back, her baby flew from her arms to land alive but broken a few feet further on. The woman in her final desperate burst of speed had completely yanked the little girl off her feet and Highness trampled her before Michael pulled hard up and turned around.

Twenty

Red's back pain had momentarily disappeared with the adrenaline surge that came when the pony heard thundered off. It came back when the crazy Muleskinner, wearing dead Pete's clothes, raced past them in some repetitious suicide scenario that seemed to precede all his recent attacks.

The big roan gelding he rode was the fastest horse in his troop, even when burdened with himself, the largest Ranger in the troop; but he was actually losing ground to the pale mule that had wrecked his spine and bitten his leg. He wondered if this was yet another action by the mule to lead him into injury - he briefly considered stopping Michael by shooting the mule out from under him.

He heard the reports of Michael's shotgun and saw him spin the mule around. He shouted at Michael and began picking targets and firing his Colts; first with the right hand and then with the left. His men fanned out and pursued their fleeing enemies, but he remained in the center of the circle of teepees, picking off men as they ran.

Almost all battles are routs after the first few minutes, and this engagement was fast concluding. Jack's men had hit the throng moments after Red's arrival and effectively shattered any beginnings of organized resistance. Comanches without their ponies were no match for the heavily armed and mounted Rangers and they knew it. Some bravely but futilely tried to make a stand but we're almost instantly cut down by pistol fire.

There were plenty of men to be seen and Red fired until his right-hand pistol was empty and his left hand had only one shot remaining; which he deliberately kept from spending. The battle inside the teepee circle had finished and the only fighting that was still taking place took the form of Rangers riding down those that were fleeing.

Red holstered the gun with one full chamber and began to reload his empty pistol. Loading a cap and ball revolver was a time-consuming task that required nearly complete attention, but he felt he had the breathing space he needed to do it. Red pushed out a wedge that held the barrel to the frame and then used the loading lever to pry the barrel free. He removed the spent cylinder and exchanged it with a pre-loaded and capped cylinder that he carried in a pocket on his belt. He pressed the barrel back into place and snapped in the wedge, which he had kept between his lips, hot and tasting of powder and grease, into place.

He had been glancing up as often as possible while reloading and as he finished he could not see any immediate threat. His and Jack's men seemed to be doing a fine job without him. Rather than pound his back with even more pain, he decided to stay where he was and wait for his men to reassemble.

He looked around for Michael and saw him, through the haze of dust and smoke and heat shimmers, riding toward where Red sat his horse. He was relieved to see that the Muleskinner was obviously alive and whole. Red surveyed the scene, seeing only dead and dying Comanches and not a single dead or wounded Ranger. As far as he could see, he was the only Ranger in any pain.

He looked around again, this time without the preoccupation of worrying over his men, and saw all the dead and dying for the people that they were and not just as non-

Texans.

"So many," he muttered. There were over forty bodies strewn prone throughout the camp and many more lying scattered over the plain. Some moved, slowly and weakly, but most were completely still. Many of the dead were women and children and there were more than a few oldsters among the dead men. Most were naked or nearly so, a few women wore buckskin tunics, almost all were barefoot. The group had been much smaller than they had thought.

Flashes of the last several minutes begin to replay themselves for Red. The bodies of those he had felled forced his mind to recall, in vividly clear images, instances which he had been too hurried to really notice as they were actually happening.

He had fired eleven rounds from his matched pair of Colts and seven of those shots had found human flesh. Red was a good shot, with over a decade of experience in mounted warfare, and that experience showed in the casualties he had inflicted on the Comanches. He did not think he had killed any women or He could not be sure.

He tried to remember that these were the people that killed so many of his fellow Texans over the years but he knew that very few of the people in this camp had actually been involved in any of that fighting. Those that had were fighting for what was obviously their land to begin with.

"A sorry business, to be sure." Red breathed out hard and shut off the memories and moralities that might plague him consciously, preferring to keep them below the surface. Neither side in this war felt that there were any alternatives, and Red, on the front lines, relied on duty, and the fact that he was white, to rationalize his involvement.

The Rangers were beginning to straggle back into camp, many of the small groups leading or dragging prisoners. The captives were all either women or children, no men would have been shown quarter. Michael, in the forefront of the returning Rangers, was riding directly to Red, the shotgun carried across his lap, the reins entwined in his grip on the trigger guard and his right hand, holding the big revolver Red had loaned him, hung at his side.

As Red watched Michael approach, the Muleskinner suddenly kicked his mule into a gallop and staring with wide eyes at Red, he raised the massive pistol and pointed it at where Red sat his horse.

And fired.

Twenty-One

The old man had been awake before dawn but had not heard the herd being driven off, as his hearing had faded in the last few years. He did hear the crackle of gunfire that indicated his people were being wiped out. He felt old and tired and beaten and, even though his people were being annihilated, he did not rise from where he lay.

He turned his head and watched the legs of horses and the lower bodies of his kin as they scrambled frantically around his teepee. He did not need to see much more than this to know exactly what was happening.

As the people he had grown up with and raised fell dead in the dirt, he felt no surprise or anger, only fatigue, and relief. He would rest a moment longer before rising. For many years he had known that this day would come and had long ago come to accept the inevitable. In his childhood, there had been hope of victory. In his manhood there been hope of a mutual standoff. In his old age, he had given up all hope.

His son had returned to him two nights past and had left again, at his father's urging, the next evening. He wondered if he had been prescient and sent his son away to be safe but he could not remember having any premonition of disaster beyond his general worldview. Also, he had only sent his son as far as the pony herd. Surely, he had returned to fight and to be slaughtered.

His hope was so long gone that he thought it would be best if his son was killed than continuing to exist in a world completely set against them.

His son's life had never been a blessed one. When he was a child there was great hope for him. He seemed to be gifted with every skill he cared to try and with the curiosity to try every skill. But to be born with great talent into a time when talent was futile, was a cruelty, not a blessing. The boy had been sexually precocious as well and that too became a curse. There were many girls and women in the camp that were available sexually. Slaves essentially; they were captives taken in raids in Mexico and Texas or against the Apache or Navajo. There were also girls of his own tribe who would sport with him at night in the pastures beyond the pony herd.

Before he turned fifteen his father recognized the chancres that marked his disease, but when his son asked about them he told him that it was nothing and that he need not worry. By that time he had given up hope and, colored by that resignation, he had in his way, told his son the truth.

After only a few minutes the shooting had dwindled to sporadic firing that was fading further and further into the distance. There were still horse's legs to be seen in front of his teepee and he assumed that the horsemen were waiting for him. He was hopeless but he had never been a coward. It was easy for him to rise and meet death.

He had taken wounds and his foot had been stepped on hard by a mare once. He felt every one of those injuries when he first rose in the morning. Now, unsteadily, he gained his feet, placed the white man's black hat that his son had given him on his head, and began to limp out of the teepee. As he stooped to duck under the flap his knees stiffened and at the same time threatened not to support him. He reached out for his son's lance that lay near him and used it as a crutch to help him remain upright and moving.

A large Texan with hair the color of the sunset was sitting on a huge horse of a similar hue, just to his right. The colorful giant had not noticed him, as he was preoccupied with his gun at the moment.

He waited patiently for the big man to kill him but he continued to sit his horse and talk to himself. He did not want to wait a moment longer for his death as his people lay dead around him and he feared he would be the last to die. A distinction he did not desire.

He stepped forward a pace and lifted his impromptu crutch to tap his doom on the back.

Twenty-Two

Michaels first shot struck the old Indian in the jaw just to the right of his chin. The big ball shattered the bone and knocked out most of his teeth before passing out the other side but failed to drop him to the earth. He stood still and bewildered, blood spilling copiously from the ragged wounds.

Red's horse jumped forward several yards and Red jerked on the reins. The big gelding spun in a half circle and Red saw what it was that Michael had shot at. He was relieved that the old warrior, lance still extended, had been prevented from stabbing him in the back and doubly relieved that Michael had not been shooting at him. He was also frightened nearly out of his skin at the thought that an obviously ancient man had come so close to killing him as he sat completely oblivious, lost in his own depressing thoughts.

Michael's second shot struck the old Comanche low in the belly and sent him to his knees hunched over like a suppliant, his hat falling off and lying like a beggar's bowl in front of him. Michael had fired while still at the gallop, decreasing the distance between himself and his target. He fired his sixth and last shot at less than ten yards. The round ball buried itself in the elderly man's shoulder just to the side of his neck but still failed to kill him or stretch him flat.

Red ignored his excited and prancing horse, controlling him automatically and only enough to be able to watch, as the Indian, that had but almost ended his life, refused to die, even though the Muleskinner was shooting him to pieces.

Michael reined in his mule in a swirl of dust just before it seemed he would ride over the Comanche. He lithely swung his leg over the pale rump of his mount and dismounted before he even came to a complete halt. While dismounting he had elegantly, without breaking his momentum, hooked the shotgun by its sling over the saddle pommel and left it swinging as he strode quickly forward to where the old man kneeled.

Without hesitation, Michael lifted the massive heavy revolver high over his head and brought it down swiftly in a flashing blue arc. The barrel struck with a sharp crack onto the back of the old man's skull, which immediately began to pour out a steady volume of dark red blood. It did what three forty-four caliber lead balls had failed to do. The time-worn man crumpled over to lie on his side in a fetal curl, his face pushing nose first into the dirt.

Red's horse was sitting quietly. It seemed almost as stunned as Red was by Michael's harsh and definitive actions. He had seen many men killed and be killed in his time on the frontier and in war, but this was very different: cold and passionate at the same time.

Michael stood over the body of the old man but was looking at the hat which lay where it had fallen. He bent stiffly from the waist and picked the hat up carefully by its brim, shaking the dust off it by slapping it softly against his trousers. He set the hat to his brow and pushed it down. It fit him perfectly.

He turned to face Red who gasped, the color draining from his sweaty face. “Damn me! That's Puritan Pete's hat, that is.”

Twenty-Three

After they had slit the throats of the boys who had guarded the herd and then driven the ponies off, the Apache scouts circled the camp while the Rangers smashed into it. As the Comanches who could, fled the camp, the Lipans rode them down, spitting them on their lances or shooting arrows into them with amazing precision as their single shot rifles had been quickly spent.

The four of them worked as a group. Not usually directly attacking any group larger than themselves, they would skirt around, picking them off with arrows while at the run. As the Comanches escaped farther from the camp, they were too spread out to pursue haphazardly, so the Apaches began to carefully choose their targets.

The four of them took time to close in on a teenage boy and an older woman merely for some sport. They killed the woman with a well-placed arrow in her chest but spent several minutes playing with the boy. Three of the scouts separated and distracted him, while the fourth swooped in and grabbed the dead woman by the hair and dragged her away. He mutilated her with his knife, slashing her skin dress open down the front and hacking at her exposed breasts in full view of the boy, probably a son or a brother, while the three others pricked at him with their lances. He scalped the woman, and as she fell away gravity helped pulled the skin from her skull. The Apache had done the scalping while on the run, holding her hair wound around one fist while his knife in the other hand cut the scalp free, guiding his pony with his knees in an arc around the boy. Seconds later, the boy was deftly hamstrung by a slash from a lance. He hobbled and crawled and all the Apaches laughed and joked and finally one stabbed him in the back between the shoulder blades.

They then concentrated on killing all the adult men that they could, as these were the ones most dangerous to their people. As the Rangers rode out of the camp in pursuit of those escaping the attack, the Lipans began to gather captives and, after only a few minutes of fighting, the Rangers too started to use their lariats to catch and bind anyone they had not shot.

Often during raids such as these, the Texans would discover white women and children who had been kidnapped by the Comanche. Liberating these captives was one of the reasons for attacking camps like this one. Sometimes Indian prisoners would be held to exchange for other captives at some future date.

Women who had been taken by the Comanche were ostracized once they returned to their homes. Their husbands and families, if they still lived, would take in the children but might turn away their mothers. The children, after a few years in captivity, would consider themselves Comanches and might be accepted by the tribe, but the women would feel themselves shamed and know quite well what kind of homecoming would greet them. Captive whites had mixed feelings about being rescued or felt they were not being rescued at all, which made the rescuing difficult and unpleasant for everybody.

Among these captives were no Americans to be saved but there were several Mexican women and their children, some half Comanche, that would be liberated. The Apaches singled out some women for themselves.

They rode into the circle of teepees, dragging and goading their prisoners, preceded and followed by the Rangers with prisoners of their own. They were just in time to see the wild Texan warrior astride the ghostly mule, savagely shoot and then club an ancient Comanche.

Although the Rangers who viewed the event were amazed by the Muleskinner's display, all four Apaches thought the scene was wonderfully amusing. All that flamboyant murderousness simply to kill one tottering old Indian, it must have been some kind of joke.

Twenty-Four

Most of the Rangers of both troops had returned and were sitting their horses or standing casually around where Red and Michael were. Red had dismounted and was standing looking at Michael, who waited calmly a few feet in front of him, a blank look on his face, holding the bridle of his mule. Red wore a grim tired expression and with his shoulders hunched forward from the pain in his back. He seemed to be, at that moment, the weariest of men.

The small area that had been the center of life for a band of Comanche that morning was now bursting with Texans and their horses and captives. The prisoners huddled together meekly; women and small children with a few elderly men surrounded by the Rangers who both watched and ignored them. Everybody was completely silent. Only a few who had seen Michael kill the old man and possibly save their Captain's life knew why the hush was appropriate. All eyes were on Red. He had his gaze firmly fixed on the Muleskinner. Some of the Rangers had forgotten that Michael had jumped the gun in leading the attack and were thinking that Red was about to thank Michael for saving him a stab in the back. Others remembered the precipitous charge of the Muleskinner and having not witnessed the rescue of their captain, figured Michael was in for a thrashing. Luke had both seen and remembered. He rode over, interposing himself between Red and the boy.

"Captain, the men are waiting to be told what to do," he said but received no reply. "You mad at that boy for what he did this morning? He fought hard all the same and kept that old one from stabbing you, I would guess that evens things out."

Red looked at Luke for the first time. "He is a strange one to be sure. You see he's wearing dead Pete's hat?"

"By God!" Luke said seeing the truth of it.

"Things do seem to be evening out, Luke."

Red turned away and yelled to his men. "Some of you scout off and look for them that we missed. Rest of you watch these prisoners and see to your horses and yourselves. Are any of you wounded or killed?" When no one answered other than with a shake of their heads, he said, "Good work, me boys. I'm proud and pleased to know and keep company with you bastards. God be praised, we're all safe and whole." The last he said quietly to himself while looking again at Michael.

As the Rangers moved off, grinning, to do as he instructed, Red spoke to Luke. "Have a look at these prisoners and see if any be white and desire returning to their people." Luke nodded and went among the captives, examining their faces and clothing and occasionally speaking to one of them.

Blackjack rode briskly into the center of the camp, smoking pistol in one hand, followed by two of his men. He slid off his horse and, handing the reins to one of them, he marched to stand in front of Red.

"A poor day for this bunch of savages. Did we take any casualties?"

"No, this one was all ours, to be sure. Though it seems that this old rascal nearly done for me." He pointed with his pistol at the dead Comanche spilled in the dirt before them and then holstered his gun.

"They are an angry sort. No matter the age, they're always murderous and vile." Jack's face showed no distaste.

"It's no distinction they alone carry, I've found." He gestured and smiled invitingly at Michael. "Come here, lad, and shake me hand. I'll be happy to see me wife and babes again because of you, it seems."

Michael almost sheepishly went to Red and held out his hand but quickly realized he was still holding the empty revolver and clumsily traded it to his other hand. Red seized the offered palm and, crushing it in his grip, pumped Michael's hand vigorously up and down.

"You used that old pistol well today. I suppose I'll be letting you keep it after what you went and did for me. What do you make of this lad, Jack? Wouldn't know to look at him that he was such a Banshee, would you?"

"I'd say he looks to be just that actually." Jack had felt there was more to the Muleskinner than was immediately apparent. "It seems you've had your revenge and more today," he said to Michael.

Michael met Jack's eyes with his luminous unblinking stare and said, "Vengeance is the Lord's." He was not disagreeing.

"Yes," Jack agreed. "The wicked are always punished sooner or later, in my experience."

"Was he wicked then?" Red asked of no one, gesturing at the old Indian. His blood had pooled and soaked into the earth, flies were abundant. He seemed to Red to be tiny and frail, barely big enough, tough enough, to withstand a strong exhalation. Red wondered if his life had truly been endangered.

He looked at Michael and shivered. The boy was crazy. He was sure of that. He could tell by Michael's eyes. But he loved him at that moment. Life was insane.

"Son," he said. "I thank you much. You keep that barker as your own. It will save your life one day as it saved mine, that I know." He patted Michael on the shoulder.

This was Michael's first experience with gratitude. He'd previously known only hostility or indifference. It shook him harder than his being crucified. Being tortured had merely confirmed his worldview; brought to fruition that which was seeded and well watered. Genuine warmth from an older person in authority was so new to him that he was rooted where he stood, reevaluating everything he had held to be gospel. He loved Red more than he loved God. He was ecstatic and terrified.

Michael stood silently, poised internally on the brink of a new universe, one that actually contained soft things as well as hard. Luke shuffled to his side and spoke to the two captains.

"I finished separating the prisoners," he gestured to the Indian captives, most of whom were sitting quietly but obviously frightened, separated from a small group of women and children. "There were no white people, just these here Mexes and their children."

They were all dressed as Comanches and most of the little boys and girls were half Comanche by blood. Luke was only sure of their ethnicity by their ability to speak fluent Spanish, so closely did they resemble their captors.

"All right. Take them and set them in one of the teepees and make sure they know we'll be turning them loose. Move the others out to that pasture 'till we figure out what will happen next."

"Okay, Red." He started off, patting Michael on the back, he nodded to the dead Comanche elder and said, "Good work there, Michael."

He told the assembled Rangers who were guarding the Comanches what Red wanted to be done, and speaking in passable Spanish, gestured for the other group to follow him as he led them past where Jack, Red, and Michael stood.

As they passed, Jack turned his back to them and said to Red, "I think we should be leaving in short order, I do not like this place. The men can travel a little while more today and then we can eat and rest, I think. I will tell the Apaches to bring back the herd."

Red nodded agreement and began to move off, taking Michael by the elbow and beginning to smile and speak to him, when he heard a shout from Jack and saw him moving on the edge of his periphery. He turned quickly, his body between Michael and Jack. He saw Captain Black bent over double, a half-breed boy straddling his back as if riding piggyback. The small brown boy had his legs around Jack's waist and one hand fisted in his hair, under his hat. Before anyone could react, the boy's other hand, holding a small knife, whipped across Jack's throat, opening a deep gouge from ear-to-ear.

The Ranger Captain desperately flung around, like a bronco bucking a rider, sending the boy sprawling and himself to his knees. Jack knelt in the dust, his hands futilely trying to stem the crimson tide that washed down his shirt front, a horrible pale look on his contorted face.

A shot boomed loudly and the boy who had been so deft a killer at so young an age, flipped back and flopped dead on the ground. Red held his smoking revolver a moment longer on the body of the boy before turning to look at Jack, who, no longer able to remain upright, fell forward, his life ebbing away only a few moments after his killer's.

The Mexican mother of the boy rushed to his side and cradled his limp body in her arms, sobbing loudly and calling on the mother of Christ. Rangers still in the camp pulled their pistols and were ready to shoot but the captives were all completely withdrawn into themselves, obviously trying hard not to be threatening to anyone. The camp was busy and alive with people who were trying to be still and subdued.

Red and Michael and Luke, shaded Jack Black's body from the harsh morning glare as they gathered in a row to one side of it. Red looked around himself at the dead and the living, the killers and the captives. The Indians were not brightly-painted, feather plumed, colorful, noble savages. They were half dressed, stone aged, and either dead or scared to death. He felt a long way from Ireland at that moment and longed to see some verdant landscape.

"Well, Jack, that day in Monterey has come back to find us both. And I am damned for it. I am damned." Turning to the Rangers he screamed, "Burn this fucking place!" The order was giving license to do much more than burn and the Rangers, charged by the sudden death of the Captain, we're ready to explode.

Red screamed to Michael and Luke, "The world is turning around now, I'll tell you. I'll not be Rangering after today." He paused, then muttered, "I'm all done."

Michael's world was once again moving through familiar space.

Twenty-Five

He sat on the bare back of a pinto pony, a dead mule deer hanging limp and lifeless across its withers. He carried his bow in one hand and a quiver of arrows was slung on his back. His eyes were fixed unblinkingly on the horizon.

Smoke rose slowly and seemed to pile up rather than drift off, obscuring the sight of what should have been his people's homes. He knew what the smoke meant: Rangers had followed him after all and had attacked his people. They would all be dead or captured. He felt cold and hardened by the sight, as if his soul had frozen. He felt a complete, overwhelming sense of isolation and desolation. He was absolutely finally alone.

He was without family without friends without a home or homeland. His environment was now completely hostile to him. His pain was so deep it was beyond expressing, and it seemed trivial and inadequate to shed a tear over the death of everyone and everything he had known.

His connections to the past and his link to the land had

been forever severed, and there remained only a bleak future. His solitude did not alter his purpose and what had been revealed to him the night before by the red stallion, now became his imperative. His people would live on, through his seed, within the white man's world.

He would wait until the Rangers had gone and search the camp for anything he might find that would aid him, and then he would go out, kill white men, and repopulate his people. He turned his pony, letting the slack carcass of the deer fall to the ground, and rode away without looking back at the burning camp.

Twenty-Six

The teepees were burning slowly and with a great deal of greasy smoke. The morning heat was made even worse by the many fires that burned in the circle. Michael walked slowly, leading the pale mule through the thick clouds of gray and black smoke that settled like a fog in the camp. Rangers, mounted and on foot, moved rapidly through the dense haze setting more fires and shooting their guns in the air and at the few dogs that had not fled.

The prisoners, Comanche and otherwise, were made to sit together in what had once been the pony's pasture; paralytically quiet and afraid as their homes and possessions were consumed in the Rangers vengeful rage.

The Apache scouts had managed to reassemble the herd and had driven it back to the pasture but the nervous animals shied away from the Comanches and the Texans who guarded them. The Apaches were kept busy keeping the skittish ponies together.

Michael wanted to take himself and the mule out of the

smoke-filled inferno and was headed across the camp towards a break between burning teepees large enough to pass through safely. He had remained by Red's side as the Rangers went about destroying the camp, but the sullen Captain had refused to move from where he stood between Jack's and the dead half-breed's bodies, even after the camp had become intolerably hot and smoky.

When Michael passed through the fiery gates and emerged out of the smoke, he caught sight of seven or eight Rangers clustered in a tight group between himself and where the captives were being held, heat shimmers waving their outlines. As he moved slowly toward them, he saw that they were all Jack's men, none of them could seem to divert their attention long enough to notice him as he passed within a few yards of them.

After moving beyond them, he looked over his shoulder to see if he could find the source of their preoccupation which had remained hidden from him by the tightly packed bodies. At first, he thought that two Rangers were wrestling in the dirt as the others cheered on their favorite. He wondered if one of them was a member of Red's troop and if he should stop and come to his aid. But the pair was not moving very vigorously, one seemed to have pinned the other down. When suddenly the man on the top stood up and Michael understood what was happening.

Michael dropped the reins of the mule.

The Ranger who had stood up was grinning as he tucked away his still erect and shining penis and fastened up the fly of his trousers. His friends slappedhim on the back while another grinning Ranger, a large man with his fly already undone, erection pointing straight out, leapt on top the naked squirming bleeding woman to the hoots and encouragement of his fellows.

Michael watched, his jaw slack, his eyes wide, as the Ranger bounced hard, up and down, between the legs of the weakly writhing woman, his body nearly covering her small frame. After only seconds, the man threw back his head and shouted out, “Lord, God almighty,” to the laughter of his onlookers. He rose quickly to his feet to be replaced instantly by another small man Michael recognized as Captain Black’s Sergeant.

Michael took several quick steps, closing the gap between himself in the crowd of men who still had not noticed him, shaking loose the braided oiled leather behind him.

“Fornicators!” he screamed at the very top of his lungs. All the Rangers, including the little Sergeant, turned dumbstruck to see the large, red faced, bug-eyed, boy dressed in black and grey, whip his right arm back and then forward with blinding speed.

The Ranger standing closest to Michael yelled and clutched his face and staggered away at the bite of the whip. As Michael continued to march forward, he brought the whip down again and again, like thunderbolts, scattering the cluster of men. None of them escaped without being stung. One, angry at the blow he received, tried to rush Michael. When he was within a few feet Michael kicked him hard and squarely between the legs, lifting him briefly off the ground. When his feet touched the earth again, his legs were too weak to hold him, and he crumpled into a fetal ball, vomiting and wheezing.

The Sergeant had rolled off the woman and, kneeling, was hurriedly trying to button his trousers as he kept his eyes on the boy, whose bulging eyes bored into him with an insane wrath. The other Rangers had all backed away from the furious Muleskinner with this punishing lash. None thinking to draw on him, they formed a ragged extended circle around him as he stepped up to the still kneeling man and the prone woman.

Michael shifted the whip expertly until he held the supple leather two feet below the wooden handle. He stood over the trembling wide-eyed Sergeant, raised his arm above his head, and using the handle as a flail struck the man a hard cracking blow across his brow. The little Sergeant fell backward, his legs tucked uncomfortably under him. Michael, breathing hard, continued to beat him senseless and bloody with the whip handle.

Stopping just short of killing him, Michael staggered backward and stood with his legs braced widely apart over the body of the moaning woman. His anger fading, Michael looked down at her face and recognized her as the mother of the boy who had slit the throat of Jack Black a handful of minutes earlier.

Her eyes had been blackened and her lips were raw and bloody, her nose was broken as was her jaw. Her long dark hair had been pulled out by the roots in clumps. His eyes wandered down, absorbed, from the face of the Mexican woman. Her breasts were scratched and bruised and one was bleeding copiously where the nipple had been bitten off. Her belly was white with dirt as were her thighs from the dust sticking to the sweat.

Michael's eyes stuck as if bound on her glistening vulva. Her legs were still spread wide, not having the strength or presence to close them, and Michael, standing virtually on top of her, could see every detail in sharp if colorless definition.

Michael stared into the exposed wound that had been her genitalia. The opening to him was a drooling maw, a chasm of infinite mystery and terror, a site of arousal and awe, that threatened to devour him whole. He wanted to rape her. He wanted to save her. He wanted to worship her and he wanted to destroy her. Her womb could suck the life out of him. Her womb could throw life screaming into the world. It was sin and sanctity all at once and it shook Michael's bones. He was lost in her, mother, whore, Mary and Mary, maternal, divine, it had the power to possess him. It called and spoke, siren-like, to the weakest basest part of him. If he took her, he would lose himself, his purpose, his destiny. She would kill him to continue him. Their consummation would consume him, and only his death would perpetuate him. It was a fangless silken mouth that could and was eating him.

Michael had thought that there was nothing more in the world that he did not understand, nothing that could frighten or move him. He stared now at what was to him both God and the Devil and felt a fear more profound and instinctual than anything he could have experienced in his mundane oblivious lifetime.

Michael dropped the whip, suddenly too hot and very dizzy, he stumbled back five paces and fainted dead away.

PART THREE: AN EXODUS

One

Mary began drinking early in the morning. The day before, she had spent all her money on alcohol and had stayed drunk. She had slept for only four hours before waking up just after dawn with the shakes and the dry heaves. She wanted some of the hair of the dog that had so deeply bitten her to ease her queasiness. She had managed to find some drunken cowboys who had spent the night playing cards and still, in the morning, had the capacity for more diversion. They bought her liquor and gave her money and Mary, smelling of vomit and cheap spirits, led them to a dusty half collapsed shed. One of the men pushed her down onto her hands and knees, lifted her skirts from behind, and thrust into her as hard and as fast as he could while his two friends waited outside.

Wincing but silent, Mary drank as fast and hard as possible, guzzling as if it were cool water and gasping an occasional breath past lips tightly sealed to the neck of the bottle. She scarcely noticed the cowboy slamming into her, gouging her hips with his grip, except as an impediment to her drinking.

In barely a moment, the one hundred proof spirits had eased her shaking, quieted her stomach, and permeated her mind with a gentle fuzzy haze, smoothing the edges and blunting the corners of her life. It numbed her in a way that made her feel light enough to float and shielded her from pain's bright flare. It was a miracle.

She mumbled and slurred encouragement to the cowboy who was jerking her against him so powerfully that her knees were skinned bloody on the hard earthen floor. She drank more, spilling some down her chin as she was thrown about but managing, all the same, to take several big swallows.

She suddenly stopped moving as the cowboy lurched to his feet, too drunk to maintain an erection no matter how hard he pushed. He stood behind her, swaying slowly, his pants around his ankles and tugging futilely at his limp member. Mary fell sideways onto her hip with her backside still exposed. The scowling cowboy tried to kick her rump with the toe of his boot but tripped on his pants and crashed sideways into the side of the shed, scraping his head while sliding down to his knees.

Mary giggled at the sight while pouring more of the bottle into her. She choked and coughed and chuckled while shaking the final drops into her mouth, her head tilted back, her tongue reaching up. She tossed the empty bottle at the cowboy who was trying to sit up and pull up his pants but it landed short and rolled up to rest against the shin.

"Have yourself a drink, my boy. I'm all done, I tell you what." Almost shouting in trying to speak clearly.

He stopped struggling with his pants, which were now around his thighs and picked up the bottle by its neck. "What are you laughing at, whore?" he said. He crawled over to Mary and using the bottle as a club, clumsily struck her a glancing blow to the shoulder, which only made her laugh the louder.

The cowboy, who was young and tall and thin, dropped the bottle and clambered on top of Mary and began choking her with both hands. Mary stopped laughing. She squirmed and tried to pry loose his fingers.

Mary was almost to the point of passing out, her vision dimming and her head pounding, when the choking stopped.

She gasped, her chest heaving, her hands massaging her neck. Although she could now breathe, she felt a sore lump when she swallowed.

The two men outside had entered laughing and pulled their friend off Mary, all of them falling down in the process. The impotent strangler remained seated as the other two laughing cowboys regained their feet and grabbed Mary by the ankles and pulled her from where she had crawled, huddled against the wall. A brief friendly shoving match ensued before one of the cowboys undid his trousers and taking Mary's hair in his fist, pressed her down and entered her.

Mary was too weak to fight effectively and almost too drunk to care, but she could not get her breath back; the cowboy on top of her was smothering her unbearably. She pushed his chest ineffectually and when she tried to bite his shoulder the man simply pulled her head away by the hair and banged it repeatedly against the ground.

What little fight she had, was gone by the time the third cowboy climbed on her, but he struck her face repeatedly with his fist before during and after.

The tall cowboy laid on his back, his pants only halfway on, and was snoring loudly, making choking sounds as well as trumpeting honks. Mary lay silent and unmoving, waiting to be left alone. The cowboy who had been punching her, was sitting near her, propped up against the wall smoking a thin cigar and chatting with his friend who stood at the entrance.

“William just can't hold his liquor, it seems.” he gestured at the snoring cowboy with his cigar.

“Been a long night all around, I believe. Can't blame the boy for sleeping it off.”

“Didn't seem to have much luck with the senorita either. Did he, honey?” The question, directed at Mary was punctuated by burning her arm with the red tip of the cigar. Mary didn't feel the burn except as a slight stinging and did not react at all.

“Here now, what are you doing that for? She ain't dead, is

she?" His concern was mild at best.

He did not respond except to climb slowly to his feet, the cigar clamped in his teeth. His rolled-up sleeves showed round burn scars of his own, old and long since healed, but still visible as spots where the black hair on his arm did not grow.

"Let's get if we're going. You take his arms, I'll carry his legs." He kicked Mary's leg out of the way and the two of them carried their companion away with them.

Mary waited for a few minutes after they left and then rolled gingerly onto her side. Moments later she became aware of something digging painfully into her leg. She squirmed off it and reached for whatever it was, coming up with a little pocket revolver. She laid back down on her side, her head angled sharply down to rest on the dirt, the gun held weekly against her chest.

The pistol made her think of her brother Beasley and how he had rescued her once before. She wanted to be rescued now. She wanted a man to come and take her to a safe place and treat her with kindness. She wanted a man who would love her and tell her jokes. She liked to laugh but no one ever tried to make her laugh. Beasley had saved her from their father but left her to a life on her own. When she saw him next, she might ask him to take her someplace else to live, but she doubted he would.

Mary had less anger and therefore less strength than she had even a week past. She was learning to drink more and be less present. Her life was becoming too small and vicious to contend with and the near-constant drunkenness was beginning to win her over to a life of passive acquiescence no matter what the circumstances. If she were able to be saved it would have to happen soon. She did not seem to be able to save herself. What she needed to be whole was not in herself to give and she was rapidly running out of hope. She knew she would die soon; her life was killing her.

She hated her father, but sometimes she missed him. He had taken everything from her and given her nothing. She had tried in thousands of ways to make him love her and she tried to make him laugh, never succeeding with either endeavor. Sometimes she thought if Beasley had not killed him, she might eventually have done the thing that would have made her father love her. When she thought this way, she physically ached, longing for that missed chance. An ache more painful than any battering she had ever taken. It made her hide: in alcohol, callousness, and violence. It made her seek in men for some spark of recognition and value, or at least of punishment for her failure, and her utter worthlessness.

"Where are you, Daddy?" she cried. "Where's my daddy?"

Two

Samuel baked his bones in the sweltering heat. It was mid-morning and he was miles from any towns or ranches. His two horses were picketed nearby, one lying on her side and, the other, a gelding, kneeling on all four knees and watching the world with heavy-lidded brown eyes. The Sun had felt so good to Sam that he had laid down on his back, in the open, his hat shading his eyes, and one hand resting lightly on the butt of the revolver tucked into his belt.

He usually awoke feeling stiff and cold. His bones ached in a deep numb way and where his ears and toes used to be, he had an itchy feeling that radiated out sharp spikes of pain. The only thing that eased the suffering was heat. Even during the warm nights, he would often wake up several times before the dawn from the pain and have to stand up and move around to restore circulation. The lost sleep made it easy and pleasant for him to nap or just rest in a dreamy state during the day. Fortunately, he had no particular destination in mind and was therefore in no hurry and could while away as much of the day as he cared to.

He looked at this time spent in the sun as trapping the warmth. He felt that if he could just lay in a large enough bank of heat during the day, he could possibly be able to sleep comfortably through the night.

In the two days since meeting Beasley Pruitt, he practiced a little every day with his new revolver. Although an excellent marksman with his rifle, he had never been a good pistol shot. The large bore single-shot pistols he had owned and carried in the mountains, were a short-range last-resort self-defense weapon, fired nearly point blank, not necessitating much accuracy. However, a six-shot repeating firearm might definitely be handy for shooting over long distances. If he had more than one shot, he would not have to wait until whoever he was shooting at was too close to be missed. He was pleased to find out that the well-balanced small caliber Colt was easy to shoot, and he was beginning to feel confident in his ability to hit what he pointed it at. It was also easier to load and he practiced loading quickly, handling the tiny percussion caps deftly with his thick fingers.

He was casually following Beasley's trail. He had no particular interest in further dealings with the man, he was just letting him be a guide to the nearest town. It never occurred to him to be scared of Beasley, should he happen to run into him again.

He slept quietly, breathing through his mouth, for almost an hour, awakening to a pleasant warm feeling in his limbs and a rested sense of vigor.

He rose to his feet, favoring his one leg that bothered him more than the other, and stretched his arms above his head, arching his back and yawning with a roaring, "Waugh," followed by a smacking of his lips. Both of his horses, startled to alertness by his noise, looked up and stared at him but did not rise.

"Now where did I set them traps?" he asked of his mounts. They regarded him silently. "I believe you are right," he said with deliberate seriousness. "You all mind the camp for me while I go check on the whereabouts of my supper."

He picked up his belt with its knife and tomahawk and wrapped it around his waist. He slung his beaded possibles bag over his shoulder and put his rifle in the cradle of his left arm, checking the cap as he walked off.

His habit was to set snares before dark then, after checking them in the morning, to lay new ones to be checked before departing.

If asked what he was, he would have said without hesitation that he was a trapper. His thoughts were almost always of trapping; it never failed to interest him. He was always curious about, and surprised by, what he trapped. Most creatures were predictable; they had habits and routines that once understood made them vulnerable. He would study what he wanted to trap, observing and noting its traits and desires. All creatures wanted something that they believed was necessary to their survival, and all creatures went about getting those things in the way they had first learned. Very few animals would, or could, deviate from their custom and methods. Most would perish rather than try something new. And that made them easy prey to the one who understood them.

He trapped animals because he understood humans all too well. They held no surprises for him. Men's motivations and behaviors were known to him because he was a man and because he was unafraid and non-judgmental of his own ways and means. Seeing himself for what he was, he was able to see others truly and without delusions. He would then know what they would do because he knew what he would do, were the small part of him, that was like them, in charge.

Nature, however, in its infinite varieties, never failed to stimulate him. It always provided him with an avenue to explore. Although the primary mind of the beast was the same as his own and his kind, they were different enough to provide a contrast. To trap an animal, he had to understand it better than it understood itself. To understand was what he wanted most from his life.

He could discern no purpose to life, no guiding hand, no ultimate goal, and yet all the tremendous activity had a certain common nature. It was chaotic and ordered, nurturing and destructive, active and still, aware and oblivious, existent and void, all at one and the same time. The paradox, for him, implied meaning but the meaning as yet eluded him. He realized at a young age that people did not have the answers to his questions so he went to the wilderness, closer to the source as he saw it, and watched and waited.

He rarely engaged in an intellectual rumination. He felt the whole and desired to be filled and then simply acted. If asked he could articulate, but alone in the mountain vastness, he'd never been asked.

He was still new to the southwest and the lower elevations, so he set traps that were indiscriminate. Whatever he caught would most likely feed him as well as begin to acquaint him with the local fauna and their customs.

That morning he had set some deadfall traps. He dug pits and, when the victim tripped the catch, a heavy stone fell to seal the opening. They did not generally kill or hurt what was caught and, if it proved inedible or unskinable, he would turn it loose.

He knew no fear of animals and the cautious process of securing a live and agitated creature was something he very much enjoyed.

He laid down on his belly, his face on the ground, one eye peering in, as he slowly lifted the stone a crack. A familiar sound brought forth a warm smile, "Waugh, hello there, little brother."

He lowered the stone, sealing in the coiled rattlesnake that was earnestly warning him off. He turned onto his back, a grin on his face, and with one hand gently shook the rattler tail and fangs he wore as a necklace, answering rattle for rattle. The snake stopped its rattling as soon as Sam began his.

"Do you recognize your own? Time to come out now to meet your brethren."

Sam rolled gracefully upright and stood with his moccasined feet on either side of the trap. He slowly lifted the stone an inch clear of the hole, being careful not to expose his fingertips to the underside of the rock. The snake inside, commenced rattling once more. Sam remained absolutely still and quiet.

The serpent first cautiously poked just it's triangular head out, it's forked tongue flicking in and out, then abruptly made a dash for freedom.

But Sam was quicker. He dropped the rock, once the snake had cleared itself and then snatched up the reptile by the very end of its segmented tail. He quickly stood up and whipped the snake in a circle over his head, like a cowboy twirling a lasso. The centrifugal force stretched the rattler out straight, preventing it from turning and striking at Sam's hand. Sam smoothly began to spin himself, his arm outstretched. Before he completed his first pirouette, he slid his free hand along the body of the snake from the tail up to just below the neck, where he pinched his grip.

The confused rattler coiled its nearly three-foot length angrily around Sam's forearm and stretched wide its jaws, trying to wriggle loose enough to sink its fangs into the hand that imprisoned it. Sam's grip, however, was like an iron band, although he was careful not to choke it. He turned the snake to look it in the eye and said, “Now you know how I got my name.” His clever snake catching trick had earned him some respect from his fellow trappers.

“You would have kept the advantage if you'd stayed in that hole and made me come to you,” he lectured, shaking his head and clucking his tongue.

He drew his long Bowie knife and, with one deft backhanded swipe, he neatly decapitated the snake, the razor-sharp blade barely missing his thumb. The head fell to the dirt and he gently kicked it into the trap's hole, it's rock lid slightly askew, while the body continued to coil and flail in his hand.

He skinned and gutted the snake as he walked to check

his other traps.

Three

His pony was quiet as a whisper as he walked her slowly through the burnt remains of his people's last encampment. He'd waited through the night, not sleeping a moment, not eating a bite, and shortly after dawn, when the Rangers took their captives - his people - and left, he entered the camp.

The dust of the departing Rangers had not yet settled as he passed the dead remains of the mutilated Mexican woman lying outside the circle of charred lodgepoles. He registered the bullet hole in her forehead but did not pause his pony. His eyes took in the sight as if it were not unusual, sparing it barely a glance. He dismounted and walked between the remains of the two teepees that had formed the gate for Michael's exit the day before.

His mind was slow to the point of stillness. An automaton with a narrow purpose, he glided softly as a ghost through the skeleton of the dead camp. The blackened lodgepoles were sticking up like the rib bones of a rotting carcass. He came only to imprint the scene on his memory and to find what might be salvageable from his life that was no longer. He marked the faces of the dead, noticing an uncle here, a first love there.

He paused at the spot where his father had kept house. The body of his aged father lay quiet and inert as a stone. He squatted in front of the corpse cataloging the numerous wounds. He studied the old man's face for a minute but the face was blank and only dead. Before rising, he gathered the lance beside him into his left hand without feeling the texture or temperature of the wooden shaft. It was his and he picked it up as if he had left it there only a moment before.

His father's lodge was nothing but ashes. He sifted through it with the lance for anything that might be left whole and unscorched. When the lancehead grated on something metallic, he bent over and brushed away the burnt remains of some hide clothing. His hand, dusted black with ash, reached in and felt for the source of the hard sound.

His fingers closed on the iron hammer, its long hardwood haft was black but not burnt. It was heavy in his grasp. It also felt comfortable and familiar. To his open and solemn mind, the tool seemed to be an omen or harbinger of disaster, a pariah that appeared to him to announce the inevitable and undesirable end of all things his.

He'd used it to crucify a white man then to kill another man. The hammer had signaled the death of the men in his war band and now it marked the end of his tribe. It was mundane and magical. Its blunt hardness was made to pound and smash; once done, the pounding and smashing set the cosmic millstone to grinding and he and his became mere grist. He would keep the hammer for he had nothing more to lose. His life was only the shade of actual existence.

He turned and headed straight back to where his pony stood. Surveying the circle of homes that were no more, he pressed the blade of the lance into the earth, securing it upright and transferred the hammer to his left hand. He then smeared the soot on his right palm across his face, darkening it into his war visage.

He had come across the trail of the white men who visited to sell guns and trade for ponies when he had been hunting. They seemed to him an inept and stupid group of human wastrels. He hoped to kill them first.

Four

Joseph and his brothers spent most of the morning spying on a little ranch. They lay on their bellies amidst a pile of boulders until the morning sun made the rocks too hot to lean upon. When the heat and the near constant bickering had made them too irritable to remain together, they walked to where their horses were being minded for them by one of the Mexicans. Joseph, the first to lose his temper, leading the way.

"You two assholes go back and join the herd, I'm going to ride up and talk to these folks," he said as he mounted his horse.

"I don't think you should be talking to them. They shouldn't get a good look at you in case we come back." Price did not really care what his brother did; disagreement was a reflex.

"We've been watching this place for an hour and ain't seen a single head of stock. Could be Comanches stole everything or they could just have everything out to graze. I either talk to them or we spend more time roasting on these rocks. You got better ideas?"

"Comanches ain't been here, we seen people about plenty. They'd be dead or gone if Comanches had been by." Price pointed out.

"He's right about that," Ocie said.

"That's all he's right about. And I'm still waiting to hear a better idea." His brothers shifted about from one foot to the other and dug their toes into the dirt but neither one spoke.

"Then why don't you two shits go back to the others and wait for me." He enunciated slowly for the benefit of the slow-witted.

"I would be very happy to do anything that would create a space between me and you, I tell you what. Come on Ocie." He walked his horse away, his brother following close behind.

"Yeah, that's right. You two boys go suck each other's cocks, maybe it'll keep you out of my hair for a spell." Joseph had his horse moving in the opposite direction.

Joseph did not hate his brothers the way his brothers

hated him. He saw them as less important members of the family than himself and therefore deserving of contempt. Having been the youngest born, he had suffered the least at the hands of their father, who had never really noticed his presence. His mother had bestowed upon him what little affection she had to give, to the neglect and resentment of his siblings. He then assumed, from the lack of beatings and the occasional soft word, that he was special. Even Beasley, who he did have at least a fear of, if not a respect for, was there in his mind to take care of him, to teach him, and to defend him.

Since he had a prince's view of himself, he expected to be treated with deference and that expectation was often self-fulfilling. Ocie and Price might nip at it, but they never bit. Beasley might beat him, but he was generally too fast to be caught and too smart not to flee, but he took those beatings as censure, not as domination. His survival he took for granted. He felt himself charming and likable from an innate specialness. The world owed him and he was here to collect.

As he neared the ranch house, he pushed his hat back to better reveal his face. The building was a haphazard construction, built partly of stone, partly of mud-brick, and finished with a little lumber. An adobe chimney was along one side and thin smoke trailed away from it in the stagnant air. Attached to the back of the house was a small barn, not really much more than a shed, and there was a thorn bush corral a stone's throw from a covered porch.

In a rickety chair on the shaded porch, an old woman sat, leaning forward with her arms on her knees and her head propped on one palm. She watched Joseph approach and called into the house through the open door. Another woman, younger, but thin and weathered, emerged to stand at the edge of the swept dirt porch and leaned heavily on a pole that helped uphold the canvas awning. She smiled at Joseph with crooked bucked teeth after he tipped his hat to her while dismounting.

"Good morning ladies."

She nodded in agreement but seemed unable to form words.

"My name is Joseph. I'm just passing on my way home. I been out to visit relations on the Rio. Saw your home here and thought I'd stop and visit for a moment and stretch out my legs. And maybe get some water for the horse."

The younger woman struggled then seemed to find her voice, "I'm Annabeth Briggs, this here is my mother-in-law. There's a pump for the well around the side." She pointed to her left.

Two boys, one a toddler the other seven or eight, both skinny and with the same mousy brown hair as the woman, came through the doorway to stand behind her skirts. "These here are Henry and William," she called into the house, "Doreen, bring out a cup for the stranger." In a moment an adolescent girl with freckles and tangled teeth came out, carefully holding a ceramic cup in both hands which she handed to Joseph without making eye contact.

Joseph took his horse by the bridle and led him to the side of the house, the younger woman and her three children followed, clustering around him as if he were doing something they had never seen before. He pumped water first into a bucket that was handy and put it under his horse's nose. he then filled the cup for himself.

"Ain't there any menfolk around?" he asked clumsily.

Annabeth stiffened. Her smile faded and she squinted at Joseph who stood framed in the glaring light. "My husband is close by," she said quickly. It was silent for an endless moment and then, feeling Joseph grin as she stared down at his boots, she stammered, "I'm afraid I can't offer you no food right now mister, I'm busy with my chores and can't take the time. So I'll bid you goodbye now that you're rested and you can be on your way."

Joseph grinned and stepped closer; so close that Annabeth stepped backward with a gasp, her boys scuttled out of the way.

"Where exactly has your husband got to?"

Annabeth did not answer except to back up another step and push her sons further out of view, her shoulders folding in and her chin pushed down. Joseph's gaze slid sideways and rested on the little girl's face. "How old might you be now, darling?"

"I'm thirteen," she whispered, her cheeks flaming crimson, her eyes darting an appeal to her mother.

"Thirteen, my goodness." His eyes slid up and down her thin frame. He leaned against the pump and looking again at the girl's mother he said, "Raise horses and cattle here, do you?"

"Some," she said, meaning horses, everyone owned cattle.

"Papa!" The littlest boy nearly shrieked, startling everyone. Annabeth's face, looking out and changing from pale to flushed, caused Joseph to turn to see a large bearded man trotting his horse purposely toward the little house. Joseph stepped out to meet him and gathered up his reins and stood smiling at the man, who did not smile back or much slow his horse.

He was tall and big-boned, with wide shoulders and a large square head. He came to a halt in a swirl of dust right alongside Joseph, pinning him between the two horses with less than a foot of space to spare. The man took in his frightened children and the look of relief on his wife's face. He had already decided that he did not care for this visitor from the smirk he wore, and his family's uncomfortableness cemented his instinct. He carried a long rifle with a full stock pointed up, he fingered the hammer meaningfully while staring harshly down at Joseph.

"Something I can do for you, mister?" He had no compulsion to use politeness he did not feel and his tone was one of threat.

Joseph understood threats. "No, no, I was just resting myself here with your family, they give me some water. I should be on my way directly."

"And you will at that," the man growled.

Joseph, awkwardly in the small space allowed him, mounted his horse and avoided eye contact. He turned his horse sharply and started walking it away. "Thank you for the visit and the water, misses," he said, twisting around in the saddle and grinning again, suddenly bold. "Perhaps I'll see you all again."

The old woman in the chair watched Joseph ride away with the same dispassion with which she had watched him arrive.

Five

Red and Michael made the best of traveling companions. Red liked to talk and Michael at least gave the appearance of listening by remaining awake and not interrupting Red's monologues. Michael was, in fact, paying attention to Red but only enough to let Red's voice penetrate the background of his awareness without being too conscious of the content of the speech. Miles wore away under the hooves of Red's big roan gelding and Michael's pale mule without Michael contributing a word and without Red pausing his discourse. Both were content with this.

Red's back still pained him deeply and the heavy stride of his horse's walking pace, bounced and jarred, keeping him alert and uncomfortable despite his continual consumption. His whiskey had run out the day before and he had switched to a concentrated distillate found in the Comanche camp that smelled of turpentine and gunpowder and had been colored brown with tobacco juice. It gave him a dull headache right behind his brow but distanced him from the pain and opened wide is capacity for reminiscing and speculating.

Michael had been offered to share in the moonshine but was unable to swallow the small amount that tried to dissolve his tongue when he had managed a companionable sip. Even several hours later and after many pulls from his canteen, his gums continued to feel prickly and his lips dry and tight.

Both men were riding in their shirt sleeves, their wide hat brims pulled down low against the glare, and their pant legs slick with sweat where they rubbed against the flanks and saddle. The butts of their pistols, Michael's one huge gun and Red's matched pair, were almost too hot to touch and were kept holstered on the pommels of their saddles with the barrels pointing forward and away in case the heat ignited the powder. Michael's shotgun and Red's rifle, were laid out cross-wise and secured to the rumps of their mounts along with rolled-up clothing and bedding and some carefully packed food. They had parted company with the Rangers that morning, Michael having worn out his welcome.

Michael had awakened late the night before in the place where he had fallen the day before that. He was groggy and weak but sprang quickly to his feet before his eyes were completely open. He tried to remember his name and where he was, but dream-like flashes of the battle and of the past few days were drifting and weaving non-sequentially through his mind. As he tried to piece it together, he was distracted when he noticed another form that had apparently chosen to sleep under the broad prairie sky next to him.

He bent over to see the figure's face, and recognition engendered the total awareness of self, time, and place. The brown-skinned woman had been shot through the head then placed like a bride by his side. He had no feelings for the woman's death. He had not been trying to save her when he had beaten back the Rangers with his whip. The idea that he had been sleeping in a parody of connubiality with a corpse did not revolt him, it confused him. The woman was naked except for the bullwhip, which was wrapped around her neck.

Still leaning over her, he reached out and, being careful

not to touch her skin, he took hold of the whip handle that lay between her breasts and gently uncoiled it from her throat without overly disturbing her head. He wrapped the whip around his waist and over one shoulder tucking in the small end and letting the handle dangle against his chest.

He could see the fires from the Ranger's camp several hundred yards away and was unmoved to join them. He was not sleepy and so he stepped a few dozen feet away from the dead body and sat cross-legged on the ground, watching the Rangers and waiting for morning.

Before dawn, he saw the stirrings of life in the camp and walked over to receive a cold and silent non-welcome from the men. Red, holding a cup of coffee, called Michael over to him and whispered to him to stay close and to keep his mouth shut. Advice that Michael easily heeded as the troop prepared to pull out.

Red had pieced together the events of the day before from the welts on some of the men's faces and the reluctance of anyone to speak plainly. He had walked out and checked that Michael was alive and in no danger of further retribution. He saw that the men had killed the Mexican woman, whose child had done for Jack, and dragged her body by the neck to where Michael lay stretched out flat on his back, his arms flung out to his sides. They had then pushed the corpse up next to Michael, throwing her arm and leg across Michael's torso in a necrophiliac cuddle.

Red had tried to lift the woman's naked body off the boy, but his back spasmed the instant he put it to work and he had to settle for rolling the woman off but not away. He found Michael's hat and covered his exposed face from the scorching rays of the sun. He hoped that what little he had the ability and inclination to do for the boy, would be enough. He caught the reins of the mule, which was standing placidly a hundred feet away, and, telling it he would shoot it if it gave him the smallest reason, he led it to where the Rangers had picketed their animals.

Red returned to his men and busied them burying the body of Captain Jack. They were too far away from any town and the weather was too hot to consider bringing him back for a proper burial. Red desired to bury the remains of the murderous little boy but he knew his men would never stand for it.

Later that evening, after the men had eaten, an introspective hush had settled over the Rangers. He stood up and announced that he was resigning as Captain in the Texas Rangers and returning home to his family as fast as possible. His men sputtered with surprise and disappointment, and Jack's men remained silent as stones. He gave no reasons when asked and placed Luke in charge of both units until they delivered the captives. Uncharacteristically he would say nothing more. He moved off to his bedding and lay down to sleep.

He'd been relieved if not happy when Michael entered the camp the next morning. Red was somewhat amazed that no one had killed him. The boy seemed to have a knack for both finding trouble and then miraculously surviving it.

Slurping noisily from his cup, Red beckoned Luke to join them. Luke greeted Michael with a stare and a nod and said, "Morning. Your mind still set on leaving?"

"To be sure," he answered in a solemn and quiet tone.

"I sure wish you'd change your mind on this, Captain."

"If I changed my mind, I'll be as dead as Black Jack. I know that as sure as God's in heaven and the Devil's on earth. Was a bad business yesterday all around, and I'm going to listen to the omens for once. I've seen my share of blood spilled in this life and me luck feels all played out now, Luke. If I don't get me arse home quick and keep it there, I'm a dead man, for certain.

"I'd like to spend some peaceful hours with me girls before I meet my maker. Maybe I'm just tired out, what with the back hurting, but I don't have the strength of faith to see me past any more hardship."

"The men will be sorry to see you go,"

"Not you, eh? You heartless bastard."

"I'd just as soon you stayed too, Captain," he protested, close to an emotion.

"Well, I won't be missing the likes of you now, will I? I'll be curled up in bed sleeping the morning away with me pretty wife, I will. You boys can keep the countryside safe without me. You take care of the lads for me or I'll kick your arse." He poked Luke hard in the chest with his forefinger to punctuate his last order. "Now get out of here before you embarrass yourself with unmanly weeping."

Luke, who had never shed a single tear in his life, asked, "What about him?" He tilted his head at Michael, who had not moved a muscle since Red had spoken to him.

"Christ on a biscuit, lad, I forgot you were standing there. You should make a noise every now and again to remind folks that you're still breathing. Ah well, you can ride with me if you like. I wouldn't recommend you stay on with the company. You're a bit more trouble than Luke here can handle, I'd wager."

"He is harder to live with and you might guess by looking at him," Luke said.

"That he is. Still, he saved me miserable life, for what that's worth. Least I can do is take him home, let me wife thank him, or kick him, as she likes. What do you say, hey? It's up to you now, son"

Michael had never considered being a Ranger. He'd never been part of a group and did not recognize the possibility. He assumed that he would be alone. Always. He had never felt he belonged with the Rangers. His new life and his old one had a definitive commonality. He was always the outsider.

There was a quality that the big Irishman possessed that drew Michael to him. Red was warm, and Michael craved that warmth from the very bottom of his soul. Inside his chilled depths, deep inside the ice cave that was his world, he longed to be with Red. To be warmed to the point of animation. He loved Red and had no understanding as to why.

"I'd like to go with you," he said.

Red did not smile as Michael announced his decision. His feelings were mixed. His invitation to let Michael join him had been more charity than gratitude. He figured the boy would be killed if he stayed with the Rangers. Perhaps not by any direct act of hostility on the part of the men, but by their failing to come to his aid, or not restraining him from charging in unprepared. He'd seen Michael fight and so had most of the other Rangers; he doubted that anyone could kill him, or would dare to try. With whip or guns, Michael fought as a man possessed and Red knew his men were afraid of the Muleskinner. Just as he was.

"Get your belongings then. We'll be leaving presently." Michael headed towards his mule.

Red stood where he was as the camp broke. When the Rangers were ready to depart, the men of Red's detachment formed a blob like line, waiting to say their individual farewells.

Stiff and formal against their unaccustomed emotions, they shook his hand and mumbled good-luck and hope-to-see-you-soon and then hurriedly mounted with a minimum of eye contact. Red's nose was running and his eyes were shiny as he responded with thank-yous and sure-will-soon and then he too mounted his horse. He waved as they departed, the captives mounted on captured ponies in the middle of the two troops.

Michael sat the mule, unnoticed, a little behind Red and watched the Rangers leave. He felt better the further away they went.

Red turned to look for Michael and was surprised to find him so close. "All right, you're ready I see. Let's be on our way. Going to put a bell on that lad." Then a moment later as they walked their mounts side by side, "Good ones, every one of them. You've family of your own, do you?"

Michael had to think hard how to answer and remained silent for nearly a minute. "My father lives in Texas," he shrugged.

"It is always hard to leave someone. When I left Ireland, I cried me eyes out and I was no lad then. Left behind eight brothers and two sisters and a dead wife..., and others."

"We came from Scotland," Michael heard himself say.

"You must have been just a tot, there's no Scott in your speech. I came a full-grown man to these shores, almost thirty, I was. It was the famine of forty-five that turned the course of life for me. Three-quarters of the country starving to death while the rest got fat. I had to leave before I started killing Englishmen. The bastards let us die by the thousands. In the harbor, where me ship left from, there was ships filled to the brim with grain and bacon and such, not coming in mind but going out. All that food grown in Ireland going off to feed the English whilst we grew thin as ghosts and died like beggars. I was so angry I thought about going to London instead of here, just to shoot me a lord or two."

"Why didn't you?"

"They'd have killed me back, to be sure. And, I didn't have a gun. Also, there was a prettiest little shanty-girl on that ship I've ever laid eyes on. Thin as a stick she was, but the sight of her made me weak. Yellow hair, and freckles on her face and neck like stars on a moonless night. When I managed to catch her eye, she smiled at me. After that, there was no power on Heaven or earth that could have taken me off that boat.

"She was crossing with her parents and little brother, but they never laid eyes on America. All three of them died in the first week. They packed us in like we was cargo and not flesh and blood, one atop the other, and no room to spare. We were hungry and weak to start with, people died the very first day. Sharks learned to follow the boat and were well-fed, to be sure. There was almost room enough to spare when we arrived in New York.

"We were married straight away. I won't say she married me for love or money. She was young and all alone in a new land and it might have been the brothels for her, for certain. But I knew she would come around in time."

"Did she?" asked Michael, vowing to kill a lord if he ever met one.

"Yes, she did." Red smiled, then opened the jug tied to his saddle beside his guns and began fortifying himself for a lengthy address on the nature of women that would last for the rest of the morning. He passed the jug to Michael.

Michael lost the thread of Red's oration just after having a sip from the jug. As the hours slipped by, Red's slurred Irish brogue lulled Michael and soothed his nerves at being alone and in conversation, albeit one-sided, with another person. After a few hours, he felt almost as though he had a friend.

Red was about the same age as his father but likable, friendly, humorous, and did not seem to hate him. That was a revelation to him. Red's unsolicited affability and openness felt so utterly generous to Michael that he felt he was the recipient of some kind of universal largess.

Michael felt, if not happy - for that was a great leap - contented. And he felt the presence of God watching over him, guiding him, rewarding him. He thanked the Lord for Red.

He studied the sweating neck of his mule as it bobbed along, at the awesome revolver Red had given him. He fingered the whip coiled about his torso and snuck a shy glance at his babbling companion.

"Thou preparest a table before me in the presence of mine enemies," he muttered.

"I'm hungry as well," Red interrupted himself. "We'll stop a bit and mess up a pan of grits."

"Okay."

Six

Beasley arrived home a day earlier than he had originally predicted. Hunger and fear had driven him to drive his horse to the limits of its endurance. They were both thin and haggard and drew stares and comments from the furtive town's people as they came through just before sunset. The low crimson and orange clouds shrouded him in bloody colors as he made his way to the stable.

He handed the reins to the stablehand and asked him if he'd seen his sister about that day. The man profusely denied having seen Mary, smiling too big and over-explaining, but Beasley, who was used to people being nervous around him, was too worn to take much notice. He told him to shut the hell up.

He left the man and confidently made his way through the haphazard maze of shacks and adobes that made up the little town that those from other towns, and most of the residents, referred to as the Asshole of Texas. It had a year-round creek and some decent bottom land suited to grow corn, with some grazing on the low hills for cattle, but most of the residents were there because they could not be somewhere better.

His sister lived in a one room mudbrick hovel with a plank roof and no windows. It had a green hide for a door. He swept the stinking skin aside and, stooped over in the narrow frame, he waited until his eyes grew accustomed to the dark.

"Mary," he called softly. "You here?"

He heard breathing in the cool gloomy interior and, from the low light that spilled through the doorway, he could just make out the small bare feet of someone sleeping on a thin straw-filled mattress on the floor in the far corner. Hunched over to avoid collision with the low ceiling, he made his way to the inert figure, carefully avoiding the detritus strewn about the floor.

"Mary?" he leaned stiffly over and shook the limp body by the shoulder.

"Ow, oooohhhh," she exhaled,

He shook her more firmly.

"Leave me be, asshole, will you?"

“Mary, it’s me. Beasley. Wake up, will you? I need you to fix me up something to eat. I am about played out.” He stood up as far as he could and, angry, prodded her viciously with his toe in her ribs.

“What, wait, Beasley is that you, Sugar?” She rolled part way onto her back and smiled, showing the gap in her teeth. “When did you arrive?”

“I just come in. You got some food handy? I had some trouble out there and ain’t et in several days almost.”

Mary stood slowly and swayed. She held her face in her hands a moment, then rubbed her back. “Yeah, course. I’ll fix you some grits and I got some bacon. You want some coffee?”

“Sure, and something to drink. Where’s your jug?”

She searched through the mess on the floor. “It’s here somewhere. I’m not awake yet, I guess. Oh, here it is, Sugar. I’ll light the stove.”

Beasley had to tip the jug far back before he could get a swallow. “Hell,” he said. “Can’t you ever leave a little in the bottle. Cork goes both ways, you know.”

“When I pull a cork I throw it away.” She squatted and fed tinder and paper into the belly of a square iron stove. She lit it with a long wooden match and fed it kindling until it was burning fiercely. The interior of the adobe was cool and the warmth was welcome to Beasley. He stretched as best he could under the low ceiling and yawned. He reminded her of when he was little.

She rushed to him and squeezed him around the middle.

“Hey, you’re making me spill.”

“I’m glad to see you. Why do you leave me here?

“Hush, and turn me loose.” She didn’t.

“Where are the others?

“Who the hell cares?” She squeezed harder and shook him. “I sent them off to do some business. They’ll catch up in a couple of days if they don’t do something stupid.” She loosened her grip and felt along his ribs.

“How come you been missing meals?” she asked.

He pushed her away a step and his face darkened in a way she recognized; he was not going to tell her the truth.

"My fucking horse got spooked by a rattler. He threw me and my pack off and bolted. It was miles before I could round him up and then I couldn't find where he threw the pack so I just headed here." He had had days to fabricate a decent story and he spilled it out with a practiced alacrity, like a nervous actor.

Mary rightly figured he had just done something foolish and was embarrassed.

"I'll make you some supper. Got some apples in a sack there too." She pointed and Beasley helped himself. He cut off slices and fed them to her as she stirred. She had trouble biting into fruit.

She made plenty but did not herself partake. She lit a candle that was stuck in a bottle like a cork, the wax from previous candles coating the sides. Her brother sat on a four-legged stool that was her only furniture and ate off a clay plate with a horn spoon. He scraped the plate gratingly with each mouthful and slurped coffee after each bite. She sat cross-legged on her mattress watching him.

"You ain't having none?" he asked with his mouth full.

"I'm not hungry. I don't feel so well." She sipped coffee and from the jug.

"Starting to warm up in here. It was cool when I came in. Been so fucking awful hot the last few days."

"Has it?"

"Sure, where you been? He studied her in the dim candle-light. "Your jaw looks all swolle." She had purple under one eye as well.

"Got in a fight," she stated matter of fact.

"You give as good as you got?" He returned to his food.

"That never happens for me. They pretty much whooped the shit out of me."

"They? What happened to that little pistol I gave you? You forget how to pull a trigger?" He sounded angry.

"Can't shoot them all, Beasley. I did take a shot at the stablehand a few days ago though." She laughed tiredly.

"Well, you missed badly then. He hadn't a single scratch on him when I come in today."

She watched him eat for a moment. "Is that all you're going to say about it?"

"What more you want me to say? I got problems of my own." He finished his food and licked the plate. He set it on the floor and wiped his hands on his trousers. Mary took that in, then laid down on her side with her knees drawn up. After a minute, she rolled and turned her back to Beasley, her face near the wall.

Beasley halfrose and duck-walked to the jug. He sat down with his back to his sister and drained the last. He belched and then suddenly felt very tired. He stretched out on his back, his elbow pressing into Mary's spine.

Mary turned after a minute and threw an arm and leg over Beasley. She kissed his neck and whispered in his ear, "Beasley?"

"What?" He was annoyed, sleepy.

"Beasley, you're supposed to take care of me," she whispered, kissing his ear. "Like I took care of you boys after Momma died."

Her hand rubbed his chest. "I need help. This life is killing me. You're my brother; you're supposed to protect me. You love me, don't you?"

He yawned, his mouth opening so wide that his jaw cracked. "Who do you want me to kill?"

Seven

"They wanted me to kill Mexicans. And they promised me land of me own. That's an Irishman's dream." Red squirmed against the hard ground, only a thin blanket as a cushion and his saddle as a rest. Michael lay parallel to him, similarly set up. They had let their small fire die after their meal had been cooked. The sun set and the moon rose.

"They were worried about the Mexicans wanting to try and take Texas back and were trying to get as many whites to settle there as fast as could be done. Lots of Germans came and they were even happy to have the Irish. There were handbills posted in Ireland with the promises of land for those who would make the trip and promise a few years work."

The moon was three-quarters and waning, bright and high. There were no clouds and the glow failed to drown out the stars in their multitudes. It dazzled Michael's brain when he looked up. Red's story was broken up by sips of moonshine and trances from starshine.

"We Irish were foreigners in our own land. I wasn't going to live unwelcome in me own home.

"Me either," Michael added.

"I joined the Dragoons when the war come. The wife had just given me a daughter and the house was not fit for a man. I've hardly been home since. Most Irish never move fifty miles from where they were born but once you start one moving, it's hard to stop him." He looked at Michael whose face was pale and spectral in the moon's light. "Time I went home and made it home, don't you agree? I've denied death by starvation in Ireland, disease on the crossing, the war in Mexico, and kept my hair from decorating a lodge pole.

"I had been thinking the boys needed me, Texas, my country, needed me. But me wife needed me, truth be told. I should have missed them more."

Red yawned and Michael caught the contagion.

"Me daughters are sweet and pretty. Started talking the moment they came out and haven't been quiet since. Drove me mad. I'm not the best at listening."

Red rubbed his head and blinked against his inebriation.

"I thought I'd just gotten to like the life. It is not dull, to be sure. I'd lost a good wife to the hunger in Ireland. Did I tell you that? Michael nodded, not sure. "Maybe I was afraid of losing another. Easier not to be near them, I suppose. Easier for me anyway."

Guilt, Michael could understand. His youth was a nearly constant exploration of guilt supported by fear. His father had ensured that Michael was made aware of his many sins and failures. Red's guilt was awash with sentimentality and regard for others and did not exist in the same cut-and-dried universe of his father's morality. Red's regrets flowed from a sadness spawned by enmeshment in life's trials and joys. Michael's guilt was a product of his inability to live up to divine expectations. Red's world was the pedestrian world of people and the heart, while Michael dwelled in the uncompromising arena of the intellect and the celestial.

Michael's upbringing had led him to believe that the commonplace was trivial, that worldly connections were inherently superficial. Only an ultimate truth mattered and all the other realities and possibilities of life were unimportant. The earthly plane was a battleground where individual souls struggled for that truth or were lost in the quagmire of human frailty. The body, the heart, were great weights dragging the seeker towards the abyss. Salvation came solely to those who could liberate their higher nature from their baser urges.

It gnawed at Michael. Could divine love and human love be connected? Could the spark of one illuminate the other?

"You love your family?" he asked, curious.

"Of course." Red was startled by the sincerity of the question. "I love them a great deal. But love can push as well as pull you."

"You feel sorry you haven't been with them?" Guilt he knew. Guilt was the sign of faith, the cross of the faithful. Guilt was created when you failed to sacrifice the flesh to the spirit. Guilt reminded you to be divine. He'd been told so. Was Reds guilt a holy reminder? Was his own guilt a misguided martyrdom?

"Yes, I do, and I am truly afraid I have run out of time."

Guilt, judgment, and redemption; all the requirements of the devout in a place Michael had not thought they could exist. Michael felt very close to Red. They had something great in common. They were two sides of the same coin. Michael cherished his guilt.

"I think me time is upon me. When I shot that boy.... I have become the wrong kind of man. Too damned to be saved. I can't see me life ahead. What do you think that means?"

Michael had changed. He had risen from the ashes of his own funeral and become an errant of the Lord.

"Fate is in God's hands," he told Red in a strong and sure voice.

That rang true to Red. He felt a softness in his bones.

"That's what I was afraid of."

Eight

He waited in the darkness. He had watched the house from sunset to sunrise. He did not really sleep anymore. He would be riding, or thinking, or at some task, when suddenly it would be hours later and he could not account for the intervening time. His waking life seemed a dream. He was never tired or hungry. He wondered if he were dead and merely a ghost. The white boy had named him Satan - perhaps he was no longer corporeal but a wraith hunting in the dream of the world.

He had followed the Pruitts' trail to this isolated ranch, catching up with, but not catching the traders. The small herd they were driving left a trail a blind man could follow; he knew he could find them again.

He had seen only one man. There were three small children and two women. He waited for the dawn. Every hour or so, he would look up and get lost in the billions of stars and rest with his eyes open.

Inside the house, all were dead to the world. Annabeth lay on her side. She wore a light thin shift and did not cover herself with a blanket. Her husband lay beside her on his back in an oversized shirt and snored softly. The two little boys slept on a pallet cushioned by straw from long-grass. The girl slept with her grandmother on top of several blankets, with one more blanket covering the old woman only. The night was warm and the air inside the little house was close.

They had come out to Texas a year before from Maryland. He had moved the family west to avoid debtor's prison after his storefront business had failed. He was a hard worker but he was not lucky. His efforts garnered little in the way of returns here any more than they had back in Maryland. They had thought to grow cotton as he had grown up on a farm and knew his way with a plow and team. But the crops had done so poorly, even the garden, that he had had to take to rounding up mavericks and mustangs for sale and trade to survive. It was time-consuming and only marginally successful. He rode hours every day. There was always meat to eat but little else. The meat was lean and dry and they had grown thinner and had little energy.

They had lost their youngest child, an infant boy, four months earlier. It had been born weak and Annabeth's milk had dried up two months later. It wasted away quietly, not having the energy to cry.

Their hold on life was tenuous and they were too worn and weary to grasp at it any more firmly. The life they did cling to, was tedious, severe, and exhausting.

But they maintained hope. It was a small and flickering glow, based on nothing more than a belief that their lives could not get much worse. And, thank the Lord, they had never been attacked by Indians.

Nine

The cold in Sam's bones woke him from a dream. He ached and burned and shivered. He stood and stamped and cracked his knuckles and spine and knees. He hopped in place, though this jarred his stiff neck and made his head ache. The cold-burn eased when his sweat broke and he paced and drew in deep breaths through his nose and blew them out through pursed lips. The air seemed to coat his insides in warmth.

In the high country, he would stamp and hop and pace but would not warm up much. The night air was so warm and wet here that he grinned and hummed a tune at how easy it had been to feel better.

He had laid a small fire in a shallow pit earlier and he rekindled it from the coals and fed it fuel. He liked the way that the mesquite burned so slowly. He would have to had collected many times the volume of conifer branches to equal what a small amount of the greasy aromatic shrub could do.

He spread his buffalo robe closer to the fire and rummaged in his possibles for tobacco and his pipe. He lit it from a coal he fished out with tiny metal tongs he kept for just that purpose. He lay back, a rolled blanket for a pillow, and produced great clouds of smoke that hung over him undisturbed by breezes. The bright three-quarter moon was directly overhead and the clouds of smoke turned the light pink.

He had learned from a educated man, that the moon produced no light of its own but only reflected the sun's brightness. His mind saw the fact of this as light and heat were incontrovertibly married and the moonlight brought no warmth with it. He thought that was a shame. He had, in the past, considered becoming completely nocturnal, like many of the animals he trapped. Moving about at night and sleeping in the heat of the day might be an answer to his issue.

But that idea made him feel lonely even in just the contemplation. Even though he had spent only the smallest fraction of his life in the company of others, living a life of unnatural sleeping and waking seemed to be too isolating. He would not be in rhythm with the rest of humanity in a very fundamental habit. He knew enough about the behavior of other animals to know that his basic requirements were in no ways different to other men's.

In thinking along these lines, he realized abruptly that he was already lonely. He knew he'd been alone, but had not, until that very moment, felt that solitude.

He followed the moon on its slow journey and thought about its reflecting again, on how it was paired and partnered by the sun. The moon was cold like he was. He considered again how being nocturnal equaled loneliness and perhaps warmth. Was loneliness the relevant factor in the equation? If he could add companionship to his diurnal life, would that somehow negate the cold?

Perhaps what he needed was someone to keep him warm at night.

Ten

Mary dreamed of a snake. She awoke with only the vague recall of a huge crimson serpent swaying rhythmically to unheard music. She had been standing in front of her father's ramshackle dwelling. Her father had been there, as were her brothers. They all stood behind her, felt but unseen, as she could not free herself from the snake's hypnotic gaze. It had not been a nightmare, she decided. The snake had not been a threat as she felt drawn to it.

Beasley slept like a dead man next to her. She was warm and sweaty where their bodies had been touching. The candle had burned out and no light spilled as yet beneath the door. She felt it was hours before the dawn.

She had been awakened not by the dream, which had been soothing, but from the aches she acquired at the hands of the drunken cowboys. Her face hurt and when she touched the bruise under her eye, she winced at the sharpness of it. Her vagina was sore and itched but she did not touch it.

The whoring punished her for a sin that was not hers. It momentarily reassured her sense of value, while permanently confirming her worthlessness.

She rolled to her side and stared at her brother. The boys were her only real connection to the world, her only touchstone. She needed them and hoped they still needed her. She trusted them as far as she could but she trusted no one else at all.

She felt let down by her brother's visit. They came as little as was possible; only, like Beasley tonight, when they really needed something. Their lives were elsewhere and excluded her. She did not think she could be wanted, so she wanted to be needed.

She could never share who she was with another and therefore it was just her body that she gave, or sold. If she showed someone her true face, let them into her mind, she risked them not wanting her. She'd kill herself if that were to happen.

She felt her drinking was grinding her down, eroding her life into a jumble of mixed unpleasantries. It fogged her mind and, at twenty-four, she was certain that her life was winding down; that she would soon simply fade into oblivion.

Though Beasley had killed their father, he could not do for every other man who had or would mistreat her, and they were not really the obstacle that needed overcoming. Her father's death had only made her life worse. More murder would not help her. She had told him about the stablehand hoping he would see she needed taking away. He just told her she needed to learn to shoot straighter.

She missed her brothers, even though one was lying next to her. Beasley would not help her. He could not. He only ever had one solution for every problem and he could not kill enough people to ease her life.

Her life with her father felt long ago and far away. And her life with her brothers was fading fast. She tried to renew her attachment to Beasley. She remembered him as a boy, always hungry and always up to something. Those memories were beginning to feel like they were not hers. She did not want to disappear.

In this rare sober moment, she all but gave up. But she was mad at Beasley and her anger had always given her strength. She fell back into sleep and dreamed again of the great benign serpent hovering over her, its forked tongue rasping as it flicked in and out.

The rasping persisted and pulled her out of sleep. She opened her eyes to see Beasley sitting in the open doorway in the sun's first light. He was sharpening the blade of a long heavy knife with rasping strokes against a smooth gray stone that he occasionally spit on.

She lifted up on one elbow, feeling nauseated, her brow pounding, and pushed her thick hair back away from her face with a trembling hand.

"Hey, Sugar. You want some breakfast?

Beasley did not look up. He wiped the blade on his pant leg and then checked its hone with his thumb.

"No," he said. He sheathed the knife and stood up outside the door, blocking the light. "I got to see a man about a horse."

Eleven

The old woman woke before the other members of the family. In the dim light of dawn, she braided her thin white hair, dressed, and went outside to sit on her flimsy chair. The air was almost cool and colors and shapes stood out in sharp definition. The orange and red hues of the sunrise-tinted clouds gave a pink cast to the land and suppressed all but the most whispering of sounds. She sat and waited for the day to explode. The morning was a time that did not last very long in the summer months. Twilight was a momentary phenomenon, lasting only brief seconds before full glaring light and overwhelming heat smashed apart any comfortable tranquility before it could take firm root.

Her years weighed heavily on her and she was capable of very little activity. She spent nearly all of every day seated right where she was; sometimes mending garments or shucking corn, but mostly staring quietly out at the horizon and occasionally napping. She spoke little and accepted every deprivation that the hostile frontier necessitated without feeling or voicing a single complaint. She enjoyed the ephemeral solitude that came from being the early riser and counted on these precious few minutes to invigorate her meager reserves of energy. Once the children were up, there would be nearly constant activity and distraction.

Inside the house, she could already hear her son moving about, getting dressed and making grunting and groaning noises, his heavy shoes clumping on the packed earth floor. He appeared suddenly in the doorway, tucking in a shirt, his eyes only partly open. He did not speak or acknowledge his mother but yawned and shuffled past her, hurrying to find a place to void his bladder.

Harriet watched him pass and turned her face once again to the now risen sun. A sharp sudden cracking noise contested harshly with the vestiges of dawn's hush. She turned her head, her eyes meandering into focus, to see the fallen form of her eldest and only surviving child, lying face down in the dirt. He had traveled only a few paces from the veranda and she could see blood pooling around his head and urine spreading from underneath his crotch.

She did not understand what had happened and was laboriously getting to her feet, when she was startled by the presence of a naked Indian standing directly in front of her. She sat back down, her legs no longer capable of supporting her, and stared open-mouthed at him.

He was a full two hands shorter than her son had been but several inches taller than herself. He was thick chested and had short bowed legs. His bones and muscles stood out in sharp relief, making him appear stringy. His long black hair was loose and on his face and body were smears of black soot and red ochre. In his right hand he held a long-handled hammer with a claw head that was stained and dripping with blood.

She crumpled in on herself, terrible pain transfixing her in a complete and non-specific way. She watched a drop of blood fall from the hammer and land whole, not flattening or being absorbed into the dirt. She felt a wound that her son could no longer feel. In killing him, the Comanche had mortally hurt her without touching her, and she felt locked in a spasm of grief and doom.

She clenched her eyes shut and tightened them against the flow of tears that was leaking out like an overflowing pot. Weightless, she floated to the ground and rested on her belly, one tear splashing off her cheeks landing round and intact in the dark shadow cast by her face. She felt warm air on the skin of her backside and legs and her body being jerked as her clothing was torn away. She felt her hips being lifted and the thin skin over her knees scraping on the hard dirt, while her nose was pressed down flat, her breath puffing up the fine dust.

He was silent, his breathing soft and inaudible, and he stopped only a few seconds after he started. He rose, his member dripping and still erect and pushed aside the door to enter the dwelling.

Harriet remained where she was, a burnt ripped feeling inside her groin. Her arm began to ache horribly and soon there were shooting pains running down its length. Harriet's chest felt tight and she could not breathe against the heaviness that threatened to crush her ribs. A trickle of sticky saliva ran from her mouth, which hung open in a silent scream. She fell hard on to her side, one hand pressed hard to her heart, the other arm bent protectively against her ribs. Her face flushed purple. She spoke in only a whisper, not an objection but a plea.

"Oh no, God no."

She did not mind the dying, only the pain.

Twelve

Michael woke well before dawn. While Red still snored, his big red nose vibrating with a ragged sound, he busied himself by saddling, bridling, and loading the mule and Red's gelding, which were hobbled and picketed separately on top of a low-rise, a few yards above them. The pre-dawn glow lighted the area where they had chosen to camp. It was an uneven hummocky place with a small stream, sheltered and hidden by a stand of tall thinly spaced trees.

Standing with the mounts, Michael had a more expansive view of the surroundings. The small height gave the advantage to see a few miles in all directions. Michael stood between the animals and watched as the sun broke the horizon and colored the long stretched-out clouds in rich fiery tones, but it was all monochromatic to Michael's eyes. His color blindness had persisted and Michael no longer noticed it. He accepted it in the same way that he had come to accept the scars on his hands.

He patted the mule's pale nose, feeling cheerful, and crooned to her. Her Highness shook her head and snorted under Michael's hand and shuffled a pace sideways. Michael felt a fondness for the contrary mule, a feeling that they were together in his mission. He thought that the finicky beast was a partner and protector and he remembered that she did try to warn him before he had been attacked those few days ago. He felt gratitude and friendship, even if Her Highness did not seem to reciprocate them.

Michael noticed when the snoring stopped and heard Red yawning and smacking his lips in the calm still quiet. He took the canteen from Red's saddle and carried it, swinging by the strap, back to the campsite.

Red was lying on his back, his head propped up on the saddlebags he used as a pillow. He turned his head stiffly as Michael approached from behind, handing him the sloshing canteen.

"Want a drink?"

"I do, but I'll settle for water, and then I think I could drink some coffee. Maybe some food as well I think before we move on." Red sat up and looked around. "Did you go and pack them up already?"

Michael nodded, afraid he'd made a mistake.

"What's your hurry, fella? Let's have us a cuppa first, at least. Go on over and bring back your shotgun and the kettle pot. I'll get the fire made again." He fished in his saddlebags and produced a brown sack of beans. Rising with a groan to all fours, he crawled around to the firepit, adding kindling and stirring for live coals.

He seemed to forget about Michael and with some difficulty, Michael realized that Red was neither annoyed or angry and just wanted some coffee. He went back to the mounts and returned shortly with a sooty pot and his shotgun.

Red had the fire going and sent Michael for more wood. He poured water from the large canteen into the pot and laid it in the flames. Michael returned with enough wood to roast a bear. Red fed some to the fire. He carefully poured some beans from the sack into a dark brown sock and tied it off close to the bunched up beans in the toe. He handed it to Michael.

"Here, you do the grinding." He settled himself back onto

his blankets.

Michael set the sock down on a flat rock they had for the purpose. He removed the caps and, using the metal butt, he pounded and ground until the contents were fine. He put the sock in the pot and replaced the caps.

They watched the water boil and when it was dark enough, he protected his hand with a thick leather square and filled two ceramic mugs Red held aloft.

"I never had coffee before coming to America. I prefer it now." He blew and took a cautious sip, smiling over the rim at Michael.

"Is it far?" Michael asked.

"Within a few days. We're making time despite me infirmity. You'll be in deep once we arrive. Me girls will have so much to tell you."

"Me?"

"Yes. You will be a lovely present for them from their Da. You'll not get a moment's peace, I'll wager." Michael seemed genuinely nervous at the prospect. "You have siblings somewhere, don't you?"

"No, just me."

"Oh, and that's a shame. The Martin clan was a wide one. I could not swing an arm as a child without hitting a brother or a cousin. Before they all died anyway."

"Died?"

"In the famine, yes. Not all, of course but many, many."

"What happened?"

"You don't know, truly?" Michael shook his head. "We all grew fucking potatoes. All of us. That's almost all we ate, morning, noon, and night; that and a little milk from the cow and something green if we had it. Then the potatoes failed. They just all died. Withered and turned gray and black. We planted all we had but none bore and we had nothing else to eat once they were gone.

"There was no work for pay either. The landlords took what little was left. Made beggars of us. I had to indenture meself to pay for the crossing but I got off it. There was a fellow named Grady, a man of much the same age as meself, on the boat who had paid upfront for his passage but didn't finish it. I told those who asked that Martin had died and I come in as Grady. I can be clever when I'm sober."

As if reminded, he finished his coffee and splashed some liquor from the jug into his cup and diluted it with water from the canteen.

"Was around this time yesterday Jack met his end. I swear I never saw that child coming. Died fast, Jack did."

"Was he a good friend?"

"No, by God, no. I wouldn't say that. I did not much care for him at all, at all. He was a pompous little bastard. I don't know that anyone will be missing Black Jack."

"What was so bad about him?" Michael was interested in Red's criteria for friendship.

"Cold as a grave he was. Never heard him laugh one time. And he was mean. Here, I'll tell you something few know. Two years ago, I think, he caught and hung some Bandido that had killed a nephew of the Governor. It was quite the business. Everyone was out for that bloody greaser including meself, but Jack got to him first and brought his head back in a jar. Caught him in some shithole on the far side of the Rio and dragged him back across to hang him. The Governor was so pissed-pleased that he gave Jack a cash gold reward and a silver inlaid saddle.

"A handsome thing it was too. Jack must have prized it greatly as he left it at home the next time he went off. When he come back sometime later, he found some cheeky fucker had admired it too well and made off with it. Jack was so displeased he dashed off pell-mell to sort that rascal out, even though the trail was cold and no one had any idea of who might have taken it.

"Makes me laugh to tell it, but I shouldn't. Shows you what a mean bastard the German was." Red leaned in. "Jack come back two months later with his beloved saddle under him. We found out later he had shot three men out of silver inlaid saddles before he found his.

"No one said anything about it. He was still a big hero." Red tossed off his drink. "Going right to hell without stopping to chat, he will. And damned if he didn't manage to drag me with him at least part way."

"Is your back feeling better?" Michael asked, no longer sure what Red was talking about.

"Better, yes. I am on the mend," he said as he got to his feet. "A good sleep, some hot coffee, and a good shit will work wonders for a man. Excuse me." He headed toward the creek.

Michael averted his eyes. He watched the last of the flames flicker. His mind started to blank and he felt the overwhelming love of God for man running through him. He never heard the mule' warning whickering or the sound of riders approaching.

"The lord is my shepherd," he muttered. "I shall not want."

Thirteen

A small crowd gathered inside the aisle of the stable. They clustered around the body of the stablehand. Some caught a look then turned away, others stayed where they were, gazing unmoving and unmoved.

He lay on his side, curled up into a tight ball, his hands clenched his shirtfront which was white that morning but now stained a dull patchy russet. His eyes were open and fixed and that was the most disconcerting thing for the onlookers. Some asked that his eyes be closed but when one old man tried, the eyelids refused to move. His jaw was fixed slack and the pale pink tip of his tongue protruded past the lips. His bowels had relaxed after death and the close warm air was thick with the stink.

Someone had gone to spread the bad news to the man's family and eventually his father hurried in and was shortly joined in grief by an elder brother. As his father vainly tried to close the dead man's eyes and straighten out legs that would not relax, he pulled a handkerchief and held it to his nose.

The brother looked about him at the crowd. He gripped his father's shoulder and offered him the handkerchief saying, "Here, Papa. Just cover his face with this."

His father took the white square and stretched it taught between his hands and carefully covered his son's face.

He stood, shoulder to shoulder with his one living son.

Those gathered in the stable took a collective breath.

"That fucking son of a bitch and his whore sister, I'll see them hanged for this." he whispered loudly.

Many in the crowd echoed his sentiment, and there was a general nodding of heads. Everyone knew who the Pruitts were, everyone knew what the Pruitts did.

The next day, after the burial, he rode out to see a friend, who had a friend, who had influence. He hoped to return with a troop of Rangers.

Fourteen

Annabeth sat on the edge of their bed. She screamed when the Comanche warrior appeared in her doorway. She was sitting, too tired to rise. She had gone to sleep exhausted and woken up weary. She had looked up expecting to see her husband, prepared to give him an encouraging smile she did not feel, but instead, she gazed at her worst nightmare.

Her scream was loud, long, and piercing, and it reverberated through the tiny house, shaking the walls. Her children sat bolt upright and stared at her without seeing the intruder in their midst. He did not move or react.

Annabeth rushed him, flinging her frail body across the room. Her thin hands bunched into fists, her lips drawn back and her teeth clenched; she snarled like an animal. She knew death was at hand, that her husband must be dead already. She feared for her life and for her children's but at the same time, she was furious. This was her life, this was its end, after so much hardship and so little joy it was to end in pain and terror.

She hammered him with her fists. She struck his face and chest, over and over, weak blows that had little effect and that he did nothing to avoid. Her voice was thick and harsh and all she could pronounce was, "No, no, no, no, no, no." Until her legs lost the strength to keep her upright, until her snarl changed into a sob. She crumpled down, still striking, at his belly, then his thighs, then the floor.

As the Comanche turned her onto her belly, lifted her to her knees, and tore away the thin shift she wore, she calmly spoke to each of her children in turn, looking them in their eyes, "Run babies, run and hide, run away, don't stop, don't come back, run. Oh, God, run. Run."

They ran.

Fifteen

Red heard the riders approaching their camp and quickly did up his trousers. He stood up and took two quick steps back toward the fire, hoping to see without being seen but he was immediately spotted by a small man atop an Indian pony.

"Hello, mister," the man addressed him. "Mind if we beg some coffee? Smells real good."

"You're welcome to what's left," Red offered and walked casually back to join Michael, who stood tall, facing the six mounted men without a trace of fear.

As Red moved, he kept his head lowered but his eyes moving, searching the campsite. He cursed softly, under his breath, realizing that his and Michael's pistols were on their saddles, and Michael had saddled their mounts. The only firearm available to them was the double-barreled fowler Michael had used to grind the beans; while the six strangers were all wearing multiple revolvers on their belts. This was bad luck, and inexperience on Michael's part and Red felt a deep-down fear that the death that he had felt closing in on him, had found him.

The little man dismounted as did two others. The three resembled each other in a fraternal way. The trio that remained mounted looked to be half breed Mexicans and Indians and from their ragged garb, low life bravos. The little man made no move toward the pot but instead picked up Michael's shotgun and turned it over in his hands.

"You all doing some dove hunting out here, are ya?" he asked of Michael.

"No," Michael replied, his tone bland, "Not doves."

"The little man looked Michael up and down, uncertain if the boy was being rude to him.

"What are you men doing out this way? Red barked, his authority coming through his voice and stance with a calm confidence that he did not feel.

"Business," he laughed as he said it, one of the two others on foot laughing with him at the inside joke.

"And what business would that be now, I wonder?"

"Family business. My name is Joseph Pruitt and these are my brothers: Ocie and Price." He did not indicate which was which. He turned the shotgun and pointed it at Red's belly. "Why don't you come over here and set down where I can keep an eye on you, please."

Red began to do as he was told, saying, "We met up with Rangers the day before yesterday that were out searching for you fellows.".

"There's always someone looking to find us."

"Well, they might be closer than you think." Red had moved to within a few feet of Michael but remained standing.

"I wouldn't concern yourself none with that. I'd say that's my problem. You got more to worry about yourself. That's a nice-looking gelding you got up there with that mule, Mister."

"Yes, and I'd be happy to keep them. Leaving us out here without horses, that's the same as murder."

"Joey, just stop talking with him and finish what you started already." Price had no tolerance for small talk.

"You all just shut up and keep an eye peeled. I'm handling this," Joseph told his brother. Price tugged his hat brim further down and spat, moving to stand next to his horse, but Ocie drew his revolver and stepped around to the rear of Red and Michael.

"I don't like the way you're eyeballing me, kid," Joseph said to Michael, though he was obviously close to Michael in age and six inches shorter. Joseph was angry now and determined to drag out the experience as long as possible.

Michael was staring hard at Joseph and had not blinked. He was wearing Puritan Pete's black hat and his blue eyes shone from beneath the shade of the wide flat brim. His pupils were huge black vacuums that nearly obliterated the irises, and his thin blonde brows lifted so high that it appeared as if he were trying to visually swallow what he was gazing at.

"He looks like a rifle I once had," Ocie said unexpectedly, drawing Joseph out of a staring contest he was losing to Michael.

"What the hell are you talking about, idiot?" He broke his eye contact but did not turn away from Michael.

"Y'all remember that old fifty-eight caliber I had a couple years back? The cap would bust but sometimes the powder would take a minute to blow, and sometimes it wouldn't fire at all. Made you kind of antsy waiting for it, though."

"I still don't know what the fuck you're talking about. Maybe you ought to just keep your mouth shut for a minute." He spoke to Red, "You see what I got to live with?"

Red did not respond. He was worried about the boy he'd been riding with, and Michael was behaving even more oddly than Red had come to expect. Michael was standing perfectly still. He was not his usual stiff unobtrusive stillness, but a relaxed calm. He was the eye of the hurricane and Red understood Ocie's reference, even if Joseph did not. Michael seemed larger than he had been, taller, broader, and much more present and noticeable than the quiet nearly invisible companion that he'd spent the last day with. He seemed confident and dangerous, a lion in repose. He was sure that the boy was going to get himself, if not the both of them, killed and could not see any way to prevent it.

Worse, he did not know if he wanted to prevent it. His pride did not take easily to the idea of being killed by a group of stupid bickering low-life horse thieves, and he had a strong feeling of being under the hand of fate. Though it might have been close to a decade since he last set foot in a church, he held unshakable belief in a wrathful, loving, judgmental, giving, and all-powerful God. This God was synonymous with fate.

If his life was no longer of his own choosing, perhaps never had been, he thought he might as well leave it in the hands of the Almighty. Fighting fate would be futile as well as sacrilegious. Reaching this conclusion soothed Reds fear and he became almost as strange and motionless as Michael. And he became curious. He stepped back a pace to better his view, deciding to give Michael his head. After all, Michael was doing better than he was.

Joseph stepped up closer to Michael and lifted the barrel of the shotgun, resting the muzzles against Michaels' chest. "This old gun of yours should blow a hole in you big enough to see through. What do you have to say about that, boy?"

Michael slowly enunciated and separated every word but spoke quietly and without inflection. "Thou shalt not kill," he said.

Joseph perked his head back in surprise and then said, "You some kind of preacher? You going to bring me to Jesus, are you?"

"Yes."

"All right, you piece of shit, you get down on your knees and start praying, I'm going to kill you in about two seconds." Joseph spread his legs for a stronger stance against the kick of the shotgun. He thumbed back one of the hammers and laid his finger on one of the triggers.

"Thou shalt not kill," Michael said again almost inaudible, he made no move to kneel. Everyone present except Michael held their breath and tensed.

Joseph bared his teeth and began to gently squeeze the trigger.

Sixteen

He trudged wearily back to where he had hobbled his pony, holding the hammer loosely in his left hand. The now hot morning sun had dried the blood on the hammer's black iron head and its long hickory handle, forming a scab on the metal and wood. He was whitened by a thin layer of powdery dirt that his sweat cut crisscrossing lines through.

His normally graceful panther-like stride was clumsy and staggering. He tripped and stumbled over rocks and in divots. Sometimes he plodded, without noticing, through low bushes, their thorns scratching the skin of his ankles. He walked stooped over and with his eyes half-closed, a trickle of drool suspended from his lips.

He automatically found the spot where he had hobbled the pony and left his garments, but he had to walk a few hundred yards further to where the grazing animal had wandered. For a moment he leaned heavily against its withers and the pinto leaned back companionly. Then he turned and slowly slumped down, sliding against the animal until he fell with a bounce onto the ground, his legs crossed in front of him. The pony stepped clear of him but stayed close enough that he remained in its shadow.

His breath was slow but labored and he made a growling noise in his throat during each exhalation, rocking back and forth in time with his breathing.

There was a loud ringing buzzing in his ears and he could see nothing much more than blurry shapes and indistinct blending colors. He was having trouble distinguishing up from down, left from right, forward from backward, and only with difficulty was he able to remain sitting upright. He felt heavy and light at the same time, too weighty to rise or lift an arm, and so airy that the infrequent whiffs of warm wind threatened to bowl him over. His stomach growled and gurgled through cycles of clenching and heaving.

He was having trouble thinking and could not seem to hold onto an image or a memory. His actions of the morning were drifting away from him like puffs of white smoke in a strong wind. But he knew who he was, knew why he did what he had done. Even if he could not clearly remember the specific actions or instances, he retained the cold angry hatred and the empty helpless feeling at his center. And he was hardened in the feeling that he was a tangible wraith, a living ghost, the final hope and lonely vengeance for his people.

White men would die, white women would carry his seed, and his people would return to grow amongst them; like wildflowers in a cornfield.

He fell forward over his legs, his forehead touching the earth and began to softly snore. He dreamed of the red stallion.

Seventeen

Annabeth lay on her belly on the dirt floor inside her home. Sunlight slanted in through the open door, carving a harsh irregular rectangle out from the shadowy interior. For the first time in weeks she was cold, but she was sweating nonetheless. Her frail form was completely naked. The bones of her ribs stood out in deep relief on her back, and her hip bones protruded enough to dig small gouges into the earthen floor. Even contained inside the small cramped dwelling, she looked tiny and fragile.

She pressed her hands against her ears but she could still hear him grunting and gibbering even though he had gone. He had not stayed long, barely a few minutes, and he had not killed her. She was surprised and unbelieving that she was still alive. She felt like a child who'd been caught red-handed in a lie or at some mischief but had somehow, inexplicably, gotten away with it. She thought that she should be relieved to be alive but could not think of a reason to be actually happy about the fact.

Through the buffering shield of her hand, she thought she could hear her name being called. Often, right before she fell asleep, she would think she had heard someone, her husband or children, calling her name and she would spark fully awake and listen for her family; only to come to the skeptical conclusion that she had imagined it. She held her ears now and assumed that she was hallucinating. She pressed her arms more firmly to her ears.

She felt a cold hand touching her foot and her breath came into her in a gasping shriek, her entire body tensing and drawing away from the touch as if it were burning instead of chilled and clammy. Her eyes burst open and she tried to crawl away, but her hands were restricted and her legs were rubbery and uncontrollable.

"Annabeth," she heard it distinctly this time. She stopped struggling and listened, squeezing her eyes tightly shut. Then she heard it again, faintly, "Annabeth."

She turned her head, twisting hard to see over her shoulder, and recognized Harriet's wrinkled face and Harriet's wrinkled claw-like hand gripping her foot.

She slipped down onto her face and her breath came out in fat husky wheezes. She started to cry, tremendous round warm tears that mingled with the cold sweat drying on her upper lip and cheeks.

"Annabeth."

"What? What, Harriet?" she asked inanely.

"Where are the children?"

"Oh! Oh! Oh! Oh my Lord. Oh my dear Lord." She heard her heart thumping loudly in her chest, shaking her body with each pounding beat. She tried to push herself to her feet again but was reminded that her hands were somehow confined. She struggled to free herself and began to panic when her thrashing only hurt her more.

"You're tied. Your hair," Harriet whispered. "Your hands is tied to your head."

Annabeth understood all at once what her mother-in-law was saying and stopped blindly fighting. Her hands had been tied with her own long hair. She reached across her scalp and touched the knotted strands on her wrist and tried without success to untie herself. As her frustration grew, she began to panic again and to flail her arms and then to pull hard trying to rip the hair out of her head. With a huge effort of will, she calmed herself and, panting, gathered her legs under her and rose to her knees.

She rested a minute, dizzy, telling herself to think it through, to proceed slowly. She looked around herself, spotting a carving knife on its hook, alongside several other implements hanging over the wooden table that was her kitchen. She awkwardly staggered, hunched over and unsteady, to the low table, colliding with it and folding over its top.

She had to stretch and stand on the tips of her toes to unhook the knife but she managed it, crying in frustration at the long minute it took for her trembling straining fingers to wiggle the knife free, then follow the bouncing clatter to the table top.

She fell flat over the table, groping blindly, and panic returning on the edges of her awareness before finally her long slender calloused fingers found the grainy surface of the knife handle and the cold hard sharpness of its blade. As she sawed clumsily at the traitorous hair that bound her, she said aloud, "Thank you, thank you, Jesus. Oh God thank you."

Her wrists and hands were bleeding from small cuts inflicted when the knife had slipped and missed. Her scalp was tender and bleeding in places, but she freed herself and was standing upright on shaking legs, panting from her exertions, almost laughing with release but not quite allowing it to exit her mouth.

She began to rush from the house, remembering all of a sudden that she was concerned about her children. She stopped when she almost tripped over the prone figure of her mother-in-law.

"Harriet?" she called, but the old woman, in her torn dress, remained still and silent.

Annabeth leaned over to shake Harriet by the shoulder and looked searchingly into her vacant eyes. She saw she was dead. She was sure of it and she gave it no more thought as she stepped over the corpse of her husband's mother and into the harsh burning sunlight.

Outside, the glaring light blinded her and she burst into a warm sticky sweat, suddenly dizzy and nauseated. The heat awakened her skin and she realized she was stark naked. Her breasts felt wet and exposed. Embarrassed and blushing, she retreated back inside the house, stepped over the lifeless remains of Harriet and the tattered remains of her overnight clothes, and rummaged for her day dress, still dirty and pungent with her sweat from the day before.

She hurriedly threw it over her head and, after putting it on backward, then reversing it, she again left the house, stepping over the body blocking the doorway.

She ran, wobbling and listing, from under the verandah.

Blinded by the sun, with eyes half closed and shaded by a bleeding hand, she cast about for any sign of her children. She was afraid to call out for fear of attracting the Comanche back to her and so she whispered the names of her children as he searched the horizon.

Her eyes hesitated then passed over, then returned to, the long prone figure that lay fully extended, arms thrust out, at the side of her little house; the bright light obscuring the details of its outline. Several moments passed quietly as she slowly recognized and realized what the elongated form was.

She went forward, one halting barefoot step at a time, then fell heavily onto her knees, the dust rising and settling as she dropped back on her heels before her husband's shattered corpse.

The earth was soaked and stained a dark ruddy brown around his head and his full thick beard was crusted dark crimson. She reached out and caressed his face and jaw without actually touching him. Her fingers and palms hovered over his dented and blood-soaked skull; reflectively reaching out but afraid and shy of actually making physical contact.

More tears threatened but the well had run dry. She cried dryly for herself in her loneliness, accepting the concrete proof of what she had already guessed.

She leaned on her dead husband's strong shoulder and pushed herself to her feet, swaying with fatigue and defeat. She inhaled a deep breath, but it was not sufficient. She forced herself to be calmer and take a deeper more fulfilling inhalation and then shouted, “DOREEEEEEN!” for as long and as loudly as she could, hunching over and wheezing with the effort.

The horrible barren silence of the dry prairie assaulted her ears. She waited, every muscle held tensely, expectantly, hopefully, disappointedly.

She looked back and forth and brought her hand to cover her eyes for a moment, too upset to maintain equilibrium. When she opened her eyes she found that she had turned around and was looking at the small footprint of one of her sons.

There were no more footprints following the one and she could not be sure if the track was new or from days before, but she started off in the direction it pointed. At first walking and then running, she headed directly into the large red fireball of the morning. The clouds were white and fluffy and no longer streaked by the sun.

Thirty paces and several turnings with the shape of the land, brought her to another set of little overlapping footprints, encouraging her to speed her pace, now more sure of her direction.

She rounded a bluff and entered the sandy dry wash and was rewarded with the sight of her daughter. She almost collapsed with relief, dipping to touch one hand to the ground. Seeing her mother, Doreen unfolded from her fetal ball and ran to her mother's arms and was squeezed into breathlessness, tears and sobs exploding from her freckled, suddenly babyish, face.

Doreen wore only a light cotton shift like her mother had worn to bed, but it was stained reddish brown over her thin thighs and narrow bottom. As Annabeth held her daughter and thanked Jesus for her life, she stared down at the blood stains on the shift. She felt the slimy fluid running between her own thighs, released by her frantic run.

"Mama," she cried, her words riding on the backs of hard sobs. "Mama, he hurt me bad." Doreen knew about sex. On the frontier, amongst livestock and in small one-room houses, the facts of life were impossible to hide and girls, only a couple years older than Doreen, were considered marriageable. She also knew what rape was and what it meant.

"Hush, baby," her mother told her. "Not out loud. Don't tell no one. Don't say it."

"I tried to fight him, Mama, I did try."

"I know, baby. Don't talk about it. You must not talk about it."

Doreen pushed out of her mother's embrace and turned away from her. She bent over, holding herself, and cried quietly, trembling.

"Doreen, where are my boys? Where is Hank and Will?"

The little girl spun around, her face pale, her eyes wide and round. She tried to speak but her face crumpled and broke down and sobs burst out of her, loud and continuous, convulsing her ribs and belly and choking off her air. She lifted a thin gangly arm, without turning, and pointed with her whole hand further down the way her mother had been heading. She did not watch as her mother ran past her and did not drop her arm.

Annabeth soon found the boys. They were lying together, legs tangled and holding each other slackly. She stood over them, her shadow cast over their broken heads like a shroud.

Eighteen

"Nooo!" Red shouted, raising his arms but not advancing.

And Joseph actually hesitated, turning to look at Red with bewilderment. Michael seized control of that moment of hesitation and stepped sideways, sweeping his hand outward and brushing the twin barrels off his chest and clamping his fingers tightly around the blued steel.

He swept the barrels out of line with himself and, in his heightened awareness did not push them too far away; he did not want them pointing towards Red. He held them firmly between himself and Red and directed squarely at Ocie.

Joseph swung his gaze back to Michael when he felt the shotgun moving. Michael's eyes locked onto his and he felt Michael try to jerk the shotgun away from him. He gripped the gun tighter, his finger, still on the trigger, clinched with an iron grip.

Michael felt one of the barrels flare with heat, and the thunderous blast deafened and set the ear closest to the blast to ringing. He whipped his foot ,with its heavy shoe, up hard between Joseph's legs and saw the little man cry out but could hear no sound. He pulled the gun free of Joseph's limp grasp. Taking a two-handed grip on the barrels, he swung it powerfully, like a club, striking Joseph in the side of his neck with the hard metal toe plate on the edge of the stock. Joseph's head folded over on his neck to rest briefly on his shoulder as his body sagged and crumpled to the ground where his head lolled unsupported.

Ocie had seen the muzzle swing to stare at him, his normally placid expression changed, in a flash, to terror. The blast of shot, dispersed only to the size of a baby's fist at that close range, slammed into his chest like a blow from a giant. His upper body was flung backward and his cocked revolver was tossed high into the air. He landed stretched flat out on his back, his arms out to the sides. The pistol fell, bounced, and came to rest touching Red's boot-toe.

Price wasted no time mounting his horse and spinning it around, jerking on the reins, his horse screaming as the bit pinched. His turning jostled and compacted the group of mounted men, throwing them into a confusion of milling, stamping beasts, and cursing men.

Michael spun the shotgun in a graceful twirl, taking hold of the stock and lifting it to his shoulder. He took careful aim at the man nearest to him, cocking the hammer and then slipping his finger over the trigger.

The man saw Michael and panicked as he stared down the barrels. He tried to turn his horse to flee but was impeded by his comrades' horses which crowded his own too closely. Michael calmly followed the man's movements, patiently tracking him until the man managed to turn his horse. The horse gathered its hind legs under it and prepared to spring forward when Michael pulled the trigger.

The man was struck between the shoulders and was

pounded flat over his horse's neck. His horse, its dead rider still in the saddle, led the way as it and the three others all sped away, finally clear of each other.

Red bent quickly to pick up the revolver and a stab of pain knifed through his back as he rose up, gun in hand, already taking aim at the men running fast and hard away from them. He squeezed off a round, holding his back with his free hand. He thumbed back the hammer but felt the action jam before it reached full cock. He worked the cylinder with one hand and the hammer with his thumb while he blew out the dust and grit sticking the mechanism. He got it working and looked up, only to see his targets fading out of range behind their dust trail.

Red turned to see Michael leaning over Joseph and working the little man's revolver free of its holster while holding his shotgun in his other hand. Red stepped closer and saw with surprise that, although his neck was clearly broken, Joseph was still breathing and his eyes were tracking Michael's movements.

Red jumped when Michael fired the pistol. A thirty-six caliber ball hit the prone figure in the chest and his breathing stopped immediately. Red watched as Joseph's eyes dimmed like a lantern being slowly deprived of kerosene.

"Sweet Jesus, Mary, and Joseph," he whispered and took a step back from Michael, crossing himself.

Nineteen

Red's parting shot had embedded itself in Price's ass. He had been leaning far forward with his legs braced in the stirrups and his rump sticking up above the saddle. Red had fired, aiming high at the fleeing figure's horse, hoping only to set him on foot. Price felt only a mild stinging and burning sensation and spared it no attention as he let his horse have its head. He was making good speed but his horse was second to and following, a horse with a dead man for a rider. It was disconcerting for him to have dead men behind him and a dead man in front of him. It made him feel that there was no escaping. He spurred his mount to even greater effort to pass the lifeless jockey.

They stayed neck-and-neck for a time, the dead man's head resting on the rhythmically pumping neck of his racing horse. His face was turned and when Price glanced over, the well-mounted corpse seemed to be watching him. For a brief hellish moment, Price feared he would lose this bizarre race and therefore his life, but his horse proved the faster and soon left them a little behind.

He did not stop, or give his fellows or his brothers a thought, until his horse halted of its own volition, entirely winded. He sat the animal as its lungs heaved and foamy sweat-soaked its hide. In a moment the other two survivors joined him, one man holding the reins of the dead man's horse, its saddle now empty.

"Hot shit! That was close, I tell you what. He killed both my brothers, I think." He was talking mostly to himself and the two others seemed to know they were not expected to respond.

"I guess he finally fell off." He nodded at the empty saddle but did not look at the other men. "That was a bad ride. Where the hell are we? We need to go back to the others."

"That way." One of the men pointed to Price's left. Price shifted in his saddle to see along the line the man was pointing and felt a stiff dull pain in his backside. He reached his hand to rub the spot, thinking it was sore from a bounce during their desperate ride. He found the spot sensitive and tender, and wet. He brought his hand around and, upon seeing the blood that stained his palm, he exclaimed, "Shit! I'm shot. I'm fucking hit. God, damn it, why does everything always happen to me?"

His face twisted when the realization of the wound brought out the pain, which then brought on the fear. Infection and poisoning bore the threat of death and most people wounded by gunfire died eventually of the complications. His head twisting this way and that, trying to get a view of the wound and making worried moaning noises until the man who had pointed asked, "You want to go get the others and go back and kill those two, Price?"

This was too much for him. He had never been in charge and no one had ever looked to him for instructions. He constantly quibbled and complained about the decisions Joseph and Beasley made but he rarely offered his own ideas, not generally having any.

After a short silence, he said, "No. They is dead, for sure. No sense getting killed over them. Those fellows were bad trouble..., bad. I ain't keen to mess with them again by ourselves. It was six of us, God damn it. Now were just three, and I'm wounded bad. I think we should go find my brother and let him figure out what to do. Yeah, we'll go find Beasley. He'll kill them bastards. God damn it."

He spurred his barely recuperated horse into motion, leaning forward off his rump and gritting his teeth. He sighed. "Ah damn! Hope I don't die. I knew that little shit would be the death of me."

PART FOUR: THE PRODIGAL

One

"Oh, and it's a fine day to be alive, to be sure. Wouldn't you agree, Michael?"

"Yep."

The sun was warm and bright, there were enormous towering castles of clouds parading through the blue. The horizon was limitless.

After several days on the trail, Red's mood had grown to be almost optimistic. Rather than confirming for him the inevitability of his doom, being attacked by a notorious gang of horse thieves and murderers had actually planted a seed of hope within him. His fatalism had to be questioned if he was able to come through a seemingly unsurvivable situation not only unharmed but victorious. He gave himself no credit for the triumph; his one shot had come late and he believed that it had not found its mark. He knew he owed his life to the quiet weird Muleskinner, again.

"You are my guardian angel I think, Michael. It is more than fortunate I met you."

"Yep."

Red was smiling, and Michael, although not actually smiling, had at least lost his normally grim and pained expression. Red had learned to accept Michael's silences and now simply talked around or through them. This made Michael feel included and accepted, and something like happy.

"We'll be home in just another day, are you looking forward to a good meal and a soft bed, Michael?"

"Yep," Michael lied.

"Me wife is a piss-poor cook, I'm afraid, but she is soft as goose down, I tell you. I'll be thanking you not to be checking that up for yourself."

"No."

"But I'll be grateful to sleep in me own bed. This hard ground has been a terrible trial for me and me poor broken back, you know."

"Yep."

In truth Red's back pain had eased considerably. Every morning he had risen with less discomfort than when he had laid down. Now he felt only a dull but persistent ache between the shoulders but without the spasms and sharp stabbing cramps that had been so overwhelming. He still stood and sat with an obvious hunch of crookedness, but movement was no longer a chore and he could ride for lengthy periods without hardship.

Red had taken guns from the dead men and some coins from their pockets but he left the two brothers and the one dead non-Pruitt where they had fallen. He wore one of the pistols, lighter than his own dragoons, which were holstered on either side of the saddle horn, in a belt rig acquired from Ocie and even slept with it on. The lighter weight was easier on his back than carrying one of the heavy dragoons. Michael had refused to wear a bandit gun but had taken to wearing the heavy Walker Colt on his left hip, modifying a saddle holster to fit his own belt. The two would not be caught unarmed again.

Red had suggested that Michael ride an extra horse and use the mule as the pack animal but Michael stubbornly refused even to consider the idea. Saying only that he preferred to ride Her Highness, then responding with no more than a shrug when asked why. Ultimately Red let the matter drop, even though it seemed strange to him. They led two horses, one behind each of them.

"And a strong drink of smooth whiskey would be most

welcome, as well." Red had exhausted his supply of moonshine two days before and was more than strongly feeling the call, having headaches during the afternoon and shaking hands and a foul mood when he drank his coffee in the morning.

"Hmm." Michael shrugged, holding back his disapproval.

"A sip now and again would do you no harm I'm thinking. Might crack that eggshell you live in."

Michael shrugged again, not sure of what that meant and beginning to feel self-conscious and a little guilty.

"And then again I don't know if I care to see the likes of you all unraveled. Y'all are a might scary even when you're restraining yourself."

"Sorry."

"Oh, there's nothing to be sorry about, son. And mind you, I'm not complaining. I wouldn't be sitting here gabbing if you weren't the banshee you are in a fight. I believe perhaps one side makes for the other."

"Yes."

"I once owned a hound dog, a redbone it was, came from good stock but was the runt of the litter. They were going to drown the wee pup so I rescued her from the cunts and brought her home for me first daughter, who at the time was not much bigger.

"The other dogs took little notice of her, they sometimes stole her food but she got on well with them for the most part, even though she never grew to match their size. Sweet animal, quiet and no trouble at all. One spring I took them all out riding with me, see if we couldn't tree an opossum perhaps.

"I remember we came out of a stand of trees into a pasture where three longhorns were grazing. They looked up at us but didn't pay us much mind after that and I started to walk me horse around them. The dogs were a bit curious though, and went to have a closer look but were careful not to get too close.

"Except that little runt redbone. She wandered up closer

and closer, a few steps at a time until she was right up to one of them. She had a dose of curiosity, that is certain.

"It watched her come in closer and wasn't worried by it and just stood there looking at her with an ugly stupid look in her eye. I whistled to me dog to come back, those longhorns can be mean when they have a mind, but she wouldn't hear of it.

"She took a couple steps closer, all ginger-like, and the cow stepped up to meet her. When the girl lowered her head me dog put her nose up, and for a long minute, they was nose-to-nose. All the time mind you, the runt dog's legs were trembling and she was shitting great piles out the other end, but she didn't back down or turn away.

"The cow was the one who broke it off, she lifted her head and, I swear it's true, looked over at me sitting there with my mouth hanging open, then she took a couple steps back.

"Me dog backed away then and came trotting back to me just as calm as you like, and a couple of pounds less heavy, I suppose. I swear I've never seen anything so brave as that among man or beast, before or since."

"What happened then?"

"Oh, the three of them beasts wandered closer. Eventually, they decided to chase us off and we had to run for it."

"No, I mean the dog. You still got her?"

"No, I'm afraid I don't. She caught the disease and went mad the next year and had to be shot. Broke me heart; had to have one of me men do it. Me little girl cried herself to sleep for days, she did."

Michael nodded in sympathy and both were silent for a moment.

"Maybe she was more mad than brave all along. The dog, I mean, not me daughter. Not backing down from that longhorn even though she was scared shitless. Was she brave or was she mad, Michael?"

"Brave."

"You think so?"

"Yep."

"Well, I suppose you might. You're a mad one yourself, you are."

Two

Price had ridden home as fast as his swollen bleeding buttocks would allow. He found Beasley at his sister's house, where he had been lying low. The aftermath of the stablehand's killing had, for the first time ever, made Beasley feel threatened in his own town. His murders and assorted assaults had gone unretaliated until now, but he seemed to have crossed a line with his latest atrocity.

When Price showed up, Mary took the news of her brother's death with at first disbelief and then hot fury. Aroused completely out of her depression, the stabbing of the stablehand had given her a great deal of satisfaction; not from the death itself but from the feelings of inclusion she derived from her brother's actions on her behalf. She felt again that her family belonged to her and that she belonged to them. but now that connection was diminished by two and Mary was angry. To be so close and then have her security once again threatened, seemed to her a personal persecution and she turned to her protector, her brother, her only friend, for justice. Mary too had crossed a line.

Beasley was not saddened in the slightest by the loss of his two brothers. There had been many a time he had come close to killing them himself and he actually felt mildly gratified, in an I-told-you-so kind of way. He felt annoyance that his brothers had been so incompetent as to get themselves shot, and burdened that nobody seemed to be able to accomplish anything without him to bark out the orders.

He was also annoyed with his sister's nearly hysterical

ravings that he do something about it. She had thrown a stool at him when he asked what she expected him to do, being that they were already dead. He left town with Price and three of their men; as much to get away from his sister, as to comply with her demands. It was also convenient for him to make himself scarce for a few days and let the town's collective hostility fade a little.

Price was not pleased to be riding again so soon. He had poured whiskey into the wound but had not had the bullet removed. The disinfecting had been painful enough to endure without having one of his men digging around in his ass-flesh with a knife. The wound had scabbed over and seemed to be healing without corruption but the scab, no matter how careful he was, would rub against the saddle as he rode, break open, and bleed.

The entire left side of his rump was swollen and purple; he had to leave his pants undone and loose, forcing him to keep one hand occupied primarily with holding his trousers up. He was unable to carry any of his weight on that side and cramped immediately if he tried, even slightly, to use the muscles in that leg. Incapable of standing in the stirrups or of sitting down on the saddle, he had to lean his body far forward and drape himself across his horse's neck and shoulders, with the saddle's horn digging into his ribs at every bounce. It was a difficult and tiring arrangement and he spent most of the time he was mounted looking at the ground passing beneath the horse's feet and simply trying to make it through one minute to the next.

Without pity for his brother's obvious pain and discomfort, Beasley set a grueling pace. Price had ridden to his brother with great speed. He'd been more numb than hurting then and made good time by telling himself that the sooner he was home, the sooner he could rest. Within three hours, however, he had been helped onto a fresh mount and hustled back out the way he had come. Only four days after being shot, Price completed his round trip, guiding his elder, and now only, brother, and three of their gang, to the sight of his lost brothers.

Beasley did not dismount to view the bodies. They smelled strongly of decay and had been nearly devoured by scavengers. The riders had chased off several buzzards when they rode up. The bald mangy birds hopped and flew reluctantly away, their full swollen bellies making their movements slow and flight difficult. But the flies were more hardy, and buzzed and gathered noisily.

"Which one's which?" he asked, his mouth tight and hard.

"That one's Joseph, and there's Ocie there. Other fellow's back there a ways." Price pointed them out with the hand that he used to hug his horse's neck. His face lying against the spine of the animal, he suddenly recalled the image of the corpse that he had raced with four days earlier and saw how he now mimicked the dead man's riding posture.

"Hope I don't die," he moaned.

"You're not going to die. Not today anyways." Beasley sat up tall and surveyed the area. "Where were you shot?"

"In my ass! Goddamnit, you know that!" Price shouted in response.

"Where were you when you got shot, stupid?" Beasley yelled back his dark eyes glaring.

"Over there, next to where that other fellow lays,"

"Shot you in the ass running scared. Y'all make me sick, I tell you what. These two are idiots but you're a fucking coward, you are. Running away from some old man like that. Letting him get the better of you." His voice trailed off.

"He wasn't an old man. What are you talking about?"

"You're a yellow bastard is what I'm talking about. I'd never have run like that." Beasley was shouting again, spittle flaking the stubble on his chin.

"You don't know what it was like. It happened too fast, I tell you. Them two killed Joey and O. in no time at all. I'd be dead here too if I hadn't run for it. You'd have done the same, Beasley, you would have, I know it." He accused and pleaded with one tone.

"I've never run in my life. Not from Pa, not from nobody, you hear me?" His voice shrieking louder. "I'll kill any man who says different, you watch."

Price decided it was best to wait Beasley's anger out. He was never sure what his brother was capable of and never, even in good health, was he able to match that anger. Price was more skilled at sullen resentment. He let the moments tick by, occupying himself with the pain in his backside, then asked, "You going to go after those two?"

Beasley did not respond, he just sat silently, breathing quickly, sweat running off his nose.

"You going to kill them for this, Beasley, are you?"

"They're my brothers ain't they?" he asked.

"We going to chase him now? I could use some rest, I tell you what." Price closed his eyes and panted noisily through his open mouth.

"Yeah, we're going after them, if one of these useless half-breeds can pick up their trail. I'm hungry right now. I think we should have something to eat before it gets too late." Beasley turned his horse and walked it away.

"Are we going to bury them?" Price asked as he turned his mount and followed his brother.

"I ain't."

Three

When Beasley and Price had ridden out to find their brother's killers, they nearly passed within sight of Samuel as he rode in from the opposite direction, leading his pack horse behind him. The crisscrossing maze of avenues that separated houses and shops did not produce any clear entrances or exits to the town, so he circled the perimeter until he found his way to the livery late in the afternoon.

He walked his horses to the entrance of the stable and, keeping his saddle, called inside the barn with loud hellos. But no answer came. He read again the sign that proclaimed the building as a place to board, buy, and trade horses then dismounted and tugged his mount inside.

He paused after a few steps, unable to see in the dimness. The light inside the stable was sliced into rows and cut into patches by the rickety walls and roof before it rested on the dirt and straw of the interior. Dust motes gently wafted through and hung suspended in the narrow shafts of light and teased his eyes to follow the beams to their glaring origins. As his eyes grew accustomed to the shadows, he saw that there were several horses and clean stalls. They all appeared to be looked after with fresh fodder, water, and salt.

He tied his horses to a stall post and stepped outside again. He did not want to simply stable his animals without first speaking to someone about the price. He had very little money and very little to trade and thought it best, as a general rule, to find out the specifics of a bargain before entering into one. He wanted his animals to have fresh hay and some rest out of the hot sun and he wanted to sell the extra horse but he would wait to find out for certain if the price suited before going to the trouble, and perhaps disadvantage, of unpacking his gear.

Outside, he was once again blinded, this time by brightness, and tugged down his hat brim to better shade his eyes.

"Been a long while since anyone tipped his hat to me in this town, Mister."

He lifted his head to see the speaker, a woman, he assumed by the soft voice, who had confused his gesture for a greeting. His breath caught in his throat. He could not see her face in the harsh glare as it was partially hidden by her long loose dark hair, but he could see every detail of her body. The sun made a mockery of her white dress, illuminating it into transparency, and although she wore undergarments, her figure was outlined in sharp definition.

She was small and thin, but her narrow waist gave her pronounced curves and as she turned toward him, the point of a firm nipple, that crowned a small round breast, was profiled briefly as it pushed against the sheer conforming fabric. When she faced him, her braced stance created a triangle of light that separated her legs. An arrow pointing into a darkness he found completely intriguing. His belly softened as he studied the shadowed silhouette of her hips and thighs.

She was only light and shadow, only blacks and whites, she glowed and yet was still obscured, and, as he studied her, Sam's back became sticky with sweat. He felt paralyzed by heat. Frozen with warmth. He melted into immobility. He relaxed into hardness.

"Cat got your tongue, Mister?" Mary lifted an arm and pushed her hair back and shook it off her face, tilting her small pointed chin up and blinked her eyes.

Four

After sleeping for nearly two days, he once again followed the trail of the traders of guns and ponies. It had taken him an hour to find his hobbled pinto, who was nearly mad with thirst, and when he watered it, he was reminded of his own thirst as well as his hunger. For the first time in many days, he ate and drank. The long overdue meal left him once again sleepy and he lay down to rest. He woke later in the evening feeling more alert and substantial than he had in a week.

He was not completely sure where he was or what he had been doing and it was only after he cut the trail of the Pruitts that he remembered he was tracking them and why. His vision of the red stallion came back to him in bright colors but without passion.

He paused when he came across the bodies of Joseph and Ocie and his trained and experienced eyes pieced together, from the clues left in the dirt, the story of what had happened to them. With a slow dawning of realization, he connected the tracks of men and animals to the presence of the Muleskinner.

At first, he felt some confusion as to who he had been tracking and why. Then he passed on to, what was for him, the equivalent of disappointment; that some of the men he had been searching for had already been killed. Then he felt a growing interest, almost excitement, in the fact that they had been killed by someone as important to him as the Muleskinner.

He did not know that Michael had been involved in the raid on his people or that Michael had killed his father. He did believe that the boy was the beginning of all his trials and indirectly responsible for the massacre; the catalyst if not the instrument, the omen if not the action.

He felt that Michael had in some way cursed him, and if he had succeeded in burning the boy to death everything would have been different, and better.

He circled his Pony around the site until he came to the trail of the Muleskinner and his companion, and kicked his pony into a trot. They were several days ahead of him and he would have some difficulty catching up.

He touched the head of the hammer which was attached to his waist by a looped strap tied to his belt and thought that this was why he still had the tool. He had a task left unfinished, a wrong that required righting. A nail was sticking up and it had snagged him.

It needed hammering down.

Five

Luke and another man stood several feet apart and conversed in quiet tones. Luke mostly listened, nodding and saying, "I see," repeatedly while the man told him of the recent murder of his son.

They were standing in the yellow haze of twilight on the dry dusty street that let into town, the city proper beginning only a dozen or so paces past them. The great wavy red ball slipped below the horizon, closing what had been a long day for Luke, and the end of a long week.

Luke and his men had delivered their party of prisoners to the Army without incident in only three day's time. The detention area was not part of the string of forts that guarded the frontier but was a supply and command center and was not walled or stockaded, being located well away from the boundary of the Comancheria. It was a jail and a camp for prisoners of war.

The men, women, and children they had captured would remain there until the Army decided what to do with them. They might be used as bargaining chips for future dealings with the Comanche; they could be traded for whites that had been taken by raiders or added into the mix as leverage for treaties, or simply relocated to a reservation, depending on what the federal policy happened to be at that moment.

Luke saw dutifully to the transfer of prisoners then conversationally he made an informal report giving the news of Captain Red's resignation and Black's death to the post officers. The Army was a federal franchise and the Rangers answered to the state government. Luke would need to receive affirmation of his command from other authorities. Talking to the military was a friendly sharing of information, not an obligation.

His business at the post took only part of the morning and, not liking as a commander to be unoccupied, he rode out that very day at the head of the overlarge combined troop to make an official report and receive new orders.

He had enjoyed his brief time of command, after only a

short bout of awkwardness, he found that he had no trouble knowing what to do or how to get it done. Much of it seemed obvious, and he realized how much Captain Red had trained him and his men to be resourceful and self-reliant thinkers. Luke knew he lacked Red's charm and ease with the men, but they seemed to respect him and not question or resent it when he asked for something to be done. Luke had always gotten on fairly well with the other Rangers and Red had treated him as second-in-command, often issuing his instructions through Luke, making it easy for the men to accept him as their leader.

There had been no particular difficulties to cope with at all during the trip from the camp to the post. Captain Black's men had also seemed to be content with his being in charge. Black Jack's leadership had been autocratic; his men had been discouraged from ambition or free-thinking and needed and appreciated someone filling the void. Above that, they were happy with the change, responding well to the looser and more congenial habits of Red's troop. Some men made overtures to Luke about being permanently attached to his troop, but he would make no promises until he had spoken to someone official.

He did not doubt that he would be given a command and he toyed with the idea of asking for Jack's troop rather than trying to follow in Red's footsteps. He could sense the unraveling of morale and fellowship in his troop and he did not know how to mend it. He was sorry to see it go, sorry not to be able to prevent it. The troop had lost some of its cohesion, there was no excitement, no order, no focus. The days dragged a little, their tasks, once familiar, seemed awkward, and some spoke of quitting the Rangers. They tried to remind each other of the glories of their shared past and clumsily encouraged each other to stick it through.

Luke, like his men, missed his Captain and appreciated him the more for not having him around. Red had made rangering enjoyable, an adventure for his men and encouraged a warm sense of camaraderie that Luke appreciated but did not seem able to foster. Many of the Rangers were actually a little scared of Luke. Red had given his men purpose, and that purpose had been grounded in intangibles. Luke understood the mechanics of the Ranger's life and work but not the method of easy leadership. Other than asking or telling someone what to do he was at a loss, unsure how to create or maintain an atmosphere that brought and bound men together.

After two days of travel, they'd reached the capital and he made his report. His superiors had made him a lieutenant and given him command of Red's unit but were assigning another to take command of Jack's;believing it best that Luke command a troop he was already familiar with. They also transferred the Lipan scouts into Luke's troop, as the other Captain refused to have them in his. Luke had no qualms about working with the Apaches and was pleased to take them on, having seen their efficiency and effectiveness as scouts and fighters. He was also extremely curious about them, taking every opportunity to openly observe them.

He was given instructions for the present. He was introduced to an angry and distraught man whose son was murdered by an outlaw in a town two days to the south and west. It was the same outlaw who led the gang Black Jack had been chasing before being sidetracked by the presence of the Comanches. Luke knew of them by reputation, he once even passed through the town they were living in. It was a disheveled conglomeration of hovels that had reminded him of a rabbit warren. He'd been traveling with Red and some of the other men to Red's ranch, having been invited to his home, which lay further south. Red referred to the little town as the asshole of Texas and they had not stayed any longer than it took to water the horses.

Luke told his men to be ready at dawn the next morning and boosted their spirits by telling them it might be possible to pay a visit on Red while they were in the vicinity.

Luke bought the man that had requested the Rangers involvement a beer and started talking to him about his son, a conversation they continued to the edge of town.

"I got one other son but that's all. We lost two little girls when they was babies, my wife died with the influenza three years back. Now that murdering son-of-a-bitch kills my youngest boy," he told him.

"We'll get them. If he don't get shot he'll be hung, you can be certain." Luke wanted to be reassuring, as Red might have been, and he knew what it was like to lose family. He'd immigrated to Texas from Missouri after the death of his own wife and children.

He had married in his late twenties and his wife had given birth to a boy and a girl in their first two years together. The next ten years together had produced no more children, but their farm was prosperous and they were content with their lives. When an epidemic of scarlet fever had decimated the countryside, Luke's household paid more than its share. All at once every member of his household except him had contracted the disease. Out of necessity, Luke became their nurse, spooning tea down sore throats, applying poultices to rashes, and sponging fevered foreheads. In four days the children were dead. His wife seemed to recover and saw her children buried but, less than a week later, she too died.

All the while he fought his family's illnesses, Luke had remained calm. At first, he enforced the calmness upon himself to help his family remain hopeful, but as they slipped quickly and painfully away from him, he became cool and then cold. He never shed a single tear, not by bedside or by graveside, and not once after moving to Texas had he ever mentioned his lost family.

After joining the Rangers, Luke found himself gravitating toward the wounded, volunteering to care for them at first, then having it expected of him. He could dig a bullet out of the deepest, most infected flesh, sew skin back together, and splint broken limbs while the patient remained alert and screaming, and he would never flinch, hesitate, or even change his expression. Men appreciated him for his talent but did not love him for it. His eagerness to be involved with the often gruesome tasks of frontier medicine, and a seeming lack of sympathy, made him appear ghoulish to his comrades, who treated him with a cautious politeness that was unintentionally distancing.

As twilight eased into moonlight, Luke recognized the wound in the man he was speaking to and understood that justice, or at least revenge, was necessary before he could begin to heal. He would find the killer and, with the same imperturbability he assumed when he attempted to save a life, he would see him dead. He promised the man that.

Six

Mary had been dry for four days, and unlike previous bouts of abstinence, she did not have headaches, her skin did not crawl, and her hands did not shake. Her sobriety had been effortless; it was days before she realized she had not been drinking. In her rage over her brothers' deaths, she had forgotten her sorrow, her self-pity, and her reliance on drink.

Beasley had left when she threw a stool at him, but she had kept on throwing things after he had gone; smashing everything breakable of the little she owned. She sweated in sheets and soaked her clothes, her loose black hair sticking to her bare arms.

She burst from the little house, flinging the door so wide that it clapped loudly against the outer wall, staggering blindly into the brightness of the narrow dirty street. She was barefoot and had a thin shallow cut under the arch of her foot from a piece of shattered crockery, it bled freely and left a red mark on the dirt wherever she put her foot down. She paced with stomping steps in front of her doorway, her fists balled tightly and pressed against her temples, the bloody blotches working out a rough circle that became more defined with each revolution.

Her pale face crimsoned and the veins bulged on her forehead and neck, throbbing visibly in time to her circular marching. Her teeth clenched tightly together, her jaw muscles swelled and her lips were sealed in a fixed line.

Although her eyes were open, they were rolled up under her lids and she saw only flashes of white light. She needed to scream but she held the sound in for fear that upon uttering it, her fury might diminish. Her head and chest were ready to burst with the energy of an angry wail but she clamped her mouth even tighter and her throat constricted, choking her in order to keep it bottled up.

She could hear nothing but the thunderous pounding of her heart against her chest and the inarticulate ranting of her own voice inside her head. As she circled the voice became slowly audible, at first just a mumbling that squeaked out between pressed lips, then, as her jaw tired and opened, words coalesced into distinct sentences.

For a moment she thought that someone was speaking to her and she stopped and focused her eyes, ready to abuse whoever might be there. Finding herself alone she realized that the voice was hers and, after listening closer, that she liked what it was saying. What it said made good sense and it seemed to be sure about what it was saying. It was the voice of someone with purpose, someone who had a cause and a reason for being.

It was an angry voice and it was the part of her that fought. Her anger had always been a short-lived, violent explosion that quickly snuffed itself out, leaving her without energy and vulnerable to the side of her that was convinced she was worthless and deserved whatever had happened. But this time the anger remained, struggling with and defeating the indulgence. She held onto the anger and the strength that stood firmly rooted in it.

As her breathing slowed down, the sweat ran in wide

rivulets down her body and she became calm. Like the eye of the storm, her passions raged around her but her center kept its stability.

She left the flimsy door open as she went back inside and soon bits and pieces of a broken home came arcing out, forming a pile that grew to include most everything she had, smashed or whole. The floor cleared, she swept the packed earth smooth, a veil of dust reflecting the strong daylight that spilled through the doorway. She then ordered the meager few belongings she had left, arranging them on a shelf and on nails driven into the walls as hooks. She carried her thin mattress outside and shook and beat the dust out of it, bringing it back in she folded her one blanket at its foot. She worked at a frenzied pace, huffing and wheezing, sweating profusely, and needing every task to be completed immediately after it was begun.

She stuffed the pile of discarded items into a burlap sack, carefully including every shard and chip, no matter how minute, and dragged it down the street in between houses until she reached the rubbish dump just a few yards beyond the town's western edge. Tired, and a little dizzy, she walked a little bit away and sat down in the speckled shade of a scrawny juniper cedar.

She rested there for more than an hour, her elbows on her bent upright knees and her head in her palms, her hair spilling forward. She watched the sun take its time setting, the sky ablaze in angry reds, and then pushed herself upright and walked slowly home where she lay down and fell fast asleep.

She slept without dreaming until mid-morning the next day and woke with a bone-dry mouth. She had no water and had broken all the jugs she might carry water with, so she walked, smacking her lips, moving her tongue, to a private bend in the shallow creek that bordered one corner of the town. She slid her bare feet into the cool water, stooped, and cupping her hands drank deeply for several minutes, pouring the last handful over her face, shivering as it trickled down her neck.

Stands of graceful cottonwood trees flanked the creek on either side, allowing only dappled sunlight to pass through. Cool water that flowed over her toes seemed to negate the heat and humidity. The gentle splashing sounds of the creek mixed with the chirping of a small bird. Mary lifted her head, strands of wet hair clinging to her face, and for the first time in years drew in a deep breath.

She was burning inside. She wanted to hang onto her anger, to her violence, and to the power it engendered. The power to resist and rail against her fate, against her past and present, the will to move deliberately forward rather than to be blown about by circumstance. She was small, she was thin, she was weak, but she was fueled by the righteous anger to an epic endurance and vigor, anger over the hostile indifference and casual unfairness that permeated the otherwise vacant space that was, to her, life.

Every day after that, she came to the same bend in the creek to drink and bathe, sometimes in the morning, sometimes later in that day, and sometimes again towards evening. She would feel her fire dampened, and her tense grip on herself soften but firmed. Sometimes the calm would last for hours, sometimes she would feel the palpitating throb of wrath rising again, overwhelming her, even as she walked back to her home.

Walking back, late in the afternoon, two days after Beasley's departure, an old man had tipped his hat to her. It seemed odd, even funny, to her at the time and the old man had added to the strangeness by his inability to speak coherently. She was flattered that he seemed so genuinely stung by her. Most people, including herself, did not consider her a great beauty. Mary believed herself to be plain at best. If she kept her lips together and hid the space between the remaining teeth, she felt she was presentable, but when she smiled, she thought her face became distorted as if reflected by a broken mirror. She supposed he simply had not seen a woman in quite a long while and it was just her gender that entranced him.

She had almost not noticed the man. Though his size and appearance were unusual, he seemed to have an unobtrusive way about him; he should have stood out, yet he blended in. She was only a few feet away from him when he entered her awareness by tugging at the brim of his black hat.

She made a few bantering and only mildly hostile remarks to him as he struggled to form words. Eventually, he managed to ask her if she knew where he could find the owner of the stable, as he had a horse to sell. She told him to try the graveyard and walked off. Just before she turned a corner and moved out of sight, she glanced back and saw the man still standing where she had left him, his narrowed eyes fixed on her.

The situation would have normally been comical to her but she frowned the rest of the short walk home. She made herself some biscuits and bacon and ate slowly, thinking about the old man. He seemed harmless at first glance, even though he was heavily armed and broad of shoulder, but there was an underlying hint of danger in him that was not shown on the surface. He acted friendly, even warm, but he did not attract or invite company. There were definite boundaries inherent in his aspect, a subtle warning that he could not be pushed or prodded. If abused or annoyed or goaded there was a risk of quick and lethal reprisal but to remain safe, one merely needed to respect his boundaries. His was a cold dispassionate ruthlessness that was completely foreign to her and her own angry brand of violence.

Mary envied those qualities. She burned and exploded ineffectually. Her boundaries changed moment-to-moment. He seemed cool and like he knew how to be quiet and still. She'd always been impatient and fidgety, chaotic and extreme, and she‘d learned to drink to subdue and anesthetize herself.

As night fell, she tied shut her latch to the door with a strand of thick twine and crawled into a ball on top of the thin mattress. She took out her small revolver and laid it on the ground within easy reach and dreamed again of a snake; of a rattlesnake.

Seven

Michael lay awake, staring up at the stars and the waning moon, while Red snored loudly a few feet away. A chorus of insects and the occasional night bird provided harmony to the strong gurgling noise Red produced with his large fleshy nose.

Michael was not kept awake by the noise. He slept much less than Red, staying awake for hours after the older man and rising an hour or two before Red opened his eyes. He seemed to need only a few hours of rest and was never tired or sleepy. He woke without grogginess and having seemed never to dream. He would, however, spend hours in quiet contemplation, his mind open and unfocused, absorbing all that his senses recorded without comment or analysis.

Tonight his sleeplessness was unusual for him for he was nervous. His mind kept slipping into focus and dwelling on meeting Red's family. He tried to plan what he might say in greeting but could never remember a precise wording for more than a few repetitions. He wondered what they looked like and how they spoke. He fretted over whether they would ask him to stay and whether he should stay. He imagined them cozy and comfortable inside their house while he sat outside in the darkness, lonely, listening to their laughter. Imagined himself inside, stiff and awkward, being expected to participate and not knowing how he was disappointing and aggravating them.

He briefly considered saddling the mule and riding away in the darkness, but discarded the idea as cowardly and rude. He pictured Red waking the next moment to find himself abandoned and cursing Michael for leaving him. He feared

Red's poor opinion more than his own discomfort. As the night wore on, part of Michael worried and fidgeted and kept him awake while another part slowly detached and observed the fearful part from a distance. After more time, the observing part seemed to be more of him and the rest dwindled to insignificance but did not disappear.

If prayer was talking to God, then Michael was listening to Him; hearing and beholding him in every aspect that his perceptions would allow: in the movement and brightness of the firmament, in the earth and rocks beneath him, and the gurgling sounds of his only friend's snoring. The presence and will of God were obvious and strong to Michael at such moments and it communicated to him that he was saved, that he need not fear.

The larger liberated part of Michael listened to and headed the Word, even as the small and desperate part of him continued to fret and squirm.

He let it squirm, indulging it in a way that he had never been indulged, being kind to that part of himself that had been fathered by unkindness and nurtured by repression. To silence it would be to disregard it. To try to kill it would be to feed it.

He would not enjoy the morrow but he was not here to enjoy. He would accept whatever the day brought to him, and, however he reacted to it, as part of God's plan for him. He did not need to understand it, only to obey it. And in the obedience, he would find sanctuary and a reprieve from himself, from the Purgatory he dragged around with him wherever he went; a reminder of his mortal frailty and humanity.

The divine and the mundane engendered each other, relied on one another, and coexisted in an uneasy truce inside Michael; allowing him to drift finally into sleep, waking every hour or so to the sound in his head of his own voice rehearsing play conversation with Red's spouse and children before nodding off again.

Eight

Sam had arranged to sell his extra horse on consignment. The brother of the dead stablehand had arrived at the livery just before sunset and, although the stable was temporarily out of business, had agreed to care for the horse and to try to sell it for a larger than usual percentage of the sale. Sam then rode a mile out of the stinking town and made camp for the night, hobbling his remaining horse and eating a cold meal of jerk meat, stale quick bread, and dried apples.

Sam's appetite was normally monumental but tonight he was barely interested in more than a few mouthfuls and then only out of habit, not tasting and barely chewing the dry tough fair. The evening was warm and wet, as it had been, and Sam was feeling the familiar ache in his bones that began as soon as the sun set, no matter how sultry the evening might be. Usually, he would build a fire and try to warm his hands and feet, but the thought of a little campfire seemed pale and depressing in the absence of the internal warmth that he had experienced in the presence of that girl.

He had been looking for a woman. He figured on finding a plump older senorita to marry and to cuddle with at night, someone all giggles and smiles who would cook and care for him. Instead, he had found, almost immediately and without really looking, a thin girl with grim humor and a hard-edge, someone all prickles and spines, but someone to whom he felt an absolute and incontestable attraction.

"I've been trapped," he told his horse, who was asleep on its feet. "I wasn't watching where I was going and I put my foot right in the damn thing."

Sam had always considered some relationships as a type of pitfall; an entanglement and incarceration counter opposed to his life of freedom and independence. Many trappers he knew took up with squaws but felt no compunction about abandoning them when the mood struck them. He had been thinking that he could find a way to connect with someone, but on his own terms, an intellectual choice, not an emotional mandate. He had hoped to be warmed and completed by a spouse and family yet remain detached and autonomous through the freedom of his own heart. He figured on being the trapper, not the trapped.

"I'd have to chew my own leg off to free myself of this one." He shook his head and frowned deeply.

He shivered and wrapped his arms tightly around himself but it was not enough. His cold, at its core, was a product of loneliness, it was much more acute and intolerable now that he had experienced, however briefly and tenuously, a true connection.

When he closed his eyes, he could see her as vividly and sharply as when he first saw her. The impression she had made on his being was deep and permanent. The image of her detailed and outlined, all bright contrast, all luminous light, and lustrous black shadow, she was glowing with radiant splendor in his head. Like a beacon of light seen in the far distance, the specter of her called to him with the promise, and more, of salvation and completion.

Sam uncovered what was for him an ugly truth that day upon seeing the girl. But an absolute truth nonetheless. Bushwhacked in plain sight. Found where he least expected it to be. In the one place he was sure it could not exist. He wrestled with the acceptance of it in a pre-ordained losing contest, a fixed fight with the truth.

Sam had always discounted people as superficial and disconnected from nature, not part of the mystery but meddlesome bystanders to it. He had looked to the wilderness and unspoiled nature instead, convinced that its savage purity was synonymous with the truth, or, at the very least, pointing directly to it.

He knew now that he was wrong. That nature was only

the setting. Only a part of the truth. The hard and disappointing and wonderful revelation, was that the rest of it lay in the bonding, connecting, and merging with others. People did not have the answers. The frightening fact was, that for him, people were the answer.

Intellect and emotion were two sides of the same whole. Ice to quench the fire and fire to melt the ice. He'd seen the winter give way to the summer and the summer yield in turn. The truth was this balance, and his life was tilted considerably askew.

His epiphany was irrevocable and would cost him dearly. He would have to change, to give up an entire way of thinking and acting. He'd even have to buck against his own character. Move against the grain. He'd followed the flow of his own nature but, like water, he had descended constantly, ending in a low stagnant place. He would have to begin to clumsily feel and fight his way upstream if he wished to reach the higher plateaus and the bright warm sunlight.

For a moment, as he faced starting over in an entirely new direction, he felt the weight of his years. His life had been good but hard, filled with joy and adventure, difficulty and suffering. He could honestly say he had no regrets, but when all was reviewed and condensed, he was left unsatisfied. He'd attacked life with great energy. He wondered, at this late point in his life, did he have the vigor to begin again?

He dwelt again on the image of the girl, on her shadows and dark places, her shell and wardings. He was curious, intrigued, fascinated. An undiscovered frontier awaited him. Dangerous or hostile, threatening to consume him. He would be like a babe in the woods, lost and perhaps overwhelmed.

Sam had never been a coward. Slowly excitement replaced some of the fear. The unknown could be awesome and terrifying in its immensity but it also drew and enticed with the promise of more.

Nine

Price tried to sleep on his side, favoring the swollen abscessed and inflamed wound on his buttock but, even though he was very drunk, he was still awake long after the moon had set; the throbbing ache and sharp spasms of pain keeping him from sleep. The wound was weeping a thin pink puss that stained through his trousers, attracting flies during the day and mosquitoes throughout the night, their wingbeats buzzing loudly in his ears.

After viewing the dry but still stinking remains of their brothers, Beasley had ridden up-wind and out of sight of the bodies to make camp and have food cooked, saying that they would look for the trail of their brother's killer after they had eaten. But when the meal was done he reached for a big jug of whiskey and made no move to get started again.

This was fine with Price. He'd slid off his horse, curled up where he landed and had not moved. During the night his rump had become worse rather than better for the rest and inactivity, and he dreaded the thought of having to climb back into the saddle.

Beasley drank in silence, sitting next to Price, and passing him the jug without looking at him. The three men with them produced a jug of their own and soon there was a circle of drunk and sweating men that were obviously not going anywhere. Several blurred hours later they were all stretched out under the night sky, snoring loudly, except for Price.

It had remained hot even after the sun went down, and the outlaws were sweating in their sleep. Price, however, was dry and although his head burned with fever, his body was chilled and shivering. The alcohol failed to relieve his discomfort and twisted it, making him feel confused and deeply nauseated besides.

The hours crept by for him like an inebriated staggering tortoise, his fever and pain pushing him into delirium. His mind would begin to think along some line and would soon be trapped in it, unable to move away at a tangent, begin anew, or conclude. In addition, his interior voice was shouting, making him cringe away from himself. The half-moon shone brightly against his shut eyes and was oppressing him with its glare. The ambient light diminished at moonset, when garish imagined colors filled his skull, slicing through his head like a sharp ax smashing into deadwood, scattering splinters of what was left of his sanity.

In the midst of this assault, a small surety began to form and then creep slowly towards the forefront of his beleaguered awareness. Gradually it began to demand notice and became another screaming voice, vying for his attention until, eventually, he said it aloud. "I'm going to die," he whimpered, bursting into tears.

The shock of hearing the thought, and the active release of crying, pushed back his delirium a few steps and allowed him the space to try to save his life.

"Beasley," he called weakly to his brother. He could hear his brother's familiar snoring behind him. "Beasley," he called again, a little stronger, but still with no response.

He could not turn over, any pressure on his hurt side would be unbearable. He called out once again louder and flailed his free arm blindly backward, striking his brother feebly on his leg, causing the snoring to choke off.

"Beasley, wake up. Oh please wake up." He struck him again, the gesture causing a quiver of intense pain.

"What the hell you want?" came a slurred sleepy reply.

"You got to help me, I'm going to die."

"Waking me up out of a sound sleep's good way to go about it. Shut the hell up, why don't you." Beasley wiped the sweat from his face with a dirty hand and rolled away from his brother out of striking distance.

"Beasley, I ain't fooling."

"I ain't either," he warned.

"If you don't help me I'll be dead like Joey and O." Beasley did not reply but the snoring did not resume.

"You shouldn't have brought me out here with you. I can't take it. I'm going to die, I know it."

"Couldn't leave you, it weren't safe." His voice was softer and he rolled back over.

"If you don't help me, you're going to lose me too, I tell you what." Price was beginning to weep again.

Beasley was silent for a long moment. Finally, he drew in a deep breath and sat up, shaking his head to clear it. "Your wound is hurting you bad? Is that it?"

"Real bad, yes. It's killing me and I'm scared."

"All right. I don't know that I can do nothing but I guess I should take a look at it." He rose to his knees and bent over the wound. He touched it with a finger, making Price yell out.

"It's all wet." He rubbed the tip of his finger against his thumb. "Ain't blood though. It's all messed up cuz the bullet's still in there. It's gone rotten, I guess. I expect we should try and clean it."

"Okay," Price agreed with a feeling of relief.

"We got to get your pants off you, roll over on your back." He was talking loudly, almost shouting, as if Price's wound had made him hard of hearing or too simple to understand. Some of the others woke from the noise but did not rise or offer their help.

"I don't think I can, Beasley, it hurts too damn much, I tell you what." His voice was pleading.

"All right, just hold still while I try to get them off." He walked on his knees and straddled Price, undoing his brother's belt and trousers. Price whimpered but did not resist or otherwise complain until Beasley began to jerk down his pants.

"Stop! Stop please, you're killing me that way."

"Well, what do you want me to do, they got to come off." Beasley was quickly losing his patience and, even though it was obvious that it was excruciating to his brother, he jerked again on the waistband, ignoring the screaming and pleading.

He stopped only when Price hysterically shouted, "You can cut them off." Beasley was tired and hungover and Price's idea sounded like less work, also it was becoming clear that Price's rear was so swollen that it would be nearly impossible to drag down his trousers.

Beasley walked on all fours to where he'd been sleeping and rummaged through his gear until he found his long knife. He returned to Price's side and began sawing through the moist trousers at the waistband.

This new procedure was not significantly less rough than the previous method of exposing the wound and Price cried and whimpered while Beasley cussed and grunted.

"It looks bad." He examined it in the dim light bringing his face close and sniffing at the putrid wound. "Ugly." In addition to being swollen, it was black and yellow with bruising.

"Am I going to die?"

"How the hell would I know?" he snapped. "Not bleeding, that's good I guess. Can't see why it would kill you, except for blood poison maybe."

"That's what it is. I'm poisoned from it, ain't I?" he shut his eyes, again afraid he was going to die.

"Yeah, I suppose it is." Beasley huffed out several breaths, unsure what to do next. He leaned back, sitting on his boot heels and tossed the knife to one side. It clanged unexpectedly, striking against the top of the whiskey jug.

Beasley reached out and picked up the jug, swirling the contents and judging the volume. He upended it and drank a deep pull, his Adam's apple bobbing with each swallow.

"You want some more?" he asked in a quiet voice, tapping his brother on the shoulder with the jug.

Price thought for a moment and then answered, "No, I suppose not. It don't help none." Price remembered feeling crazy and was afraid it might return. He felt a little better in spite of all the struggling and being shifted around. His brother, though not encouraging or gentle, was at least trying to help him and that made him feel slightly less hopeless if only for a moment.

Beasley poured whiskey over the wound, moving the Jug in circles to be sure of covering all of it.

At first, it felt cool and therefore good to Price. But in an instant, he began to realize what his brother had done. Coolness turned to burning and was quickly followed by searing, and then scalding, and a pain so intense that his mouth hinged open in mute drooling screams.

Ten

Tracking the Muleskinner had been a slow and frustrating experience. He lost their trail several times and had to spend hours searching to pick it up again, only to lose it a half hour later. In two days he had covered only several dozen miles and instead of shortening the distance between himself and his quarry, he let them increase their lead, leaving him farther and farther behind.

It was not that the trail was cold but that he seemed to have a difficult time concentrating. Tracking involved constant attentiveness and a nearly complete state of devotion, and although he had been considered highly skilled in the craft, even among a people renowned for this ability, he found himself mentally and then physically wandering off course. He would find the trail and begin to follow its primarily straightforward course, only to end up miles away with no memory when his open attentiveness to his task had turned into a self-absorbed trance.

Before midday a foggy fatigue set in and he stopped his staggering progress to eat and rest, two things he had done little of over the past two days.

After eating, the fatigue was transformed into drowsiness and he soon fell asleep, the reins of his pinto tied to his wrist. He dreamed from the very moment he closed his eyes, vivid images that unhurriedly stretched and contorted as he wandered lost across the vast desolate expanse.

In his dreams, he was a ghost, unable to impact his environment or influence any of the vague entities he encountered. He haunted his own mind. The people inhabiting his dreams did not notice him, they walked right through his insubstantiality. If he spoke there would be no sound, when he reached out there was no touching. Only garbled, distant sounding noises penetrated to him and shapes became indistinct and unidentifiable when he attempted to focus on them.

He moved without course or destination, blown about like a tumbleweed in a fickle wind. His thoughts were the mere impressions of will and emotion, inarticulate and expansive like irregular ripples radiating out from a stone dropped into a stagnant and murky pool.

Even though his progress was undirected and his influence unfelt, he knew there were purpose and meaning in his wandering. His mood was unsatisfied, hungry, questing; not searching, he was trying to find. He was not acting but he needed to accomplish.

Time was not passing but it was running out and he had a sense of urgency that was not being prompted or goaded by anything he could grasp. The landscape was disintegrating, fading away into void, and the encroaching oblivion terrified his soul.

He was forgetting what actually was, and how his perceptions held it together. Himself slipping into nothingness. Slipping away from time and space, from cause and effect.

His people regarded dreaming as sacred, as a window to the truth, that was more real than real. Questions could be asked while waking, but knowledge might come when dreaming.

The feeling grinding into him from these dreams now was that he could no longer differentiate between the world of spirit and the realm of matter, that there was no difference, only perception and experience. He had no knowledge of separateness. He would not know when he awoke.

Several hours later he sat unmoving astride his pony. He was no longer really following any trail. He was simply roving the barren landscape with little will and no clear intentions. He was actually backtracking in his confusion.

After the massacre of his people, he had followed the trail of the Pruitt gang. Then, responding to the track of the Muleskinner, he had changed course and pursued another quarry. As if in validation that his world had become nonlinear, that circumstance and happenstance were evolving around him, that he was unconsciously generating coincidence, that he did not need to act, only to let the winds blow him, he came again into the presence of the Pruitts or, more accurately, they came to him.

They would have ridden right up to him if he had not swung his pony off the trail a few hundred yards before. As it was, they passed within full sight of each other, though out of pistol range. They were led by a half-breed Indian who was obviously following sign. All of them eyed him warily as he faced them without moving.

He waited until they were out of sight and then fell in behind them. They were on the trail of the Muleskinner, and now he had all his enemies in front of him. All his tasks were merging.

Eleven

Mary had thought that she was alone as she cooled herself in the creek. The townspeople had been avoiding her, shutting her out for the part she had played in the death of the stablehand. Not bold enough to confront her directly, they expressed their hostility by their absence, and although she appreciated the privacy, she also recognized that the general mood was ugly and that she would eventually have to look to her own safety. When they stopped avoiding her, it would turn mean, so she kept her pocket pistol loaded and within easy reach even as she bathed her feet and legs. When she heard the voice call out to her, she was startled and reached for the revolver even though the voice was soft and friendly.

"I sincerely didn't mean to scare ye. I must be in the habit of moving quiet." Sam was dressed in his buckskins with his rifle but was not mounted. He stood at the edge of the creek, being careful not to wet his toes.

Mary lowered the pistol and replaced it in her pocket, she had no fear of the mountain man. "You want something from me, Mister?" She turned away from him and picked her way deeper into the creek, away from Sam. Holding her skirts up, she placed each bare foot with care and then tested a foothold before committing her weight.

"Just want to share a little of this crick with you if you don't mind. Perhaps have a little company." He studied her ankles and small feet as they appeared from and disappeared into the rippling water. The hem of her white skirt was edged darker where it became soaked. The clean wetness made her pale skin turn glossy white, and sparkling droplets trickled from her raised arched toes as they emerged.

"I don't do that no more." She spoke without anger or bitterness, simply stating a fact. Tones of mild surprise were mixed with the pride in her voice.

"Ye don't talk anymore?" His brows rose with genuine confusion. Mary laughed and the sound to Sam was an echo of the creek-flow's gentle warbling.

"If talk is all you want, you're welcome to stay. You might be the only one in this asshole of a town will still speak to me." The pride was still in her voice, though tempered with irony.

"Trapping can be a lonely life. Sometimes what you miss the most is someone to converse with. Many is the time I found myself in the middle of a long talk with my horse. It don't seem strange until you think about it later. Sometimes ye need more than you let yourself have, I suppose." He wondered if he was talking too much. He tore his eyes away from Mary and sat down on a smooth round stone. He could feel the cold from the stone drawing the heat through his buckskins and a shiver ran through him, followed by a ripple of pain. He heaved himself up quickly, as if he had been burned rather than chilled, and settled into a comfortable squat with his heels flat on the ground.

"Not much to trap around here, is there?"

"Ye might be surprised." He smiled and tipped his head down to hide it from Mary who had turned to look at him.

"I don't like surprises." Her voice was quiet.

"Why is that? I can't think of anything I like more than being surprised." Sam shifted his rifle from the crook of his arm and placed the butt on the ground, using it as a staff to steady himself as he stood up.

"If you can't see something coming it's hard to get out of the way." Most new things were bad things in Mary's experience.

"I understand ye, I do." Sam hung his head and thought for a moment. "I suppose ye want me to go then?"

Mary looked at him with confusion, and then understanding, and then softness. "I didn't mean you," she said gently. "I don't mind you being here." She saw his face switch from dejection to relief, which surprised her. She did not dislike it.

Sam could not understand this woman. Everything she did or said was unpredictable, surprising. He wanted to trap her but felt like he was caught. And she had not even tried to catch him. She did not even want him.

She was hot. He could sense the heat from where he stood. He had become expert in finding sources of warmth and, though he did not know how she generated the heat, he responded to it by instinctually gravitating towards it. He'd been looking for someone; a woman to match him, to balance him. Instead, he had stumbled into someone who overwhelmed him. She had the potential, without effort, to absorb him, as fire absorbed fuel. And he craved the absorption. He did not know how to make that happen. He would have to move slowly, deliberately, he reasoned, coaxing her, one false move and she might bolt.

"My name is Samuel Johnson. What might your name be, Miss?"

"Mary Pruitt."

"Mary, that's a nice name." He tried complimenting knowing some people like that. "Pretty."

"Mary Margaret Pruitt," she said sing-song.

She sat down on a stone on the opposite side of the creek and downstream a few yards from Sam. She combed her fingers through her long loose hair, her quick fingers working out the snarled tangles.

"You sell your horse?" she asked.

The question startled Sam. He'd been preoccupied with watching her. "Naw, not just yet. Might have to stay here for a time," he said.

Sam's attraction to her was obvious to Mary, as it would have been to anyone watching. Always, in her experience, when men had wanted her, they'd been brutally direct and never wasted any time in courting her. Sam's hesitation and clumsy schoolboy caution were intriguing to her. No one had ever thought enough of her to be put off by her.

Patience was a novelty in itself to her. She had little and had never known anyone who had much more. Sam's slow carefulness in the face of his obvious ardor fascinated her. As she observed him from the corner of her eye, he did not fidget or shuffle his feet, he remained calm and still, a fixture in the landscape. When he did move it was with an economy and grace that was elegant and odd in such a big man, carrying some of the relaxed stillness into his movement, giving it power and gravity. She could not imagine him rushing or hurrying, he appeared as if he would always be wherever he wanted to be before he needed to be there. Mary had never planned ahead, rarely thought beyond surviving the moment. Her sense of time was vague at best. She was always a step or two behind her circumstances and therefore never prepared, and usually applying too much force in compensation. Sam looked ready for everything. Everything except her.

"You come down here to cool off, do ye?" he asked lamely, feeling stupid the moment he said it, flushing beneath his beard.

She did not answer but flung her hair back over one shoulder and leaned forward, lifted her skirt up high, and dipping her hands in the flow, smoothed water up and down her legs.

"You hot, Mister?" she teased him.

Sam's forehead was indeed beginning to shine but he shook his head no, not ready to speak.

"Why don't you get your feet wet?" she purred. "It's nice, I tell you what."

"No, miss, my old bones can't take any cold like that. I'll just watch y'all, I suppose." He actually backed away from the creek a step while speaking, just the thought sent a chill through him, the sweat drying on his brow.

"How old are you?" she asked bluntly but casually.

Sam's sighed with the remembrance of his years. "Oh, old enough to be your pappy, probably." He was actually closer to her grandfather's age.

Mary paused mid-step and regarded the mountain man more closely. And, in a dreaming quiet voice, she said, "I guess you are at that." She studied the seamed face with its deep cheerful crow's feet and the salt and pepper streaked beard. She noticed his large heavy hands, liked their character and the relaxed straightness of his fingers.

Mary felt herself growing flushed and warm.

Twelve

They rode around a stand of oaks and came in sight of a little ranch house at midday. It was a three room, one-story building, made of plank lumber laid clinker and built on a stone foundation with a stove pipe chimney and a wood shingle roof. It was situated the end of a shallow valley dotted with oak and covered with tall brown grass. Outcroppings of sharp white rocks jutted up and lay littered about. The shallow creek, only a few feet wide, trickled windingly through, bordered on both sides by thick shrubs and stunted trees. It ran from behind the house, around the base of a little hill they had crested and out of the valley. Two piebald horses were grazing part way up the side of the valleys northern slope and an open shed barn stood behind and to the side of the house. Before they could get within two hundred yards of the front porch a red-haired girl, followed closely by four dogs, burst from the open door and ran with all their might to meet them.

She was only a young child but her thin little legs pumped under her simple brown dress with a machine-like persistence that ate up the ground with incredible appetite. She was like a small rodent whose tiny stride is overcome by its frequency; the dogs in pursuit were only barely keeping pace. Her arms labored furiously and her mouth was wide open with a rapid breathing and inarticulate screaming. Then, as she drew closer, she flailed her arms above her head and shouted as if it were possible that she might not be noticed.

Red reined his horse to a halt and Michael stopped his mule beside him, but neither man dismounted. Michael marveled at both the speed and intensity of the girl, neither decreasing as she neared. Her father smiled with his entire face and shouted a whoop of greeting, leaning down and scooping her up; breathless, she flew up to meet him. The dogs, all hounds, milled around the horse's legs, sniffing excitedly but instinctively knowing to stay clear of Michael's unpredictable mule.

He hugged her and she kissed his cheeks and lips and they both were laughing. Red said in a soft voice, "Katie, me little darling, how have you been?"

"I'm well, Dad. I've been a big help to Mum, you can ask her. Did you bring me a present?" She had an Irish lilt to her speech as well as a slight lisp.

"Why yes, as a matter of fact I did. I brought you a big brother. His name is Michael." He nodded his head towards the Muleskinner.

"You're not me brother," she told Michael after giving him a searching look.

"No," Michael answered, blushing and not sure what to say. His worst fears coming to light.

"Oh, there is herself now." Red was looking at a blonde woman running towards them, slowed by the child in her arms. "Have you ever seen a prettier girl in all your days, Michael? Here, take me daughter now." He thrust the girl to Michael, who did not know which girl Red meant, and she sat herself on his lap. Red dismounted and ambled unhurriedly to meet his wife.

He gathered wife and youngest daughter in one embrace and kissed first one and then the other with loud smacking kisses and spoke quietly into her blond hair for several minutes. Red gestured with his head towards Michael and the woman stole a glance at him. Her face, partly hidden by Red's shoulder, was thoughtful. Michael could hear them speaking together in Irish. Michael awkwardly held the child steady between his large hands and was very conscious of her every movement. The girl, however, seemed perfectly comfortable and contented where she was, patting Michael's leg with her hand as her parents talked.

'You're not me brother truly?" she asked, twisting to look up at him, her unruly hair brushing his chin.

"Michael, come down from there and say hello to me rib." Red, appearing at his stirrup, was reaching up to take his daughter who dropped heavily into his hands, causing his back to clinch and a grimace to twist away his smile.

"Rosie, this is the boy who brought me home safe."

Michael slipped off his mule and stood in front of the woman, staring at his hat that he held in front of his belly with both hands and mumbling quietly, "How do you do, ma'am?"

"I'm pleased to meet you, Michael. I'm grateful to you for bringing me husband home safe and whole. God bless you and welcome." She shifted the tow-headed two-year-old in her arms to her other hip.

After a moment of silence, in which Michael shuffled from foot to foot, Red said, "If you're waiting for more conversation from him, darling, I'd best warn you, Michael likes to keep a bit of mystery about him." He set Katie on the ground and she went to stand next to her mother.

"Well, there's more than enough talkers in this house that we won't be feeling the pinch. Be a nice change to have a quiet man about, to be sure." She smiled and laughed at her own joke.

Michael then took, for the first time, a close look at Red's wife. He was surprised by what he saw. Rose was younger than Michael had expected. Red was more of an age to be her father than the father of the two children. She had yellow blonde hair that was long and tied into two braids with cloth ribbons. She was a foot shorter than her husband and so thin and light looking that it would have taken three of her to equal one of him. Michael, who was only an inch smaller than Red, felt large and clumsy and like he was towering over her. She looked up at him, unconcerned about any size difference, her blue eyes searching his, her small round mouth open in a smile. Michael had indeed not ever seen a prettier sight. In a country where the sun was so harsh, it was rare to see someone with fair skin. Rose's complexion was milky and her nose and cheeks were splattered with small freckles. Michael thought she embodied the ethereal, beautiful qualities of an angel.

"Damn, shit!" she yelled abruptly. "I left the supper burning I have." She thrust the child at her father and ran back to the house, lifting her skirts to free her legs, and running almost as well as her child had.

"I told you she was a piss-poor cook. Never made a decent meal in her life. The woman could burn water." He gathered the reins of his horse and started after her, the hounds falling into step with him. "You'll be missing trail rations before long, I'll wager. This is me little baby Kerry. Here, shake hands with her."

Michael awkwardly shook hands with the girl, who smiled and said, "How do you do?" very seriously.

"Oh, what fine manners you have, darling," Red crooned to her.

"Dad, did you bring that horse for me?" Katie asked as she ran up beside Red.

"No, Katie." He took her tiny hand in his large one as she walked beside him, Michael trailing behind and leading the mule and the pack horse that she referred to. "He's not a good horse for a little girl and mind you stay away from that white mule, mean as a bear it is. Nearly done in your old man. Eats human flesh she does, took a bite out of me leg."

She looked over her shoulder at Her Highness with fear and quickened her pace to stay ahead. "She won't hurt me brother, will she?" she asked, meaning Michael.

"No, Michael has a way with mules, he does."

"Where did you find him?" she asked.

"He found us, you might say. Anyway, he rightfully belongs to Michael."

"No, dad. Where did you find me brother?"

"Oh him. Found him nailed up like Jesus and a half on fire, I did." He turned to Michael and winked at him. Michael felt uncomfortable being spoken of so openly but was also grateful that he did not have to answer the girl's questions.

"Dad!" she complained, throwing out the word and pouting her lips. "Tell me truly."

"'Tis the God's honest truth, I swear it to you." She twisted her neck and studied Michael doubtfully.

As they approached the house, she squirmed loose of Red's grip and dashed inside, dogs again in hot pursuit. Red handed the reins of his horse to Michael and said, "That child never walks when she can run. Would you mind seeing to the animals? There's a shed behind. You can turn the gelding loose to graze but maybe you should pen the other two."

Michael nodded and led the three animals behind the house as Red stomped across his porch and into the house, his boots loud on the raised wooden floorboards. Michael, once alone, exhaled strongly with relief and set about unsaddling the mounts and brushing them quickly with a stiff bristle brush he found. The sweating animals drank deeply from the half-full trough and when Michael turned the roan loose, it dropped to its back and rolled vigorously in the dirt before walking off to join the other two horses on the slope.

After he was finished, he could think of no more tasks to do. Michael stood stiffly in the hot sun and wiped the sweat from his brow with his sleeve, staining his gray shirt darker, and wondered if he should go to the house or wait for Red to invite him in.

He paced a little and fanned his face with his wide-brimmed hat and eventually paced to the front of the house one slow step at a time. He stayed outside even though the door was open and he could hear the family talking loudly to each other. He walked in small circles, breathing in the hot weather and feeling flushed. He wished he were not there but somewhere off by himself where he did not have to worry and wonder about the scene he had dreaded finally arriving. Now that he was actually there with them, he felt completely alone.

He decided he would leave as soon as possible, today, now. God had not saved him just to have him standing around. He had seen Red safely home; it was now time to go. He started back to saddle the mule but stopped, thinking he should tell Red that he was leaving and that he could keep the pack horse Red had said belonged to him.

He turned again to face the house, steadied himself with a deep breath and stepped onto the porch where three of the hounds were resting, lazily thumping their tails in greeting as he walked past. He cautiously approached the door and peeked inside.

"Michael!" Red shouted loudly at him, making him jump. "There you are, boy. I thought maybe Indians got you. Come in here and sit down to this delicious supper." The four of them sat around a square wooden table, Red on one side, Katy opposite, and Rose between them with the youngest on her lap. There was one unoccupied chair opposite Rose and Red pushed it out for Michael with his foot; a plate with fried potatoes, beef, and boiled greens already laid for him.

Michael hesitated then sat down, his foot nudging a dog underneath the table. He picked up a fork and began eating, keeping his eyes on the food.

"Michael was on a cross like Jesus and on fire, Mum," Katie told her mother excitedly.

"Katie! Don't say such things," Rose reprimanded.

"But it's true, Mum. Dad swore to it," she protested.

"John Martin, what foolish thing have you been telling this silly girl?" she asked her husband.

"It's true. Ask him if you don't believe me."

All talk and movements ceased as the family turned its entire attention on Michael. With a mouthful of burned potatoes Michael chewed a little longer, then swallowed. He did not speak but instead set down his knife and spoon and held out his hands palms upward and displayed red and puckered stigmata scars.

Rose gasped and crossed herself and Katie almost stood on her chair as she leaned in for a closer look. Red reached out and pushed Michael's hands gently down. "That's enough now, let's finish our meal," Red said with quiet authority, then adding gently, "Sorry, Michael."

Michael blushed with embarrassment, certain he had offended, even though Red had apologized to him. He continued eating without tasting.

"Would you like some more to eat, Michael?" Rose asked sweetly.

Michael had just finished and, although he was still hungry and did indeed want some more, he shook his head no.

"I warned you about the food, didn't I?"

"You mind your manners, John Martin or you'll be cooking for yourself, you will."

"The food was good, ma'am. Thank you."

"So, here's a gentleman you could learn from, John." She smiled at Michael and frowned at Red.

"Or a flatterer, I could learn from."

"You need no help there, husband."

Katie quickly finished eating and asked to be excused. She kissed her father and ran outside. Rose set Kerry on the floor and she crawled down under the table where she talked quietly to herself and the dog in mixed English and Irish about some make-believe game. Red leaned back in his chair, tilting it on two legs, and brought out his pipe and tobacco from his shirt pockets. Rose lit his pipe for him, smiling and meeting his eyes as their hands touched.

"I have some news to tell you." He held to her hand.

"And what might that be?" She narrowed her eyes.

"I've resigned me commission. I'm home for keeps." He let his chair fall forward with a clap, startling the dog.

Rose sat back down in her chair, her interlaced fingers between her knees and an astonished look on her face. "Oh, is it true? Is it really true, John?"

"Yes, you'll have your hands full with me here now. I'm a rancher, it seems."

"Oh, thank the dear sweet Lord." She closed her eyes and crossed yourself. "I was mad to ever let you go off to fight in the first place." She leaned back in the chair, more relieved than happy.

Red's self-satisfied smile faded as he saw relief flood his wife's face. He realized all in a moment, how he had chosen to ignore her distress. He never spoke about the death of his first family, but the loss had kept him from his second family. He'd always felt pressure from Rose during his short visits, a clinging attachment that was painful to return or acknowledge for fear of a second great loss. After losing her parents to disease and being alone in a new country, Rose had eagerly accepted Red's advances, only to find herself lonely and at risk of losing a husband. She'd been filled with hope and excitement when she had taken ship from Ireland, feelings that were crushed by the deaths of her parents then renewed by her marriage to Red. But his long dangerous absences had engendered only fear and loneliness, not security and reassurance. Their pasts had pushed and pulled them apart for all of their married life and they had never truly spent time as husband and wife. Rose had accepted much of her pain as normal, but Red knew the difference. He knew from his first marriage what it was supposed to be like, what it should have been like, what it could have been like.

He laid his smoldering fragrant pipe on the table and reached out for his wife's hand. "Rose dear, I'm sorry. I'll make it up to you. I will, I promise." His eyes were misty with a sense of his own loss, for his first wife and for what he had missed with Rose. He very much wanted to mean what he had said.

She lifted his hand and kissed the thick fingers and pressed them to her cheek, her own tears spilling over and clinging to the hairs on the back of his hand. She wanted very badly to believe him.

Michael curled inward and faded into invisibility, his eyes on Red's pipe and its gray spiral of smoke, leaving Red and Rose completely alone.

Thirteen

Michael sat in a hard wooden kitchen chair with a high back that he had pulled out onto the porch. After their meal, Red had gone into the bedroom to lie down and sleep, saying that he had missed his bed and that his back was paining him. Rose was busy with chores in the house, leaving Michael to amuse himself. He offered to help with the work but Rose told him that there was nothing to be done with an extra set of hands and that he should do as he pleased.

Feeling out of place and purposeless, he settled in on the porch and watched Katie romp with the dogs by the creek bed. He did not feel like he was intruding; Red and his family were too warm and including for that to be the problem. His continued uncomfortableness was more that he did not know what his role was, what his tasks were, and how we should occupy himself.

In a situation like this he needed to be guided, to be told what to do. Being a part of something was unnatural and new to him and he did not know what it involved. In is very brief time with the Rangers he had been supervised or actually taken care of, and he really had nothing to guess at. His work with the Rangers was part of His work, his destiny, and he had been a willing initiator.

He sat nearly motionless for over an hour watching Katie inexhaustibly run circles around the baying hounds, busily gathering stones and sticks and transporting them to a central site in some grand building scheme.

Michael turned his attention to a scraping sound that preceded Rose's rear as she backed out the door, dragging a chair for herself. Michael stood, thinking that he should help the slight woman with her chair, but he had no opportunity as her body blocked his way and she was quickly done and sitting while Michael was still considering how to be of service.

"It is too hot to be inside, you have the right idea staying out here, you have." Her face was flushed and strands of yellow hair clung to her damp forehead. She had a bowl with pea pods and, as she sat, she stripped the peas out.

"Red still sleeping?" he asked, even though he knew. He just wanted to say something, to not appear as stiff as he felt.

"Yes, yes, no one likes the rest like me husband. A lazier man than me husband you will not meet."

Michael had noticed his friend's liking for reclining but had not made a judgment about it. He tried to accept everything Red did and was, that way he remained free to like him.

Rose's nearness made Michael extremely self-conscious. He sat with both feet flat and his knees bent at right angles. His back straight as a pole. He did not even move to brush away a fly buzzing noisily near his face.

As Michael pretended to be watching Katie, Rose examined Michael, not surreptitiously but openly and with curiosity.

"You're a big fella, you are," she observed. "not as big as Red but you're near as tall as him and strong. I like big fellows. They make me feel safe." She settled her narrow shoulders deeper into the chair. "Me dad was a small man."

"He died on the boat," Michael stated bluntly. "Red told me," he added after a moment.

"That's so. John was me rescuer. Would have gone hard for me if he hadn't taken a fancy to me. I'd be some rich woman's maid in Boston or New York, or worse, instead of out here, owning property, with a family of me own." She shook her head in wonder. "You should have seen him, took care of a weepy little girl and got himself out of indenture and into a home in Texas. Just as though he had it all planned."

"Red told me how he tricked them." Michael smiled, feeling in on the joke.

"Oh, they didn't believe him for a moment, Michael. The big bully threatened to beat the hell out of them and they took his meaning. Him pretending to be me dad; I told him it wouldn't work."

"He said he pretended to be someone else." Michael was not disappointed, he did not care if Red told the truth. He was only a little confused.

"That's just because he doesn't like to admit he's old enough to be me father." She patted Michael on his leg, causing him to tense his muscles, partly in shock and partly from pleasure, though the gesture itself seemed innocent enough. "You're close to my age, I would be guessing." Her hand seemed to perhaps linger a moment too long.

"You must be happy Red's home for good." Michael was wishing that Red would wake up and join them. He was uncomfortable to the point of physical pain.

"I'll believe that when I see it. It seems as though I hardly know him sometimes. He hasn't been home more than a month at a time since Katie was born." Furrows appeared in her forehead. "I don't know to be glad or angry when he comes home."

"You're just lonely, that's all." Michael had no trouble recognizing loneliness.

"That's all?" She smiled her eyes widening. "What could be worse?"

Michael closed his eyes and remembered his solitary life, estranged from his family, separated from the rest of humanity in self-enforced exile. Rather than reacting with resentment like Rose, he became colder and less alive. He'd never contemplated how his loneliness was eating him, wearing him down, but he identified with Rose's desperation and knew that in his own, less passionate way, he'd been miserable.

"It's easier being a man, I think." She looked at the heavy revolver sitting in its holster on Michael's left hip. "You can come and go as you please, can't you?"

"I suppose." Michael did not understand how that would be better. It certainly allowed him to avoid contact and that was easier for him. He always wanted to leave and always dreaded arriving. "Where would you go?" he asked her.

"Oh, with my husband, you know, or him with me." She smiled for that was a happy thought to her but at the same time her voice choked and thickened.

"Like I did."

"Yes. I should be jealous of you, shouldn't I?" she laughed, a sharp unmusical bleat. "Oh now, don't look so worried, Michael. Truth be told I'm happy to have another man about. Here I am usually a man short. Now I've got one to spare, don't I?" She patted his leg again.

Michael had been less lonely during his time with Red and the Rangers, but they had kept a respectful distance, not penetrating where they were not invited, nor willing to share in return. Red had talked nearly nonstop but he was really mostly talking out loud to himself. Michael did not know how he felt about communicating so intimately, and with a pretty young woman. It was a little like talking with Red, but better. And worse.

Michael's eyes drifted over and lingered on Rose's breasts.

Katie charged up the porch and stood on the steps. "Michael, will you come help me?" Dogs gathered and flopped in the shade of the verandah and panted noisily, flipping out big drops of saliva that stained the floorboards darker.

"Katie, perhaps Michael is tired and doesn't want to play now," her mother gently suggested.

"I'm not tired." Michael stood up quickly and stepped towards the little girl, who took his hand with both of hers and took him along faster than he could walk, forcing the two of them to lean away from each other, Michael backward and Katie forward, counterbalancing.

Dragging him to her worksite beside the creek, his heavy shoes scuffling with short steps, she put him to work carrying stones that were too heavy for her to lift. She directed and chattered and he obeyed and listened, serious and intense, not knowing that he was supposed to be playing, not knowing really what play was.

Fourteen

Mary knew where Sam was camped and in the hour before sunset when the heat was first waning from oppressive to just warm, she gathered the dumplings and chicken stew she had made and walked, in her quick stomping pace, out to the edge of town. Balancing a cast-iron lidded Dutch-oven in one hand and a sack of prunes and apples in the other, she forded the creek, soaking her heavy shoes. The shoes were hand-me-downs from her little brother Ocie; from a time when he had actually been as little as she was.

Sam had made his home less than half a mile out of town along the same creek she bathed in and, although she could not see him as she approached, she could see his horse standing tied to a tree.

She added extra clamor to her already noisy stride as she came close, to announce her coming. Only the horse seemed to take notice of her however, and she stood looking around. She called out, "Hey, you here? I brought some food."

Sam appeared before she finished speaking, making her loud tone unnecessary and humorous. She broke off with a laugh and said, "Hey. I brought you some supper." She lifted the stew pot a little, showing him.

"Well now, that is a fine thing. I believe ye have made yourself a friend." He smiled at her and it was infectious enough to make her smile back, although she kept her teeth hidden.

"It's a rooster chicken with dumplings," she explained, setting the pot down next to a cold firepit, the cast iron ringing against the stones that circled the shallow ash filled pit.

"I could have guessed." He nodded. "There is nothing wrong with my sense of smell." Sam nearly danced as he moved to Mary and, setting down his rifle, he pulled a blue and white blanket from the neat stack of his goods and spread it on the ground. "If you want to set there, I'll make us a fire."

"The stew is still hot," she touched the side of the metal.

"It's me that will be needing the fire. I chill easily," he explained, "And the light will be pleasant after the sun finishes its work."

Mary slipped her feet from the loose shoes and stretched her legs while Sam took wood from a pile and artfully arranged it in the pit. When it was burning fully, he sat down right next to Mary but without touching her.

Mary brought out two spoons from her pocket. "You hungry now? Cuz we can eat if you want."

"Young woman, I am close to starved," he assured her.

"I didn't bring no plates, we'll have to share."

Sam had more than one tin plate with him but he said, "Oh, that's fine."

She placed the pot between them, sliding over to make room, and set the lid upside down on the blanket. They ate, the quiet broken only by Sam's generous praise of her cooking and thoughtfulness. Mary enjoyed the compliments and marveled at the gusto with which he ate. No one in her family had ever shown a big appetite. They preferred to drink their meals and made only token overtures towards actual sustenance. Mary herself was thin to the point of gauntness and she only nibbled while Sam gobbled unabashedly.

"That was a most welcome surprise," he said as he picked the pot up and scraped the bottom with his spoon.

"Well, you said you like surprises."

"I do, thank you. What is in your sack?"

"I have prunes and apples. You want some?" She untied the knot and handed him a handful of prunes while taking an apple for herself.

Mary looked around herself in the dimming light and then asked, "Y'all got a knife I can cut this with?" Biting into an apple was an awkward gnawing procedure for her.

Sam drew the big Bowie knife from its sheath at his hip but instead of handing it to her he casually took the apple and cut off a dainty slice.

The apple was small and green and dry but Mary did not taste it. The next slice Sam handed to her she did not touch with her hands but took with her lips, letting him feed her. She was beginning to feel flush again.

"What prompted in you the idea of bringing me supper?" he asked, as he carefully slipped a thin piece between her lips.

"I don't know." She lowered her eyes "I just felt like it, I suppose." She moved closer to Sam, her leg and shoulder against his.

She looked down and then around, nervously avoiding eye contact and feeling a little hesitant, even bashful. She did not understand her caution. She'd always been straightforward and even bawdy with men. Sex did not embarrass her.

Beneath her thin garments and on her bare arms, her skin was tingling and goosefleshed where it touched against Sam. Her stomach was quick and queasy and she felt a knot twisting in the middle just below her breastbone. She felt that she could not form coherent thoughts or manifest those thoughts into articulate speech. Her head buzzed. She felt weak.

"Sam"

"Yaw?"

"Nothing." She'd not meant to speak out loud.

"Stars are coming out," he said as the last of the sun's light faded and stars that eluded direct inspection in the soft afterglow we're beginning to appear. Sam patiently waited for more to emerge and accept attention. He'd taken a greater interest in the night sky since traveling south; since he spent a good portion of the night awake. The mountain's sky was most often overcast and too cold to allow much more than huddling by a fire. But the southern plains with their vast flat expanses, warm evenings, and huge heavenly vault made stargazing an inevitability.

"I've come to notice the stars since coming south," he

told her. "I like their orderliness."

"What do you mean?" His deep tones were soothing.

"Well, the constellations, and the way certain ones come out first. They're reliable. Sailors, I have been told, can find their way by them as good as by a compass."

Mary raised her eyes, inspected the sky. "I can't see what you mean. It looks to me like someone threw a handful of rock salt or like when you smash a bottle how the bits of glass scatter all over."

"Look there." He pointed and Mary sighted along his arm, resting her cheek on his elbow. "See how they look like a dipper."

"Course. Everybody knows that one."

"That's their habit. They always come together like that and you can always find them in the same place if you look at the right time. They're predictable, that's how you can come to understand them."

"What do you want to understand them for?"

"Ye must understand things, or else you'll never know how best to use them."

"How do you expect to use the stars?"

"To find my way maybe. I suppose I really don't know. Not yet anyways."

"I don't think you can understand anything," Mary stated. "It all just seems so wild. Everything changes so fast. I feel one thing like I'm sure of it one day and then the very next day it seems upside down. It's all a mess, I tell you what."

Sam was quiet, absorbing what she had said, putting it with every other thing he knew about her. It was the most she'd ever spoken to him at any one time and he thought it might be important if he wanted to understand her.

"Perhaps then, it's a little of both. Perhaps ye need some wildness and some sameness to make sense of it, I don't know. I know that when you're cold, ye want to be hot and when you're hot, ye want to be cold. Things seem to need their opposites, don't they?" he looked right at her and reached across to gently lift her chin. Her eyes met his and did not shy away but surrendered.

"Yes, they do," she whispered.

Mary's face drifted closer to Sam's but stopped before contact was made. Her hesitation was not lost on Sam, who patiently waited, keeping the proximity.

Whores did not kiss. Kissing was intimate. It cannot be faked or misconstrued. No one kissed unless they meant it.

She was close enough to smell Sam's beard, it smelled rich and masculine. She inhaled him, his breath, streaming out of his nostrils, was inebriating; her head swam. She was aware that he was greedily absorbing her exhalations as well, exchanging life. One breath, one body,

She knew his heart at that moment. She acknowledged her own heart. With relief. With no conditions. With abandon. She loved him back.

It was glorious.

She kissed him. Slowly. Tenderly.

Fifteen

While Michael was being bossed about by Katie, Rose went inside and burned another meal. The smell of scorched possum woke Red, who stomped outside and called Michael and Katie inside. He embraced his daughter and patted Michael warmly on the back as they passed through the doorway.

Rose instructed Katie to set their table and asked her husband to light the lamps, leaving Michael standing awkwardly unoccupied again. Seeing him standing in the doorway, Rose approached him smiling. Standing extremely close, so close Michael could smell her, she unfastened his gun belt.

"No firearms at the table," she told him as she buckled the

belt into a loop and hung it from a peg on the wall that also supported Red's twin pistols.

When Rose's fingers had touched his belt, they'd pressed lightly into his belly, Michael had reacted with paralyzed shock. His breath did not move either in or out and he did not blink. He did not hear a word she said as he stared at her moving lips, and it was not until a minute after the gun was hung up that he understood what she had said and done. He'd been sweating when he entered the house from his play with Katie but the sweat turned cold and his legs weakened and shook. He wanted her to touch him again.

Red's loud voice filled the room as they ate their meal, scaring Kerry, whose eyes filled with tears and had to be comforted by her mother on whose lap she sat. Katie chatted about the fort she and her brother had built and Rose giggled as Red teased his daughters jovially. Michael remained silent, neither talking nor laughing but often stealing glances at Rose, his skin coloring at each peek.

After the meal, Red smoked his pipe and drank his whiskey, offering some of each to Michael. When he declined both with a shake of his hea, Red offered some to Katie as well, who accepted but her nose would not let her, the fumes making her face crinkle and her blue eyes water.

Rose came into the room having left to place a limp sleeping Kerry in her small bed in the other room. She scolded her husband, calling him by his full and correct name, and told Katie that it was time for her bed.

Without protest, Katie kissed her father, and then a surprised Michael, good night and led her mother away by the hand. Rose reappeared only after a quarter of an hour of murmured dialogue.

Red told Michael that he could sleep in the kitchen but Michael said he wished to sleep on the porch, not at all an unusual thing for country people in the summertime. Rose spread quilted blankets for a mattress and a pillow stuffed with chicken feathers and fussed about a great deal, on her hands and knees, trying to make Michael a cozy nest. Red toasted goodnight to Michael from inside the house and called for his wife to hurry herself to bed.

"Smells like it might rain," Rose remarked as she paused at the doorway, turning to face Michael. "Still, I suppose you'll stay quite dry all the same."

Michael only nodded in response.

"Well goodnight then, Michael," she said with a small shy smile and turned to go inside; Michael's mumbled good night following after her. The light drifted from the kitchen and dimly reappeared in the window of the bedroom, casting a reflected glow on Michael as he lay down fully clothed on his bedding.

The house was built in a straight line. The large kitchen in the middle and two smaller rooms extended out to each side. Red's bedroom was the room to the left if facing the house, Katie and her sister sharing the room to the right. The covered wooden porch ran only the length of the middle room, flower gardens occupying the space in front of the other two wings. There were no windows in the kitchen, just the door, but the side rooms had large shuttered windows looking out onto the flower beds. Shadows of Red and Rose flickered behind the thin curtains.

Michael rested quietly on his back and could not help but listen to Rose's muffled giggles and Red's rolling voice from behind the walls; inarticulate but obvious in their meaning.

The sounds continued but softer then the light went out, putting Michael in near total darkness. Several minutes passed and the voices fell silent, Michaels ears reaching out for them despite himself.

Rhythmic squeaking and bumping noises began. The bouncing, rocking sounds occasionally punctuated by low deep moans and sharp high exclamations.

Sixteen

Miraculously, Price was feeling better. He no longer ran a fever and the throbbing lancing pains had diminished to a bearable level. He was very tired and extremely weak. Staying mounted on his walking horse's back required almost more strength than he had left, but he managed it for the entire day.

They had not made great progress. Price's condition slowed them to a crawl. Frustrated but accepting, Beasley called a halt just at sunset.

He was not concerned with the lack of progress. Beasley had had a very sensitive feeling that nagged at the back of his mind for the final several hours on the trail. He did not like encountering that lone Comanche, even at a distance. If he had learned only one thing in his years trading with them, it was that the Comanche were always dangerous and usually unpredictable. Seeing one did not mean that there was only one, and he and his men might be greatly outnumbered. He also reasoned that if he had been a friendly Comanche, one that they knew, he would have come forward and greeted them, but he had not. And he could not shake the feeling that they were being followed.

Trusting his instincts and obeying his fear, Beasley set his men, except for his wounded brother who was already fast asleep, on watches. Beasley took the first shift, wanting to be alone with his unease. Fear made him edgy and anxious. At such times people irritated him more than usual and he was quickly reaching his threshold. He also did not relish the idea of keeping lookout in the dead of night.

As he watched, he paced, keeping a sharp eye out and starting at every noise and rustle, real or imagined. He sipped at his jug, careful not to pull on it too deeply. He needed to remain sober enough but he wanted to hide in drunkenness and soon, despite his best intentions, the balance tipped away from sobriety. By the time he came into the light of the overly large campfire, barking at another to take his turn at guard duty, he was staggering.

He spread a blanket next to his brother and stretched out on his back. It took several more drinks, this time guzzling. After only a short time of watching the stars spinning over him, he drifted off and was soon snoring loudly.

One of the two men, for the moment not on watch, gingerly crawled over to where Beasley lay and lifted the heavy sloshing jug from his slack fingers. Grinning, he crawled back and sat down next to his fellow, they began passing it back and forth.

An hour later both were passed out. The procurer of Beasley's jug was asleep sitting up, propped on his saddle, legs crossed in front of him. The jug, resting on his knee, was steadied by one inert hand. The other man was curled up on his side. Not bothering with a blanket, he slept in the dirt.

The moon, approaching its new phase, was barely a sliver and the stars shown extra brightly and numerous for the lack of competition. The man on watch could gage time by the progress of the moon and know when to wake his replacement, but the thin crescent cast little light and, although he remained awake, having a healthy fear of Comanches, the darkness was nearly total and he doubted he would be able to see anyone coming.

Sweating, he paced outside the perimeter of the campfire's glow and avoided looking towards the fire to keep his eyes adjusted to the dark. He kept thinking he saw a movement but always, on closer inspection, it turned out to be nothing.

Alone in the darkness, his nerves fraying, his vision limited, and his hearing diminished from overexposure to gunfire, he felt like a sitting duck. He carried his revolver cocked, his finger on the trigger, and walked a circuit crouched over in a defensive hunch.

He looked up to check the advancement of the moon but was momentarily unable to find it. Fast-moving thick clouds were rolling quickly across the sky, blocking out the stars and screening all of the moon save for a hint of glowing yellow light. As he searched the vault above him, a whiff of warm air tickled the stubbly hair on his face, breaking the close stifling stillness like freshwater stirred into stagnant.

The hairs on his arms and the back of his neck stood up and he felt a tingling sensation rush up his spine. Short moments later the quiet was split and shattered by a blinding flash of lightning so close to him that the roll of thunder was instantaneous and overwhelming.

The brief flash illuminated the looming figure of the Comanche they had encountered earlier that day as he moved swiftly forward like an angry ghost, not more than ten feet behind the man whose job it was to watch for him.

Seventeen

The kissing became cuddling. The cuddling became fondling. And the fondling became urgent. Mary had never felt this way before. She'd had sex with dozens of men but had never once felt what it was to be aroused.

Her actions had little to do with Sam's love-making. He was slow and patient, kind and gentle, strong and passionate, all good things to Mary, but the difference was in her. She wanted Sam. She wanted to embrace him, to love him.

They removed each other's clothes. They caressed and explored. She stroked and kissed his many scars. She touched his feet and ran her fingers unhesitatingly around the bumps where his toes used to be. He squeezed her soft places and traced the indentations and valleys between her bones. He kissed where her flesh rose and delved curiously into the crevices.

Mary's breath was deep but inadequate. Her skin was flushed and hot to the touch, all pinks, and reds, and milky whites. Her hair was everywhere, in his hands, in front of her eyes, in their mouths when they kissed. She pressed and rose against him, unable to get close enough, touching constantly and completely, but not satisfyingly. She wanted more of him. She wanted all of him. She could not think, could not form words. Her eyes were wide open, deep black pools that obliterated her dark brown irises, and she saw only impressions, colors and shadows that blended and evolved but never coalesced into recognition. She felt insubstantial but so heavy that movement was an effort. And all the while she did not feel like herself.

Sam drank Mary in like a rare and mysterious potion. His life up until that point was mostly solitary. His lovers he could count on one hand with fingers to spare, but he was not inexperienced with women. The few lovers he had known had been the object of his intense scrutiny. He may have only played on a few choice violins but he fiddled like a virtuoso. He took time, enjoying every new place, and marking her reactions and responses. She was resilient and supple in his arms, tiny and fragile-seeming, almost childlike. She tasted of salt and honey and her odors were sharp and stirring. He wanted to envelop her and to crawl inside her. He wanted to stop and draw back to contemplate her beauty, her warmth, even her wretchedness. To behold her, to worship her as a shrine. He marveled at her innocence, her purity, her guilt, and earthiness. She was awash with life; to him, at that moment she was life. He could forgive her any sin because she was natural and morals did not apply.

Thunder and lightning burst and crackled around them but they accepted it without pause or commenting vocally or internally. It was noticed only as they noticed the ground supporting them, Mary feeling in complete rapport with the tempest.

"Oh shit," she said as he penetrated her. "Oh," she thought.

Eighteen

He drifted into The Pruitt's camp silent as a ghost. Their fire had died somewhat but still gave enough light to illuminate the faces of the snoring men, who had not been much disturbed by the weather. The lightning and thunder had moved farther away and now was only rolling like a timpani drum rather than booming like a cannon.

He stood directly in front of the drunken figure that was asleep in a sitting position. He bent over, reached out, and gently removed the man's wide Sombrero hat and carefully set it on the ground beside the man's knee.

He stretched up to his full height and held the hammer above his head like a lightning rod. He closed his eyes and breathed in deeply the warm heavy air. The sheen of sweat on his body reflected the flickering glow of the fire. His face was smeared black and streaked with red. He held himself perfectly still.

He waited to feel the moment but to do so he needed to concentrate, to gather himself together. His breathing brought in the fragmented bits of his spirit, weaving them together until he felt tangible. The process was slow and required several minutes of total absorption. He nearly gave up, feeling himself fraying and splintering faster than he could reassemble. But his will was strong and still centered in his task, in his vision, and he persevered.

Just like the instantaneous sparking and striking of the lightning, he whipped the hammer down in a fluid arc, almost too fast to be seen even as a blur. He struck his mark dead on without even really opening his eyes, the iron head striking the sleeper's temple with a crack like close thunder.

The skull broke and bled profusely but the sleeper did not awake, and never would. He tumbled over on his side, turning and falling toward the fire. The jug of corn whiskey he had been unconsciously supporting on his knee fell on, and then rolled off, the top of his sombrero. It continued rolling the two feet down-slope to the fire and turned when it struck the ends of the wood to present its open mouth and gurgle forth its contents.

After a pause, the spirits fueled an explosive flare, shooting blue flames as tall as a man into the damp air and illuminating the camp for several seconds, as brightly as if it were daylight.

The sudden noise and commotion roused Price from his exhausted stuporous sleep. He opened his eyes and, short of breath, screamed weakly but persistently at what greeted him: white teeth flashing in a blackened face behind a veil of bluish flame. Bright eyes lanced through the shimmering wall and held his, stifling his screaming and freezing him in place.

The flare-up died, shrinking down and fading away as if it had never existed, only a faint twinkling blue glow remaining, playing over the red and orange fire with dancing accents. Blinded by the sudden darkness, Price lost sight of the warrior and, when his eyes adjusted moments later the apparition had disappeared.

The incident was so fleeting and so confusing to Price he wondered if he had dreamed it, or seen a ghost. He pushed himself up and propped himself on one arm. Able to see over the little fire, he caught sight of the dead man who lay on his side. The eyes, open and staring, though rolled partly up into his head, were looking his way.

Price shuddered. Dead men always seemed to be staring at him. He realized he alone was up and moving and, afraid he might be the only one left alive, he began screaming again, this time loud enough to wake the dead.

Nineteen

For the first time in weeks, Michael dreamed. The thunderstorm had moved on. Rain had fallen only briefly as it passed but it left a clean smell and an extra layer of thick humidity. The soothing sound of rainfall and the blanketing warmth made him drowsy, though he had not been tired.

He dreamed of a big table in a small room where he was eating a meal with his father and mother. They laughed and they screamed, making jokes at each other's expense and leaning close to whisper to each other all the many things that could not be said aloud.

His mother wore an encircling crown of red roses and kept placing and smoothing a napkin on his lap. His father's hair and beard flamed and sparkled bright red and he constantly reminded Michael to remember the tenth commandment. His mother whispered to him, red lips brushing against this ear, her hand in his lap. "Honor thy father and thy mother."

"Michael!" his father commanded. "Switch with me."

Michael stood up, but his mother reached out to stop him. She told him to sit down and then replaced the napkin, now filthy and ragged from falling to the floor. Her hand emerged from his lap holding the large Walker revolver and she said, "I'll hold this."

"My father gave it to me," Michael protested meekly.

"No firearms at my table," she sternly told him, placing the pistol in her own lap and out of view.

"Switch with me, Michael, me boy," his father said again, this time in friendly tones.

His father made no move to change places and Michael's mother began crying. She extended her arm to him, holding out a fragile glass cup.

"Fill it," she screamed in a thick Irish brogue.

Tears clouding his eyes, Michael scanned the huge table and lifted a pitcher from its center. Carefully, his hand shaking, and still crying, he poured a thin stream of soft white milk into his mother's cup. As he was pouring, he became aware of a sour odor wafting up from the milk and, suddenly made nauseous by the stench, he turned his face away. The cup ran over, spilling the viscous milk onto the floor.

His father shouted at him, pointing at the spilled milk, saying, "Remember the tenth commandment!"

His mother drank deeply of the obviously spoiled milk, rivulets running to either side of her chin as she noisily slurped. When she finished, she showed the empty cup to Michael and said, "There's none for you now."

The roses in her crown wilted and the thorns glistened with big drops of bright red blood that was not hers, for her skin was clear and unscratched. She offered it to him.

"Red blood," she said. "Blood is red."

"Remember the tenth commandment," father warned him again, his voice weak with age.

"Honor thy father and thy mother," his mother explained, nodding her head, her mouth rounded open.

"That is not the 10th," Michael whispered to himself, puzzled. "that is the fifth."

"Five will get you ten, I'd wager," his father laughed.

Twenty

When Price finally succeeded in waking his brother, it took another twenty minutes to make him understand and then believe what he was telling him. Beasley examined the bludgeoned corpse lying by the fire, and then spent a few long tense minutes staring into the darkness.

"The horses are still here, that's good," he finally said.

"We going to get the hell out of here, Beasley? I'm fit to travel, I tell you what."

Price was more scared than fit but his fear gave him energy and he wanted to be home safe and to get very drunk.

"We are not going out there while it's still dark. Could be more than one of them waiting for us."

"There ain't but the one, I tell you. If there was more, they would have killed us by now," Price reasoned correctly.

"Just shut the hell up. We'll wait till first light." Beasley had always been a little afraid of the dark. "We need to build up that fire, we got any wood left?"

"That was all we got." He sounded downcast. "Maybe we should wake Chico, make him go get some more." He referred to their only living companion, who snored loudly, his legs outstretched, next to the dead man. Chico had stirred and woken when Price started screaming but had passed out again when he had stopped.

"No, he'd just get himself killed. We might need him." Beasley was pacing quickly in a narrow oval.

"He don't look like he'd be much good to us anyhow. He's drunk as a bastard." He could smell the liquor from where he sat, even over his own saturated odor.

"Son of a bitch has been at my corn whiskey. Nearly drank off the whole jug." Beasley weakly kicked the sleeping man in passing. He raised his hand up and held his head. "My head is pounding something awful." He glanced at the dead man's wound and shuddered.

He stopped his agitated pacing and dropped down to sit on his blanket next to his brother. He drew his revolver and cocked it and Price followed his example. After a few minutes rain began to fall and, although it did not last a long time, the heavy drops finished off the fire's feeble glow, leaving them in nearly total darkness.

The night slowly and ponderously withdrew, grudgingly giving up its reign until it all at once was defeated by a hot and quick sun. Price and Beasley exhausted by their intense vigil were left jittery and pale.

Beasley woke the drunken Chico by hitting him repeatedly with his hat. Before the man was completely awake, Beasley had him off in search of their missing comrade. He returned without good news.

"Go saddle the horses and get ready to get away from here," he snarled his words, his pistol still in his hand.

"What if he follows us, Beasley?" He could not get the image of the black faced, bright-eyed apparition from his mind.

"We can be home 'fore dark if we ride hard." Beasley holstered his pistol and rearranged his gun belt, feeling more confident and hopeful now that the sun had risen.

"Are we going to keep after Joey and O's killers?" He was relieved to be going home but a little curious as well.

"Don't see how," Beasley snapped at his brother. "The rain will have washed out their trail and our tracker is lying there with his fucking head all smashed in."

"That's good! I don't want to spend another night on the trail with that fella lurking around, I tell you what."

"Get your ass mounted and let's get moving," Beasley ordered as soon as the horses were saddled.

Price slowly and gingerly mounted and lay over the neck of his horse. As they kicked their horses into a jolting trot, the dust swelling up and around them in spirals and whorls, he said "Mary ain't going to be happy."

"Mary ain't ever happy."

Twenty-One

Mary woke before the dawn. They lay naked and exposed to the stars on top of a buffalo robe, their flesh moist where they touched one another. She stretched her naked body in the almost cool air, disentangling herself only partly from Sam's intertwined limbs. She moved slowly and carefully, trying not to wake him, wanting him to continue in this contented sleep, wanting to give herself a moment alone.

She felt renewed and relaxed, and a smile kept returning to her lips no matter how often she pushed it away. She was also angry with Sam and afraid of him, but only smaller and more distant parts of her submitted to those emotions. Her past railed and warned but her present remained unconvinced.

The stars were fading in the blue glow of false dawn, the sky clearing of storm clouds, no rain having actually fallen on them for all the clamor. She held onto Sam's sinewy arm and burrowed deeper into his embrace, comforted and reassured by his weight and musk where normally she might have felt confined and put upon.

She knew it had been her decision to seduce Sam but at the same time she understood that he had been seducing her. She did not mind his actively pursuing her, it meant that their attractions were mutual, and she felt more bonded to him knowing that his desire was as strong and irresistible as hers had been.

She wondered what would happen next. She made no plans, had no fantasy for the future, she always let the present unfold from one development into the next without anticipation. The habit had been born of the expectation that she had no real future to count on. She always fled from her past and dreaded her future.

She thought that Sam was someone who could effectively plan and think ahead and she was hoping, but not doubting, that his plans included her, and them, and they could manage to be together.

It was not distrust or lack of faith in his character. She did not trust either Sam or herself, much less that there would be a place for her and them in the future, or that there even would be a future. She was only ever sure of two things: how she felt, and that life is mostly random. She assumed some people, like Sam, could successfully predict and adapt to what was to come. But it was beyond her how to accomplish this, as her best attempts in the past to control an outcome had only led to bad becoming worse. She might concede that maybe other people's futures had some pretense of order, but not hers.

The bindings of her past were looser now. Her anger at her brother's death and her connection to Sam had done a great deal towards freeing her from the history that impelled her misery. She knew that the strength to be brave flowed from that anger, but she did not yet fully comprehend how her relationship to Sam enabled her to release so much of the past. But she did know that the present moment was no longer an agony.

She also knew without doubt that she would never go back to whoring. She would kill herself first. She knew that the whoring and the drinking had been her way of hurting herself, a slow suicide. But a part of her remained hungry for life and for love and had not allowed her to end her days quickly, although she had many times held the little pistol and contemplated. Now she felt that to move backward would be unbearable and she would surrender completely rather than accept something less.

She would also not hesitate to kill anyone who tried to impede her. It's not just her own life that she held cheaply but all life. The only thing she thought more worthless than herself was everybody else. Sam's presence only scratched the surface of her sense of self, only released the smallest fragment of hope. He was like a cork lifesaver thrown to a drowning woman, cruelly cast overboard, crying out as the ship sailed swiftly away. And even though the ocean was vast and wide, she would cling to Sam with all her might and be ever grateful even as the waters enveloped them.

She drifted back into sleep and dreamed of a snake. Dreamed that she lay naked and safe, wrapped in its coils.

Twenty-Two

Red stomped onto the porch where Michael sat, his boots rattling the floorboards. All four of his dogs, roused from a lazy pile, jumped up on him, tails wagging busily, and he greeted each by name, with much rough petting and patting. He grinned and leaned against the door frame. “A good morning to you, Michael, me boy.”

Michael nodded without looking up. He'd been awake for an hour and had listened to a repetition of the previous night's romantic noises. He sat fully dressed in the high-back chair with his dark hat pulled low over his forehead.

Rose stepped out to stand next to her husband. Red put a bear-like arm around her shoulders and kissed the top of her head, at the line where her blond hair was neatly parted. “Did you sleep well out here, Michael?” she asked.

Michael nodded yes and stared for a moment at the woman. She almost glowed. Her smile was radiant and her disposition sunny. Her cheeks were flushed and whisker burned, her body relaxed and sensual as it melted into Red's. She seemed heavy and dreamy. Michael paled and turned away.

He opened his mouth, ready to announce that he was leaving but was interrupted before he could begin by Rose. “I'll be making the coffee and the breakfast now. I'm starved, I am.” She kissed Red with a loud smack then went inside, a wide smile covering her cheerful face.

Katie blew past, bearing a milking bucket and yelling, “Morning, Dad, morning, brother.” They both waved but did not call out as she left them no time. They dogs gave chase.

Kerry walked carefully through the door, held on to Red's pants and peaked at Michael from around her father's legs. “Say good morning to Michael, dear,” her father gently urged her.

"Morning." Her voice was just barely above a whisper and her eyes were wide and curious.

"Good morning," Michael politely replied. She released her father and quickly stepped over to Michael and resting her hands on his thighs, pushed herself up onto his lap. She looked back at Red and grinned at her accomplishment while Michael went rigid with surprise. Red chuckled at his child's behavior, and Michael's discomfort, and turned and went inside to get his coffee.

Left alone with the little girl, Michael tried to remove her from his lap but she resisted and squealed with displeasure as he tried to pick her up or push her off. She held tightly to his clothing and squirmed so effectively he could not maintain a grip. "Go on, get down now," he ordered.

"No." She whined the word so loudly that Michael desisted from trying to remove her, afraid that Red would think he was hurting her. Michael blew out his own breath with frustration and tried unsuccessfully to relax and ignore her. Kerry turned her back on him and leaned against his stomach, playing with their fingers by bending them back one at a time, satisfied with her victory but not gloating.

This was the second time in two days he had been forced to hold a child. It was the only two times he had ever held a child. It was the only times he had ever held anyone. At the moment he did not like it. Holding Katie the day before had been easier. He had known that he was giving her a ride on his horse and that any contact was incidental. Kerry, though, was on his lap for reasons only she understood and Michael, feeling disconcerted from having had to listen to Red and Rose's noises, was extra prickly and desperately feeling in need of some time to himself.

He sweated and wriggled under the child interminably when Rose emerged. He hoped she would take her from him but it was her other daughter that she was looking for.

"Katie," She called, and then more softly to herself she said, "Now where did that girl get to?"

"I believe she went to milk the cow," Michael offered, wanting to be helpful also wanting to be noticed in his predicament.

Rose only smiled at him when she looked his way and said, "You've a way with children you have."

Michael almost groaned.

"Me girls love having you here," Rose's eyes played slowly over Michael and settled on his face. She rested one hand over her belly and rubbed it slowly back and forth. I like you being here as well, you know."

"I'll be leaving soon," he blurted out his voice tight and strained.

Rose, her eyes on him but focused far away, did not respond to his statement. It was as if she had not heard it. Her non-reaction was so complete that Michael wondered if he had actually spoken aloud.

It was not unusual for people to ignore or not hear what Michael said. He spoke quietly and so seldom that people learned not to expect expression from him and so did not pay him much direct attention. As a result sometimes, Michael felt totally invisible. He'd placed so many walls and barriers around himself that often people were not able to see him. In his time with Red, the older man had often spoken over him or just forgotten his presence. And Michael had let him. Just as he always had. Just as he did now with Rose.

His head was beginning to ache. It was another warm morning, no cooler for the sparse rain that had fallen in the night. Michael was sweating so much he seemed to be melting, though it was no hotter than it had been the day before. He trembled and felt weak. His stomach churned.

The child on his lap, the presence of Rose, the closeness of the family, the heat, his dream, Michael felt he was beginning to fall apart. It was too much and too different. And when he looked at Rose, he looked too long and too longingly. When she looked at him, he had to repress an urge to strike her. He was reaching past his limits every moment he stayed, he did not know how much longer he could persist.

Rose took a step towards Michael and his entire body clenched, all the color draining from his face. Without noticing Michael or seeing his distress, she simply picked up her child and walked into the house, saying something about the food being nearly ready that Michael did not really register until she had left.

As soon as he was alone, Michael lurched to his feet, panting and almost on the verge of fainting. He clenched his fists and made small dancing steps in place. He opened his hands and placed his palms over his eyes, rocking back and forth. He stumbled off the porch, his knees almost giving out from the unexpected step down. The sudden blaze of unshaded morning sun struck his head like a mallet and he became intensely light-headed.

He felt disassociated from his body, airy and insubstantial. As his body staggered on rubbery legs, his mind became focused on the bright white illumination that filled his skull, and a sense of peace slowly began to settle over him like a cool dazzling mist.

He perceived two visions simultaneously, as if each individual eye captured its own distinct image. He saw his surroundings, colorless and shifting, tossing and spinning like a view from shipboard. And he beheld, still and tranquil, the soft loving rapturous white and gold light that enveloped and held him.

Gradually, the two perspectives began to overlap and although they were not able to merge, they settled, unantagonistically, one behind the other and together they faded slowly into indistinguishableness.

His detachment restored, Michael congealed his liquid seeming legs, straightened his stooping torso and wiped the cold drenching sweat from his face with one shaking hand, breathing deeply, suckling the last remnants of divine grace. "Thou restoreth my soul," he muttered.

"I what?" Katie stood before him, a quizzical expression

on her little face. She was nearly doubled over with the weight of the bucket, her shape washed out and indistinct in the harshness of the background light.

"I didn't say anything." Michael's own face was puzzled.

She shrugged and continued past him. Michael turned to watch her. She laid the milk on the porch and then crawled up the steps, using her hands to support her. As she gained her feet, one of the dogs passing her side was nudged by another dog and bumped into her, knocking her off balance. She exclaimed with a sharp oops sound but caught her balance before falling, only stumbling one step. Her leg, however, brushed against the bucket and tipped it over. The milk flowed out of the bucket in one quick rush and spread out over the floorboards, trickling through the cracks between the planks.

"Uh-oh," she said slowly. She watched the milk drain away while the dogs quickly tried to lap up all they could. Red emerged holding a clay cup and surveyed the scene. "Well, there's a fine breakfast for you lot," he told the happy hounds.

"Katie, you clumsy girl, what happened here?" Rose stepped out, frowning at the mess.

"Scarlet tripped me," she explained, rubbing her shin bone where it had scraped against the bucket.

"To be sure," Rose nodded. "Are you not hurt?"

"I'm fine, Mum."

"Go on, eat some breakfast then. These beasties will clean this up I'm sure." She ran her hand over Katie's head as she passed by her and into the house.

Michael was awestruck.

He shuffled slowly up to the house as if magnetically drawn, his jaw hanging slackly.

"John Martin, these dogs of yours are wearing me thin." She playfully pushed her husband on the chest, not budging the big man an inch but making him grin.

"They're right rascals they are. They did this all deliberately, I'd wager."

Rose turned to Michael and explained as if seeking justice from a neutral third-party, "He's always bringing me home these strays and then leaving me to look after them."

"These are fine good dogs, they are," Red protested. "And Scarlett is the best tracker in Texas."

"For all the good that does me. You're just a weak hearted man when it comes to strays, you are." She looked at Michael, afraid he might take the reference personally but he was just standing there with his mouth open.

Michael had been sure that Katie was going to get a whipping but she had escaped without even a reprimand. He was shocked that a familial incident like this had ended in caring and humor rather than violence and shame. It seemed fair and correct as well, appropriately lighthearted and forgiving. There was anger and resentment spilling over from other times and places, but it was not being misdirected on to an innocent child.

His mind reeled at the implications. This was how it could be, how it should be, but had not been.

"I'll be leaving soon." This time he spoke clearly and even the dogs paused to regard him. Red regarded him closely.

"You should stay a while at least, Michael, we're happy to have you here with us." surprised at Michael's directness. Red squared his shoulders and faced Michael, looking him in the eye and stepping down to join him.

"I thank you, but there's somewhere I need to go."

"I'm sorry to hear that, son, I'm grateful to you for saving me life and hoped to be able to repay you." He stepped forward and put his arms around Michael and hugged him so hard that Michael's spine popped. "You will always be welcome in this house."

Michael accepted the hug with some hesitation and, although he very much wanted to return the embrace, his arms hung limply at his sides. He tried to raise his arms several times but always lowered them again. Finally, he just let them hang, and melted into Red's warmth.

Twenty-Three

Luke led his Rangers into town late in the morning and started asking questions. He examined the stable where the Pruitt's latest felony had taken place but could gather no intelligence as to the whereabouts of Beasley Pruitt and his three brothers. They did learn that Price Pruitt had come into town wounded but had left in the company of Beasley and three other men. No one knew where they were bound or even the direction they followed.

Luke wanted to question the brothers' sister, Mary, a prostitute with a reputation for violence that was impressive on its own, but she had not been seen much for a couple of days. He set two of his troop to watch her hovel of a home and with the rest of his men rode out of town at the canter. They had learned that the Pruitts maintained their family's ranch, complete with a rundown house, a short ride from town where they were known to corral horses and lay up.

The dilapidated one-room adobe was the sum total of the Pruitt family heritage. The boys and Mary had all been conceived and born there. When the father, who had outlived the mother, had died under questionable circumstances, the property had come to the eldest son. Beasley, like his father before him, had not wasted a minute in improvements to the property and the two decades of neglect were evident. The barren dusty ground on all sides of the broken-down dwelling was littered with dung and buzzing with flies. Tall brown dead grass surrounded the mouth of the well and the lone tree within a hundred yards of the house was a scorched and charred skeleton of an oak with the remains of a flatbed wagon leaning heavily against it, only one rusted wheel still standing.

In front of the house, and to the side of the well-worn path leading up to it, there was a corral of sticks and thorn bushes that contained over a dozen Indian ponies. The day was hot and the ponies were sweating and haggard, they're corral unshaded and without a water trough.

Three men were relaxing in the shade offered by one wall of the house. One sat on an upright stump of firewood, the two others were on the ground leaning against the wall.

The Rangers saw them before they were spotted and Luke acted quickly. Splitting his men into two groups, he ordered the charge, sending half the men around the back to cut off any retreat, the other half, with himself in the lead, headed straight in, guns drawn and calling for their surrender.

The three men leapt to their feet and ran. One dashed inside the house, but two headed directly away from Luke, drawing their pistols as they ran and snapping off several unaimed shots without taking the time to stop or turn.

The shots missed widely and Luke fired into the air and again shouted out for them to give themselves up. As the words left his mouth, a rifle shot from inside the house whizzed past his ear with a high-pitched whine and struck a Ranger behind him in the shoulder. The wounded man managed to remain in the saddle and keep riding but the attack inflamed the anger of the troop, who immediately opened fire in earnest.

The wall of the adobe was quickly peppered with a hail of bullets, chips and chunks of dry mud breaking away and scattering amid puffs of fine dust. When the Rangers neared the house, they jumped free of their mounts and recklessly charged inside. The first Ranger through the door was hit in the knee by a ball fired from the outlaw's revolver but before he collapsed, he fired his own pistol, and with better aim.

His shot struck his assailant in the throat and would have killed him had not the next several men through the door fired several rounds each into the falling bandit, ending his life before his limp body hit the dirt floor. Thick gray smoke from the pistol fire hung heavily in the air as the Rangers helped their fallen comrade outside and dragged the bullet-ridden carcass of the dead man into the light.

The other half of the split detachment had headed off the two outlaws who believed in discretion. They threw down their pistols and raised their hands, calling out for the Rangers not to shoot them. The men were quickly surrounded. Several Rangers dismounted and roughly kicked and pistol-whipped the two to the ground, where they tied their hands behind their backs with strips of rawhide. They were then jerked to their feet and lariats were thrown over their heads and cinched tightly around their chests. the Rangers half led, half dragged, their captives back to the adobe, where the rest of the troupe had assembled.

Most of the dismounted men were gathered around the two men who has sustained wounds. Luke asked them to be laid out in the shade of the wall where only a few short minutes earlier the bandits had taken their ease. The captives were brought up and kicked to their knees and left to bake in the sun. They kept their bleeding faces down but stole quick furtive glances at the Rangers and at each other.

Luke squatted next to the Ranger that been shot in the knee. The man's face twisted and his fingers clenched and opened spasmodically but he held his leg still while Luke used a scarf to tie a tourniquet around the thigh.

He hurried with the leg, wanting to get to the other wounded man. He knew that the leg wound he was treating was serious and that the man might lose his leg but the others man's wound gave him greater concern. The shoulder was bleeding profusely, soaking through the wadded cloth pressed tightly against it by a friend. The man, whose name was Andrew was obviously disoriented, his face was ashen and his eyes were rolled up into his head. His consciousness maintained only a flirting presence.

Luke lifted the bloody cloth, exposing a neat clean hole

from which blood grouted in rhythmic spurts with the man's accelerated heartbeat. The bullet had entered just beneath the collarbone and Luke checked for, but did not find, an exit wound, though he did feel that the scapula had been splintered. He could not tourniquet this artery, it was too deep and protected by skeleton and thick muscle. Other than keeping pressure on the entry, he knew of no way to quickly stop the bleeding and suspected that the situation was hopeless.

He calmly asked for and received more cloth that he held in place, feeling the pulse of life diminish with each beat. In less than two minutes, the dim spark in Andrew's eyes faded and his body fell limp, as if exhausted. In another short minute the man blew out a short harsh breath and did not breathe in again. Luke stood up, wiping the blood from his hands with one of the unused scarves.

"He's gone," he said simply and without inflection.

He returned to his work with the leg wound, loosening the tourniquet and washing and disinfecting the gash. "Go find me some straight sticks about a foot-and-a-half long," he requested of no one in particular. The bullet had bounced off the knee cap, shattering it and gouging a deep furrow in the thin skin. When Luke discovered the true nature of the wound he removed the tourniquet and bandaged the gash. When the sticks were brought to him, he quickly splinted the leg, causing the already agonized Ranger to suffer a great jolt of pain when he forcibly straightened the leg.

He had Rangers prop the man against the wall and give him some water to drink and some liquor to console him as he contemplated whether he would only limp or whether he would have the ghost of a leg and a crutch to remind him of his life as a lawman.

Men whispered and shouted, congratulating each other, and some looked meaningfully at the two prisoners. "Should we hang them now?" one of them, a short man without a beard and a healing welt from Michael's whip's lash to the side of his left eye, asked in a loud clear voice.

"Not yet, Matthew." Luke examined the captives for the first time. The men seemed to be Mexican, perhaps with some Indian blood. He wanted information from them and he knew what would scare men like these.

"Matt, signal the Apaches to come in. Maybe we give these sons of bitches to them."

At the word Apache both men started and looked at each other with worry. Being hung would come as no surprise for them. They had never expected to live to be old. But being tortured to death by Apaches was a nightmare they had dreaded their entire lives.

Matt rode his horse a short lope away from the house and stood up in the stirrups, firing his pistol over his head twice and waving his Red Scarf vigorously back and forth. Several minutes later the four scouts magically appeared, riding their ponies at a walk from the opposite direction.

Luke stood over the cowering bandits, his shadow falling over their faces and said, "I need to know some things. I need you boys to tell me some things. You sabe English?"

"Yes, we speak English," one of them answered but both of them avoided making eye contact.

"I'm looking for four men. Beasley, Price, Joseph, and Ocie Pruitt. I know you're in with them and I want you to tell me where they are and I want you to tell me right now."

"Joselito and Ocie are con Dios," said the man who had not as yet spoken.

"They're dead, you mean?" Luke asked skeptically and a glanced dramatically at the Apaches.

"Si, is true, I swear. I see it with my own eyes. They were shot, one week ago." The cringing man squinted up at Luke and spoke without hesitation.

"Where? How'd this happen? Who shot them?"

"West of here. Two days maybe. Two big Hombres. Pistoleros. One ride a white mule. The other a red horse. They killed them two boys bad. And one other, they shoot Price too but he live, I think. He go back with Beasley. They go get them." He hung his head as he finished speaking.

"A white mule?"

"Si."

"The other fella, got a red beard? Barbarossa?"

"Si. Ranger I think, like you." He nodded his head as he spoke, His companion nodding his agreement in harmony.

Luke turned slowly and walked away from the two men. He approached Matt, who had remained mounted, and, looking up at him, shaded his eyes with his hand as he tipped his head higher than the brim of his hat could screen.

"Seems Captain Red and that crazy Muleskinner come across these fellows and killed three of them. Least that's what these two piles of fresh shit seem to be saying."

Matt shook his head and whistled, touching the mark to the side of his eye. "The Captain's already done most of our job for us. Him and that fucking Muleskinner are a dangerous pair."

"They say that the others rode out after the Captain." Luke studied the ground. "No way of saying if they're telling the truth or not, though." He tugged at his hat brim.

Matt thought that bit of news over, first staring down and then scanning the horizon before saying, "I don't think your Captain would let the likes of these trash catch up to him."

"Don't seem likely, I admit, still...." Luke scuffed his boot toe in the hard gray dirt, working out in his mind the best course of action.

"Matt, take six men and the Apaches, head down to Red's ranch and see if he made it home all right. If he's there tell him what's happening and he'll tell you what he wants you to do from there. If he ain't got back yet, get the Indians to find him for you."

"Alright."

"We'll wait here for a couple of days, see if them bastards come in. We'll rendezvous at Red's no matter what, so if you have to go out looking for the Captain leave word with his wife which way you headed and I'll try and find you all. Send one of them scouts looking for us, that'll help."

"Alright, hope this turns out okay."

"You had best get started. Pick your men and take the extra mounts, y'all want to make good time."

Without a word, Matt kicked his horse into motion.

Luke stood where he was for time and then walked back to stand in front of the prisoners, most of the men gathering around him. "Dig a grave for Andrew," he said staring cooly at the two men but not addressing them. "And get a rope and hang these sons of bitches."

Twenty-Four

Mary was happy. She was in love with the mountain man and he made her happy. Both of those facts were disconcerting.

She strolled rather than stomped back to her little house late in the afternoon. She'd spent the day with Sam, talking, eating, and cooling herself in the creek while he made jokes and made her smile so widely and genuinely that she showed the gap between her teeth without self-consciousness. She had left him at his camp, kissing him reluctant goodbyes with deep lingering passion, to return to her house to check if her brothers had returned or left word for her.

She more than partly hoped that they were not back yet, she did not know how they would react to her new relationship and she was not eager to try to explain it to them. It probably would not interest them at all and that was the reaction she dreaded the most.

As she turned into the narrow lane that led to her home, she walked past two tall, well-armed men who sat in the shade of a covered porch, sipping liquor and smoking cigars, watching her with narrowed eyes as she passed by.

She returned their looks without shyness and wondered if she knew them. One of the men tipped his hat, smiled broadly, and greeted her politely. Her face, loosened by Sam's clever charm, returned his infectious smile, but she snapped it off when the man reacted visibly as he noticed her two missing teeth. She turned away quickly and with a hardness creeping into her gait, hurryied the last little bit to her doorway.

She swung the door open and glanced back down the lane and saw that the two men had risen and we're still watching her, talking to each other but in hushed tones. She paused with curiosity but she dismissed their interest as the usual type of attention she received from men and went inside, tying off the door and hoping that they would leave her alone.

She lit a candle to bolster the dim light, her eyes being adjusted to the afternoon's bright glare, and set about gathering together her possessions. She intended to live with Sam and she did not intend to stay in town. He'd said he wanted to travel further south and that he wanted her to come with him. That was all he had said, not giving a destination or a reason, but it was all that she really needed to hear and she had not thought to ask for more details.

She stuffed clothes and a few personal items all into the same burlap sack; surprisingly little was left after her manic house cleaning from a few days before. Her lack of meaningful material items first depressed and then, upon reflection, reassured her that leaving was the best thing she could do. Her life here amounted to very little and all she was really leaving were bad memories and bitter associations. She hefted the far from full or heavy sack and wished that she might leave those final few things behind as well but relented under practicality.

She sat down wearily on her mattress and rubbed her small hands through her thick tangled hair. Her life to this point scrolled through her mind in a blurry alcohol misted parade. Mary had always tried to avoid reflection, it brought her only anguish and resentment, never insight or change. But today it carried her towards regret.

She felt wasted and cast off, drained, as if she had been denied some benign indifference on the part of the world and that she had failed to rise above its harshness, merely surviving. She vowed that she would never be a silent partner to circumstances again, that the world would not be allowed to prey on her, that she would claim her due rather than simply, foolishly, biting back. She felt she was owed a life for the one she had missed. She accepted that she could collect that debt only from herself.

She laid back on her bed and closed her eyes, feeling comfortable and sleepy. She needed to pass by the stable and pick up Sam's extra horse, now her horse, on her way back to him and she did not relish the idea of appearing at the scene of Beasley's crime. She held no guilt for instigation of the murder but wanted to avoid, if possible, any confrontation with angry relations. Sam would have spared her the issue if he had known, but she had not cared to share that part of her past with him, or any other part. She decided to nap a while and collect the horse after dark. Also, she had slept so little the night before and the hot afternoon was acting as a irresistible soporific.

Whether her brothers returned or not, she was leaving in the morning with Sam. She could not leave a note for them, for she could not write and they could not read. She had to take a chance and leave word with a neighbor. She rarely spoke to the people whose homes bordered hers and they, though hardly paragons of virtue themselves, did not seek out her company. But she knew one or two by name and that was good enough if she could only figure out what she would say, other than goodbye.

She had virtually raised the four boys and was feeling cowardly and negligent for leaving but she also could not bear to remain and watch them die, one after the other: that was an obvious inevitably. She was also terribly afraid that the surviving two older boys would not return from the errand she had set them. She'd rather leave than face that.

Her life would never be her own unless she was free of her brothers as well as her past. Being a catalyst or witness to their deaths would mean a permanent bonding and unbreakable bondage to them and an end to her hope.

Twenty-Five

Michael exhaled many deep sighs of relief as he rode further and further from Red's happy home. He had left almost immediately after announcing his intentions. The perplexed family had, much to his embarrassment, each insisted on hugging and kissing him goodbye. Katie, crying and red-faced, had refused to let loose once her small but strong arms had encircled him, and her father had to gently pry her from the helpless and flustered Muleskinner.

Her Highness also seemed to share his relief at being alone and in motion again and, even in the sweltering heat of midday, she ate up the miles at an amazing rate, almost trotting in her enthusiasm. Michael gave the mule its head for he wanted to make the little town that Red had told him was on the way north before it became too late. He had left without taking any supplies and, in the suddenness of his flight, neither Red nor Rose had thought to equip him. He hoped to be able to purchase what he needed and move on without having to wait until morning, but even at Her Highness's fast pace it did not seem likely that he would arrive until after sunset.

He had collected and packed his shotgun, which was tied, loaded and capped, behind the saddle. He wore Red's revolver, butt forward, on his left hip and his bullwhip was coiled cleverly around his waist and torso. His black flat-brimmed hat was pulled low over his face against the harsh light and his gray shirt was buttoned all the way to the top and stained darker gray with sweat where it stuck to his back. Her Highness was slick with sweat and the white hide reflected the bright light, making her outline indistinct in the shimmering heat waves. From a distance he would seem to be a black figure floating above the earth.

Michael's hurry at first was to get away, not to go toward, and as the miles grew between himself and that which he fled, he became less frantic, but still urgent about his progress. He was on his way home and, though the idea of a home was vague and troublesome, he was anxious to be there.

He wanted to see his father. He wanted to tell him what he had become and how he found a place in the world that was at God's side. He imagined the scene of his homecoming. His father would be standing in front of the small house, his back straight and his countenance grim, his eyes looking deeply into his son's as Michael dismounted and approached him. There would be no need to speak. His father would see and sense the profound and glorious changes in his only child, and pride and approval would well up in the old man. Slowly his father would reach out his hands and firmly grip Michael by the shoulders and Michael would bow his head in humility at his father's blessing.

As Michael rode, he replayed the vision in his mind again and again, making small changes and embellishments with each repetition. Hours passed by; Michael oblivious to his surroundings and the mule never flagging her quick gait.

He had forgotten his dream from the night before but, in between his hopeful daydreaming, his mind wandered to the wife of his only friend and how it felt to be held and hugged by her at his departure. She thrust herself to him full length, the top of her head tucked just beneath his chin, errant yellow hairs tickling his face, her body alive and warm against his.

He had never been held by a woman before. He had no memory of his mother embracing him, other than when she had bathed him, she had avoided touching him, even in an incidental manner. Rose's flesh had been supple and soft, the skin of her arms was so silken to Michael that he had let his own course hard palms stroke up past her elbow in an uncharacteristically uninhibited moment of wonderment. Her smell enveloped him and her body seemed fragile and childlike, yielding and frail. Michael had felt tall and powerful in comparison, and for the first time in his life, he noticed his masculinity as a distinct and separate identity.

When self-consciousness returned, he had flushed deep crimson on every square inch of visible skin. His breath shortened and became ragged, and he could only look down at Rose's feet as she stepped back from him. She spoke to him, her high voice tingling through his awareness without imprinting its content, while Michael nodded and studied her bare feet, noting their narrowness and how tiny her toenails were. He felt saddened and wished for her to touch his head the way he had seen her pet her daughters and speak to him in the soft gentle affectionate tones she reserved for her family. But as the flush on his skin contracted and centered in his groin, he withdrew from all sensation and wilted away under a surge of guilt that quickly came, leaving him cold and distant. Within minutes he was riding away, not once looking back to wave a last goodbye.

The afternoon dwindled into evening with Michael oscillating between the past and the future, between the persistent sensual memory of a woman's soft arms the optimistic fantasy of his father's love. Just before the blood red sun dropped to his left, streaking the low tangled clouds with vibrant pinks and oranges and bathing the landscape with sharp contrasting light, Michael caught sight of his first stop over, a cluster of squat square buildings that appeared in the clarity of sunset, less than an hour's ride ahead.

Michael smiled and grunted and urged his pale mount to continue its efforts, promising a good currying and good feed in reward if the town should boast a livery.

Twenty-Six

Beasley, Price, and the only other surviving member of their gang, Chico, rode into town just before sunset. They had pushed hard all day, stopping only to rest their exhausted mounts for only the shortest possible time. Beasley could not shake the feeling that they were being closely followed but he would do nothing to prove or disprove the eerie sense and simply pushed their pace faster when the feeling was strongest.

The three men were dusted nearly white and were drenched in sweat as were their lathered horses. Just short of entering town, Beasley pulled up his horse and the other two men and the extra horses Chico was leading gathered next to him.

"We made good time. I think I could sleep for a week, I tell you what." Price's face was pale and he looked worn to his limit. The tense night and the hard-riding would have been difficult even for a healthy man but Price was left feeling weakened and without resources. He was ready to give up and would go whichever way the wind blew. There was no more fight left in him, his voice had been soft and toneless.

"I'm thinking maybe we should go straight to the ranch." Beasley was worried about the town's hostile attitude toward him. He had hoped to be gone longer than he had been and without his brothers - Price was obviously useless - he felt vulnerable.

"If you want." Price was numb with fatigue. He lay draped across his horse's neck, His legs hung straight down not in the stirrups, his arms weakly embraced his mount.

Beasley studied his little brother and was suddenly

afraid he might die. Far from feeling sentimental, he was only sure he did not want to be around if Price was not going to live and he decided that he would risk the trip into town to dump Price off with his sister. He was not anxious to see Mary either, knowing the nagging and reprimands he would receive.

"What are we waiting here for, Beas?" Price's voice drifted over to him. "You scared to go into town?" The question was innocent, Price was too weak to consider baiting his older brother.

"Shut the hell up. I'm trying to think here is all." The pressure of the last few days boiled over and he decided he was sick of running and would face whatever lay ahead, even if it meant risking his life. "If they try and fuck with me, I'll see them sorry for it." He kicked his mount's ribs and the tired animal picked up its drooping head and sluggishly plodded into motion.

Price fell into step behind him but Chico held back a little. They entered the town by the most direct path, the one that would take them past the livery.

Twenty-Seven

Luke watched the rider's swift approach from almost a mile away and even in the fading light of sunset he recognized the horseman as one of the two he had set to watch the whore's house. Anxious for news, he walked out away from the clustered group of Rangers to meet the rider.

The horse slowed to a walk is it came close to Luke, the rider waving a greeting. "The girl's back," he told Luke. "But no sign of the boys, I'm afraid. James is watching her now."

Luke considered silently, his head bowed and his feet making small scuffling steps. "Alright," he said quietly, his eyes scanning the horizon, squinting into the last rays of the sun. "You change horses and we will ride in and talk to her."

The rider dismounted to walk back alongside Luke. "Looks like you had some doings here," he said as he noticed the two bodies hanging from the side of the house. The lack of trees had forced the Rangers to execute the prisoners by swinging a rope over the roof of the house and hauling the bandits up by their necks, their backs scraping against the wall, until their feet were just off the ground and then letting them slowly strangle.

"Yep, Andrew got killed and Simon took one in the knee. We killed one more inside the house but none of them are Pruitts." The information was offered dispassionately.

"Will he make it?"

"I expect he will if the leg don't have to come off. Won't ever work right though."

The other Rangers stood and gave their attention to Luke as he stepped in their midst. "The whore has come in," he announced. "We're going to ride in and question her. The rest of y'all should stay here in case them boys return. Post guards and don't let anyone take you by surprise."

The Rangers nodded and chorused their understanding then went back to their smoking and conversation. Luke strolled off to saddle his horse. Tired by the long active day, he took his time. There was no cause to hurry. He doubted that the woman would yield much in the way of real information and so, when they rode off in the twilight, they rode at a comfortable pace.

Twenty-Eight

Mary awoke just after dark. She wiped the sleep from her

face with a rub of her hands and yawned deeply. She lit a candle, taking one final look before leaving.

The room was nearly bare and seemed completely lifeless, as if it had been abandoned months before and showed no sign of its previous occupant. There was nothing to indicate that Mary had been years here, no clue as to who she was and what her life had been like, other than illustrating the emptiness and pointlessness of her existence.

The candle flickered in the wind from her prolonged and powerful sigh, casting jumpy shadows and making her once familiar surroundings seem strange and unfriendly. She had not even left and already she felt as though this house were not hers.

"Hell, all those years," she said. "I never belonged here, I tell you what."

She went to the house next to hers, separated by a patch of tall weeds, and banged noisily on the door, but to no effect. She tried the house across from hers where an old Mexican woman lived with her grandson, but still no one emerged at her knocking.

"Damn it!" she angrily kicked the flimsy door, causing the entire building to shake and rattle. She stepped back from the door and turned, considering whether to try a third house or to just go, and saw that she was being watched. One of the two men who had greeted her when she came home earlier that day was still there, sitting quietly in the dark, his eyes fixed on her.

She stared back for a moment, at first simply confused and curious, then irate and defiant. She stormed back into her house and picked up the sack containing her belongings. She pulled her pistol from her pocket and checked that the percussion caps were in place and, satisfied, replaced the five-shooter.

She paused as she stooped to extinguish the candle, her face poised above the tiny flame, her lips puckered but not yet blowing. She straightened and, her face contorting in an angry frown, dropped the sack and picked up a jug that rested in the corner of the room nearest the door. The whiskey jug had spiderwebs gently attempting to hold it in place. She swirled and then uncorked the jug pouring several cups of nearly pure alcohol in a puddle onto her mattress, splashing it around to try to cover all of the surface. She tossed the empty jug aside and it fell onto the dirt floor with a dull heavy clunk. She swayed briefly, the strong odor steering her to wish that she had tasted some before pouring it all out. She caught up her bag of goods and with the other hand, picked up the candle and, leaning far over, carefully set the little flame to the edge of the mattress, patiently waiting until I caught.

With the mattress sprouting a vibrant blue flame behind her, making her shadow leap ahead of her, she exploded out the door saying loudly, "Next time maybe y'all will answer when I come a-knocking," as she passed into the calm night air.

She stopped in front of the man who'd been watching her and said, "What are you looking at?" And when he did not speak, "You like what you see, cowboy? Want me to suck your cock?"

He pulled back deeper into his chair and dropped his eyes and still did not answer.

"Cat got your tongue?" she glared at him, the dim light hiding her face within the hood of her long hair, daring him to speak.

Twenty-Nine

Sam sat in front of a small campfire. The dry oily wood burned hot and smokeless and he kept his feet so close to the flame that the leather of his moccasin soles had begun to smolder and he had to remove them, but still his feet ached.

Earlier that afternoon he had followed Mary into the creek and it had chilled his feet to the point where they seemed unable to rewarm and walking had become painful.

Mary had left him several hours earlier and had not wanted him to accompany her for reasons she seemed guarded about, and Sam had not pressured her for an explanation, preferring anyway to build a fire and try to restore his circulation. He missed her and was anxious for her return, anxious to spend another night in her arms and inside her. Every few seconds his mind returned happily to thoughts of her and he would smile to himself, sometimes even laughing aloud. Before his feet had chilled, he had felt supremely relaxed and fulfilled, quietly at peace; which was to him better than outright joy. If he concentrated, he could feel the imprint of her lips lingering from her parting kisses and he found that the remembrance warmed him a little. He associated her absence with the return of his chronic cold pains and found it hard to remain still and wait for Mary to come back to him.

After the sun was tucked well under the horizon, his aching began to subside and he stirred himself long enough to make coffee, grinding it with the box-shaped grinder he had taken from Beasley. He tapped the revolver tucked uncomfortably inside his waistband and wondered if that too would prove useful.

At the moment his hand touched the smooth walnut of the pistol's butt, he felt a prickly feeling ripple up his spine and he froze in mid-movement, all his senses straining. Sam was a rational man, but he had learned from hard experience to listen to and trust his intuitions. It was something tangible that was tugging at his mind, something perceived below his awareness. Then, when a rare light breeze came, he knew. He could smell an Indian. They had an odor, just like he had, and this one - he was certain it was only one - had it strongly.

He drew the pistol and stepped quietly out of the glow of the fire light and tried to relax his eyes to more quickly accustom them to the darkness. He left his rifle where it rested against the saddle, the barrel pointing to the starry sky, the pistol being a smarter choice in the limited visibility.

He knew his adversary was as much in the dark as he was and that the cat-and-mouse they were playing was as much a matter of patience as skill. A trapper and a hunter for more than thirty years, Sam had survived by being very good at this type of game, and, at that moment, he forgot his pain and his Mary and he began to enjoy himself.

The mountain men were essentially in a constant state of war with the people on whose lands they were trespassing. Sam had killed before, however, he did not enjoy it and he never took a scalp. He would avoid violence if possible.

Minutes passed and Sam began to wonder if his adversary had withdrawn. He decided on a different tactic.

He risked a moment when the fire died down to quickly step through the low light and retrieve his rifle, moving back into shadow just as quickly. He stealthily traveled away from his camp on a curve and set up within rifle range, watching the fire, rifle to his shoulder, hammer cocked, waiting for a silhouette.

He heard movement behind him and ducked and turned keeping the rifle poised. He smiled when he saw a pinto pony in Indian harness. He saw that it was hobbled and grazing in the sparse grass near the creek, unconcerned with him. He approached it cooing. It raised its head to study him but did not move away.

He examined the pony for a minute then returned his attention to his camp. He worried that Mary might come stomping back and into the situation. He considered his options.

Thirty

As Michael rode up to the stable, he glanced back over his shoulder, having the sensation that he was being watched. Even in the darkness he could make out the shapes of several riders, two leading unmounted but saddled horses. A third was leaning low on his horse's neck and talking loudly enough for Michael to make out sounds, if not words, and pointing Michael out to the man who rode abreast of him. The three of them came to a complete halt when Michael returned their stares.

He turned away and rode his mule in through the open stable doors. A warm yellow glow from a brightly burning oil lamp lit the interior and a man was methodically pitchforking alfalfa into a stall. Only two horses occupied the stable with the man and, as Michael dismounted, he greeted the man with a quiet hello.

"If you're looking to keep your mule here, you'll have to see to it yourself," the man warned him. "That was my brother's job. I'm just working it cuz he got killed and I ain't got time to do much. The place is for sale but you can keep your animal here for a while, long as you see to it yourself."

"That's fine. Can I get some feed for her?"

"Yeah, but like I said, do it yourself." He speared the pitchfork into the stacked alfalfa bales and stepped up to stand in front of Michael. "I won't charge you none for some 'falfa but we ain't got no oats or hay left."

"Okay. I'll be gone come morning anyhow. Is it all right if I sleep in here tonight?" Michael had had this same conversation a hundred times.

"Yeah sure, don't make no difference to me." He studied the tall broad-shouldered young man dressed in dark drab clothing and a black hat whose wide flat brim shadowed and obscured his face. "Don't like being in here myself on account of this is where my brother was killed."

Michael said nothing in response, he just continued to look at the man. "Got stabbed to death by an outlaw." Michael remained steadfastly uncurious so he dropped his head and moved around him saying, "I'll be on my way then. There's a brush and pick on the wall there if you want them. That mule looks hard rode. Just put out the lamp when you're done."

"Okay." Michael led Her Highness into an empty stall and removed the bridle from the steaming animal as the man walked out without wasting another word. He uncinched the saddle and hung it over the rail between the stalls. He shifted his gun belt so that the revolver hung further behind his hip and more out of the way and uncoiled the whip from around his torso, draping it over the stall gate, which he left open.

He found the brush and other tools hanging from rusty nails, brought them back and began to groom the wet and dirty mule. The stiff wire bristles of the brush loosened the grit from the mule's back and Michael did a thorough job, cleaning all of the sweat caked dust from the legs and belly. The rhythmic monotony of the work and the solid feel of the handle snug to his palm, it's leather strap tight over the back of his large hand, as he stroked the mule's hide was a reassuring and calming activity. It had been more than two weeks since he had been by himself and after a refreshing day alone, the familiar tasks brought him back to his old life and the security he had always found in solitude.

He did not hurry but lingered, redoing what had already been done, his mind drifting along, becoming absorbed and still.

Thirty-One

"Course I'm sure it's him. How many fellows around here ride around on a white mule and carry a double barrel." Price remained mounted, slumped over the neck of his horse. His tone was surly, though he kept his voice lowered.

Beasley had dismounted and stood next to his brother, their heads almost level with each other. "Big fella. Didn't see his friend nowheres though. The red-haired fellow I mean."

"He's in there by himself. You going to go in there and shoot him now?"

"No, sounds like he's in there with someone." The muted sounds of conversation were audible. As Beasley stared into the dimly-lit interior of the stable, he could see no movement other than the flickering of the lamp.

Just then a man stepped out of the stable and walked directly past Beasley and the two others. He stopped dead in his tracks when he lifted and turned his head and saw the group of men and horses standing motionless only a few yards to the side of him. He took a slow step back as he recognized the men, his mouth dropping open and his eyes widening with apprehension and alarm.

"What the hell you looking at?" Beasley snarled in a whisper. The man backed away another step but did not speak. The glare in Beasley's eyes made the man's legs tremble and he began to lift his hand in a pointing gesture but lowered it before it had risen halfway.

"Cat got your tongue?" Beasley asked.

For an answer, the man backed away another step, then turned quickly and, with many anxious looks over his shoulder, he hurried away at a fast jogging walk.

"Better get this done and get the hell out of here," Beasley whispered as he watched the man disappear. "You two stay here and stay quiet." Chico only nodded and Price did not speak or move as his older brother quickly and silently approached the open doors from the side. The light from inside spilled out and washed over the tops of Beasley's boots as he peered around the door's frame before entering. As he passed inside, he drew his knife. The blade where it jutted out from Beasley's tightly clenched fist glinted, reflecting the soft yellow lamp light.

Thirty-Two

He had thought to surprise the white man as he rested, but the man had surprised him by suddenly jumping up and disappearing from the cone of red light. This was to be the second night in a row without sleep, the second night he would spend stalking and killing white men in the darkness.

He had followed the gun traders without being seen since they had broken camp just after dawn. They had ridden at a furious pace throughout the hot and windless day, giving him no opportunity to attack them again and no chance to rest. As they approached the sanctuary of a town, he swung away from them and rode a circuit around the town like a wolf surveying a flock of sheep. In a short time, he spotted the glow of a campfire and had dismounted and prowled silently forward for a closer look, the hammer sliding easily and comfortably into his hand.

Carefully staying far enough from the man's horse that stood hobbled out of the light of the fire that it would not hear or smell him, he circled to the other side. He came just come close enough to see that there was only one person and that was when somehow his presence was noticed. One moment the man was oblivious to his imminent death, the next he was smoothly in motion and had vanished from sight.

His eyesight was poor at night and so his progress was slow but he diligently, but circuitously, moved closer to the man's fire sure that he was unseen and undetectable. He just needed to be patient; more patient than the white man.

He stopped moving for several minutes, lying prone on the warm ground and listening intently. He heard the sounds of wind and thought he could hear the whispered conversations of ghosts brought to him in tangled snatches. He listened and pieced together what they were saying. They were addressing him, telling him wake up.

With a sharp exhalation he woke. The camp was quiet and when he looked to the fire, he saw it was lower and that the rifle was gone. The horse was still resting quietly and nothing else seemed to have changed. He wondered if he was remembering the rifle being there or if he had dreamed that part.

He edged back, taking a great deal of time and care. When he judged he was far enough, he came to his feet and made his way back to where he had hobbled his pony. A hobbled animal will still wander but it cannot wander far and cannot run further quickly enough to avoid capture when approached. It was not where he had left it but was a hundred yards nearer and closer to the creek.

He called softly to it as it seemed unusually wary and it calmed and moved slowly toward him. He greeted it with a pat and untied the hobble from the horse's front legs. He leaned against it for a reassuring moment as weariness threatened to overwhelm him. He may even have begun to drift off again when he was roused instantly alert by the unnatural sound of metal gears clicking into place.

With no hesitation, he vaulted onto its back and jerked the reins away from the noise and kicked his mount. The pony gathered its hind legs under it to leap forward as the gunshot thundered behind him.

Thirty-Three

Her Highness shifted uneasily, snorted and blew out her breath. Michael immediately stopped grooming her, becoming aware as if waking up, and straightened his back, turning his head to look and reaching out attentively with his hearing.

The mule was definitely nervous but Michael could not see or hear anything that might be the source of her agitation. His arm, with the brush still strapped to his hand, fell loosely to his side as he stepped from the stall. His left hand rested on the bullwhip that was draped over the stall gate, his fingers pinching the oiled leather as he searched the shadows. A cricket chirped persistently somewhere out of view.

Behind Michael and coming from inside the next stall, he heard a soft scuffling sound and a sharp intake of breath as Beasley burst out at him, the knife thrusting low and fast.

Michaels spun to face him and caught Beasley's wrist but without completely stopping it and only slightly deflecting its course. Michael stifled a yelp as the blade gouged into his abdomen just above his hip bone, and entered his body several inches. For a moment the two men struggled, Beasley furiously trying to plunge the knife deeper in and to twist the blade, Michael holding fast to his wrist and fighting back.

Beasley's charge had pushed Michael back and pinned him against the rails of the stall gate. Beasley leaned into his effort, adding his weight and leverage to his wiry strength. Off-balance, with his hand occupied, Michael had no room to retreat and no way to free himself and so they remained for a long moment locked into position, their feet scraping and shuffling under them. Their labored breathing loud.

Thirty-Four

The range was close and the visibility poor and so he used his new pistol. He took his time and let the Comanche mount, waiting for that moment while the pony gathered itself and the Indian would present a broad target. But as he mounted he swung himself low over the neck and part way off the side of the animal using it as a shield. Sam fired but was high. He had no qualms about shooting the horse out from under the man but he felt he could bide.

The pony tried to charge when kicked but could not get its hind legs into position. It pirouetted instead, kicking out, then rearing up. The Comanche fought for control and to stay mounted and shielded. All of which he attempted one-handed as he still held his hammer. As he came around, another shot boomed out. He saw the muzzle flash and the grim face behind it but this time the shot went wide as the whirling mount twisted him away.

Sam laughed evilly. He had noticed the pony's unusually long tail that nearly touched the ground and had tied the pony's tail to one of its hind legs in the brief time he had had after spotting the Comanche coming back. Now the confused and panicked beast was circling like a dog chasing its tail. He cocked the hammer a third time.

The Comanche's horse reared again and he aimed it at Sam. The animal rose up, several feet in front of Sam who calmly waited for it to settle, ready to fire nearly point blank. But as it came down on its front legs the Comanche was not there.

Sam sidestepped quickly to see around the horse and the Comanche was upon him. He fired at the same time the hammer whipped forward striking the pistol and smashing Sam's thumb. The ball caressed the Indian's ribs, chipping two but not breaking either and passing through the flesh of the broad muscle near his armpit.

The hammer came toward his head on the backswing and Sam stepped back and leaned away, the heavy head missing his nose by inches. The still exasperated horse whirled and its heavy head slammed the Indian's hip as he raised the hammer and stepped toward Sam, knocking him off his feet and sending him sprawling.

Sam was on him before he could rise. He kicked out at the

man's head and, though his arms came up in time to deflect kick, he was knocked to his back. He rolled away coming to his feet and bounded forward hammer high. Sam could not cock the gun with his smashed thumb and when he tried to pull the hammer back with his off-hand it stuck, damaged by the hammer blow. The Comanche almost upon him, he dropped and rolled like a log. Unable to stop himself, the Comanche tripped over the log and fell hard on his face.

Sam dropped the pistol and as he rose up, he pulled his tomahawk free with his right and his Bowie with his left point down. The two faced each other for a breath.

"WAUGH!" Sam charged, his face savage.

The pony, finally torn free from its tail, bolted and struck Sam from behind, spinning him around but not knocking him down. Still gaining momentum, it sped past and the quick Comanche sidestepped and, gripping round the pony's neck, swung himself up and they galloped away into the dark.

"Well, shit," Sam said when he had caught his breath.

He sheathed his knife, retrieved his pistol and rifle, and walked back to his fire, now only coals, speaking soothingly to his horse and flexing his bruised thumb. He wanted to and should have saddled one of the horses and headed out in pursuit of the Indian or packed and moved his camp, but he did neither. He was waiting for Mary.

He tossed the pistol on his buffalo skin. He built the fire back up. He examined his thumb which was swollen but still moved. He took up his rifle and stood well outside the light, staring into the darkness toward the town.

He waited, wondering aloud, "What the hell is keeping that woman?"

Thirty-Five

She passed a hurrying figure in the dark street without pausing or reacting to him, but she hesitated as she approached the stables, for her way was blocked by two men and several horses.

With some effort in the darkness, she realized that one of the men was her brother Price and, slowly at first and then with more speed, she neared, and became certain. She walked up to join them, calling out as she approached.

"Price, is that you Sugar?" He did not look like himself to her. The last time she had seen him she had hardly taken notice of him, having just been delivered notice of Ocie and Joseph's death.

He lifted his head off his horse's neck and twisted to see his sister coming toward him carrying a sack in her hands. "Yeah, it's me all right."

"What are you doing here?" she asked, noticing that he did not look well and reaching out a small hand to stroke his head which still rested on his mount's neck.

"I'm waiting on Beasley," he answered her and smiled foolishly, his normally surly demeanor softened by weariness and pain.

"What are you talking about? Where is Beasley? I need to tell him I'm leaving." Her voice became tight and a little stern. She thought he might be drunk.

"He's in there, with that mule riding son of a bitch what killed Joey and O." He spoke without inflection and then rested his head back down and closed his eyes.

Mary gaped at him for a moment then looked hard to the open doors of the livery stable, shaking her head with confusion and then with understanding. "What are you doing out here then? Get in there and help him, you fools."

"Beasley told us to wait for him."

"You idiot, get in there." She tugged hard on his shoulder and pulled him from the saddle then helped to steady him as he stood swaying on his feet, his back resting against his exhausted and immobile horse.

"But Beasley told us to wait out here and be quiet, I tell you what," he protested weakly, his eyes open only a slit.

She grabbed his sweat-soaked shirt front and shook him. Her head, with its tangled mop of dark hair, wobbled with the effort. She glared up at him from under his chin. "Do like I tell you, dammit!"

"I don't know, he's a big fella, shoots straight too. I best stay here." Price sounded bored.

Mary no longer listened. She shoved Price on his way and pulled Chico from his horse, pushing him forward as well. Chico complied, but no more willingly than Price had. He was healthier, though, and was soon walking ahead of the limping Price, both men drawing their revolvers and plodding cautiously towards the light.

Mary gathered up the reins of the horses and held them tightly, nervous and tense, but confident that the three of them could easily kill one man. She mounted one of the horses, ready to hand the others off to her brothers as they emerged and ready to ride off as they made their escape.

Thirty-Six

As Michael wrestled for his life with Beasley, he began to feel strength rather than fatigue building in him. His head buzzed, his vision shook, and a part of his mind retreated to make room for the power flowing into him, flowing through him. He felt a lightness of being alive and a singularity of purpose materialize and harden in him. He raised his right arm and swung it down in one short powerful blow.

Beasley's head was lowered, his right arm pushing on the knife, his left arm across Michael's chest to pin him and to keep his own balance. He looked up and his grimace turned into a flinch as he saw the unavoidable strike that was aimed at his face. The wire bristles of the brush, weighted by its heavy wood back, bit into his face and ear even as he turned away from it, knocking his hat off his head, ripping open hundreds of thin gouges, blinding him in his left eye. Before he could recover, he was struck again. This time the force of the blow staggered him and he lost his grip on the knife handle. The third blow sent him to his knees.

Michael heaved himself from the gate rails and shook the bloody brush from his hand. He steadied himself with his left his hand, it rested again on the coiled bullwhip. He took up the whip in both hands and stepped forward to stand over Beasley. Beasley knelt in the straw and dirt, his face unrecognizable and spilling a steady torrent of thick red blood. Michael looped the whip over Beasley's head and jerked it tightly around his throat, hauling Beasley upright, bracing his knee against the outlaw's back. Michael's breath was deep and even.

Beasley had begun to try to draw his gun but blinded by the blows and the blood, he was having difficulty finding it, the holster having been pushed back behind him during the struggle. When the leather tightened suddenly, choking off his air completely, making his pulse pound in his head, he forgot his pistol and reached up to pull the loop from his throat, but his hands and neck were slick with his own blood and he could not grasp the slippery whip well enough to ease the pressure. His consciousness and strength fading quickly, he groped blindly for Michael, managing only to grasp his shirt and imprint a smeared dark stain but not pushing him off in the slightest.

Beasley's hand released its hold and fell limply to his side but Michael continued to squeeze the loop tighter. The body hung slack and heavy for a dozen seconds before Michael let him fall away from his knee. He slipped slowly down to the ground, the whip uncoiling as he dropped. His face pressed flat in the straw and muck and he lay with his hips jutting up and his knees curled under him.

Michael exhaled. A drop of sweat beaded on the end of his nose and fell, splattering audibly in the tense silence on the leg of Beasley's trousers. He let the now loose ends of the whip slide from his fingers. He straightened and hitched up his belt. The barn in the soft light glowed with colorless vibrancy for him and he could clearly differentiate every straw, every grain in the wooden planks, every bit of dust that wafted through the air, disturbed and freed by the struggle. It was beautiful.

He heard the men enter and saw them before they saw him. The first man through was dark-skinned and dressed like a ragged Vaquero. Another, heavy on his feet, crouched behind him, obscured from Michael's sight.

The Vaquero instantly raised his pistol and fired at Michael the moment his darting nervous eyes noticed him. The shot whizzed past Michaels head, the man's aim high and wide, smoke from the pistol reaching out for him. Michael drew his big revolver smoothly and then unhurriedly raised it to arm's length as a second shot missed him to strike the stall gate with a loud crack and spray of splinters. Michael thumbed back the hammer, aimed, and fired, a great gout of smoke and fire spewing from the muzzle, wrestling with the smoke from the two previous shots, and an ear-shattering roar shook the rafters.

The bullet struck Chico in his belly and passed through his body to strike Price in the ribs over his heart. Both men staggered backwards several steps and out the wide doorway to crumple in a heap upon each other in the light spilling out at the stable's entrance.

Price's short rib was shattered, doubling him up in intense agony. His pistol dropped from his hand and he clutched his side, gritting his teeth.

The lead ball passing through Chico had slashed through his abdominal artery. He bled profusely internally as well as from the massive exit wound for several seconds then died from the loss, although only a few drops stained his shirt in front.

Michael appeared in the doorway, shrouded in smoke and silhouetted by the soft light, the pistol hanging by his side. He gazed at Chico and the unmoving Price then looked up suddenly to meet the wide eyes of a dark-haired young woman, sitting a horse in the darkness across from him. Their stares locked and lingered; hers shocked and horrified, his blank, cold, and otherworldly.

Michael calmly holstered the revolver, his hand brushing the hilt of the forgotten knife that protruded from his side. As if noticing for the first time that he had been stabbed, he examined the handle for a moment, then gently grasped it with his thumb and forefinger. He withdrew the slick bloody blade from his body with no more gravity than if it were normal to be sheathed there. Once it was free from his abdomen, he dropped the dripping blade onto the earth at his feet.

The dark-haired woman kicked her horse and bolted past Michael and out of town the instant the knife hit the ground. One of the other horses followed her for a space then slowed and turned, aimlessly walked a few steps, then stopped completely.

Price groaned loudly and made Michael notice that he was alive. Michael placed his hand on the butt of his gun but the spirit had left him and he hesitated to draw. He was joined by the Ranger who had been watching Mary, who came at a run with his own pistol drawn. He came right up to Michael, studying the tableau and then Michael's face.

"I know you," he said. "You're that crazy Muleskinner."

Thirty-Seven

Mary raced out of town as fast as the tired mare would carry her. In the black obscurity of night her panic eased and she reined her horse in, searching the darkness to get her bearings and trying to remember which way to go. She spotted a dim glimmer from a campfire and prodded the reluctant horse toward it while looking fearfully over her shoulder the way she had come.

She was greeted at the fire by an anxious Sam who, rifle in hand, grasped the reins of her horse and fairly jerked the animal into the light. He helped Mary down and accepted her into his arms when she threw herself toward him. He squeezed her tightly and made soothing noises as Mary cried loudly and tried without success to form clear words.

Sam was not an excessive drinker; life in the mountains prevented ready access to alcohol and he'd never developed a great urge for it, but he nonetheless kept a bottle of grain spirits handy for medicinal purposes. He led Mary to his fire and set her down on his buffalo robe. He set his rifle aside and while she panted and sobbed, he rummaged through his carefully packed gear for the little clay jug.

"Here, steady yourself with some of this." He handed her the jug and squatted flat-footed next to her and helped her trembling hands hold the jug to her mouth. She swallowed several times. The familiar burn down her throat never tasted so sweet or necessary. She remembered the dreamy release alcohol brought as it coated her belly with warmth and sent a flush of red to her cheeks.

"They killed my brothers." The words spilled out and she stared at Sam with disbelief. "Now they're all dead."

"Your brothers got killed tonight?" She nodded in response.

"Just now?" She nodded again, waiting for him to understand.

"Was it Indians?" he asked.

"No." She drank deeply from the jug, spilling some down her chin. "It was the man on the white mule."

"On a mule? Tell me what happened."

"He shot them. He's the same man what shot my other

two brothers. Now he's shot and killed all of them and left me all alone." She started crying again, this time softly.

"Why did he shoot them?" All things had reasons to Sam and he was trying to understand.

"I don't know!" she snapped at him.

Sam stayed quiet for a moment thinking through what he knew about the situation and what he did not know, then choosing his words carefully, he asked about what concerned him the most.

"He isn't going to try to kill you too, is he?"

"He looked like he was going to kill everybody." Her voice sounded far away to Sam and she stared right through him. She shivered and then shook her head and raised the jug again. "His eyes were evil."

"I'll finish loading the horses and we'll move out." Sam rose to his feet and picked up his rifle, surveying the darkness for signs of life.

"What? Where are you going?" There was panic in her voice, though softened by a slur.

"We'd best go."

"What? Are you a coward? We can't run away. We gotta kill that son of a bitch." Her voice was hoarse and ragged and she glared angrily at Sam.

He backed up a step and his face closed down as he weighed his options against what he wanted and what he needed, against what it might cost him.

Seeing his hesitation, Mary softened her demeanor and became placating and pitiable. "Please, Sugar, you got to help me. I can't do it by myself, he'll kill me I know it. I can feel it." she cried gently. "You'll leave me too, I'll be all alone." She crawled to Sam and clung to his buckskin leggings. "I'm scared, Sam, I'm scared."

Sam did not mind if someone was in pain, for pain with a constant. He did not sympathize with sorrow, for loss was inevitable. But what tugged at his heart, what tripped his logic and engendered an impulse to intercede was fear. Fear was his own impetus, what brought him close to the truth and what pulled him short of it. Wanting to ease his fear was what made him want to understand, and by understanding he hoped he would be freed. Fear was what drove him into the mountains and solitude, away from life and its chaos in the delusion that he would find order and understanding. His disconnection was the source of his fear and unity had been the relief.

He had tasted union with Mary, he'd discovered love's lack of rules, and found some happiness, and now he saw revealed in her, a fear like his own. And he felt an even deeper union with her, a recognition of her. And his heart spoke out.

"Hush there, my darling." He held her and comforted her the way he had wanted to be comforted. "Your Sam ain't going nowhere without his Mary. I'll keep you safe," he promised. "And I'll kill that mule rider for certain."

Thirty-Eight

Luke had heard the shooting and he and his companion had sprinted their horses towards the source of the shots but they spent some time searching through the warren of narrow streets before finding a small crowd gathered around one of his Rangers, a duo of dead outlaws, a barely living unconscious outlaw, and a bleeding Muleskinner. They dismounted and shouldered their way through the onlookers.

"What has happened here?" he asked kneeling to examine the bodies that had been carefully arranged for viewing. They'd been laid out side by side with their backs propped up against the outside wall of the stable. Price had been set next to his brother. The lamp from inside the stable had been brought out to illuminate the area for the crowd that included, Luke noticed, the stablehand's grinning father and brother.

"Michael here killt these three. Seems two of them is Pruitt's. This one here is Beasley Pruitt," the Ranger with Michael explained, nudging Beasley's body with his boot toe.

Luke stood up and looked at Michael. Taking in his wound at a glance, he asked brusquely, "Where's Red?"

"At his home. I left him there this morning." Michael's face was pale and his voice tight.

"Why did you kill these fellows, Michael?"

"They tried to kill me."

"You? You know why?"

"They're evil."

Luke dropped his eyes away from Michael's unblinking certain stare, "I suppose you're right about that. Let me look at your side."

Michael laid down next to Price and rested his back against the wall. Luke paused at the sight of the four men sitting together, the killer posing calmly with his three victims, he knelt down and began to clean and dress the jagged cut in Michael's side, asking the Rangers to fetch his needle and thread from the saddlebags.

Thirty-Nine

He rode several miles before stopping and examining his wound. The ball had torn across his ribs without penetrating his body. Though his ribs were chipped and bruised they were not broken. But the flesh was ripped and ragged. It bled freely and streamed all the way down his side and leg, pooling in this moccasin. It was tender and swollen and he had to be careful not to let his arm hang down and rest on it.

He had done nothing to stop the flow of blood. If he bled

to death it was not his concern or his place to interfere. His life would unfold or dissolve of its own inertia and he need only behave according to his vision. He dismounted and stood beside his pony, leaning heavily on its withers, suddenly very weary.

As he sagged against the animal, he heard the steady clopping of an approaching rider. He peered over the back of his pony and saw a man riding a pale mule. His head was down and he rode slumped over and holding his belly. He rode blindly and without any awareness of his surroundings and, even though he passed within a few yards of the Comanche, he was completely ignorant of his presence.

He watched the ghostly rider pass without revealing himself but something nagged at his mind, a familiarity, a recognition. He had some previous knowledge of this man but he was having difficulty concentrating. He was having difficulty staying awake.

As the rider disappeared into the darkness he slumped down behind his pony, the image of the rider's hat lingered in his eyes and stayed with him as he fell limply to the earth and passed out with his eyes open.

Forty

An hour after first light, Sam left Mary at his camp and rode into town to collect his horse and found that the livery had been turned into an expedient morgue and jail. Price, who had survived his injuries and his doctoring by Luke, lay in the back on a bed of straw, guarded by several Rangers who lounged in the shade inside and out front. Chico's and Beasley's corpses lay inside a stall, covered by a canvas tarpaulin that left their boots sticking out. Sam smiled broadly and greeted the group, saying he'd come to collect his horse then asking about what had happened.

"We caught us some outlaws here and at their ranch." They were proud and pleased and gregarious, happy to boast and be praised. "Going to hang this one." He swung his head in Price's direction, smiling broadly as he delivered the news.

"Seems like they gave you all a fight." The smell of gunpowder clung to the walls in the warm still interior. Patches of blood stained the ground and the signs of struggle were readily apparent to a tracker like Sam.

"Yeah, they did, but they got the worst of it, I tell you." He squared his shoulders and several of the men chorused their agreement with laughter and whoops.

"Y'all in this fight?" Sam was puzzled.

The Ranger looked down, shuffled his feet, pinched the end of his nose, and adjusted his hat. "Well, not this one. I was in the fight at the ranch though, lost a man out there. Another got hisself crippled."

"How'd you get all these folks?" He wandered over to the stall and leaned on the gate, idly fingering the wood splintered from the gunshot. He could not tell anything about the two men under the canvas beyond their size and footwear.

"Well ah, that was one of our, well he used to be a Ranger, that is he rode with us for a time, a muleskinner is what he is I suppose. He killed those two men and wounded that one hisself."

"A muleskinner done this?"

"Yeah. He's a mean one, I tell you." He swallowed loudly. "Tell the truth I'm glad he's gone." The Ranger fixed his hat again then crossed his arms over his chest.

"Gone?"

"Yeah. Left early while it was still dark. He ain't really a Ranger like I said, just rode with our Captain for a time is all."

Sam stayed and made pleasant conversation for a few more minutes, then with his horse in tow he headed out of town. Once out of sight of the Rangers he circled the town, searching the ground as he went. He followed the track he had spotted near the stables and picked up again as he headed east. Mules were very similar to horses in the imprint of their shod hoof but the way they walked and how they carried their load was markedly different and Sam knew one when he saw it.

He followed it for less than a mile and then turned his horse and headed back for Mary.

Forty-One

Luke had sewn Michael up then watched as the stoic Muleskinner saddled his ghostly mule and rode off long before first light. He'd bound Price's ribs with strips of cloth and questioned him, finding out about the death of his two youngest brothers. He then found the wounded man a place to sleep and tried to make him as comfortable as was possible. He sent one of the men back to the ranch house to fetch the rest of the troop then he found himself a soft pile of straw and slept soundly and without dreams for the rest of the night.

He awoke the next morning at dawn and during his breakfast of coffee and grits he was interrupted by some townspeople who asked him to join them; that there was somebody they wanted him to see and speak with.

Luke was led to a small but clean house, where, in the closeness of a square hot kitchen, he was introduced to a gaunt woman named Annabeth and her quiet daughter Darlene.

An hour later he came back to the livery and told his men that they should be ready to travel again soon.

"First we're going down and pick up the boys from Captain Red's. We're going to need them 'Paches for this one too."

"What about the prisoner? I don't think he can ride," said the Ranger who had accompanied him to town the night before.

Luke took a moment, like a man remembering an important task he had left undone. “Get a rope,” he ordered. “We'll do it right here.”

He walked slowly over to where Price lay, curled up on his side with his back to him and gently shook him. Price let out a long low groan but did not roll over. “Get up there, Son, we got to get on with this.”

“Get on with what?” Price asked in a sad sullen tone. “I ain't in no shape to go anywhere.”

“You're not going far. We're going to hang you right here, boy,” Luke explained patiently.

Price was silent for a long minute and then began to weep. Luke stood still and said, “You must have known we was going to hang you.”

“Yeah, I supposed. I was just hoping I guess.” his voice was choked and teary.

“You want something to eat first?”

Price thought for a moment. He thought he should stretch his time out and get a last little bit of life but he was not hungry and felt too weak to try to force himself to eat. Finally, he said, “No, I do not, I'm not hungry. I’d go for a drink of whiskey, if I might.”

Luke stepped away and then returned with a small bottle. He helped Price into a sitting position, which put pressure on the broken ribs and made Price whimper. He held the jug to his lips and Price drank deeply, wanting to be drunk and oblivious; he did not think he had the courage to face his execution sober. Luke let him drink as much as he wanted and then set the bottle on the floor. "It's time,” he announced.

“Can I see my sister before you hang me? I'd like to say goodbye to her.” The whiskey was beginning to soothe him and it stopped his crying.

“Don't know where she's gotten to, else I’d fetch her for you,” Luke apologized.

“Yeah, she said she was leaving. I'm sure she lit out when

we saw us all shot."

"She was outside?"

"Yeah, she sent me in after Beasley."

"Surprised that Michael didn't shoot her too."

"He probably should have. She holds a grudge, my sister does."

Several Rangers carried Price and set him on the bare back of a horse. They stood to the side of him and used their hands to hold him steady as he was led to the center of the stable. A rope had been thrown over a sturdy rafter and tied off at one end. The other end was made into a slip knot and secured around Price's neck as his hands were tied behind his back.

All this was done with quick efficiency and it seemed to Price to take no time at all. He found that he did not need to have courage, that his pain and trials were almost too much to bear and that this conclusion to a life that he had considered unfair and harsh towards him especially, was fitting and normal and a relief.

Luke appeared at his side and Price saw him as if in a dream, indistinctly and difficult to focus directly on. Luke's words wafted up to him like soft chimes from a silver bell, "You have anything to say for yourself before we do this?"

Price remained silent so long the Rangers assumed he had nothing to say and begin to lead the horse out from under him, not stopping when Price finally did speak.

"This comes as no surprise to me." His voice soft and forlorn. "Everything happens to me, I tell you wha...."

Forty-Two

Mary paced back and forth impatiently with her stomping stride in front of Sam as he dismounted and hobbled the horses. She held the jug in her hands and she reeked with the smell of it.

"Did you see him? Did you see the murdering bastard?"

"Naw. He's gone." Her face cycled to anger and disappointment and anguish as she digested that news, marveling Sam with her facility with feeling. She demonstrated more emotions in five minutes than he did in a year.

"They bury my brothers yet?

"No." Sam wanted to be truthful but decided not to mention that Price had been still alive but destined to hang.

"I found his track, though. We can follow him easily enough but he's a day ahead." He paused, thinking carefully before speaking. "Mary, there's some things you haven't told me. About your brothers."

Mary became serious and still, meeting Sam's eyes and deciding on the truth for this moment. "I know they was bad, Sam. But you didn't know them when they was babies. I raised them, they're like my own children. They was my family. My family, Sam. We watched out for each other, they fought for me. Now this one man's killed all my family, not just Beasley and Price but Ocie and Joseph too. One man's killed all of them."

Sam considered for a moment and then wilted under her pleading stare. "Alright, I understand you. Blood is thicker than water. We should get started after him." He smiled, reassuring her, and she dove into his arms, squeezing herself to his chest.

"Oh, Sam honey, I need you so much now. You'll take care of me, won't you?" He crooned answers as he returned her embrace, and kissed the top of her head. She turned her face up to his and pulled his mouth to hers. Her taste was salty from tears and perfumed with alcohol.

Sam was unnerved by the way his life was out of his control, but he had no ability to resist her passion, or violence, or closeness, and soon they were lying on his buffalo robe and he was lifting her skirt up over her hips and loosening his belt. He squeezed her small breasts and accepted her tongue in his mouth. His erection searched for her and she wriggled to help him. He slipped easily inside her and she gasped and closed her eyes, arching her back and drawing away from him, then pressing closer to him. Her legs wound around his waist and she crossed her ankles, locking him into place. She ground against him in tiny circles and throwing her head back, her mouth wide open but soundless, she trembled and cried out. She pressed her face into his shoulder.

Sam listened to her panting gasps as she eased her legs from around him and he began to rhythmically thrust himself in and out. He quietly let go, relaxing into it. His body softened and melted hot over her. She accepted the full weight of him, merged rather than smothered, soaked in sweat, and breathing each other's breath.

Sam made food and then packed their things but did not load or saddle the horses. The sun was high and beat down with its full strength, it would be hard traveling and Sam said it would be best if they waited until late afternoon before departing. Mary fanned her legs with her skirt and nodded.

They ate their meal sitting in the shade next to each other, their legs rubbing and Mary leaning against Sam's arm and shoulder.

After they had finished Mary stood up and said, "There's something I need to do, won't take me long."

"I don't know that you should go to town. Those Rangers may still be there," Sam warned.

"I ain't really going to town, Sugar." She smiled at him genuinely but with tightly clenched lips.

Mary stomped off, her short legs stretching out with each stride, making her feet land hard and flat. She passed through their bend in the creek without noticing or feeling sentimental and skirted the town's buildings. She encountered no one as she walked, the townspeople had gone inside to hide from the midday heat, and came finally to a slope of low hillside that was overgrown with weeds.

There were several tired-looking crosses planted askew and one actual headstone that was less than a foot high. The majority of graves, however, were left unmarked. She went to the freshest grave, a mound of earth only a little more than a week old and not yet settled and leveled.

She stood over it for a moment and then squatted down on top of the mound, hiking up her skirt. Some of Sam dribbled out of her as she waited but she finished what she came there to do and stood up again saying, "I told you I'd shit on your grave. Beasley killed you. Now he's dead, but I'll have the last word on this, I tell you what."

Forty-Three

As the Rangers left town towards the south, Luke saw two riders moving east. He noticed them only in passing and was prepared to forget them but the Ranger riding next to him was one of the men who had been placed to watch for Mary.

"Luke, that there's the whore," he said, pointing.

"Her brother said she was leaving. Who's that riding with her?" he asked afraid he might have missed a brother.

"That's that trapper what come in the livery while you was gone," another Ranger volunteered as he joined the conversation and scrutiny of the two riders.

"What trapper?" Luke asked.

"Came by the livery to collect his horse. Didn't say nothing about the whore, though. I think he was shitting us maybe."

"Shall we round them up, Luke?" Asked the first Ranger with some eagerness.

"No, I don't see why. We don't need them now. This business is done."

Luke and his men arrived at Red's ranch before midnight and Red and Rose came out and greeted the troop; the big Irishman clapping them in on their backs and calling them by name. The Rangers had set up their camp in front of the house and Luke and Red went inside and sat across from each other at the table, a dim lamp between them and a whiskey jug at Red's elbow. They talked for more than an hour, comparing stories of Pruitts and muleskinners before getting around to Luke's present business.

"Her name was Annabeth and they had a place about two days out from here."

"How many did she say was in on it?" Red's interest was keen.

"That's one of the strange things. She was sure there was just one of them."

"It's not unheard of but it's strange. Has he struck anywhere else?

"Nope, not that we learned of leastways." Luke shook his head, staring through the table top. "This is a bad one though, bothers me."

"You've seen worse, you have," Red reminded him. "We've all seen worse. Some of us have done worse."

"I don't know about that. I think it's that it's peculiar that it bothers me. He killed the men folks only. Now that ain't so strange but he didn't take the women or the children captive."

"He's by himself, traveling fast, didn't want to be slowed down with captives," Red conjectured.

"That's just it you see, he's not making war or even stealing, he's just out killing and raping."

"That's what making war is, Luke." Red drank, mulling over his own statement, absentmindedly petting the hound under the table with his bare foot. He'd been excited when the half of the troop appeared the day before and had spent an evening drinking and chatting with them. When Luke arrived with the rest of the troop he began to feel tired and sad and could not explain why.

His own father had never gone more than a few miles from where he'd been born but nonetheless had never been home, preferring to spend whatever time he could away drinking. He was absent so much that Red remembered him chiefly as a set of sounds that came in after dark or as a snoring bulk under a heavy quilt. He had a few sharp and vivid images of a large red-faced angry man with huge fists that broke his bones and scraped his skin. He had never known who his father was or what had been in his heart.

He could not leave with Luke in the morning. One Indian, even a Comanche on a killing spree, did not warrant his return from retirement. And he was ashamed of himself wanting it to be otherwise.

"You never did catch up with the sister?" he asked, breaking the silence.

"No, she was always a step away from us. She headed out for good after her brother was shot. We caught sight of her moving east with a trapper as we left that shithole."

Red thought for a moment; the connections between things beginning to trouble him. Then asked, "Which way did young Michael go off?"

"East as well as I recall. You think she might be following him?"

"Maybe that trapper can track."

"Maybe, didn't seem likely at the time but her brother said she was one to hold a grudge."

"I think you should send some boys out to run them down, just to be sure, I mean."

"Be tough to track the two of them, that's a well-used route they're all on. None of my boys can track good enough, I'd need them Apaches for it and I'm going to need them to find me that Comanche."

"Send a couple along," Red suggested.

"Only one of them talks American or Mexican. They're no use split up." He was quiet for a moment, observing Red. "I wouldn't worry about that boy, Captain, he seems to be able to take care of himself all right."

"That is the God's truth."

"I guess I'll get some sleep, we'll be leaving at first light. Good night Captain." Luke scraped his chair away from the table. He tipped his hat and smiled at Red and walked out the open door.

Red tilted his chair back, running his hand through his wavy thinning hair. He watched Luke leave and leave him to his familiar solitude, alone with his family, and unable to distract himself. His wife had heard all his stories, knew all his lies. He was surrounded by the people closest to him and he felt he had no one to talk with.

He patted his leg, calling the Redbone Coonhound that lay panting under his foot. The dog stood up one paw at a time and shuffled closer, resting her head on Red's leg.

"There's a good girl, Scarlett." He rubbed her head and ears. "Best tracker in Texas you are."

Forty-Four

Michael rode almost without pausing for several days, the tireless mule bearing him forward at a steady pace. The wound in his side, although uninfected and sewn shut, often broke open and began bleeding whenever he twisted or arched his back. Mounting and dismounting succeeded in opening the gash nearly every time, no matter how careful he tried to be and although the bleeding would soon stop, it always left him shaking and queasy.

At the end of a day's ride, he would be weak and tired and would often not remember to eat. He would sleep only a few hours, at first stiffly on his back with his hand covering his wound. Then, as the days passed and he neared his destination, he began sleeping longer, curled up with his belly to the hard ground, squirming and muttering with dreams. His days were dreamy and indistinguishable one from the next.

In the final few miles of his journey, he was jogged from his trance by familiar landmarks. Flashes of memory, long suppressed, surfaced and faded in a moment, leaving him breathless and pale. As he approached the small two room adobe and wood house, shaded by a large Sycamore and set only a dozen yards from a dry creek bed, his anxiety grew and a cold sweat broke across his face and back.

He did not know if anyone still lived in the house; he had not been there for years. Part of him hoped it was abandoned and that he could remain there for a time by himself and try to understand what it was he wanted, why he had really come. He was feeling a helpless fear but was unable to turn the mule another way.

He had seen and experienced little of life and the world between the time he had last seen the house and before his scourging by the Comanches. And in those years, he had never considered returning. When he emerged from his chrysalis, as it was stripped from him by the bullwhip he now wore around his waist, leaving him exposed to the universe, he had seen a new destiny, a place for him to exist outside of his shell.

He was here to find out if his transformation would make a difference. If he could bring his past into alignment with his present. He hoped it would be possible to understand his childhood from the vantage point of his epiphany. He wanted, he slowly realized as he dismounted, his existence to be acknowledged.

As he approached the door it swung open and his father emerged, little changed from when Michael had last seen him, though he appeared smaller from Michael's adult height. He looked his son up and down with a solemn expression. Then in a strong Gaelic accent, he asked, "Who the hell are you?"

PART FIVE: SOME REVELATION

One

Mary shifted her hips in the saddle, trying to find a position that was at least tolerable; having given up on comfortable after the second day out. She had ridden often in her life but rarely for more than a few hours at one time and never for days on end. Her thin thighs and rump offered little padding and the soreness had penetrated right through to her bones. When the day was don, her legs would cramp and throb making sleep difficult and unsatisfying. Sam's buffalo robe, even doubled over, was cushioning only for a short time before the hard and stony ground would assert itself. The nights were as difficult as the days.

Sam, however, journeyed unperturbed by anything except his inability to tolerate cold and rode with stoic ease. He enjoyed Mary's company even if her mood was often less than congenial. He enjoyed coaxing a smile from her, massaging her sore body, feeding her, and being inside her. He suggested once that they slow or stop and let her heal but she would not have it. Her refusal had been manic and forceful and it took some time before she calmed and would speak civilly.

Quarreling aside they made love for hours every night and again in the morning. Mary consumed him like an inebriant. With tireless and steady energy, she indulged in him to excess. The alchemy of their two bodies conjoined pushed back her confusion and chaos and made her feel safe and happy.

When that security faded, she would wither into a quiet sadness reviving only to try again.

Sam mistook the sex for love and mistook the sadness for sweetness. Sam's perspicacity was dulled by the smoke that surrounded her fire. He was warmed by her, no doubt, but the fire was consuming too.

He was only a little uncomfortable with the idea of violent revenge. The blood feud was common in the hills where he had been raised. As he considered Mary to be his wife, then her brothers where his brothers-in-law. There was an obligation to kin and to justice that was ingrained so deeply that it could not be dug out. But Sam was a thinker and he considered what the Rangers had told him about the Pruitt's habits and he was mostly convinced justice had been best served by their deaths. He felt a lack of moral high ground beneath him but Mary was his wife. And he felt as she did that the mysterious Muleskinner would come for her too.

He had never killed a white man. He had killed in self-defense, not in anger. And he had killed the red man with an attitude of superiority and, when he thought of them, he felt no remorse. What unsettled him was that he knew he could kill for his woman but it would not be for love: it would be for fear of dying cold and alone.

Two

Red walked his roan gelding at a steady pace. His hound Scarlett, as ruddy as the horse, sat perched on the saddle in front of him, his heavy arm steadying her though she comfortably balanced.

They had easily picked up Michael's trail east of the little town and, though Red had ridden hard and fast many times in his tenure with the Rangers, left on his own he was someone who invariably strolled rather than hurried. His backache had lessened during his time at home but riding was still uncomfortable and he stopped frequently to rest and drink. He gained no ground on the Muleskinner.

When Luke and his troop departed, Red had announced his intentions to his wife in a loud and righteous tone. Making his case for seeing to the safety of someone he owed his life to. Rose, who knew him better than she had a right to, considering their age difference and his frequent long absences, had turned her back to him and remained silent. She did not come out to see him off.

Kerry did not fuss when he kissed them goodbye. Katie was more upset that he was taking Scarlett with him. They were accustomed to his leavings. Red had packed and loaded his horse and led it to the front of the house. When Rose did not come out, he entered and announced he was leaving. With her back to him she said in a tight voice, "Well, you had better be going then, hadn't you?"

Red shuffled his feet for a moment and said, "He's just a boy, Rose."

"He's my own age, near enough," she snapped.

He left. Katie held the other dogs leashed as he whistled and coaxed Scarlett to stay with him. He rode to the east of the little town and followed the route out Luke had mentioned. He had taken some of the mule's dung he had collected from his barn and held it to Scarlett's nose. The hound's sides worked like bellows as she huffed and examined the scent; reading it with a depth that would embarrass a scholar. With Red's encouragement and praise she picked up the trail in twenty minutes and bayed and led on, tail wagging with a surety beyond all doubt or reproach.

Red noticed that Michael's trail was mingled with the prints of several other horses and an unshod pony. Feeling validated in his concern for the Muleskinner, he pushed back his guilt a notch but did much hasten his pursuit.

Even bearing Red's considerable weight, the horse could cover more ground than the dog and even a poor tracker like Red could follow the trail of people and animals that flowed in Michael's wake, and so he rode double with Scarlett when she tired. The big horse's stride was long and smooth and the dog sat the horse with serene aplomb.

"For a quiet child, that boy attracts a great deal of company, I was never so popular meself." He rubbed the dog's knobby head and pulled her long ears. She flipped her head back and slapped her wet raspy tongue across his whiskered chin.

"That's the only kissing I'll be receiving for some time. If we get home. I may be sleeping with you still." He frowned realizing he had said if, not when.

"Damn that boy," he whispered. "And damn this pack of disciples wandering through the desert after him, fools and cripples all of us. He's leading us to our maker's doorstep, to be sure."

He twisted and stared back the way they had come. "I have to be wondering who might be following us now, don't I?"

Three

The sun seemed to melt as it sank, spreading out in a bloody stain on the line of the horizon. Low long wispy clouds subtly changed hue, hushing the world. The sunset was a beautiful thing and Luke relaxed and let himself enjoy it until it all turned to gray.

They had buried the bloated stinking corpses of Annabeth's family in back of the house. Annabeth had saved them from scavengers by dragging the dead inside the house and closing them in. She had been too weak and too scared to linger and bury them herself. She had not informed Luke of the grisly scene she had left for him to discover as they forced open the door.

She had laid the boys on their bed but had left the old woman where she lay and had pulled the heavy body of her husband to just inside the door. All of the dead were open eyed and staring. They had had to back away from the house and gather in breath and hold it before running in to drag the bodies out into the fresh air.

Scratching out shallow graves in the hard dry dirt had been a tough task in midday heat and had consumed most of the afternoon. The Apaches found sign and validated that it had been a lone Comanche. Luke decide to rest there for the night and start fresh in the morning.

The morning led them to the bodies of two more men; their skulls picked over but showing dents from heavy blows with a blunt weapon. They had been well armed and capable men but had been killed quickly without a struggle. Tired of digging, they left them where they lay.

They tracked the Comanche back to the pathetic little town they had just departed. The Apache scouts pieced together a confusing series of events describing an odd battle between the trapper and the Indian that had left the Comanche wounded and bleeding.

As they followed the trail it became stranger and more disconcerting to Luke, as it seemed everyone he knew was following the Muleskinner's path; only ahead of him and his troop. It appeared that the unlucky and dangerous boy was being pursued by the vicious and bizarre Comanche and by the trapper in company with the vengeful whore sister of the four outlaws that Michael had killed. And between all these ferocious and terrible people and himself and his Rangers was the large unmistakable hoofprint of his Captain's roan and the toed track of his coonhound.

Luke did not understand how the Comanche fitted into the puzzle of the parade but he could certainly guess at the motives of the other participants. The Indian was the wild card and was Luke's primary responsibility but he worried about his captain; that he would not be in time to come to his aid should he blunder into a situation that was larger and more complex than he could know. He conjectured that that the Comanche and the weird Muleskinner were somehow linked and destined to meet but he did not favor one over the other, believing both to be supernatural and incomprehensible and that they would have to sort the matter out between themselves. Luke could pick up the pieces later.

As the sunset died, he decided that the best course, the best choice, was to ignore his duty and hurry on to the aid of his friend. He wanted to find Red and keep him from the Muleskinner and his travelling circus of death.

Four

"The Lord is my shepherd, I shall not want. He maketh me to lie down in green pastures. He leadeth me beside the still waters: He restoreth my soul: He leadeth me in the path of righteousness for his name's sake. Yea, though I walk through the valley of the shadow of death I will fear no evil." Michael recited the psalm for grace with head bowed and hands folded in all humility. His father sat opposite and mouthed the words.

Their day had dragged past with less than fifty words passing between Michael and his father. There had been impersonal queries as to each other's health and some vague inquiries as to plans for the future, leaving hours of awkward silences.

Both Michael and Gabriel often left the confinement of the house and each other's company on some thin pretext: Gabriel to see to some unimportant chore and Michael simply wandering with the idea that he would revisit some place or thing that he had not thought about for years and that did not move him when he saw it.

Eventually the time for an evening meal neared and Gabriel ludicrously asked Michael if he were staying for supper. Michael pretended to consider the offer, as if he might have a pressing appointment elsewhere, then mutely nodded, wondering if he could take for granted his intention to stay the night, and questioning whether he wanted to.

Gabriel prepared an uninspired, uncelabratory, and meager meal which he uncerimoniously plunked down on the same plain table Michael remembered from his childhood. They scraped their chairs close and Gabriel folded his hands, bowed his head, and asked, in an echo from years earlier, "Michael, will you say the grace, please?"

Michael felt the last half dozen years scatter from him like dry leaves in the cold winds of fall, and he was once again a thin preadolescent boy living in terror in his own home. He swallowed hard and tried not to falter as he choked out the psalm. When he finished, his father reached for the biscuits and butter and began eating.

After, Gabriel rose and removed a steaming kettle from the small iron stove and poured hot water into the porcelain teapot that had survived the journey from Scotland. It reminded him of his mother's hands. After the tea steeped, he poured it into two chipped cups and they both added a great deal of cream and a scant teaspoon of molasses to their cups in turn and spent several minutes mirroring each other, even adopting the same bunched posture, elbows on the table.

Michael recalled the rich brew: creamy tea and buttery oats had been the substitute for mother's milk and kindness. He had not tasted either since he had left.

"Good tea." His remark was hesitant and quiet and went

unnoticed. Michael realized his father had grown hard of hearing.

"Good tea," Michael spoke louder and clearer.

"What? Oh, aye." The older Burns ran his hand through his thinning gray hair as he answered wearily; his hand crooked and shaky, speckled with dark spots. The Texas sun and the frontier had aged his father harshly. He was once tall and imposing to Michael but now was frail and human.

"Will you be spending the night?" he asked, his tone indicating his preference.

"No," slipped out immediately. But, considering, Michael realized he would rather be anyplace else. This was the most he could hope for from his father. Gabriel's love was not there to be given. And some acknowledgment that he was a son and not a stranger was not forthcoming.

"It's time I went to sleep then. You'll see yourself off, I suppose." Gabriel rose and washed his cup in the metal basin of water that resided on a sideboard, then washed his hands and face in the same water.

Michael stood, his head nearly touching the roof beams. His anger was righteous.

"Don't you have anything to say to me?" he asked in a voice too loud to be unheard or ignored. The words and the courage coming from a strength that he had come to treat as a welcome guest.

Gabriel did not turn but he trembled angrily and hesitated. Michael knew he had been heard and understood and his wrath rose, doubling every moment his father continued not to do the right thing. A word, a gesture, a pained expression, any hint would have satisfied.

The revolver appeared in his hand at the end of his outstretched arm, fingers white on the grip, his aim stone steady. Once more in desperation, he asked, "Don't you have anything to say to me?" His clenched teeth barely let the question escape, his tone both pleading and demanding.

Gabriel snorted a brusque laugh devoid of humor;

Michael had heard it many times. "You want to talk?" The inflection rhetorical, derisive. he did not turn. "You've never said more than ten words to me in your life."

Much depended on that answer for both of them. Michael thumbed the hammer back; the ratchet grinding loudly.

Five

He had been close but he had had no opportunity to attack the well-armed boy. The Muleskinner had spent little time out of the saddle. The constant riding coupled to the aching weeping wound along his rib had left him weak. Also, the white mule gave him a queer superstitious feeling that his intuition insisted he follow; he would not attack while the boy was astride the mount. The fight with the mountain man had shaken his confidence and his belief in his intangibility, making him adopt caution.

After several grueling days, he had followed his prey to a small lonely house several miles from a settlement. He watched from hiding as the boy entered the house and was greeted by an elderly man. As the day slowly wore on, he caught several glimpses of the Muleskinner and the old man but as the sun set his eyes grew heavy and his sight blurry and he fell asleep sitting up.

His sleep was shallow, dreams mixing with what passed before his hooded but open eyes. After an hour he was startled awake but could not say what had roused him. Before he could quite piece together his dreams, Michael came bursting from the house, his heavy shoes clumping loudly, hushing the crickets. He watched the boy quickly saddle the mule and ride away.

The Comanche waited for more signs of activity from the

house but when none came, he rose and slipped closer. He was not worried about losing the Muleskinner, the boy could ride far and fast but he left a clear track. As he approached the house, he drew the hammer from its place on his belt, wiggling his wrist to feel its heft. The old man he had seen earlier had reminded him of the man who had shot him and now the two were linked together in his hazy mind.

He still remembered and kept his intention to catch the Muleskinner and finish what he had begun less than a month earlier, but there was time to visit the house, just as Michael had.

Six

Sam lay on his back and let his eyes sweep the broad night sky. Even though he could smell a rain coming, the stars were unobscured by clouds and he took in the panorama before letting his gaze rest on the bright moon.

He was relaxed and warm to the bone, his mind was lazy and content, and Mary, covering him like a blanket, writhed slowly but persistently, her intensity and absorption uninhibited by Sam's inactivity. Her broken and bitten fingernails digging into his chest, plucking at the short soft hairs. Her slightly open mouth drooled, and her closed eyes teared, her long loose hair clinging to her damp back in tangled clumps. Sam's hands rested idly on her bent straddling knees and his fingertips fluttered over the soft skin, caressing and tickling his own nerves with her smoothness. They breathed deeply and evenly, in time with each other.

The moon floated through its arc without the lovers reacting, continuing their relentless slow rhythm as if times grinding progress had ceased. Sam's stamina in love making had moved from control to an unconscious reluctance towards fulfillment, something which sometimes frustrated and worried him and at other times allowed him the space to appreciate their enmeshment. Mary, however, had found grooves and paths that led directly and repeatedly, sometimes grandly, to culmination, and she could doggedly pace these routes until Sam's body would finally give in or give out.

Mary grew weaker after each peak but rather than slide down the far side she would quickly set up for a new pinnacle and push on determinately.

When Sam swiftly and surprisingly filled with heat and pressure and exploded into a short precise release, she collapsed, panting and dizzy. She stroked and hugged Sam, kissing his chest affectionately.

"Sometimes I think you're trying to kill us," Sam mumbled into the night, more thinking out loud than trying to begin a conversation.

"It is like dying a little," her voice was soft and not particularly directed at him either. She toyed with his snake fang necklace, fingering the rows of the hard shell of the rattle.

"Why would you want it so bad then?" Surprised and curious, Sam struggled to look at her, pressing his chin down on his chest, his nose tickled by her hair.

Mary lifted her face and twisted her neck to kiss him gently. "It all stops for a moment," she breathed the words into his mouth.

"What stops?" She remained silent and so he asked again, "What stops?"

"Everything. It's the only time I'm not truly alone." She rested her cheek on his shoulder and shut her eyes, her hair spilling over her face.

Sam let it go, another bit of her he would never understand. They lay unmoving and quiet, both concentrating on the sensation of Sam shrinking and slipping out of her. Mary separated into loneliness. Sam was released from absorption. Both anticipated reunion.

Mary slid off, their bodies slippery with sweat, and melted to Sam's side, her hand reaching to caress his slack member, probing for life and will.

"No use flogging a dead horse," he told her.

"I think there's some spirit left in this snake yet, I tell you what." She grinned. There was a strange stickiness to him and Mary brought her hand close to her face to see. "Seems I got you a little bloody, Sugar."

"What do you mean? Are you all right?" The depth of his concern shocked and pleased her.

"It's all right, it's just my time is all. A little blood won't hurt you none."

Seven

Scarlett rested her head on Red's thigh and snored softly. Red lay fully dressed but barefoot on top of two blankets, his upper back and head propped up by his saddle. His pipe was cold in his right hand and his jug leaned against his ribs while he patted his dog's head with his free hand. Drowsy, and the pain in his spine numbed, he watched as the last little flame in the small fire he had built dwindled and died.

"We are cold and alone now, Scarlet." he was sweating in the stillness. His shirt stuck to his back and belly and the dog occasionally stirred, lifting her head to pant. The dog's open jaws suggested a smile and Red felt that the dog understood his humor, or at least humored him.

"That boy travels fast, he does. We're nowhere near catching him. Don't know what his hurry is, the weather being so fine and all." He took a deep drink, managing the heavy jug with one hand. "We'll find him though, he has only half a Texas to hide in. Should be easy to spot him from all the Comanches we're bound to run into, eh?"

He took off his hat and languidly fanned his face, his thinning red hair stuck to the sides of his head retaining the hat's shape. "Good that I have only daughters. Don't have much luck with boys, it seems. Even you're a girlie, you are." He fanned some warm air over the dog, who picked up her head and panted into the breeze, her eyelids droopy.

"Just as well, I suppose. Here I am, the war hero, Texas Ranger captain..., shooter of little boys. Just like Little Blackie. He come to a bad end, but he had the last laugh on me." Red's mind wandered among images as his mouth rambled the words: still pictures of dead boys and smoking pistols, bleeding slashes, and eyes lifeless and vacant.

"Dead boys is me lot, to be sure. Saw me little brothers die of hunger. Then me wife..., and me first born. He would be near Michael's age now." He sighed deeply and drank deeper. "Never told Rose about him, just you Scarlett, no harm in me telling you, is there?" He rubbed and tugged on the hound's long soft ear. "She does not need to know about that, she thinks me useless enough as it is. And she's right, I'd wager."

He corked his jug and slid down a little on his saddle. "Ah my, will you listen to me, the gloomy fellow. This whiskey must be lazy. It's not doing its job at all." He closed his eyes and let the heat nudge him into sleepiness.

"Texas..., I thought it'd be a lot further from Ireland," he mumbled. "Life is shit."

Eight

Michael had ridden for several hours, giving the mule its head, leaving direction and destination to the animal's whim. As Her Highness slowed and then wandered to a stop, he dismounted, unsaddled, and set up his Spartan camp.

He lay down and let his eyes drift without focus across the freckling of bright stars. The moon low on the horizon, ready to set, it's size, magnified by the low hills it rested on and casting a sickly yellow pallor onto Michael. He was tired but wide awake. His lids were half-closed, hooded and glassy. His body relaxed like spilled water and he did not twitch or shift after he lay down. His breathing was so shallow as to be mistaken for dead.

The mule, hobbled, whickered and snorted, stamping and pawing the dirt. Michael neither moved nor changed position, and Her Highness eventually quieted and stood still but did not sleep.

The moon slid under the earth and Michael let it pass without a blink. His revolver in its holster, dug into his hip, numbing his leg, but he did not alter his position. The knife wound in his side itched but he did not scratch.

Quickly the sky clouded over and warm drops of rain splattered noisily on Michael's stiff dirty clothes. The rain came in short powerful bursts, stopping and starting again every few minutes, and not amounting to much. It failed to cool the night and added a steamy clamminess that weighted the air. The atmosphere pressed down, hushing the crickets.

Nine

All four of the Apache scouts ventured ahead during the night, leaving the Texans to their coffee, whiskey, and sleep. They followed the tracks in the bright moonlight and passed, in succession, various others on the same trail, without themselves being seen or noticed.

They passed Captain Barbarossa and his red long-eared

tracking dog, both of them snoring loudly, and the big roan horse asleep on its feet. They passed a white man having sex with his woman under the stars and heard their moans and their quiet conversation. They passed the house where both the deadly mule rider and the rampaging Comanche had paused, and found a dead old man. And still they followed the trail, clear now for the lack of new tracks overlaying the old.

After many hours of fast riding and only several hours before dawn, they caught up to the mule rider. He was lying on a blanket in a fireless dark camp, awake, and, although the ghostly mule snorted and stamped, the boy remained unaware of them. They did not announce themselves; they had a wariness of the crazy and perhaps possessed white man. They had seen him fight and it had made an impression.

They had no real interest in the ex-ranger. They'd only come upon him in their pursuit of the Comanche and they lingered near the white man's camp out of confusion and an inability to pick up the Comanche's trail. They knew he had visited and observed the white man, that he had crept close enough to speak with him, but after that his movements became unclear and difficult to follow.

The Apaches gathered together in a group and discussed the situation. All agreed that the Comanche was close by and had probably observed their arrival and then moved off, hiding himself and obscuring his own trail. But where he was hiding and how far off he had moved was unknown. They all offered their thoughts freely and each opinion was carefully considered before a decision was made to split up.

One would ride back and bring along the Rangers, guiding them to the mule rider's camp where another would wait. The remaining two would move off together to explore trails and clues and if the Comanche was found, one of the pair would ride back to bring the news while the other kept an eye on him.

The warrior sent to bring up the Rangers, rode at a fast pace, wanting to regain the troop by morning. As the storm came, he slowed a little, the thin rain obscuring his vision. Thunder rolled at regular intervals and lightning flashes blinded him, illuminating the countryside from miles around.

He had only traveled a few miles when an especially close and loud thundercrack split the air. Deafened, he still heard, or perhaps simply sensed, the rapid pounding approach of hoof-beats from behind him. He turned in time to see, with dazzled eyes, a horse and rider and a blurred arm that whipped a heavy headed club, already too close to avoid.

At Michael's camp, the Apache who had stayed had dismounted and hid amidst some rock and brush, forcing his pony to lie down with him, making sure he had a clear view of the boy even after the moon had set and the rain began.

Only a little more than an hour had gone by, when he was surprised by the sound of a rider. He twisted slowly and was startled to find that it was Frog who had gone to bring the Rangers. In the dimness and through the last of the rains his eyes could clearly make out Frog's pony and shield and thought he must have found some sign of the Comanche to have forsaken his task and returned so quickly.

Stepping from his hiding spot, he made a soft hissing noise to catch Frog's attention, who noticed him and turned his pony, picking up his pace to a fast walk.

As he neared, it occurred to him that something seemed unusual about Frog, his hunched posture or the way he guided his pony. By the time he understood it, it was too late.

The Comanche kicked the pony into a sudden sprint and spitted the Apache through the chest with Frog's lance. Leaping from the back of the pony, he stood before the dying man before he had even time to fall. They both gripped the lance and kept eye contact while the hammer whipped forward.

Ten

Sam and Mary followed Michael's tracks, left mostly unobscured by the rain, and came to Gabriel's house at midmorning. Sam, ever bold, decided it would be clever to simply approach the house and ask after the Muleskinner. Mary remained out of sight as Sam ambled his horse into the yard.

As he dismounted, he realized that something was amiss. The door was ajar but not far enough open to let in a breeze and there were several tracks, including moccasin made imprints that had survived the rain, that were fresh and led into the house. He unsheathed his rifle from the fringed buckskin scabbard under his stirrup and cocked the piece, pushing open the door with the muzzle.

As soon as he had stepped through the doorway, he knew intuitively that no one was present, no one who still breathed. Gabriel had wasted no time in rotting and the sour odor of decay hung heavily.

Sam shuffled around inside, sniffing and poking, scanning, but not touching or disturbing the puzzle of what had happened. Mary appeared in the doorway, her shadow spilling in and shading Sam's legs and causing him to turn. He had no thought of sparing her the sight of a corpse, Mary was not the squeamish type.

"The Muleskinner do him in?" She stared dispassionately at the corpse, which lay on its side and face, the thin gray hair stained reddish brown and clumped stiffly together around a gaping hole that had been the back of a skull. A shattered teapot lay in shards on the floor near him, only the spout still whole.

"Hard to say," Sam mumbled. "Head's stove in. Can't say for sure what done it, unless I cut him open."

"Don't do that. Leave the dead in peace, I say." Mary stepped over the threshold and began to rummage through the cupboard and chests. Inside one she happily discovered a not quite full jug that smelled like corn whiskey. She sipped generously several times, her shoulders drooping and her eyelids fluttering.

Sam watched expressionless and then said too loudly for a small space, "I'll get to burying him then."

"What? What the hell for? He's no friend of ours. Just leave him lay and let's go."

Sam set his rifle on the table to took hold of Gabriel's legs and began dragging him out. "Won't take long. I'd want someone to do the same for me should I die alone."

"We ain't got time to spare for foolishness, let's just go, damn it." Her voice rising in both pitch and volume, her words slurred.

Sam did not argue but adamantly continued his dragging, banging the lifeless head on the one stone step that led up to the door. Mary plopped into a chair, loose as a ragdoll, slamming the jug down on the table, causing Sam's rifle to jump and bounce. She grimaced and made inarticulate angry grumbles while fanning her face with one hand, the other twiddling the open spout of the jug.

After a time of sitting and sipping she began to feel better than she had in a week. The light sheen of sweat, that was a constant even in inactivity, felt cool in the shadowy interior and the pain and stiffness in her legs and hips lessened, drawing back from her attention.

She was beginning to feel ready to sit there and not move for as long as the jug lasted, but the sounds of Sam digging and grunting drifted in through the dead air and reminded her that she was mad. She surged upright and tripped out the door, placing herself behind Sam, the old man's body on the ground between them. She assumed an impatient pose, and watched down her nose as he toiled shirtless at his digging.

"You're taking your sweetass time about this. That murdering bastard's getting away from us, I can feel it."

"I don't expect a few more minutes is going to make a difference either way. If you want this to go quicker y'all could lend a hand." Sam almost smirked.

Mary remained almost silent while Sam finished his digging. He dragged and rolled the body into the shallow ditch and scraped dirt over it with the short-handled spade.

"A lot of work for nothing, if you ask me."

"Like I said, I only hope someone will do the same for me when my time comes. I don't like the idea of feeding the buzzards." Sam wiped his brow and studied his handiwork. he gathered a few large stones and placed them atop the grave mound.

"Don't see what difference it makes. When you're dead, you're dead." She nodded her head with certainty and stared off into the shimmering distance.

"You're right," he said with woof. "I just don't like the idea, I suppose."

"Someone's coming." She pointed with her arm fully extended and Sam saw the single rider and dog; wavy forms rippling through the heat and glare.

"I don't care to be here to meet that fellow. This isn't a good time or place." He planted the spade in the ground as a pitiful headstone and turned to retrieve his rifle from the house. Mary stayed close to him, grabbing the jug off the table at the same moment that Sam lifted his gun.

Outside, Sam helped Mary into her saddle, almost tossing her, and after a last studying look at the steadily approaching rider, he gathered up the reins and, swinging up onto his horse, led them off at a trot.

Eleven

"Now there is an unfriendly pair." Red told his dog. "And here I was hoping for some company; no offence to you."

He studied the couple riding away. "That would be the little whore sister and her tracker friend, I'd wager."

They came to the house and Red paused, looking at it. "Now, who the hell lives here?" Scarlett leapt to the ground and Red followed less agilely. He approached the house with one pistol drawn.

"Hello the house," he called. "Captain John Martin, Rangers, coming in." He pushed open the door. The smell of death was strong and the room had been ransacked. "Didn't think those two were common enough for this."

He searched methodically. In the second room, bedside, he found an old Bible. In the family tree he read, "Gabriel Burns; Michael's Da, I suppose."

Outside he noticed the fresh mound of overturned earth. Standing graveside with Scarlett wagging her tail and sniffing in rapture, he said, "I think I know what I'll be finding here. Still I'd best be digging him up to be certain. Won't be nice for me back. Kind of them as to leave me a spade."

He moved some stones and scraped rather than dug. His fifty-fifty chance paid up as the face emerged. He knelt stiffly and pulled the head, up grasping the shirtfront, loose dirt slipping off him.

"I believe I see a family resemblance here. Or maybe it is just the look of death" He turned the head and saw the damage to the skull. "'Twas some mischief involved, it seems." He lowered Gabriel and stood. "Well, old man, who done you in? You're not so fresh as it could have been those two. Was it that handy Comanche?" He hoped it hadn't been Michael.

"You're not saying, eh? I'd best go ask those two sweethearts then." He covered Gabriel up again, giving him his second burial in one morning, and added a few stones of his own. He left the spade where he had found it, in case those who followed might need it.

Twelve

The two surviving scouts draped the bodies of their dead across the ponies they rode in life, and rode hard for the Rangers. They were displeased. They had been badly humiliated, beaten at a game they were the masters of. They felt they now understood the true supernatural nature of the Comanche. He was a walking ghost and would require a different level of tactics. They were not without their own sorceries and they could bring overwhelming force to bear.

The deaths of their kin meant that their resolve was fixed. They would never stop, never deviate; they would see the Comanche dead no matter the cost. The Apache grew no corn, their lands could barely support lizards. They accepted that enemies both tangible and unseen surrounded them in constant hostility; they understood violent and cruel deaths were foreordained. They survived by taking and being the most indurate, the most savage, and the most willing to cut a throat or sacrifice a life. They would always prevail. Their commitment to their persistence was universal. Their anger was deeply ingrained from centuries of hardship. They were reconciled to pain and deprivation - that was fate - but they would never not fight that fate.

They were not discouraged. They were determined. They were not defeated, they were enraged. They would ride back and bring up the dimwitted slow-moving Texans and then they would hunt down this demon Comanche, this ghost that stalked, who had halved their number in a night, who had killed their kin. They would see his skin flayed, his flesh burnt, and his eyes torn from his head

This was a bad day, but it was one among so many. The Muleskinner, the white mule, the demon Comanche, the red captain, the trapper, the Rangers, they were all allied against them and they would survive them all, they would see them all dead. They could survive anything. They were at war with the world. They were Apache.

Thirteen

Michael rode with purpose again. He had risen before dawn saddled Her Highness, and tugged the reins in a specific direction. He pulled the brim of his hat down against the glare of the rising sun and kicked the mule into its tireless jarring trot.

Michael had found a sense of himself, revealed by the lash of the Comanche and he had lost his willingness to reside in the shadows of life. In his fractured inarticulate way, he wanted and needed desperately to confront the truth. He did not think of himself as brave, just invulnerable, and helpless. He was clenched tightly in God's fist. He would be safe if he could only survive the pounding.

There was a palpable urgency in this posture. His face was fixed on the horizon, his torso leaned slightly forward. His relaxed legs seemed to merge with the quickly shifting white legs of the mule.

The wound in his side broke open from the bouncing gate and a stain of fresh thin blood spread out over the existing dry blot. He displayed no discomfort and his back was as rigid as a fence post. He sweated freely but drank no water. The edges of his vision blurred and blackened and when his eyesight cleared, he found himself still in the saddle and being hurried unerringly on his way.

The mule stopped when it needed to, rested for a brief time, and then slowly came into motion again, gathering speed as she went. Highness drank deeply at the infrequent creeks that were slightly swollen from the thundershower, before splashing through, high-stepping in the muddy water. Foam fell from her hind and shoulders as it trotted, splattering down to the dry ground in sheets.

After only a short few hours, Her Highness seemed to know where to go and required no direction or urging. Michael eased in the saddle, his face still fixed on a long sweep of the horizon, but his body relaxing and melting into the mule. He let his mind soften and go with the passing landscape, his fate once more in God's hands.

Fourteen

As the afternoon wore on, Sam became convinced that the big man on the roan horse was following them. He had doubled back twice, leaving a drunken, nearly comatose Mary alone for a half hour at a time, and he'd seen the red-haired trio clearly following, at a little more than a mile behind on the first instance and a little less than a mile on the second trip. He would have felt confident about out-distancing them were he on his own. There had been many times that he had had to run for his life, but Mary's inexperience and inebriated lack of equilibrium sorely hampered them.

He knew that he and Mary were possibly wanted because of the association with her nefarious brothers, but Sam had not thought that Mary's involvement with their activities would warrant any determined pursuit. He was surprised, but he also realized that there were many things he would never know about his companion. Although they talked a great deal, Mary was always guarded and rarely spoke at any length or any detail about events from her past. Her precise relationship with her brothers was unknown to him and specific answers would not be forthcoming. Mary may have committed foul murder for all he knew.

The trail wound around several low rocky hills, outcroppings and mounds that could only be considered more than that relative to the flat expanse they commanded. As they pushed on, Sam, who had been keeping a sharp eye to the ground, quickly dismounted and began to search through the rocks and low brush to the side of the trail. He stooped, suddenly disappearing, and then reemerged, spinning like a desert whirlwind.

Mary, who had not seen him jump from the back of his horse, was startled to see him suddenly appear at ground level and watched in disbelief as he spun, whipping a four-foot rattlesnake out in front of him by its tail. When the snake straightened from the force of Sam's spin, he slid his hand down its length and pinched it tightly just behind the head. He had barely stopped moving before his knife whirled from its sheath, flashed in the bright light, and decapitated the writhing coiling serpent.

"Why that was splendid, Sugar." Her words slurred and she squinted to try to focus. "I've never seen anything like that before, I can see why they call you Rattler."

Sam grinned and strutted a little as he walked toward her. "It's a trick I learned as a boy."

"Is that our supper?" She wiped a hand across her flushed and sweaty face, smearing her features. "I'm not much hungry now, to tell the truth."

"Naw, this here's bait."

"You going to trap a something for later? It ain't that late, we can go further today. I'm not so tired." She knew Sam usually set snares at night.

"Naw, darling, this is to catch us a man." He wiped the bloody blade on his buckskins and sheathed it.

"The mule rider?" She was attempting to concentrate.

"No, that nosey gentleman that's been tracking us. I'm

going to put a stop to that." He squeezed the snake, forcing blood and bile out of the severed neck, spreading it around the rocks and brush before dropping the still undulating carcass to the side of their trail.

Mary watched him puzzled; his ways and means were as much a mystery to her sometimes as hers were to him. When he finished, he swung gracefully into the saddle and kicked the horse into motion, leading them forward several hundred yards before turning, doubling back in a loop, and heading up the side of one of the low hills that commanded a view of where he had caught the snake.

"Y'all wait down there out of sight till I say you should come," and, handing the reins of his horse to Mary, he dismounted, drawing is rifle from its place.

"You be careful, Sugar," she said as he walked away from her, heading further up the hill and out of her sight. She moved herself and the horses around the side of the hill as Sam had told her and climbed slowly and stiffly from the saddle. She was sweating and sobering, biting her fingernails and squirming with impatience.

It seemed to her that hours passed and she fought with difficulty the rising desire to go up the hill and find Sam. She would call out to him every so often, but softly, almost in a whisper, unable to restrain herself. Her skin was pale and her eyes were wide and round, she shook. She had lost all of the men in her life to violence and, although her confidence in Sam was unshakable, her faith in the fairness of life was not worth an expletive. She never questioned the necessity for violence, even though its consequences invariably careened or rippled towards her.

When the shot came, muted but unexpected, she jumped and cried out, her hands leapt to her head and clutched handfuls of hair and her feet slid in the loose gravel as she scrambled up the hill.

Fifteen

Luke watched the Apaches ride in, his face hardening beyond his normal banality at the site of the two dead scouts draped over the backs of their ponies. He pulled his hat from his head and wiped the sweat from his brow on the back of his arm and then fanned himself slowly with the heavy hat.

"I hope that Muleskinner didn't kill our scouts. Several Rangers we're near enough to hear and nodded in appreciation.

Luke spoke at some length with the evasive and sometimes simply unresponsive Apaches, who seemed preoccupied and intent upon dealing with their fallen comrades. He learned that they had encountered the Comanche and that it was he and not Michael who was responsible for the two dead warriors. Luke shook his head and whistled in wonderment at the prowess of a man who could sneak up on Apaches, and wondered again if Captain Red had any chance alone.

They were under a high hot sun, out on the hard rocky ground, the three of them squatting, two across from him while he asked if they had located Captain Red and received only nods of affirmation and nothing more no matter how many times or ways he asked. His inquiries after the whore and the old man or Michael met with the same sparse results. The old Luke would have admired these men as they frustrated his every effort to pin them down, but the burden and responsibility of command had dulled his interest in the indecipherable. They're careful but casual ability to thwart his authority did intrigue him but he needed to know and lives depended on him. He found himself getting angry and he had not been angry for years.

He stood up and stomped away from the scouts and

they're dead. He paced up and down a short line, suddenly changing his direction as he thought up and dismissed his options. Finally, his mind was set and fixed. He marched back and stood between the living and the dead Apaches and told them that they would forget about the Comanche for the time being and lead the troop directly to Captain Red.

His display of autocracy and decisiveness engendered no reaction at all from the stone like warriors. Luke was certain that they had understood everything he said; he had quickly figured out that their inability to understand English was a convenient contrivance and so he did not repeat himself. Several minutes passed in a silent standoff and Luke believed himself victorious as the two began speaking softly to each other in their own language.

They stood at the same moment and one of them nodded his head in acquiescence. Much to Luke's astonishment, they saddled up and appeared ready to do as he had demanded. Luke shouted at the men to mount up, as he moved quickly to his own horse. His anger evaporated and was replaced with a hopeful enthusiasm; they would be in time to aid their Captain after all.

Sixteen

Red kept his horse just behind his dog which, nose to the ground, ran at what for the big Roan was a jerky trot. They followed a winding route that led them through a series of low rocky hills and hummocks. The sun was lower than its zenith and was shining into Red's face beyond the ability of his hat to shade, making him squint.

The surroundings and his limited visibility made him wary and nervous. He constantly scanned the hilltops for signs of ambush but the glare made persistent observation difficult. He tried his best to keep moving quickly until they were once again out in the open.

Even though the dog had the scent and lead him unerringly, he was considering whistling the hound up into the saddle to hurry their progress, for he thought he knew where Michael was headed. Having spent considerable time with the boy, he'd gotten to know something of the Muleskinner's ways. Michael was odd but he was not unpredictable. Without someone to tell him almost exactly what to do, Michael was generally at a loss. Although a fanatic and a loner, he had little will or initiative of his own. Michael had tried to return home but, as the corpse of his father mutely but succinctly testified, that had not worked out. With unequal parts of intuition and deductive reasoning mixed and blended by inebriation, Red was confident he had guessed Michael's destination.

Red pursed his lips and began to whistle, but Scarlett had found something of great interest and was oblivious to him. She circled something Red could not quite make out in the bright light and sniffed and slobbered excitedly. As Red drew up he could discern that it was something bloody and mangled, whether it was a human body part, not something rare enough in his experience, or the remains of a small animal, he could not tell from his high seat. He stood in the stirrups and leaned forward, preparing to swing his leg over the horse's rump and dismount, when Scarlett flinched and the sound of the rifle shot floated through the thick hot air.

Red froze for a split-second, his eyes widening with horror as he watched his dog fold in on herself sideways, quickly, like a bear trap snapping shut. She then staggered a few steps, her four paws dancing lightly on the hard dirt, then collapsed, wriggling and writhing, desperately but futilely trying to regain her feet. A great gout of blood spurted from the ragged hole in her side and the pained betrayed expression slipped from her soft brown eyes. Her movements ceased abruptly and a moan drifted out with her last breath. Red and his dog kept eye contact until Scarlett's light went out.

Red slammed back down into the saddle and jerked the reins, spinning and rearing the already electrified horse. He spurred directly towards the hill that the shot had come from, dropping the reins and drawing both pistols, screaming his furious banshee cry as the roan thundered forward.

Without any apparent target Red fired his pistols one at a time, leaning forward against the rush of the horse, a bloody red glare fringing his vision. The grey smoke from the pistols clouded and swirled in his wake, mingling with a dust kicked up by the pounding hooves.

As he neared the base of the hill Red caught sight of the sniper as his head and rifle barrel lifted from its rocky cover at the top of the hill, and he snapped off one hasty shot before smoke belched from the rifle's muzzle. The gelding continued running for two full strides and then pitched forward onto his knees, his large head digging into the ground and its hindquarters lifting.

As the horse went down, Red was thrown forward and flipped over to land on his back ahead of the dying horse. He skidded the length of his body and rolled part way onto his side before stopping with a jerk. He had desperately held onto his pistols, even cocking the one he had just discharged while hurtling over the roan's head. Red surged to his feet and, with only a quick backward glance at his horse and an angry yell, he scrambled up the side of the hill; brute strength overcoming the lack of firm footing and propelling him to the top of the hill in only a few seconds.

He burst onto the summit firing both revolvers simultaneously. He recognized the older man who had been escorting the whore, even though he had only seen him briefly, and at a distance, the day before; the man's dress being distinctive. He was finishing loading the rifle, pulling the ramrod from the barrel and watching as Red fired upon him.

Both of Red's shots kicked up dust and ricocheted with a loud whine missing their marks by inches. In a rage, Red dropped his guns and launched himself through the air, his hands held like grasping talons before him. The heavy barrel of the Hawken rifle clubbed down on his back is he slammed into the mountain man's torso and brought them both to the ground.

Red wrestled on top of his opponent and shoved the gun away with one hand as his other, balled into a huge tight fist, powerfully slammed across the old man's bearded jaw. Red pounded with the one fist as Sam, dazed and fighting to remain conscious, curled his arms and legs together in a protective ball. Red jerked the gun away from Sam and continued to flail and pummel the retreating and beaten man with both fists. Red's breath was a gasping wail and his chest heaved from his exertions. His face purpled and throbbed.

With ears deafened from gunfire and eyes clouded by dust, madness, and smoke, Red still heard and then noticed the frail weaving woman who stood before him, needing both hands to pull the hammer back on her small pistol, her wild hair swirling and her face contorted into a wide-eyed snarl.

Though the muzzle bobbed unsteadily, she was close enough to be generally on target and Red stopped in mid-punch, his enraged brain struggling to comprehend. Before he had a chance to calm, his body bolted up, his bear like bulk towering over the slight woman. As he grabbed and deflected her aim, she pulled the trigger.

The little ball slashed across Reds shoulder, gouging a deep furrow and cracking his collarbone, but he reacted only by yelling and punching her on the side of her head. Her legs went weak and she began to fall before the back of his hand swung back and whipped her head to the other side. She dropped to the ground, her legs melting out from under her and her chest leaning against Red's leg.

As Reds actions began to return to his conscious control, the pain in his shoulder grew from an ember to a blaze. The fractured bone hurt when his chest moved to breathe and he could not calm or slow his needy lungs.

"Damn!" he cursed in a whispered rasp. "Just what I fucking needed." His front now hurting more than his back, he almost laughed before he remembered that his dog and horse had just been killed.

"You fucking bastards! I. ..." he had begun to turn when the tomahawk blade bit deeply into his spine, severing the cord that carried thought from his head to his body. Red fell with the softness of a ragdoll and the heaviness of a slaughtered bull. He landed on his side, the tomahawk still embedded where his neck met his shoulders and swaying, like a slowing pendulum, in time with this diminishing breath.

Before he died, Red's eyes shifted and looked up into the face of Sam who stood above him and then into Mary's, her face only a foot from his own and told them, "Me wife will never forgive me now."

Seventeen

He heard the sharp cracking sounds and was aroused from his stupor, his blurred and exhausted mind lured and caught by the call of gunfire. He'd been sitting on his pinto pony, his eyes open but unfocused, a string of sticky drool hanging from the corner of his mouth. He'd doubled back on his trail to throw off the two Apaches who had been searching for him and towards morning, as it became clear he had eluded them, he had drifted into his unasleep, unawake state, that constituted the only rest he now knew.

He was lost and a little confused about what he wanted to do, but it seemed simple and obvious to move towards the sounds of conflict and his pony started off in that direction before he had made a decision. As he rode the shots stopped, but by that time he had pinpointed their source as the top of a nearby hill. He held back, unable to see who or how many had been doing the shooting.

He carefully and slowly moved around the hill while still mounted and look for clues as to what was happening. He found tracks that he was already familiar with and a dead dog and dead horse that he recognized. From these he was able to discern the participants if not the outcome and that was enough for the moment. He quickly withdrew out of sight of the hilltop but kept the hill in view.

As he waited and watched, his mind cleared a little and he remembered his purpose and task, and his pursuit of the Muleskinner. He knew where to find the white boy's trail and he did not imagine he could lose him. He also was beginning to believe he knew where the boy was headed. His encounter with the Apaches had irritated him and he was no longer in the mood to tolerate anyone dogging his trail.

Over the next hour, he caught several glimpses of the old man and his woman but saw nothing of the big red-bearded man who had ridden the gelding. He assumed that the old man had killed the big Ranger in the gunfight he had heard; a fact he was ready to believe as he held a high opinion of the old man's abilities.

An hour later, the moon rose opposite the setting sun. It was full and would light the night like a lantern. He fingered the hard head of the hammer and settled in to wait for nightfall. As the minutes passed, he picked at the abscessed scabbed groove along his ribs and grew ever more impatient but held himself in check. He would not be overconfident or underestimating again.

Eighteen

"That fellow nearly took my scalp." Sam's arms were bruised and bloody and his jaw was swollen and achy. Two of the teeth on the top and right of his mouth were loose enough to wiggle with his tongue, which he had bit. "I don't believe he broke my jaw though. Lucky for that."

"What the hell happened?" Mary remained where she was, lying on the ground a foot from Red's body, as Sam bent down and, with his foot on the dead man's back, jerked free his tomahawk.

"I shot his dog. It seems he was very much fond of it." He returned his weapon, tucking it through his belt behind his back. He retrieved his hat from where it had fallen during the fight and slapped it repeatedly on his leg to shake off the dust.

"You shot his dog! What for?"

"I had hoped that if I shot the dog he'd run for cover, being caught out in the open like that, and we'd ride away. I don't believe he could have tracked us without the dog, ye see, then we would be free of him. I did not want to kill him. But he took it all personal and charged right for me, so I shot his horse out from under him. But the angry son of a bitch still kept coming, got up here before I could reload, wouldn't think a big fella like him would be able to move so fast. Seems I misjudged the whole thing start to finish."

"I believe he wasn't the scary type." Mary spoke softly while studying the body.

"This is a sorry day."

"You killed him for me." Mary scrambled to her feet and walked unsteadily around Red to stand next to her man and hold his arm.

"I did not intend to. But that does not make a difference to him now. What's done is done. Don't know how I could have figured the whole thing so wrong." Sam shook his head, more bothered by his plans going awry.

"It appears I'll be digging a second grave today."

Nineteen

The Lipans rode at the head of the hard riding Ranger troop, keeping the Texans from being distracted. They led them in a wide arc around the trail of the Muleskinner, taking them hours out of their way but avoiding any chance of encountering Captain Red-Beard or the old man and his woman.

It would be dark soon and the Texans would insist that they stop for a meal and perhaps the night, putting them still further behind the fast-moving Comanche. They had few options. The Texans could be stubborn and difficult to control, and they needed them.

Just before dark, Luke did command that they stop and make camp. It had been a long tiring day of hard travel in difficult heat and he was satisfied that they had gained ground on Captain Red and would catch up to him the next morning.

As the men made small fires and prepared food, Luke unrolled his bedding and sat down. He noticed that the Apaches had unsaddled their ponies and that they were saddling fresh mounts. Luke sighed deeply shook his head, and laboriously climbed back to his feet and shuffled wearily over to the scouts.

"What are y'all doing? Don't you want some food?"

Turtle shook his head no and bent down to cinch the saddle tightly but said nothing.

Luke sighed again, "Where are you going?" he asked directly in a louder, more insistent tone.

Turtle paused long enough to point upward with his chin and then began wrestling with his reluctant horse's head to fix the bit.

Luke looked upward and saw that the sky was filling rapidly with dark heavy clouds and noticed that the already humid air was becoming even more saturated. "Storm coming," he observed and nodded in understanding. They would need to secure the trail before the impending rain washed away the tracks.

The two Lipans leapt into their saddles in synchronized motion and waited, looking down at Luke patronizingly for permission to leave. Luke stepped back and resignedly waved them forward. He did not watch them leave as he walked back to his bedding and lay down. He hoped to get an hour or two of sleep before the sky opened up and the furor came.

Twenty

Michael walked the mule to the edge of the little creek as the sun, obscured and dulled by low black storm clouds to a bloody crimson smear, paused before setting behind him. He dismounted and let the reins drop. The exhausted mule hung its head and did not move, too tired even to travel a few feet more to drink from the rippling creek.

The water was shallower and the flow narrower than Michael remembered, the burned husk of the wagon had fallen off one wheel and spilled some of its charred load. Nails lay partly obscured in the dirt, reddened with rust. The clean white skeleton of the mule that had been killed for meat by the Comanches was jumbled and rearranged into an unrecognizable beast.

He stood with his feet casually braced, his head tilted slightly downward and his dirty sable hat pulled so low as to touch his eyebrows. His plain shirt was buttoned to the top and tucked-in at his back and belly; the sleeves, too short for his long arms, we're unfastened and rolled up to his elbows. The massive revolver dragged the belt with the silver Mexican buckle, to an exaggerated slant at his left hip, and the braided leather whip was coiled diagonally over one shoulder and around his waist, before being tucked into itself.

The sun reluctantly drained away and Michael remained motionless. Only when engulfed in nearly total darkness did he hesitatingly abandoned his vigil and move to unsaddle and water the mule.

He ate no food nor made a fire but simply unfurled his bedding and stretched out as he was, removing only his hat, which he rested on his chest. His hand unconsciously covered the knife wound in his side and the damp spots that stained his shirt. As the night grew deeper and the air filled with warm moisture, Michael became feverish and stopped sweating for the first time in weeks. His mind reeled between unfinished thoughts and unnamable sensations, the festering wound sparking sharply and painfully across his belly and a nonspecific fear chipping out and a rotting away his sense of time and place.

He was tired and weakened from travel and lack of sleep, and meals, and the festering wound. The anxiousness kept him from a sleep that might heal him, or at least ease him. He became chilled and began to shiver, his teeth chattering loudly. He could smell rain coming. As he hugged himself in an effort to be still and relax, he began to feel that he must act if he were to survive, that being passive to his pain would only prolong it and, though he was without energy, it would be better to make an effort in his own behalf.

He slowly and shakily came to his feet and gathered kindling and wood from the ruins of the wagon and the broken kegs and piled them next to the wagon. He took planks and made a shelter for the fire, by leaning the boards against the wagon, leaving wide spaces for the smoke to escape, and built a large bright fire. He uncoiled the whip from his torso and set it next to his hat but kept his gun belt on. He dragged his bedding under the wagon and sat as close to the fire as possible without being burnt; first facing the fire then turning around to warm his back.

When large fat drops of rain began to sizzle and steam in the blaze, he tipped his head up and opened his eyes to be blinded by a brilliant spark of lightning that whip-cracked across the sky and made the hair on his arm stand up.

"Storm's here," he mumbled to himself. "It's going to come down fast and hard now."

Twenty-One

"We had better get us off this hilltop before we're struck by lightning." Sam stood over the fresh shallow grave and spoke over his shoulder to Mary, who sat hunched several yards behind him, drinking from her jug. "I'm going to need to make a fire. I worked up a sweat scratching out this fella's bed, I'll be feeling a chill soon. Hot meal would help some too."

"I can warm you up." Mary suggestive voice brushed him like a cold wind.

"I just killed this white man," he told her in a stern tone. "Don't think it would be right."

"That son-of-a-bitch help killed my brothers. I'll shit or fuck on his grave as I please." Sam winced under the heated violence of her words and he knew, without having to consider it, that she could not be reasoned with or turned aside. How she felt was how it was. And Sam respected that logic even if you could never understand it.

"Don't know what difference it makes him being white anyhow," she muttered.

"There's an order to things," Sam asserted as he turned and went to sit beside her.

"Not that I can find. Dead is dead."

"Maybe so," he sighed. The daylight had faded as Sam had

worked at his digging. The ground was stony and he had not brought the spade with them from the farmhouse, forcing him to dig Red's grave with the tomahawk that he had killed him with.

"I'm not used to all this digging," he said after a few minutes. "I'm already starting to stiffen up."

"Stiffening up is a good thing, Sugar." she leaned into him. As Sam dipped his head to kiss her upturned face, he smelled and tasted the powerful odor of alcohol and saw that Mary was too drunk to focus her eyes or perhaps even to stand up. He was tired and feeling his age and injuries, too tired to fight Mary's stubbornness or to carry her down the hill.

They lay back and grappled clumsily with each other, pushing aside clothing and kissing whenever their open mouths came close. Mary was not able to coordinate well enough to stay on top of Sam and eventually slid off and lay on her back, pulling Sam down on top of her.

Sam entered her abruptly. Her eyes clamped shut, Mary whispered, "Daddy," inside a deep moan and Sam ground in deeper still, trying to bury himself. Rain splattered on his back and on Mary's bare legs, which she raised and crossed over Sam's hips, locking him in almost too tightly for movement.

He wondered peripherally if it was the killing that had kindled his fires but when he remembered it he felt only ambivalence. But the killing had marked his relationship with Mary, given it permanence. He had sometimes wondered during the time he had been with her if she might leave him. She was unpredictable and changeable. Today he had killed a total stranger for her, and he knew that she would not leave him.

The realization gave him a moment of fear but it was only a reflex and he surrendered to a part of himself he had not known existed and into a feeling of more than simple contentment. When Mary moaned and clutched him tighter, he moaned back as the inevitable overwhelmed him even as it overcame her.

Sam lifted his head to hover over hers and smiled into her half-closed eyes. He kissed her and noticed how her hips cradled his. She smiled back, a lazy toothless grin and released him from her embrace.

"I'm hungry." She had never asked for food when there was drink available.

"I'll build a big fire and make us something special. Maybe some fried apples and onions." He stood and began to turn when the hammer struck him on the side of his head. His head turned as if to have one last look at Mary. He fell to his back at the Comanche's feet. The Comanche dropped and straddled him, a thin rusted knife in his off hand. He dropped the hammer and grabbed the leather thong that held the fangs and rattle. He pulled and Sam's chin lifted. He dragged the knife across Sam's throat severing the thong and cutting Sam deeply.

Sam had felt the ground come up to strike him and had begun to grope for his weapons but lost all use of his limbs as an icy chill flooded through him. He shivered and wondered how the rain and heat had so quickly turned to snow and cold. He had been told as a boy that hellfire and damnation awaited him. He did not believe in an afterlife, but thought it would be a miserable joke if hell actually existed and then turned out to be cold.

The dark clouds had blocked all moonlight and the hilltop was shrouded in black. The rain that had been falling erratically was beginning to make a concerted effort, splattering consistently and growing in intensity, muffling sound. Mary could not tell what had happened. Sam lay dead at her feet, and she knew only that he had fallen. A lightning flash lit the hilltop and she saw in that second her only anchor to life dying under the knife of a demonic savage.

Paralyzed and unbelieving, she felt herself being pushed back and turned onto her belly, her skirt lifted. She did nothing. Mary had been raped many times in her two decades;

it was no surprise. Her hand, of its own will, rested on the butt of her pistol inside her skirt pocket but she had not the strength to use it. The Comanche shoved away and stood and Mary rolled to her back and looked up at him, ready for death. Another bolt, louder and more vivid than the first slashed through the dark and displayed him standing holding his bloody member.

As the thunder rolled and cannoned, the man howled and screamed and slapped his palms to his face, streaking the black soot with the blood of her womb.

Mary understood intuitively what she had inadvertently done, how she had wounded Sam's killer by her very nature. Her disgust with his weakness overcame her resignation and she drew the gun and fired all five rounds.

Twenty-Two

The Apaches rode as quickly as possible but were slowed by the rain and poor visibility. They were having little luck finding the Comanche's trail. The storm had been sudden and violent washing away prints, forcing them to follow other sparse clues: broken shrubs, pressed down grass, overturned stones. It required much more time and attention and a great deal of guesswork. They were also less sure if they were following the right trail and not the Muleskinner's.

It had taken hours to cover less than a dozen miles. The rain, however, had begun to ease and the sky to open, bright moonlight making their way clearer. The trail led them along a shallow sided ravine, dug out by a narrow creek. As they traveled, the creek began to rapidly rise. They hoped the trail did not cross the creek as it soon would be too high and too swift to ford.

The pale light was harsh and hard and defined the land in sharp edges. The swollen creek rushed with a grinding roar. The heat and heavy damp were overbearing and the night conspired to make the Apaches tense and uneasy. It seemed that nothing lived here. That this was a land inhabited solely by ghosts.

Unafraid of anything that breathed, their relationship with the unseen was hostile and a source of dread. They were confident in their ability to escape or overcome tangible difficulties but nature's wrathful and malevolent side was often invisible and mysterious.

It made their present task more heroic. The Comanche was perhaps not completely natural but spectral in part, dangerous on many levels, a monster to be exterminated.

Twenty-Three

He pushed his pinto hard through the blinding rain, eating up the miles even as the earth washed away beneath the pony's unshod hooves. His mind heaved with a violence that matched the thundering storm. Defiled, stained, marked, wounded by the bleeding of a woman's mystery. He could not fathom the repercussions. Already doomed and wraithlike, he could not imagine what new contortion would ripple through and twist his soul further.

When the lightning flash had revealed his contamination, he had staggered back in shock, stepping on the round side of Mary's jug, which rolled out from under his foot, spilling him onto his back just as the shots screamed through the air where he had been standing, the muzzle flash illuminating the woman's arm and the strained angry face behind it. He turned onto his belly and scrambled away like a dog, the jug sticking in his hand when he leaned on it to leverage himself to his feet, and remaining with him as he bolted onto his pony's back and sprinted away.

The weary pinto had kept up a strong canter as he guided it unerringly to the birthplace and the catalyst of his brutal odyssey. No longer having any doubt as to the destination of the Muleskinner, he hurried to the rendezvous, ready to settle and rewrite his destiny. The storm seemed to ride with him, keeping pace, sweeping him forward.

The jug sloshed as he rode and its open mouth spilled liquor on his hand. He knew the smell and taste of alcohol and remembered what it had done when it he had seen it spill into the fire, rolling from the dead Mexican's fingers. His hand was a grasping one, always reaching for, and finding, a tool, a whip, a hammer. If he had picked it up, he must have wanted it, had a purpose in mind. He held it more carefully.

This night he would reach a conclusion. He wanted to set his world back on a balanced path, or extinguish his own half-material existence. It needed to be finished, for he feared the light of day shining on his polluted manhood. He had little time left to remain potent. His power had been infected and he could feel it leaking out. He did not know if he could be cleansed or redeemed but he did not want to keep dwindling away. If he could kill the Muleskinner. He would stem the flow of his life's ebb, plug the leak that had come when he had failed to kill him one long nightmare earlier.

Still hours before sunrise, through the thinning curtain of rain, he saw a dim flicker of orange firelight and the broken shadowy bulk of a burned wagon. He dismounted before his pony came to a stop, smoothly slipping from its back but staggering and soft-legged as he hit the ground. And, with the hammer in one hand and the jug in the other, without any attempt at stealth, he weaved closer to the wavering glow.

Twenty-Four

She had kept cocking back the hammer and pulling the trigger even after all five chambers had discharged. Deafened and blinded by the roar and flash of the little pistol, she sat with her legs stretched straight out in front of her, her narrow chest heaving as she gulped for breath. The revealing lightning remained frustratingly dark for several long moments before once again flashing and illuminating the hilltop.

Mary saw herself all alone. The horses hobbled though they were, had abandoned her and were nowhere in sight. She had seen Sam's body lying still at her feet in the brief moment of brightness but failed to immediately recognize it. After the darkness had again covered her, she pieced together the scene in her mind with the out of plac, limp figure, sprawled on his back, his head tilted up and his arms thrown wide as if ready to embrace.

She tossed aside the revolver she still held at arm's length and crawled quickly over to the body, recognizing the feel of his clothing and beard and understanding the sticky wetness under his chin. As her eyes accustomed to the blackness they filled with tears which became lost amidst the raindrops that filtered through her hair and washed over her face.

Sam's corpse was already cold to the touch. His clothes were soaked through with the cool rain and stuck to the pallid skin. His eyes were closed and his inertia was so complete that he seemed as if he had been dead for days rather than minutes.

"He should have killed us both. I should be with you now." Mary's lament was soft and weak, it did not carry under the blanketing noise of the rain.

His form seemed smaller than when he had been animate. His graceful economy was reduced to utter and simple immobility. In life, Mary had seen Sam remain motionless for hours but his being had been concentrated, giving him tangible presence even in repose, like a snake at rest but unmistakably alive. Now he was only a collection of bones and flesh, empty and derelict, hollow. There was no Sam there at all, as if living had left no trace.

Twenty-Five

Michael felt warmer when he awoke and, as he opened his eyes, he believed that he must have slept through until morning, for there was a soft glowing light seeping in through his interwoven eyelashes. But the light was flickering and blue hued and there was darkness back-dropping the glow.

As Michael realized he was on fire, he lurched to his feet, holding his arms out to his sides as he inspected and accepted the blue flames that dances and fluttered from fingers to shoulders. Making a human cross, he glimmered and stood in bright highlight against the shadowed landscape and cloud darkened horizon, a grotesque beacon on the flat sweep of the Texas plain.

Michael's skin blistered on the backs of his fingers and the itchy, stinging pain interrupted his astonished paralysis. He spun slowly and ineffectually flapped his arms, the quirky bashful flames were fanned into momentarily flaring. Panic and anger began to rise and overwhelm him and black smoke began to smolder from him has his clothes started to burn. His blundering steps brought him closer to the swollen and now raging creek, the level having risen to reach the tops of the slope of the ravine. He fell the final steps, his face and chest splashing into the fast-flowing water, which tugged at him and dragged him into a twisted pose that made turning, rising, or rolling over difficult and he thought he would drown.

As he thrashed and sputtered a calm begin to seep into him from the outside, like the cool water that soothed the burns and smothered the flames. When he eased his flailing a little he felt the current's pull and it occurred to him that he might be able to swim with it and to safety. He relaxed and pushed deeper into the stream.

The rush of water grabbed him with an alarming swiftness and power and carried him a dozen yards in a single heartbeat. But it spun him and spit him up onto the bank far enough that he could lift himself up onto his forearms and free his body from the tendrils of flow that still hauled at his legs.

Shoes slipping in the mud, he dragged himself clear with the strength of his arms alone. Free of the water he rested on his belly, his chest heaving against the wet sand as he struggled to catch his breath. He had not as yet had time to consider how he came to be on fire, but he now imagined that he must have rolled into the fire that he had slept so near for warmth.

The sound of Her Highness snorting and stamping brought his head up and he realized that he had been hearing it, but not listening, since he had awakened. When he looked around he found himself only a body length from the Prince of Darkness and the Lord of Fire.

Michael could easily have slid back into the creek and let fate, luck, and the swift water carry him away. He could have trusted in the Lord's mercy and, cradled in his watery hand, floated far from the reach of his tormentor. That was why the water was behind him, the choice and the temptation.

Michael stood tall and faced the Comanche. He did not feel strong or brave or invulnerable, merely resolute. The calm that had settled into him when he was immersed in the creek had stayed and become commitment and congruence. No part of Michael wanted to flee. His need to believe that life was more than the harsh fabric of the everyday had brought his ordinarily divergent wants into accord. If he failed to meet his task, he would surrender all hope that there might be a just center around which the world turned and that the finer lighter tones that he'd only recently glimpsed, might color his remaining days and his life beyond.

Without anger, without righteousness, purely in his own self-interest, he took a step towards Satan. He drew his revolver, the handle slick in his grip, and thumbed back the hammer while he stared into the Comanche's eyes; the whites gleamed, with a hard sharpness against the streaked black war paint.

The trigger's pull felt light as a feather as Michael squeezed. The mechanism tripped with a suddenness and Michael felt the hammer falling the long way to the anvil. The percussion cap burst with a quick crack but the chamber, filled with damp powder, failed to spark and remained silent. The terrible boom and gout of orange flame that should have erupted from the muzzle, never came, leaving Michael holding only an empty threat.

Twenty-Six

Luke was unable to sleep. He'd sat with some of his men under a tarpaulin during the rain and then he'd laid down on top of it after the storm had passed. The air was more than warm and he was tired from the hard riding, but when he closed his eyes, his mind, usually practical and steady, had refused to relax.

He was uneasy that his scouts had led them in one direction and then had ridden off in another. He was worried about the fate of his predecessor, a man he admired and liked. He was disturbed by the nature of the Comanche that he had been pursuing, who seemed unpredictable beyond the ordinary, random and dangerous as a lightning bolt. He was afraid for his men. It was one thing to be one of them, to tend their wounds, to be a companion, it was another to be responsible for them, and to send them to their deaths.

He had felt a certain equilibrium prior to being placed in command. A stasis of emotion that had allowed him to survive the death of his family and to be the unperturbable doctor to Red's Rangers. But responsibility was eroding his stony detachment. Most of the men in the troop were younger than he was by many years. Red had been his senior in age as well as rank and, when he had retired, Luke had lost his fraternal anonymity and inherited the role of father and the involvement and worry that went with it.

He thought he knew why Red drank.

He had not trusted the Lipans but he had relied on them. In the quiet of the night he again second-guessed that decision. He had wanted to follow Red but thought he needed to catch the Comanche. Once more he wondered if he would be too late. He had never wanted to lead the troop but there was no one else and, on that decision, there was no turning back. It was time for him to lead and be the leader Red had been.

Luke stood up. He fixed his hat to a more serious angle and shouted loudly for his men to, "Get to your feet, boys! Saddle up, we're pulling out in five minutes."

The men were used to early hours but it was still several hours before sunrise and they muttered irritable curses while doing as they were told. They mounted and assembled. When they were awake sufficiently to wonder what was possessing their lieutenant, one of them thought to ask, "Where we headed?"

"I have an idea I know where that Muleskinner might be and I believe that's where the Captain and that devil Comanche are going to be."

"Where's that?" Another asked.

"Where we found him in the first place. It isn't that far from here. We can be there an hour or two after dawn."

"Hell, let's get going then," a third Ranger urged and the

rest of the troupe excitedly chorused their agreement a moment later.

Luke smiled. These boys, his boys, were good boys.

Twenty-Seven

He dropped the empty jug, the contents of which he had poured over the sleeping Muleskinner. He had almost laughed to see the white man burning bluely, his arms lifted as if he were once again nailed to the side of the wagon. But though the boy burned, he did not seem troubled by it and it turned from gratifying to freakish.

When the Muleskinner dashed suddenly to the raging creek and hurled himself face first under the water, he let go of the burning stick he had plucked from Michael's fire to touch him to light. He watched from the bank as Michael was nearly swept away, and as the boy pulled himself to his feet, he drew the hammer from his belt.

He waited unperturbed as the boy drew out his gun and did not flinch when the trigger was pulled. He felt half immersed in death and was not worried about bullets or pain. The little bit of dying he had left to accept, was so close as to be inevitable. He had been shot once and survived to kill the clever and dangerous old man who had shot him. This boy has never been a serious threat, only a pebble he had stumbled over.

When the pistol failed to discharge, he lifted the hammer high and, screaming a horse whoop, launched himself at Michael. He covered the distance between them in an eye blink. His arm whipped across with the full force of his twisting torso and running leap, the iron head aimed unerringly to shatter Michael skull. Michael smoothly lifted his arm and stepped into the blow, his forearm colliding with a bruising impact against the wooden haft and his ducking head crashed into the Comanches jaw, making the man's teeth clack noisily together.

They immediately closed and began to grapple, clumsily unable to grip each other well with the one free hand each had available. They tried to strike with their weapons but were too close and too tangled to apply much force and the blows went largely unnoticed. The Comanche quickly thrust upward with his knee and the Muleskinners lungs emptied with a woof but before his foot came back down, Michael twisted him off balance and they both fell to the ground, landing on their sides with enough force to make their bodies bounce.

They rolled over and back several times, first one on top, then the other. Ultimately Michael's greater weight and size enabled him to pin the other down and sit upright, his knees straddling the Comanches hips. As Michael raised up, the warrior used the distance to strike him a glancing blow, the hammer nicking Michael's forehead and making his vision swim with colorless sparkles. He struck back with the heavy revolver, clouting the man on the shoulder near his neck.

Both men grabbed out with their free hands to keep the other from striking again. They wrestled in a stalemate of control, Michael stronger and in a position of greater leverage but the Comanche quicker and more flexible. Michael's determination gave way to rage, prodded by desperation. His mouth hung open and gasping grunts and choked whimpers came involuntarily with his breath.

Their thrashing grew in intensity until neither one was able to maintain their grip on the other. As Michael broke free, he whipped his arm back and forth flailing without aim. His eyes bulging out, he incongruously yelled, "OFF SATAN."

The Comanche covered and protected himself with his arms, pulling his head down like a turtle retreating into its shell. His arms were battered and torn but not broken. He lost his grip on the hammer as it was knocked from his hand, landing out of sight above his head. Both hands now free, he rolled and pushed himself from under Michael's weight. But before he could scramble away, he was bludgeoned on the side of his head, a heavy blow from the barrel of the pistol. The edges of his awareness blurred and his vision darkened at the periphery as he collapsed onto his belly, struggling to remain conscious.

Michael floated to his feet, holstered the gun, and moved with long quick strides to where he had been sleeping only minutes before. He stooped down and scooped up the bull-whip, grasping the wooden handle and shaking loose the coils. The Comanche had managed to rise to his knees and had paused to steady himself before attempting to gain his feet when the lash struck him across the back. Michael was expert with the whip. His skill and size combined to produce instant welts wherever the supple leather landed. Even as the whip snaked out again and again with great speed and accuracy, the Comanche, like a man walking into a hurricane wind, brought his feet under him and pushed himself upright, again trying to shield and defend himself with his bleeding arms.

His rage unbounded, his teeth clenched and his lips snarling, Michael cleverly wound the whip around the Comanche's ankles and viciously jerked his feet out from under him. Michael reversed the whip in his hands and, stepping closer, began beating the prone rolling figure at his feet with the whip's heavy wooden handle.

The fall to the ground had shaken him out of his stupor, and his own anger flared to white-hot intensity. As Michael rained down blows upon him, he snatched up and caught the wooden grip. He pulled hard and though Michael staggered, he did not tumble. Winding his hand in the braided leather, Michael pulled back. The tug-of-war lifted the smaller man to his feet and dragged him forward, his heels digging furrows in the mud.

Separated by three feet of arms and leather, the two whirled in a spiraling dance. They spun each other to within several feet of the still rising creek. Choppy muddy water, swollen by the rain, surged past with the speed of a sprinting horse. Their battle reduced itself to a struggle for possession of the whip, both combatants panting and tired, unable to strike a blow or do more than keep their grip and their feet. Their eyes burned through the moonlit air; Michael's wild and frenzied, the Comanche's hooded and glinting. Their feet shifted and slipped with each pull and turn but never left the ground. Michael's hands throbbed and purpled from the tightening coils, the Comanches finger's drained to whiteness.

Nearing exhaustion, they both ceased their swirling efforts and leaned back, keeping the whip taunt between them. The Comanche's back was to the plunging waters, Michael's weight counterbalancing him.

He held still for a moment, poised on the brink, then with squirming wiggling sculling grinding rotations of his feet the Comanche began slowly but inexorably to drag Michael down slope.

Michael desperately started to unravel the whip from its strangling biting hold around his hands and wrists but the effort lost him his leverage and his feet slipped out from beneath him, sending him to his knees and elbows. For a brief second, the coils held and he was jerked to the feet of his enemy.

Michael twisted and looked up into the black featureless face of Satan, who gathered up the slack in the whip and heaved mightily. But Michael's hands were no longer entangled and and he let go of the whip. The Comanche fell backward into the raging current, releasing the whip too late. Michael scrambled backwards on his hands and knees. His eyes followed the water which he had seen envelop the Comanche, but the flailing warrior did not reemerge; even the splash was lost amid the roiling hillocks and depressions.

Michael crawled clear of the creek before sitting up, still searching the water and banks for any sign of his adversary. Movement to his side made him turn and jump to a crouch. He saw not the Comanche but two mounted Apaches, who towed a pinto pony behind them. They drifted dreamlike slowly past the Muleskinner, never removing their eyes from his, and then once past, kicked their mounts forward and raced off in pursuit of the fleeing water that had taken away the Comanche.

Michael dropped down to his knees in the hard clean light of the full moon, too tired to wonder.

Twenty-Eight

Luke and the Rangers sighted the burnt wagon two hours after dawn. Their horses lathered from the hard riding in the blistering heat, themselves tired and sweaty. Luke scowled, disappointed and irritated that neither Red or his roan were anywhere to be seen. he was not sure how he felt about seeing Michael and his pale mule.

The Muleskinner was sitting on a blanket, the blazing sun rippling and distorting his image, his back to the oncoming Rangers. He sat on the top of the slope that led down to the creek, which no longer was in flood and now flowed gentle and shallow, though the banks were cut deeper and at a sharper incline.

"Hello Michael," Luke called when they were within earshot. The boy turned slowly and stiffly, his eyes peering from beneath the brim of his dark hat. He made no reply and did not stand or move to greet them.

Luke signaled for the troop to dismount and the men led their horses to water at the creek, parting and moving to either side of Michael like a river divided by a boulder. Luke handed the reins of his mount to another and walked over to stand and look down at Michael.

"I thought I would find you here." He did not smile when

he spoke and Michael did not look up. "I was hoping to find Captain Red with you. you ain't seen him?"

"No," he said softly.

"He was following your trail," Luke said, as if the fact made Michael somehow responsible for knowing where Red might be.

"He was following me?" Michael was surprised and when Luke only nodded in answer, Michael lifted his face to see him.

"What happened to you?" Luke asked in a dispassionate monotone, seeing the marks, bruises and cuts, on the boy's face and arms.

Michael had washed himself and his clothes in the creek at daybreak and had put them back on to keep him cool as they dried, but his body and face showed the ugly signs of a struggle in deep purple, black, and yellow contrast against his fair skin. "I cast out Satan."

Luke had nothing to say to that but after a long moment's pause, he sighed and asked, "You hurt anywhere bad? want me to have a look at you?"

"No." Michael shook his head and turned back to what he had been doing when Luke arrived. He had broken down the revolver Red had given him but that had failed to kill the Comanche. He'd removed the caps and the nipples they covered and was painstakingly pushing the tightly fitted balls and damp powder out of the chambers.

"Your gun get wet last night in the rain?" Luke asked.

"No."

"You should probably clean your shotgun as well."

"I forgot about that." Michael's hands hesitated as he pondered that.

Luke shifted from one foot to the other, hot and uncomfortable, he let some time pass before asking, "You ain't seen a lone Comanche, have you?"

"No." Michael finished cleaning the gun, reassembled the pieces and reloaded it. He holstered the revolver and slowly, with obvious pain and stiffness, came to his feet. "Red was following me?" he asked.

"Yeah. We've been trailing him for days now, him and a renegade Comanche. I think my Apaches have led me astray though."

"They come by here last night, went that way." Michael pointed downstream.

Luke's gaze follow the finger. "I suppose we'll be heading after them. You coming with us?"

Michael's decision was slow in coming. "No."

"Just as well," Luke said frankly.

Twenty-Nine

Mary had worked all morning and into the afternoon on her knees. She scraped at the ground under the blazing sun to dig Sam a shallow grave beside the one he had dug for Red. His cold body was stiff as old dry wood by the time she dragged it the few steps to its resting place and began to cover it over.

When the body was hidden, the rocky dirt piled into a low mound, she stood and, with weary steps, retrieved Sam's rifle from where it lay next to his buffalo robe. With both hands, she carried the heavy gun to the head of the grave. She pushed it into the ground, muzzle first, working it in deep enough that it stood upright and steady on its own. She took the snake fang amulet with its severed thong from her pocket and tied it to the trigger guard.

Affixing the marker had drained the last of her energy and she slipped down to kneel, bent forward and head bowed as if in prayer, at the edge of Sam's grave.

The sound of footfalls crunching up the hill behind her brought her chin up but did not turn her head. The unmistakable clacking ratchet of a pistol being cocked and the feel of the barrel, hot from the sun, pressing through her thick hair to the back of her skull, failed as well to greatly arouse her interest.

"Who is buried there?" The voice quavered but remained low and distinct.

"I buried Sam in this one." She spoke quietly and steadily. "That there is a big red-haired lawman that was chasing us."

His shadow fell over her as he moved to her side, lifting the muzzle from her head but keeping it leveled and cocked. "Did you kill him?"

"No." Mary stared down at where Sam's face would be staring up from under several inches of dirt. "Yes."

"Did you kill Red?" Michael asked more specifically.

"Dead is dead, what does it matter?" She lifted her eyes and studied Michael's shaded face with her eyes, sore and blurry. "Well speak of the devil."

"It matters." His voice quivering again.

"You don't sound so sure."

"It matters to you." He pressed the gun to her head again, his meaning clear in the hard edge his voice had acquired.

Mary laughed, her mouth opening with a sobbing sound. "You think I care?" A little of her fury still surviving. "You expect me to beg? Or tell some lie?" She pressed her head into the muzzle.

"I just want to know who's responsible." Michael's own voice rose in anger.

She snorted and said, "Me too," and dropped her eyes as her rage fizzled out. "I thought it was you for a time." She shook her head. "I could have just gone south with Sam like he wanted."

"I know you?"

"I'm Mary Maggie Pruitt," she sing-songed. "You killed my brothers."

"They were not good men," Michael asserted without pausing to consider.

"Is that why you done it? I suppose they had it coming to

them. You didn't know them when they was just boys though, they weren't always so wicked. Life has a way of changing things. They did not have no chance at all, I tell you what." She ran shaking fingers through the tangles of her hair, revealing her dark eyes and low forehead. "I was no help to them. I don't think I did one right thing in my entire life. All the men in my life have come to a bad end now. There ain't no one left but me."

"You shouldn't have killed Red. He was a good man. He was my friend." The long barrel of the gun shook as his grip tightened.

"Oh, there's lots of things I shouldn't have done. Didn't seem like I had no other choice at the time. What a fucking waste it all was, I can't even really remember much. I was drunk a lot. I'd rather forget most of it anyway, I suppose" She snapped her attention suddenly to Michael as if she had momentarily forgotten that he was there. "You done any better yourself? You want me to feel bad about your friend?" She met Michael's eyes, her expression genuine and, in spite of her words, apologetic. "I think I'm all out of sorry. Sam was a good man too, first I ever met, the only friend I ever had."

There was silence for a long moment, Mary kneeling with her head down again, Michael standing completely still.

"You going to shoot me now?" she asked without looking up. Michael did not speak or move. "I am not a good woman. Sam could have had a good life if he hadn't taken up with me. He was smart, clever. Don't know what he wanted with an ugly whore. I loved him though. I can't remember if I ever told him that."

Michael slowly began to take a step back, his hand, holding the gun, lowered an inch. Mary's head came up quickly and she turned on her knees to face Michael. "Where you going?" she asked.

Then, "Where are you going, Sugar?" A grimaced smile scarred her face. "I don't want to be alone."

Michael froze in mid-step, in mid-gesture. Mary reached

one hand slowly up and covered Michael's, her small thumb overlapping his finger inside the trigger guard.

"Don't you want to stay with me? I'll make you real happy." Her other hand crept up to gently hold and stroke the smooth round gun barrel.

"Oh, sweetie pie, you're so big." She spoke directly into the dark muzzle.

"I'll give you your money's worth." She kissed under the tip of the barrel, the words and actions familiar and meaningless to her.

"I'll hum you a nice lullaby." She slipped the barrel into her mouth whispering, "Give mama what you got."

The bark from the Colt rolled like thunder across the plain, echoing interminably in the still afternoon.

Thirty

Luke sat his horse and, with the rest of the troop gathered in a semicircle, stared down at the four dead bodies. He'd ridden in the direction that Michael had pointed for several hours, following the creek as it meandered generally south, picking up a trail of three ponies, two mounted one lighter. They veered away from the creek's course when the tracks diverged and when they spotted vultures circling only a few miles distant.

The horses were lying one hundred yards apart but the two Apaches were laid one on top of the other. All four showed large bloody head wounds. Their weapons were scattered around them and Luke could see clear signs that they had been killed in separate places and then dragged together. He could find no sign of the third pony or the killer, though he had little doubt as to the man's identity.

"Looks like our scouts were kind enough to bring that Comanche his horse."

"Hell of a way to thank them," said the Ranger to Luke's left.

"He killed the scouts but that Muleskinner lived. Damn strange." Luke lifted his eyes to circle with the buzzards.

"What now, Luke?" asked the Ranger.

"Yeah, damned if I know."

Thirty-One

Michael lingered only long enough to bury Mary, pushing the loose mound of dirt from the top of Sam's grave away and setting the small woman beside him. When he lifted her, he was surprised at how feather-light she was in his arms and again when he placed her on her side, how small she seemed next to the tall mountain man. Her face, unmarred, struck him as childlike and he lingered, looking down at the two before pushing the mound back over them.

Michael left the rifle standing where it was but picked up every other gun he could find. Red's two big dragoons he holstered in the rig he retrieved from Red's saddle, which he had cinched to Her Highness, replacing the poor saddle he had inherited from Puritan Pete. He loaded Mary's little pistol before tucking it into his waistband. He left the hilltop leading Sam's horses, wanting to put some miles between himself and the graveyard before night fell.

His anger over the death of his friend and benefactor had dissolved the moment the gun had fired. His wrath was God's wrath and both were satisfied when justice was served. For him there was nothing more to consider.

He went south on a straight path for the next few days

avoiding all towns and people, eating from Sam's stores and grinding beans in Beasley's coffee grinder to drink in the morning as he had with Red weeks before.

When he made Red's ranch, Katie had come running to greet her big brother. To his relief she did not ask about her father. They had left separately and she did not assume that they would return together. But he was not so lucky with Rose.

Michael floundered through the heaving sea of emotion that Rose generated. Loving and bitter, she said prayers for her husband and cursed his name. She remembered him fondly and resentfully. And she would look Michael in the eye and ask him what she and her children were to do now.

She spoke as if she assumed Michael would be staying and he said nothing about leaving. Just after sunset she dumped some blankets on the kitchen table and, after a few more minutes of crying and an embrace made awkward by Michael's stiffness, she wished him good night.

Michael sat on the porch in the warm muggy air and thought about Rose and her family and how Red had been with them and what it would be like if he stayed. He thought of chores he could do and projects he might start and imagined Rose cooking him suppers and Katie sitting on his lap at the table.

Through the window he listened to the squeaking of Rose's bed as she tossed and turned and his brow furrowed.

Rose slept later than usual the next morning and, after rising and dressing, she stepped into the kitchen and called for Katie, who was standing on the porch holding the baby. She soon found that Michael had ridden away during the night, the fact disturbing her less than she would have imagined. She made breakfast and fed herself and her daughters, smiling at them and speaking softly and reassuringly.

Miles to the south, under the blazing midday sun, mounted on the pale mule, Michael's mind wandered and skipped through indistinct and colorless memories of the past month; a fragmented parade of images, punctuated sharply by the faces of dead friends, relatives, enemies, and women. It rolled across his inner panorama like a thunder-clap. Finally grinding to a stop with the face of the Comanche slipping beneath the heaving waters.

The blackened face with its piercing dark eyes lingered, gradually chasing him from his reverie. Michael shivered, then after a moment twisted his neck to look behind him, but saw nothing but flat barren land, rippled by heat shimmers, stretching off out into eternity.

Her Highness walked doggedly on throughout the hot afternoon, and every few minutes Michael turned and looked over his shoulder.

The End

Made in the USA
Middletown, DE
30 March 2022

63384861R10217